PRAISE FOR THE NOVELS OF

Suzanne Forster

WITHDRAWN

"[a] hard-edged, sexy romp."
—*Publishers Weekly* on *Blush*

"A gripping novel...depicting the darker side of the rich
and powerful that includes intrigue, sex, lies and possibly
murder. The reader will not want to put the book down..."
—*New Mystery Reader* on *The Lonely Girls Club*

"Intelligent, psychologically complex and engaging..."
—*Publishers Weekly* on *Come Midnight*

"Forster's name has become synonymous with taut,
suspenseful and wildly sexy novels that are
hot enough to melt asbestos."
—*Romantic Times BOOKclub*

"The attraction was palpable, and [the] love scenes were
hot...a romantic suspense novel I can recommend highly."
—*All About Romance* on *Every Breath She Takes*

"Interesting and appealing characters, great pacing and
interaction, an original plot line...strongly recommended."
—*The Mystery Reader* on *The Lonely Girls Club*

Suzanne Forster

Tease

Spice

TEASE

ISBN 0-373-60506-4

Spice and Colophon are trademarks used under license and registered in
Australia, New Zealand, Philippines, United States Patent and Trademark
Office and in other countries.

www.Spice-Books.com

Printed in U.S.A.

Tease

Prologue

"Whatever you do, Tess Wakefield, do not come."

Had she actually said that out loud? Tess tried to open her eyes, but her lids were uncontrollable. They quivered like feather fringe. God, she must be glowing like a beacon. Sensations were lighting her up from the inside, crackling like the filaments of a neon tube.

Had he heard her? What would he do? Take it as a challenge and increase the pressure? Or lighten it and drive her utterly mad? It wouldn't take much. He could so easily sweep her up and fling her over the edge.

With one finger.

With one more breath on her aching nipple.

One more feather stroke.

Why didn't he just get it over with? Why did he leave her alone for so long? He came when she least expected him and touched her in intimate places. One finger gliding through her wetness, and then he was gone. The way a child steals icing from a cake.

Two fingers rolling her nipple.

Tight and tender.

Teeth on her rump.

How long had he been doing that? Hours? Days? She didn't know anymore.

But he didn't know how strong she was, how ardently she had fought to take back control of her life. She could not be broken, even if it was joy that poured from the cracks.

Someone was laughing, shaking with laughter. Him? No, it was her. Tears soaked her face and salted her tongue.

Was he even there? Or was she imagining a lover worthy of the Marquis de Sade? A demon with the patience for whatever time it took.

Was any of this really happening? The water dripping on her body, splashing between her legs and becoming more intense with each drop. It was a torrent now. She was becoming the water, flowing, dripping, melting like a glacier in spring. How did she stop this flood?

She forced her eyes open and saw them staring back at her. Eyes. Everywhere. Hypnotic and black as cherries. Her own eyes, heavy with sexual desire. Begging. Release me. Don't let me writhe and thrash like this, helpless. Electrical current grounds me. Lust cracks me like a whip. I am what you have made me, a whore for pleasure. But I will fight you to prove that I'm not. And I will win.

"Put your hands against the wall. Spread your legs."

Was that his voice? Was he speaking to her? Was that his hand on her naked flank?

Oh, God, no. Another touch. Another feather stroke, and she would be gone. Shattered.

She was ready to climb out of her own body, shed it like a snake, anything to escape him. She grabbed hold of the metal bars, quivering, waiting for pleasure that was unbearable. It took her all the way to heaven and back. All the way to hell. She could not let go. She would shatter into pieces.

One touch and he would break her in half.

Whatever you do, Tess Wakefield, do not—

One

Twenty-five days earlier…

No point packing the vibrator. Tess Wakefield had zero interest in sex. She'd been doing without it for the better part of a year, and that year *had* been better, thank you. No more bikini waxing unless she felt like it, no more inspecting her backside for unsightly blemishes or plucking the odd hair from the knuckle of her big toe, which hurt like hell.

No more penises or anything that was attached to them. Men were high maintenance. Well, most of them anyway. They needed all that ego-stroking and fawning, and they didn't even care if you lied about how wonderful they were. They'd rather you fake orgasms than admit to not having them. *Think about it.*

And they were wimps, too, when it came to the important things in life. Squeamish about a little honest emotion. Terrified of giving up their freedom. They weren't looking for partners in life. They wanted groupies. Wannabe pop stars, all of them, in search of an adoring audience. And all that pretending to love football when you were freezing to death and had to pee but didn't want to risk hepatitis in the event bathroom.

Well, this groupie had turned in her backstage pass.

She tossed the vibrator into one of the boxes that would go into temporary storage and turned back to the array of clothing on her bed that still had to be sorted and packed. Thank goodness her new employer, Pratt-Summers, was handling most of the move to New York for her, which included the generous offer to use one of their corporate apartments until she could find a place of her own. She'd been offered the prestigious creative director position, and she had to look professional. That meant black, and lots of it. On the other hand, this was an advertising agency and they tended to be casual. It was also February, which meant jeans and sweaters, except for client visitation days when everybody wore suits like big boys and girls.

Tess knew a little something about ad agency protocol. She'd been with Renaissance Marketing in L.A. for the past eight years, doing everything from answering the phones to running the creative department to pitching and winning multimillion-dollar campaigns. Now, finally, it felt as if all the hard work and long hours had paid off. She'd given it her all, and maybe too much, considering how everything else in her life was withering from neglect.

She picked up her off-the-shoulder jersey sheath,

briefly tempted by the thought of the New York club scene, then relegated it to the storage box. The dress was too red, too tight. It shouted *take me off*—and a couple other things that ended with *off*.

Her conversion to celibacy had come immediately after the breakup with Dillon, her let's-wait-until-the-perfect-moment-to-announce-our-engagement fiancé. That perfect moment was never, of course. Too late Tess had discovered that Dillon was involved with another woman, his mother. She steamed the wrinkles from his boxer shorts and enzymatically cleaned his contact lenses for him, while Tess could barely handle the instructions on a box of laundry detergent. The fact that Dillon had made his mother break off the engagement with Tess confirmed her suspicions about him. He was high maintenance *and* a commitment-phobe.

That had seemed obvious to Tess, but her always brutally frank friend, Meredith, had disagreed. "*You're* the CP," she'd told Tess, who'd protested, "How could *I* be the commitment-phobe? I'm the one getting dumped." And then it had hit her. Maybe she was choosing CPs so that *she* didn't have to commit.

She knelt to pull the plug on her clock radio and saw the time. "*Ten?* It can't be." She'd been up since 6:00 a.m. How did it get that late?

Pratt-Summers had arranged for a car to take her to the airport, and a moving van to pick up the last of her boxes. The van was due in thirty minutes, and not only did she have to finish packing, she had to get the apartment presentable. She was subletting her one-bedroom place furnished, and the tenant had agreed to a month-by-month arrangement, just in case Tess found herself packing for a flight back.

Not that Tess expected anything to go wrong. She was eminently qualified for the job, according to Erica Summers, the CEO at Pratt-Summers, who'd interviewed her personally just three weeks ago. But how often did a creative directorship of a large Madison Avenue ad agency come along?

"To most thirty-two-year-old ad execs? Never," she said, aware of the flutter in her voice. God, she was nervous.

This job was huge. New York City was huge.

Maybe she wanted to miss the flight. She couldn't even seem to make up her mind what clothes to take with her, and there was no time to call her brutally frank friend to discuss it. Meredith, voice of clarity in a jumbled world, steadfast shoulder, mother confessor and occasional scolding conscience. Were there any Merediths in New York?

Tess's spirits sank with her shoulders. She looked around the place, marveling at the chaos. It could have been declared a disaster area. Fortunately, she saw the problem immediately.

She wasn't dealing with Bank of America's automated voice-mail system. She only had three options to worry about. Get rid of the crotchless day-of-the-week panties that Dillon gave her, obviously without his mother's knowledge. Toss out anything else that brought the word hot to mind. Then pack the rest and go.

One week later…

"The best way to open the mind is to open the body. If one is closed, the other cannot be open. Breathe through the soles of your feet. Listen with your fingertips."

Tess spoke in low, modulated tones to the five men and women lying on their backs on gym mats, arranged in a circle and forming rudimentary U shapes with their bodies. Their arms and legs were straight up in the air, reaching toward the ceiling, some steadier than others.

"Can you feel the energy flowing and your mind expanding?" Tess asked. "Focus on the base of your spine. Is it tingling?"

"Something's tingling." Carlotta Clark giggled.

"Would you tell Carlotta to stop looking at my balls?" Andy Phipps, who lay on a mat opposite her, tugged at his baggy gym trunks in an exaggerated attempt to cover himself.

"If you had balls," Carlotta scolded in her sexy, hiccupy voice, "you'd be begging me to look at them."

Andy lifted up on his elbows and appealed to the group with eyes as big and velvety brown as instant pudding. "You're my witnesses, people. She's harassing me again. I'm being har*assed*. That has to be obvious to everyone here."

Andy suddenly collapsed, his elbow knocked out from under him by Jan Butler, a plump graying copywriter on the next mat. "She may want you, Andikins, but is she woman enough? Can she take you to Jannie Land?"

Andy seemed to be considering the idea. The others

began to cheer him on. "Breathe through your balls," someone suggested.

Tess rested her hand on her hip and watched their antics with amused forbearance. It wasn't the relaxation break she'd had in mind. She'd had plenty of experience with ad agency brainstorming sessions. They needed to be loose and free-flowing, but this bunch was flowing all over the place. What they needed now was direction. Tess's specialty.

She stepped into the center of the circle to restore order. "Back to your mats, wild things. Let's finish the exercise and get on with our brainstorming."

Jan gave Andy a wink.

Andy's skinny legs boinged back into the air. "Don't blame me if someone else loses control," he warned Tess. "This position drives the ladies crazy."

"We'll bear up," Tess assured him. Andy's diminutive frame, rag-mop dark hair and dimples did seem to bring out the vixen in the over-fifty set, but Tess was hot for his fertile brain. And it hadn't taken her long to figure out that he could be counted upon for comic relief, even when he wasn't trying to be funny. He was in his mid-twenties, fresh out of grad school and a gifted illustrator. He'd been at Pratt-Summers just a month, which was three weeks longer than Tess had been here, but he was shaping up to be a key member of her creative team. He was bright, verbal and a bottomless pit of ideas. Exactly what Tess needed, considering that she'd been assigned the lucrative—and problematic—Faustini account. The leather-goods franchise was in big trouble. The Faustini name had always been associated with meticulous handcrafting and old-world elegance, but that wasn't selling in a culture that prized everything young and hot. Faustini's management wanted to expand beyond briefcases and luggage. They were after a chunk of the luxury leather clothing and accessories market, and that couldn't be done without a total image overhaul.

"Nine thousand and ten thousand," Tess said, counting out the final seconds of the position. "Okay, last chance to check out Andy's balls. Now, lower your legs slowly, and don't forget to breathe."

They all copped a look, including Brad Hayes and Lee Sanchez, the other two males in the group. Brad was a thirty-year-old communications major from Harvard, and Lee was the team's prematurely balding marketing whiz. Andy rose to a sitting position, as red as a stop sign, but seemingly pleased by all the attention to his male anatomy.

Tess had held this morning's brainstorming session in the company gym so she and her team could take Qigong breaks. She'd expected skepticism toward the martial arts technique, especially from some of the agency veterans, but at least everyone had agreed to give it a try.

"Tell me again why we're doing this?" Brad Hayes asked. "I tend not to do things I can't pronounce."

Carlotta snickered. "Do you even need to ask, Brad? Tess comes from la-la land."

Tess took the jab in stride. In the week she'd been here, she'd picked up on some animosity from Carlotta, who'd been at Pratt-Summers longer than anyone else on the team. Tess could think of two reasons. Carlotta didn't believe that Tess had the creative chops to handle the job, which was understandable. Tess had yet to prove herself. Or Carlotta felt the job should have been offered to her, which was a bigger problem, but Tess was optimistic that she could handle it with plenty of diplomacy, and maybe some plum assignments.

"It's pronounced *chee gung*," Tess said, answering Brad. "*Qi* means life force, and *gong* means accomplish through steady practice. It works wonders for me. Keeps the blood flowing and the ideas coming."

Tess dragged her mat into the circle on the other side of Andy Phipps, not wanting to come between him and Jan Butler. It was time to get back to work. She'd been brought in as their boss, so it wasn't surprising they were a little wary of her, but she hoped to quickly melt any resistance. The team was on a tight deadline with the Faustini campaign. The starting gun had gone off even before Tess arrived, but she did not intend to lose this race.

At least she'd had some experience with bonding and leading. She was more concerned about the other task Erica Summers had given her. Pratt-Summers had built a reputation for brilliant innovation. They'd won nearly every industry award for their avant-garde designs, but they were also becoming known for their arrogance and lack of communication with clients—and it was costing them business. Tess had been brought in to do what spin doctors were supposed to do—create a new image for the agency's clients, but she'd also been tasked with creating a new image for Pratt-Summers itself.

Now, *there* was a challenge.

And worse, Erica had asked her to keep quiet about it. She didn't want to ruffle feathers. Creative types were sensitive about being handled, she'd cautioned, as though Tess weren't a creative type herself. It was Tess's ability to successfully straddle the two disciplines—account management *and* creative—that made her the perfect covert agent for change within the creative division.

"Let's talk about the Faustini account and don't be shy." Tess coaxed the team with her hands, like a traffic cop beckoning cars to advance. Too bad she didn't have a whistle. "Any new ideas since our last session on Faustini? Somebody toss something out. Anybody. I don't care how wild it is. How do we make Faustini's new leather boots a must-have item?"

Andy had arranged himself cross-legged on his mat, continuing to tempt the ladies. "We don't," he said. "We start with the briefcases, their signature product. First, make the cases sexy, *then* introduce the boots."

"Good luck making a briefcase sexy." Carlotta shook back her claret-red waves and played with the zipper pull of her Lycra warm-up suit, as if to say now *this* is sexy.

Tess would have guessed Carlotta to be in her late thirties, but thanks to the wonders of cosmetic surgery, she was, and probably always would be, ageless. It was tempting to think she'd been hired to boost male morale, and maybe their testosterone. But, to date, Carlotta had racked up more awards for her ads than any other Pratt-Summers creative. She was kick-butt in more ways than one.

Andy sprang up and went to get a sleek black leather case he'd left under the basketball backboard. Tess recognized it as a Faustini. She watched with interest as Andy dropped to his knees on his mat, took a pair of sheer red panties from the case and glanced up, a wicked gleam in his eye.

"A man can't spend *every* weekend working," he said, letting a beat pass. "Faustini. Work hard, play hard."

He'd given Tess an idea. She reached over and touched the lid of the case seductively, swirling her fingertips over the silky leather. "It's so soft," she cooed in a kittenish Marilyn Monroe voice, "and you're so successful."

Andy arched an eyebrow: "You're into leather, too?"

"Not leather," she scolded. "Faustini."

Tess and Andy grinned, high-fiveing each other. "Not a bad thirty-second shot," she said.

"Or!" Carlotta squealed. "Picture *me* as a dominatrix, a bullwhip in my hand. "You're not carrying a Faustini?" She cracks the whip. "Take that!"

The enthusiasm was contagious. Soon, they were talking over each other, but the suggestions got more and more outrageous. Tess hated to be a killjoy, but she'd already met with Alberto Faustini, the company's rather stodgy founder, and he didn't want anything far-out. He'd told Tess to come up with something provocative, but nothing X-rated, and that was despite strong opposition from his new partner, his twenty-two-year-old wild-child daughter, Gina, who favored vampires, sexual bondage and other gothic images. Fortunately, Gina Faustini didn't sign the checks.

"Guys," Tess said, "we want to seduce customers not shock them."

"Why not shock them? Before you can seduce them you have to get their attention."

Tess wasn't sure who'd spoken until she noticed her team members looking over her shoulder. She whipped around, saw the source of the disembodied voice, and was glad not to be hooked up to a lie detector. Her sweaty palms would have shorted the machine out.

How long had *he* been standing there?

She'd never met Danny Gabriel, but even if she hadn't seen his likeness plastered all over the agency walls in photographs with business giants and celebrity clients, she would have recognized his personal trademarks—the bare feet, the worn blue jeans and the flowing hair he'd gathered into a loose ebony braid.

Here before her was the agency's image problem in the flesh. Not his clothes, even Gabriel donned a suit on client days. His attitude. He was Tess's codirector—and the infamous advertising savant she'd been brought in to teach some manners. The Faustini account had been his before it was given to Tess, and rumor had it that he'd been replaced because he sided with Faustini's daughter.

What was he doing here now? He'd been in Tokyo all week, drumming up international business, which was his new focus, according to Erica. Tess was supposed to have been formally introduced to him tonight at a dinner with Erica and the board members. She was nervous enough about that. If Carlotta was the agency's diva, then Danny Gabriel was its rock star.

Tess sat there, thunderstruck, aware that she wasn't racking up leadership points with her silence. Her team knew him, but they seemed to be speechless, too. Either they were intimidated or expecting a confrontation. There was a good chance that Gabriel saw her as an interloper.

She *was* an interloper. And this could be a test, but of what? Her worthiness to walk the same ground he did?

She rose to her feet, accomplishing it with surprising grace. "My, my," she said, her tone both friendly and challenging. "I've heard so much about you. Danny Gabriel, right? I'm Tess Wakefield."

She waited for a reaction before offering her hand. He looked almost approachable, except for those eyes. Sharp. Serrated. Like a cutting tool. They reminded her a little of someone else's eyes, and it was just enough of a resemblance to make her thoughts heat with unwanted memories.

He nodded, his expression warming slightly. "Faustini management doesn't know what the hell they want," he said. "The client rarely does, so it's our job to tell them."

"Really? *Our* job?"

They shook hands, and she covered his with both of hers, pressing down firmly. His focus sharpened. Possibly he was just realizing that she might be a worthier adversary than he'd thought.

"But shock value has a way of backfiring, don't you think?" she asked.

"For people like me, yes. Not for you, though. You can get away with anything."

"Excuse me?"

He just smiled. "You have a free pass—in advertising and in life. Use it."

"What free pass?"

"Your sincerity. The good-girl thing. It sells, especially when it's used to sell something bad. People might not line up to buy bibles from you, but they would buy sex. They would buy leather, even if it came with whips and chains."

"Really."

He nodded. "You make the bad stuff okay. If a sweet thing like you is a little bit kinky, then maybe kinky is okay. You give people permission to do what they secretly want to do."

"Sweet? You're quite sure of that?" Tess had never been called that before, and it didn't strike her as a compliment, no matter how he couched it. Her naturally curly blond hair was cut in a bob, on which she spent a fortune for frizz control, and she still had a bit of California tan and a few freckles left. But she was no angel. Her past might shock even him. As for her work, of course, she was passionate and sincere. If you didn't believe in the client's product, you had no business trying to sell it. That was her motto. Obviously, it wasn't his.

"Shock them, Tess," he continued. "It's the only way you're going to get their attention."

Neurons were firing in her brain, sending out orders to tighten muscles and tendons, her jaw being the target area. She fought the desire to remind him that he was giving advice to his *replacement*…then arched an eyebrow and said it anyway. Indirectly.

"Shocking the client will accomplish nothing, except to lose us the account, and I don't need your help with that." *Thwap*.

"I meant shock the public, not the client," he replied, nonplussed.

"That's not necessary, either. People don't appreciate being made fools of. You might get their attention once, but you'll never get it again."

He rubbed his jaw, seeming amused. "You have much too high an opinion of your fellow man."

Present company excepted, she wanted to say, but held her fire. She usually kept a pretty good grip on her emotions—Meredith liked to call it a headlock—but anger wouldn't get her anywhere with him anyway. She needed to stay grounded because this guy was a raging river. He held nothing back, and she didn't have that luxury. She had to preserve her energy to save the account that *he'd* put in jeopardy.

"Are you done with the gym?" he asked. "It's reserved on Friday mornings for murder ball. You and your team are welcome to join us. Carlotta has a mean serve."

"Murderball?"

He grinned. "Dodgeball where you come from."

So that's why he was here. Dodgeball. Not because he couldn't wait until the evening to meet her. Figured.

"They may want to play," she said, referring to her team, "but I have some calls to make. Give us a minute to finish up our brainstorming session, and we'll be out of your way."

"Take your time." Suddenly warm and friendly, he

worked open the top button of his white dress shirt. "I need to hit the locker room and change first, anyway."

She mumbled something about seeing him at dinner that night, and then turned back to her team, not surprised to find them riveted. The gym virtually hummed with tension. A corpse would have been sitting up.

"Let's meet tomorrow morning in the Sandbox," she told the team, referring to one of the agency's many themed conference rooms. "I know it's the weekend, but we have a deadline bearing down on us like a tsunami."

Andy rose first, picking up his mat. "So, what kind of a campaign is this going to be? Shock and awe?" He grinned, apparently at the possibilities. "I'm sure I could come up with something that would put Faustini management on life support."

Hmm. Andy may have just handed her the perfect opening. She had no idea whether Gabriel was still behind her, but she hoped so. This was her chance to make an impression on all of them, but most of all, she wanted *him* to hear it.

"Keep in mind," she said formally, "that it will be difficult for Faustini to pay their advertising bill if they're on life support. They *are* the client, and without them this agency wouldn't exist. They've hired us to do a job. Let's do it. Let's give them the campaign heard around the world. But don't forget that the client has to like it first or no one else will ever see it."

Tess couldn't tell whether they were with her or not, but she wasn't finished. "It's not us versus Faustini," she said. "It's us *and* them. We're a team, and they're part of it."

Her team gave her a smattering of applause, and she curtsied. Tess waited for Gabriel to say something, and the silence became awkward. She glanced over her shoulder and saw that he'd already left. So much for the crusading speech.

As she knelt to pick up her mat, she had the feeling the murderball game had already started, and there were only two players. This was a one-on-one with Danny Gabriel, and she was the rookie, fighting for a piece of the star player's turf. And maybe for her career.

Two

Tess hovered in the narrow stall, trying not to drop her purse, or anything else, into the sleek, low-slung toilet. She'd just finished her business when a man had entered the bathroom and taken the stall right next to hers. Now she was stuck. Or rather her outfit was stuck. Her cotton gauze jumpsuit had been perfect for the Qigong session that morning, but it should have come with assembly instructions for all the hooks, snaps and tabs. Now she was having a slight wardrobe malfunction. She'd ended up with a hook and nothing to attach it to but a snap. And she couldn't very well leave the stall half-dressed with a dude next door.

The agency's bathrooms were coed on the theory that new experiences were stimulating and enriching—and Pratt-Summers was known for providing their creative staff with plenty of stimulation. The coffee lounge offered more choices than Starbucks. It also had an oxygen bar, a tea bar and a gourmet snack bar, featuring exotic dark chocolate from around the world that was said to be as potent as prescription mood elevators. Anything to keep the ideas coming.

Tess had worked straight through lunch on the Faustini account, and this was her first break of the afternoon. All she wanted to do was pee and get back to her desk. But it looked like she was going to have to take herself apart like a model airplane and start over.

The adjacent door opened and banged shut.

Tess hesitated, listening. She could hear him washing his hands and chatting with Mitzi, the mysterious washroom attendant, who seemed to be on a first-name basis with everyone at the agency. Apparently she was as much a fixture as the bathroom's fancy gold faucets. Tess had heard through office scuttlebutt that Mitzi had been with the agency through every management shake-up, of which Tess was just the latest. She not only guarded the bathroom and the adjoining lounge, she ran an aromatherapy concession, did reflexology and was rumored to be a licensed acupuncturist.

Tess gave up on the jumpsuit. Let it flap. She might flash a few people, but her white cotton sports bra wouldn't give anyone much of a thrill.

She rolled her neck, aware of clicking noises. A massage would be wonderful, except that Mitzi made her nervous. The washroom attendant looked to be in her mid-forties, attractive in a strange way. She had severely cropped hair, an olive complexion and dark, expressive eyes. She was also short-waisted and pear-shaped, with the lowest center of gravity Tess had ever seen, which probably made her a powerhouse masseuse. And to her credit, she kept a beautiful bathroom. There were orchids everywhere, plush rolled towels, pearlescent hand lotions and the place smelled luscious. Today, it was essence of an English rose garden. But on Tess's first day at the agency, she'd smelled something she couldn't identify, and Mitzi had explained that she'd been using oil of hemp for a massage.

Hemp? Could Mitzi add drug dealer to her list of specialties?

Tess had given her a wide berth after that, but she seemed to be the only one who was concerned. As far as Tess could tell, Mitzi was widely revered for her advice on everything from health to dating and relationships. She got more respect than the CEO. Right now, she and the unidentified man were discussing his blood pressure and she was recommending that he burn candles during his power nap.

"Lavender, geranium or neroli," Mitzi suggested. "Lavender is good for dandruff, too. Makes a wonderful tonic for the hair, and if you put the buds in a dream pillow, it will help you sleep. But be careful, you might see ghosts. And, by the way, I have plenty of that ylang-ylang soap you like. You know, the libido-booster bar with just a touch of nutmeg."

The man's embarrassed chuckle made Tess wonder if Mitzi had winked at him. Libido booster? Dream pillows and ghosts? No wonder he had hypertension.

Tess had decided to wait until the transaction was over. She couldn't be sure the man wasn't Danny Gabriel, and she didn't want another awkward encounter with him now. Their dinner tonight would be plenty soon enough.

The moment she heard the man leave, Tess let herself out of the stall and went to the long bank of sinks to wash her hands. Mitzi, keeper of the towels, was seated on her stool at the end of the long counter, her many products displayed on wall racks behind her. She watched Tess intently, ready to hand her a towel when she was done.

Tess thanked her and grabbed some paper towels instead. "In a rush," she said, taking a moment to scrutinize herself in the mirror.

Good girl? Her? What had Gabriel been thinking?

She pulled on a tight curl, trying to get it to relax and dangle in a provocative way. How did she get stuck with yellow bedsprings for hair? She'd always wanted to be one of those fey beauties whose hair went flying every time she gave it a little shake. The kind who gave men whiplash when she strolled by. She sighed. Not in this lifetime.

Still, she hadn't had that much difficulty attracting men, especially back in college. She'd gone through a wild-child phase when hormones and adrenaline had uncorked inside her like a magnum of champagne. Reserved as she'd been, she'd gotten bold enough to flirt, and that was all the encouragement certain boys had needed. Suddenly, she was wildly popular. Not for any of the right reasons, of course, but the boys' reactions had taught her that being sexy was about much more than one's appearance.

Too bad she'd been riddled with guilt the whole time. Being "bad" had only been fleetingly good. Mostly, the experience had left her confused about her sexuality and her urgent need for male attention. And years later, when she'd finally figured it out, the answers hadn't been pretty.

The bathroom door swung open behind her, and a small pack of women burst into the spacious room, laughing and talking, probably on a break.

Tess thought she recognized them from the Research Division but couldn't be sure. She'd been introduced around by a Human Resources person, but she'd met too many people that week. It was all a blur.

"Last night was a Rolling Thunderclap," one of the women said as the three of them entered separate stalls. "It was loud and fast, and there were reports of smoke coming from my ears."

"Reports? How many people were there?" the second woman asked from her stall.

"Just me and my boyfriend, but he gave me updates on the half second."

"Sounds more like a Shake, Rattle and Roll to me," the second woman said. "Were there coital quivers? I'm a Mountain Fountain girl, myself."

"And I fall somewhere between Napping Kitten and Arctic Silence," the third said. "Therapy was suggested."

Mountain Fountain was a Qigong position, but Tess was pretty sure they weren't discussing martial arts. She moved aside as the women emerged all at once, not unlike synchronized swimmers. They washed their hands, thanked Mitzi for the towels and disappeared into the adjoining lounge.

Tess glanced at Mitzi, who shrugged. "This month's *Cosmo* has a Name Your Orgasm quiz," she explained. "Apparently, orgasms can reveal hidden aspects of your personality. If you're limited to one kind, it means you're not expressing yourself fully as a human being."

"Ah." Tess nodded. 'Nuff said. She gave her hair another tweak and frowned. A giant sigh escaped her. Limited to one kind? She should be so lucky. What *was* an orgasm? She couldn't remember. Most of hers had been pretty forgettable anyway, if she was being honest. No Rolling Thunderclaps. Even all the heavy breathing in college had been only briefly exciting—and definitely not worth the self-recrimination afterward.

Mitzi was watching Tess with a knitted brow and enough concern to send Tess running. She reached for the Faustini bag the designer had given her, along with a pair of their gorgeous new stiletto boots. Each of the team members had received some Faustini launch products as gifts, and to better help them sell the line. Pride of ownership was a prime motivating factor, and old man Faustini, as everyone called the sixty-two-year-old founder of the company, was smart enough to know that.

"Gotta go," Tess said. "Work to do." She gave Mitzi a reassuring nod, but it didn't seem to register. Mitzi's health-o-meter was engaged.

"Female trouble?" Mitzi said. "Let me guess. PMS, right?"

Tess was too startled not to respond. She was premenstrual beyond belief, bloated and incredibly hormonal. Worse, she'd never been hornier. She glanced down at her body. "Does it show?"

Tess's period was nearly two weeks late. Probably stress. She definitely wasn't pregnant, unless this was an immaculate conception. She hadn't had sex in months, which seemed to be affecting her cycle.

Good for creativity. That's what she'd been telling herself. Theoretically, pent-up sexual energy could be channeled into other things, like work. In reality, though, she was getting more frustrated, not less, despite the distractions of a new job and a new life. At this rate, her sexual energy would soon be the equivalent of a black hole, sucking up every productive thought she had. Too bad she hadn't been assigned to come up with an ad campaign for porno flicks.

Mitzi was off the stool and down on her knees, searching through the cabinet beneath the sink. "Maybe some clary sage and juniper-berry tea? It balances hormones, and it's a powerful diuretic. You'll pee like a racehorse."

Tess reached for her purse. "Does it come in bags?" she asked, ready to buy on the spot. What did it cost? Fifty bucks a bag? Sold. Anything that equaled less bloating was gold.

"Aha!" Mitzi beamed as she pulled out a small box of tea bags.

The transaction went quickly, and the price was fair, but it all felt vaguely illegal to Tess. Maybe because Mitzi had literally gone under the counter to get the tea.

"Did I hear a man in here earlier?" Tess made small talk

as she waited for Mitzi to process her charge card. "I met lots of people this week, and his voice sounded familiar."

"Did you meet Danny Gabriel?"

Tess tried not to act startled this time. "Yes. Was it him?"

"No, but that's who you were thinking it was, am I right?"

"I thought it *might* be him. Are you supposed to be psychic or something?"

Mitzi wrinkled her nose at the idea. "If the first five senses work, why do you need a sixth? Good eyes and ears is all it takes around here."

Laughter drifted from the other room, where the women were hanging out. Tess wondered if they were still comparing personal bests or had moved on to something else.

She signed the credit card slip Mitzi pushed toward her and tore off her copy. "Thanks for suggesting this," she said, picking up the box of tea. "I'm sure it will help."

Mitzi had her PDA out and was busy making an entry. It was probably how she kept track of sales or inventory. "You're welcome," she said, not looking up, "but I think you might need more than tea, dear."

Tess was already heading for the door. "Thanks, but I have plenty of soap and candles. This will be fine."

"*Tess Wakefield.*"

The urgency in Mitzi's voice made Tess hesitate. She turned to see Mitzi coming after her with a halting gait. Tess wondered if she was much older than she looked, or if she'd been injured somehow.

"Is something wrong?" Tess asked.

Mitzi handed her the credit card. "You forgot this."

"Oh, thank you." Tess took hold of the card, but Mitzi didn't let go of it. Instead, she frowned, her dark eyes boring into Tess's, as if she was searching for something.

"You don't know anything about this place, do you?" she said.

"New York?"

"Pratt-Summers."

"I know it's one of the best ad agencies in the country."

A sniff of derision. "And you came here with the highest hopes, thinking this was your big chance. But it could just as easily be your downfall. Not everyone is your friend."

Tess tugged the credit card free. "What are you talking about?"

Mitzi shrugged, as if to say she'd done all she could. She reached up to pat Tess's face, and it was all Tess could do not to shrink away.

"Why is it that we always want what we can't have?" Mitzi asked, lowering her voice. "Use your senses, all five of them."

Tess wanted to make light of the woman's intensity, but she couldn't quite break the spell Mitzi had woven. "I will," she said.

"He has a secret."

Tess blinked. "He? Who?"

"Danny Gabriel. You only think you know him."

"I don't know him at all."

"Good, you understand." Mitzi nodded. "Don't take the people you work with for granted, especially if they have power over your career. I just don't want you to be blindsided." She started back to her stool. "It could happen."

Tess was becoming exasperated. "Are you going to tell me what you're talking about?"

Mitzi shook her head. She tsked. "My problem is I talk *too much*. Ask anyone. Pay no attention to me. You're busy. Go back to work. You're a good girl, solid. You'll do fine."

Tess had been blown off before, but Mitzi was a maestro. Tess didn't much appreciate the good-girl remark, either. It was the second time today she'd been called that, and it was making her feel like a virgin being groomed as a sacrifice to the advertising gods.

The gallows humor was meant to loosen the knots in Tess's stomach, but it didn't work. Was that why she'd been brought here? To be someone's scapegoat? To draw fire? Every office had internal politics, and she already knew something about this company's problems, but Mitzi seemed to be suggesting there was more going on. And Mitzi might actually be in a position to know. Her bathroom was the equivalent of a locker room/spa where people came to hang out and gossip.

Tess debated the wisdom of trying to pry more information out of the washroom attendant. Maybe it was a sign that the three women reappeared from the lounge, saying they wanted to look over Mitzi's wares. Tess noticed how chatty and personal they were with her. One of them asked her about her acting job. Apparently she had a bit part in an off-off-Broadway play. Another kidded her about her sexy new haircut.

Tess made it a point to say hello to the women before she left, and to thank Mitzi again for the tea. A woman with enemies couldn't be too careful.

Relief washed over her once she was out the door and heading back to her office. Maybe from now on she'd go to the downstairs bathroom. Better for the hypertension, which she probably had by now.

It was mid-afternoon on a Friday, and the twenty-eighth floor seemed quiet as she traveled hallways that curved and meandered to evoke the tributaries of a river. You could get seasick trying to get around quickly. The walls were covered with murals painted by some of the agency's artists. One was a whimsical underwater motif with sea creatures who'd been given the faces of various staff members. Tess hadn't figured out what the deeper meaning might be, but she hadn't failed to notice that Gabriel was a dolphin. Better than a shark, she supposed.

Tess passed the art and production studio on the way to her corner office, but avoided looking inside. She didn't want to be tempted. She loved seeing the ideas become reality, and this studio was spectacular, large and magnificently equipped. But she couldn't dawdle any longer. It felt as if the entire day had slipped away from her, and tonight's dinner was going to be another time-suck. Worse, she would be spending it with a bunch of people who made her nervous—and apparently had secrets that could blindside her. Great.

"Where is it?" Tess hesitated in her office doorway, talking to herself as she peered at her desk. Her heart jumped painfully. "Where's my PDA?"

Her personal digital assistant was also her cell phone, but there'd been no place to attach it to her jumpsuit when she went to the Qigong session, so she'd left it on her desk. She'd set it on the lead-crystal box that had been her going-away gift from Renaissance. She specifically remembered doing that.

Tess didn't have an assistant. She did her own scheduling via the PDA's digital calendar and memo pad. It contained all her appointments, her address book, even her various passwords. All her vital information was stored on that contraption! She would rather have lost an arm.

She began to search her office, starting with the drawers of her desk, which was a rather strange-looking antique made of rattan and glass that creaked under any kind of weight. Actually, the entire office was strange, although Tess loved the wraparound windows that surrounded her from behind. She wasn't as crazy about the enormous German Messerschmitt airplane nose coming out of the wall facing her desk. The last occupant had clearly been a World War II nut. There was a glass case of army divisional patches, of which the 101st Airborne Screaming Eagle was her favorite. That was one pissed-off bird. If she could ever remember, she would have to ask why all the paraphernalia had been left behind.

She'd been told she could redecorate on the company's budget, but there hadn't been time to think about that. Meanwhile, she wanted to duck every time she looked up and saw the plane. She felt like she was about to be strafed.

"Where the hell?" She lifted a stack of account files and searched through the rattan baskets sitting on the credenza behind her desk. Nothing. The PDA had vanished. Maybe she hadn't left it on the crystal box?

She noticed her quilted coat hanging on the coatrack and reminded herself to check the pockets. At the same time, she saw the blinking message light on her office phone. She'd missed that completely when she came in.

She picked up the receiver and punched in her voice-mail password. At least she had that one memorized. The disembodied electronic voice told her she had several new messages, and she raced through them until she got to one from Erica Summers. The CEO's musical voice filled her ear.

"Tess, I just found out that Danny Gabriel can't make our little dinner tonight. He left a message saying that he'd run into you this morning and was very favorably impressed, so didn't feel a pressing need to attend tonight. Apparently he's up against a deadline." Erica sniffed. "We'll just have to muddle through without him, won't we? Looking forward to it, Tess."

Tess hung up the phone and swore softly. Gabriel had just blown her off, and he'd used the company CEO to do it. The guy had balls. He would be conspicuous by his absence at dinner tonight, an obvious sign to the board that he didn't consider his new codirector important enough to bother with.

Tess had feared the dinner might not go well, but this was ridiculous. She took a deep breath, willing herself to let it go and get back to work. She still had to find her

PDA. There was no time to waste on professional ego trips, and she felt certain that's what this was. But a half hour later she'd given up on the search—and she was still steaming over Danny's slight. She couldn't concentrate on anything but her outrage, which wasn't like her at all.

The desk gave out a noisy groan as she rose.

So, Danny Gabriel was impressed, was he? She was about to make an even deeper impression on him. It was almost four o'clock by her watch. He shouldn't have left the building yet, if he truly had so much work to do. She had no idea where his office was, but she would search until she found it.

Three

Tess clicked down the hall in her high-heel boots, pencil skirt and black velvet Edwardian jacket. It was five-fifteen, and she had forty-five minutes before the limo was scheduled to pick her up for the reception. She'd decided to change into her dinner outfit and let Gabriel get a look at what he'd be missing—and call him on his blatant attempt to undermine her on her big night. You never got a second chance to make a first impression, and this was her chance with the company brass, which he very well knew. She even managed to get the kinks out of her hair with a special spray that relaxed and defrizzed. It had loosened her curls, and now they were bouncing all over her head. Extra-large silver hoop earrings and a kiss-my-ass attitude rounded out the look.

She'd also had two cups of Mitzi's tea. No one could say Tess Wakefield didn't live dangerously.

Check it out, Gabe, baby. This is the lady you kicked to the curb. Maybe you should watch your shins. She's wearing boots.

Tess had never felt so tricked-out and sexy. It was almost fun. She figured it was the PMS or the tea, but either way, she had a few choice words for her codirector. She'd called the agency's receptionist for directions to his office, which had turned out to be quite simple. He was on the opposite end of the building from her, in his own corner office.

The twenty-eighth floor was now a ghost town. Tess didn't see another soul as she crossed the building. Everyone had gone for the weekend, but if Gabriel really had a deadline, he might still be around.

His office door was open when she got there, but she found no one inside. The room was mostly windows and traditional in style, which surprised her. She'd expected to find a dark, artsy lair, with decor that might even be mystical. One of the many rumors about him was that he had Native American blood. Instead, everything was mahogany, beautifully carved with reflecting-pool surfaces and damask upholstery. It reminded her of a federal court, except for the two walls of posters showcasing his ads.

Tess took a moment to check them out. He was very good, but she knew that. What struck her was the unexpected way the ads were displayed. On one side of the room, they were bright and upbeat, with vibrant colors and attractive models. On the other side, the ads had a dark edginess that bordered on sinister. But, even more perplexing, on the abutting wall hung just one poster—a misty pastel of a child in a swing, rising toward the setting sun. It almost looked as if she were going to slip off the seat and fly away.

What a strange juxtaposition, Tess thought. It was enough to make you wonder if Gabriel was bipolar. Mitzi had said he had a secret. Tess was curious whether the ads might have something to do with that, but there wasn't time to explore. She turned and saw a set of double doors that led to what looked like a conference room. The doors were partially open, and she could see movement inside. Maybe he was in there, preparing for his deadline.

Tess peeked through the doors and saw Gabriel bent over a storyboard, probably checking out the sketches for a client's television spot. "Am I interrupting?" she asked, opening the doors.

He glanced up at her and did a double take. She couldn't help but notice the way his eyes narrowed. Whether it was appreciation or appraisal, she couldn't tell, but his gaze was riveting.

"You're perfect," he said. "Come in."

"What?"

"You're wearing boots, a skirt. It's perfect." He beckoned her over to him. "Come on in."

Tess didn't move from the doorway.

He took a chair from the conference table and rolled it to within a few feet of where she stood. She had no idea what he was doing as he positioned the chair in front of the doors.

"Right here," he said. "Come over and sit down, *please*. I have something to show you."

The please did the trick. She couldn't resist conviction.

She walked to the chair, aware of him standing there with his hands on the leather back, as if he were about to give her a ride.

"Are you going to tell me why I'm doing this?" she asked, wondering what would happen to her very skinny skirt when she sat. Surely he wasn't angling for *that*, a leg shot.

"All will be explained," he assured her, "but not yet. That would ruin it."

He stopped her before she could sit down. "Let's fix that skirt first," he said. "Here."

He actually came around the chair and turned her toward him, then spun her skirt until the slit in the back was running up the side of her leg. With any encouragement at all, the opening would now reveal an eyeful of caramel thigh. Thank God for liquid stockings.

"Mmm, yes. Perfect."

It was almost erotic the way he said that word, *perfect*. Like a man whispering something dirty in a woman's ear.

He sat her in the chair and knelt in front of her, apparently to do some more adjusting of her person.

She pulled back as his hand grazed her leg. "What *are* you doing?"

"Relax," he said, "trust me, *please,* this is important."

She wasn't as taken with his conviction this time, but she was very curious.

"Unbend your knee. Here, like this." He inched her left

leg forward a little and then propped her sleek laced boot on its spiky heel, with the tip pointing in the air.

"Good," he said, rising to look at her. He nodded, murmuring something about how perfect this was under his breath.

Interesting that she had to focus on what he said. It was entirely possible he was doing that on purpose, making her listen. He had a reputation as a persuasive pitchman, a closer, as they said in sales, but there was nothing overtly aggressive about him. Even now, he came across as supremely laid-back, and yet he radiated energy. It was like droplets sizzling on his skin.

She'd heard all the rumors, that Danny Gabriel was deadly smart and blindingly handsome, almost his own species. She'd heard them. She just hadn't wanted to believe them. No wonder they needed someone to corral this guy.

He studied her, his features knit in concentration.

"Lean back and support yourself on the arms of the chair," he said, giving her direction as if they were on a photo shoot. "Good. Now relax and arch your spine. Can you give me a little more bend? Try to relax and arch your spine."

Tess drew herself up and felt the chair move. "The wheels are going to roll out from under me."

"Here, I'll steady you." He moved behind her and gripped the chair. "Try it again," he said. "Lean into the arch and tilt your head back. God, *yes,* that's great."

Tess's spine bowed with tension, locking her in place. At that moment, all she could see were the edges of him, a blur. But when his head came into her line of sight, and he looked down at her, she suddenly felt vulnerable.

She started to sit up.

"No, wait," he said. "This is important. Look at me. *Look at me, Tess.*"

She held on to the chair, steadying herself. As she gazed up at him, she could feel her jacket fall open and her skirt creep up. She was balancing herself with the heel of one boot. Her other foot had lifted off the floor.

What must she look like? What the hell was he doing?

"How much longer?" she asked, annoyed. "I can't hold this."

"Just a few more seconds." He pulled the chair back toward him. "We're almost there, and you look hotter than hell. Don't think about anything but that—how hot you look. *Amazing.*"

His voice dropped low and sexy. He was still murmuring as he bent down and fitted his mouth to hers in a weightless kiss. Tess's grip tightened. Her whole body quivered as she struggled to get up, but there was no way possible. All of the laws of gravity and physics were against her, and with his mouth locked to hers, she couldn't move.

"Perfect," he whispered against her lips.

Tess's body reacted to the extreme vulnerability of her position. Her flesh felt as if it had caught fire. Her nipples zinged to life, hardening instantly, and the cotton crotch of her panties should have been steaming they were so damp. What was happening? She could feel herself lubricating down there, blushing with shock and excitement.

He broke the kiss, freeing her, and Tess sat up too quickly. Dizziness washed over her. She'd been upside down so long the blood had left her head.

"What kind of stunt was that?" she asked, fighting to get her bearings.

"No stunt," he said.

"You *kissed* me."

"Yeah."

"Yeah? What do you mean *yeah?* This is an office. We're coworkers. Who the hell do you think you are?"

"True, but let me show you why I did it."

Before she could catch her breath, he was standing in front of her. Tess stole a glance at his crotch—and hated herself for it. Did she really care whether or not he'd been as turned on as she had? There was no hope for her.

"Look at that," he said, pointing to her legs. "It's perfect."

The man was a broken record. *"What's* perfect?"

"What you did when I kissed you." He knelt next to her. "Look at how you're sitting—the way you raised your right leg and hooked your toe under the left."

Tess saw that the tip of one boot was tucked under her other calf. "So what?" she said. "I was trying not to fall over."

She settled both feet on the floor, still too dizzy to stand.

Gabriel rose and went to the double doors, drawing them together but not closing them. He left an opening about six inches wide, and then he came back to her.

"When I saw you in those boots it gave me an idea for an ad," he said.

"An *ad?* Why didn't you just say that?" So much for being turned on.

"It wouldn't have worked. I had to catch you off guard to see what your legs would do. Can you imagine what a shot that would be for your Faustini ad? Think print campaign, maybe even billboards."

He gestured toward her chair and the door, setting the scene. "You're sitting there, like that, but the camera's outside the doors, which are open just enough to show your legs levitating."

She sat forward. "What are you talking about?"

"Imagine someone standing outside these doors, looking in. What would they see through that opening? Your legs, right? Your boots, Faustini boots. It's the perfect tease."

"Actually, they wouldn't. These aren't the Faustinis. I changed for dinner."

His brow furrowed. "For the sake of argument, they are, okay? And that innocent bystander out there can't see anything but your boots. She can't see me, or what's going on in here, but she knows damn well by the way your boots are behaving that you're not taking dictation. What does that say to her?"

"Wear Faustini and people will sexually assault you?"

"Wear Faustini and life will *surprise* you."

"There are some surprises I could do without." Tess got up and whipped her skirt around the right way. She was done playing along. "All of this was about Faustini? *My* account?"

"Yes, but you don't have to thank me."

She emitted a sound of disgust, and he actually cracked a grin. "What are you, eight years old?" she asked.

They locked stares, engaged in a steamy visual battle. After a moment or two, Tess began to feel a little ridiculous. Maybe he wasn't the only one being childish. But as she glared at him, she noticed something she hadn't seen before, a small crescent scar on his upper lip, near the bow. Her stomach dipped, and something even deeper fluttered in the most pleasurable way. *Damn.* The scar turned his mouth into a sensual wonderland. It was wicked. You couldn't see a mouth like that and not think about sex.

What would that feel like?

Not a question Tess wanted to contemplate. Thank God, she was highly skilled in the art of denial. Give her a couple more seconds, and it shouldn't be a problem.

Perhaps, though, she could create a little problem for him. She smoothed her outfit into place, remembering why she'd come here. Someone needed to catch this man off guard and show him how it felt.

"Are you checking me out?" he asked. "Because I could swear you were checking me out."

"Murderball must be dangerous," she said, walking over to him. She touched his scar with her fingertips. If she was nervous it didn't show, and that was all she cared about at the moment.

"*You're* dangerous," he said.

"You aren't kidding." Tess angled in for a kiss, but he stopped her. He gripped her arms and held her off, staring at her as if she'd gone crazy. She could almost hear those droplets of energy sizzling on his skin. She may even have caught their scent, a fiery male essence that made her throat ache. Something about all this thrilled her. Maybe it was taking a chance, calling his bluff, if that's what he was doing, bluffing.

"Okay," he said softly, "let's get dangerous." He yanked her close and kissed her.

The flutter in Tess's gut turned bright and sharp. In her mind, she could see that damn sexy scar, but she couldn't feel it on her lips. The only rough sensation was his hands, molesting her arms. His mouth was soft and hot. It was luscious. The sound vibrating inside her was a growl. A tiny voracious growl.

A startling hunger overtook her. She wanted her hands free, not to break away, but to clutch him. It didn't seem possible that she was suddenly greedy for more. For something wild and deep. As deep as the sea. A kiss that would drag her under and drown her.

Her nipples brushed against his chest, and again, hardened uncontrollably. A sensation she hadn't felt in months flared in the pit of her belly. God help her, that was hot.

In her mind, she saw the two of them spinning in the chair, whirling like tops, her facing him with her legs spread over the chair arms and him beneath her, anchoring her with his brick wall of an erection, thrusting madly, fucking like bunnies—

What? Was she crazy?

Was it the tea? Mitzi's psychotropic tea?

Her fantasies hadn't been that energetic in her college years, had they?

The questions brought her back to reality. Somehow Gabriel had turned her around, all while kissing her ardently. Clearly he was going to take this further. Next, he would be scooping her up in his arms and laying her out on the conference table.

She gave his shin a sharp little kick.

He swore and released her.

She stepped back, panting. "You kiss good," she said.

"Jesus, so do you. I'm coming to that dinner tonight. In fact, I'm taking you *home* from that dinner tonight."

She drew herself up. "No, no you're not. Tonight is about my work, and my work is not about kissing, in case you hadn't noticed."

He nodded, but she had a feeling he would have agreed with anything she said at that moment. He seemed far more interested in her mouth than her point. There was a time, not so terribly long ago, when Tess would have succumbed in a New York second to the charms of a man like Danny Gabriel. Make that a nanosecond. She'd been a total pushover, a wuss in every way. Of course, that had to stay her secret. She was stronger now. She'd had a lot of practice not having sex. The denial thing.

And more important, she hadn't made her point yet.

"Canceling out on the dinner," she told him, "was petty and insulting, *Mr.* Gabriel. I guess I may have you on the run, hmm? Otherwise, why would a man of your stature have to lie your way out of my dinner?"

He started to speak, but she overrode him. "I may not be a genius, but I'm damn good at what I do, and I deserve respect."

He began to shake his head, but she wasn't listening to any lame apologies. "I think we're finished here, at least I am." She tweaked the lapel of her jacket, shot him a burning stare, and turned to find a distinguished-looking man in an immaculately tailored suit standing in the doorway. Obviously he'd heard every word.

Gabriel spoke from behind her. "Tess Wakefield, meet Oliver Handel, the vice president of international marketing for the Kashogi Corporation."

Shit. It looked as if Gabriel had told the truth. She was staring at his deadline. Possibly, her inner-life coach might have some advice for her at this inopportune moment?

Don't ever let them see you sweat, Tess.

The self-talk that most people called an inner voice had always come to Tess in the form of old television commercials. It was probably what had led her into advertising. And in this case, it was exactly what she needed to hear.

She made no attempt to make herself presentable. That would have drawn more attention to the fact that she wasn't. She walked straight over and took the man's hand, shaking it firmly. "Mr. Handel, how do you do, sir? Such an honor, really. It's a great pleasure to meet you."

Handel returned her grip. He smiled, chuckling aloud. "You have *my* utmost respect, Tess, if I may call you that. I'm sure Daniel deserved every word of that lecture."

Tess smiled knowingly. "He's just brilliant, isn't he?" she said, deciding to take the high road. She'd already expressed herself to her complete satisfaction, and maybe it was karma that Gabriel's client had shown up. "And now, I'll leave you two to your meeting."

Tess turned to Gabriel. "We'll miss you at dinner," she said with a wicked little lilt in her voice.

"I'm sure." His response was as dry as dust.

On the way back to her office, she retraced her path through the deep-sea aquarium. Pleased with herself, she grinned. Maybe *now* she'd be able to get some work done. She had an ad campaign to come up with, but it damn sure wasn't going to feature levitating boots.

Four

*H*e was down on one knee, rearranging her legs and inadvertently brushing against her bare skin. He'd removed her boots, leaving her legs and feet exposed. Why had he done that? He didn't seem to understand that his fingers tickled like feather fringe, and his skin was the richest shade of tequila gold she'd ever seen. He touched her ankle, innocently positioning it, and streamers of light shot up her thighs, straight to her sex.

No, straight to her pussy, she thought, giving in to a wicked urge to use the bad-girl word. The words and images assaulting her overheated brain were bordering on lewd, but they might be the only way to get this man's attention.

He cupped her calf with his palm, and her pulse raced out of control. His hands were warm, strong, smooth against her flesh. He was going to wreck her. Now he was playing with the back of her knee, lingering in that secret, unbearably *sensitive spot. If he went higher, she'd faint. If he didn't, she'd explode.*

Fainting was less dangerous.

"Danny," she whispered. She drew up his head, gazed at the crescent scar on his lip—and didn't know whether to kiss him or slap him silly. How could he not know what he was doing?

Desperate, she inched up her skirt, letting him see that she wore no panties. "See that?" she whispered. "It's a pussy, in case you were wondering. Help yourself, for heaven's sake. Stop making me crazy and make me co—"

Tess slapped the desk with her palm. This *had* to stop. Her eyes snapped open, and she breathed out an exasperated sigh. She'd been drifting off into crazy X-rated fantasies all morning. And they all revolved around her spread-eagle legs—and *him*. He didn't get all the credit, though. This was at least partly biological. Could doctors induce periods the way they induced labor? Her never-ending PMS was killing her.

And, she'd figured it out. Now she knew who he reminded her of with his cut-you-like-a-knife eyes. Tess prided herself on having left her past behind, but there was one man who'd touched a chord that wouldn't stop resonating in some darkened corner of her mind. If every woman had her indelible bad-boy experience, then Professor Jonathan Wiley, her theater arts instructor in college, was Tess's, except that he wasn't a boy. He'd been her phantom of the opera, in a manner of speaking, but without all the soaring romance—and his image had come to her during her fantasies about Gabriel.

Not good, she thought. Nothing about this was good.

She drew herself up and surveyed the chaos on her desk. It was Saturday, but she and her entire team were working this weekend in order to be ready for the pitch to the Faustini brass next week. Even Erica Summers had agreed to make herself available, probably to set an example for the troops.

Tess's desk was strewn with eight-by-ten glossies that had been sent to her by casting directors. She'd spread them out hoping that photos of fit young male and female models would inspire a killer idea for the Faustini promotion, but no such luck. Some of the women were promising, but the guys reminded her of southern California's yuppie bikers, who dressed up in black leather and swore off shaving for the weekend. A couple of them were cute, but definitely not the millennium outlaw with the soul of a poet she had in mind.

Tess sorted through the glossies one more time, creating a stack of hopefuls. Too bad she couldn't blame her fantasy trips on pictures of buff bikers. Unfortunately, Danny Gabriel's sneak attack had triggered the daydreams, and she hadn't been able to concentrate worth a damn since.

The welcome dinner with the board last night had gone as predicted. Gabriel was conspicuous by his absence and probably on everyone's mind the whole time. Certainly he was on hers, the snake. Sure, he'd been acting as if he wanted to help her with the campaign, but she had to wonder if that wasn't about hiding his real intentions. He was a saboteur at heart. And she didn't need one of those. She was doing well enough on her own.

What had happened to that headlock she was supposed to have on her emotions? More than likely, she was suffering from simple estrogen overload. In theory, the human body was like a hydroelectric dam, which overflowed if left untended, and she was definitely untended. All she needed to do was open the sluice gates a little, and the quickest way to do that was with some good oldfashioned masturbation—or what her mother had called "naughty fingers" when Tess was growing up.

The Queen of Euphemisms, her mother. "In the family way" meant pregnant and the birth was a "happy event." The bathroom was "the smallest room in the house," and a woman's period was "a visiting friend." Tess's favorite—"tired and overemotional"—was how her mother described her father when he got carried away with the communion wine.

God bless them, her parents could never have been accused of neglect. Tess was a desperately wanted only child, and her mother had anxiously attempted to control every aspect of her daughter's existence. All in an effort to protect her, of course—from life's pain, from its ridicule and shame. Sad that her mother had resorted to ridicule and shame, herself.

Tess had been shy and overweight, and her parents had tried to embarrass her out of both. Her mother had weighed Tess before every meal, bought her clothes that were too small and put her on her first medically supervised diet at five. Five? *Mom, what were you thinking?* The debating team and the glee club had been Dad's idea. Under all the pressure, Tess had developed a stutter.

Fortunately, she'd outgrown it *and* the weight, which had turned out to be a combination of baby fat and adolescent rebellion. But when she'd slimmed down in college—and started getting attention from boys—she'd gone a little crazy. Enter the wild-child phase. She'd been looking for love in all the wrong places, needing to prove to herself again and again that she was desirable to men when what she'd really wanted was the love and acceptance she didn't get as a kid.

Most of the boys she was with couldn't handle the sex part, much less provide any sensitivity toward her emotional needs, which even she wasn't aware of at the time. Tess could barely remember the encounters, probably because she didn't want to think about all that furtive groping in hallway alcoves and the sweaty fumbling in parked cars. But there was one guy she did remember.

What a wicked kinky dude Jonathan Wiley was. Not a boy, a man—and maybe a demon escaped from her id, if anything Freud had said was true. Wiley had quietly insisted that she had talent and could have a big acting career, if she wanted. Yeah, sure. She'd barely heard that part, given the blazingly erotic stuff he'd whispered in her ear during their after-hours coaching sessions.

Tess remembered his suggestions in far too much detail: *If I had you where I want you right now—naked with your bottom in the air—I wouldn't know whether to swat you or lick you like an ice cream cone.*

He'd talked about restraining her with the ropes that hung from the stage rigging, freeing her from her clothing—and her inhibitions—and arousing her until she fainted dead away. He'd been particularly obsessed with her ass, and all the amazing things he could do to it, including love bites and erotic discipline. Spanking, to be exact. He'd whispered about disciplining her in ways that had made her hair stand on end, but only to bring her the most intense pleasure, *of course.*

Honestly, he'd frightened the hell out of her, and she'd run for her life. She was only eighteen. But much of what he'd said and done had stayed with her, and as she'd matured into her twenties, the fear had faded, and she'd become secretly fascinated with some of his suggestions, especially the darker ones.

That had scared her a little. Still did. Especially given that just thinking about it made her hot and twitchy. Like now.

"*Enough,* Tess," she warned. "You're not a college kid anymore, and Danny Gabriel is not an incarnation of Wiley." *Despite the sensual features and the seductive ways. All Gabriel did was kiss her.*

She got up from her desk and went over to the water dispenser, hoping a cold drink would put out the fire. On the way she passed the Messerschmitt mounted on the wall. "Give it your best shot," she said softly. "I'm pretty fast."

She drank several tiny paper cups of water and went back to her desk. This wasn't her first time dealing with sluice gates. She was a healthy thirty-two-year-old woman, who'd been celibate for a very long time, and she'd had to find creative ways to deal with the situation. Quite by accident, she'd discovered a certain yoga position that had brought about some spontaneous relief. It might even have made the *Cosmo* orgasm quiz.

She needed to start doing yoga again. Quickly.

She was thinking fondly about her version of the full lotus position when the phone rang. It was the landline, which reminded her that her PDA was still missing. She'd looked everywhere, including the lost and found in the coffee lounge. She'd stopped by security this morning and reported it. She'd also picked up a replacement phone, but it contained none of her vital information, of course.

She went back to studying the glossies as she picked up the receiver. "Tess Wakefield," she said.

"I know who you are. I just don't know why you're not here."

Tess had a moment of confusion. The male voice struck a familiar chord, but she didn't know how to respond. It had to be Danny. "Where are you?"

"Waiting for you down here in the Sandbox."

"The Sandbox? Why are you there?"

"Tess, hello! It's Andy. We're *all* waiting for you down here in the sandbox. You called a team meeting this morning, remember?"

Tess fell back in her chair. Suddenly her heart was pounding when before it had been utterly still. She'd just daydreamed her way through fifteen minutes of the session she'd scheduled with her team. And after all the pep-talking she'd done, trying to impress upon them how important it was for them to be prepared. Oh, yes, she definitely needed to get busy with those naughty fingers.

* * *

"Okay, this is major," Carlotta told the team. "We choose one man and one woman with tremendous potential, and we call them Faustini spokesmodels. We create images for them that are totally distinctive, maybe something like Darth Vader for the man."

Tess had been hoping for something other than Darth Vader, but Carlotta clearly loved the idea. Her expression said she was waiting for affirmation, applause, something. Her shapely butt was perched in a belt swing that hung from the ceiling on chains. Andy had taken the other swing, right next to her, and the rest of the team was sitting around the conference table, which was an old-fashioned picnic table.

Of all the agency's themed conference rooms, the Sandbox was the favorite, probably because it suggested a day at the beach. Only a wall-size wipe board and a flip chart said business as usual. Otherwise, the wedge-shaped room was lined with real bamboo in naturalistic planter boxes, and the floor was exotic pink sand, imported from somewhere in the South Pacific. The rustic table could have been found at any state park, and the ceiling was painted sky blue. Several large skylights washed the room in sunny yellow.

Natural light, bare feet and sifting sands were supposed to inspire greatness, apparently. Mostly, they inspired Tess to nap like a cat in the sunshine, but that was about it. All this outer pressure and inner tension was getting to her.

"Batman and Catwoman?" Andy suggested.

"That's distinctive?" Carlotta's tone dismissed him.

"With my idea, we save the client money because the spokesmodels do the entire campaign, *and* we create magnificent brand identification."

"Only if the models are magnificent," Tess countered.

"They will be—"

"Listen to this," Brad cut in. He rose from the picnic table, his bare feet squishing in the sand. "We set the photo shoot in one of those hot new S&M clubs in the city. We'll find ourselves the fucking Prince of Darkness and outfit him in Faustini."

"I love it!" Carlotta squealed.

Tess wasn't thrilled with the concept, nor did she think Faustini would be, but she was curious where her team might take it. "What about the woman?"

"Streetwalker chic? Gothic glam?" Brad offered his suggestions with a shrug. "I disagree that we need to be distinctive. Faustini already is distinctive. We need to get low-down and dirty. Make people notice."

"What's wrong with pulling women's underwear out of a briefcase?" Andy said, apparently referring to his idea from yesterday.

Tess reached for her tote, where she'd put the manila envelope with the glossies. A moment later she had the pictures fanned across the picnic table like a large deck of cards.

"Good luck finding Darth Vader in this bunch" she said, "and by the way, I'm not sold on the club idea."

Jan Butler got up from the table and went over to the wipe board, where she grabbed a grease pen and wrote two words.

"Performance advertising," she said, turning to the group. "We hire actors in all the major cities to walk around in their underwear carrying Faustini cases, chanting 'Clothes don't make the man, Faustini does.'"

"And get our client charged for indecent exposure?" Tess shivered.

"*Or,*" Butler said, not giving up, "we could hire the actors to be human billboards, print Faustini across their foreheads and send them into the streets. It worked for a company named SnoreStop."

Everyone laughed, but it didn't work for Tess. "Sorry," she said, "it's back to the drawing board, everybody. I really am sorry."

Andy fell out of the swing and onto his knees, pretending to collapse as he sank into the sand. His meaning was obvious. Tess was asking too much. It didn't escape any of them. Nobody looked happy about her announcement, and neither was she. They were working 24/7 now, and they were running out of time. The meeting with Faustini was scheduled for late next week, but prior to that there was a dress rehearsal for Erica. If the boss wasn't happy, Tess was screwed.

Tess quelled the urge to end the meeting with a pep talk. She couldn't very well whip the group into shape when she'd just nixed all their ideas and didn't have anything to offer herself. It was up to her now.

"He's *hot,*" Mitzi said as Tess came out of the stall.

"Who's hot?" Tess straightened her jeans and cashmere turtleneck as she walked to the counter, wondering if the sweater's oatmeal color was washing her out a bit. She used to be a blue-eyed blonde. In this light everything looked dishwatery, even her eyes.

She glanced over at Mitzi, startled to see the washroom attendant holding up a glossy of one of the male models from the stack Tess had left on the counter.

"That's my work you're going through," Tess said.

"Of course." Mitzi seemed confused. "That's why you left it out, isn't it? A lot of the creatives consult me on their ideas, and I assumed— What? You didn't want me to look at the pictures?"

Tess felt as if she should be angry, but she didn't have the energy. "I was in a hurry. I left it on the counter because it was awkward taking it into the stall."

"I see. Well, if you don't want my input, that's strictly up to you."

Mitzi was quiet for exactly two seconds. Tess counted. One one-thousand, two one-thousand.

"But if I were you—" Mitzi flapped the picture, a young stud in a black biker's jacket and low-slung jeans, "I'd give this cutie a Faustini briefcase with fake dials and have him turn it on like it was a boom box. He could be walking down the street with it, bopping along, and suddenly there are a bunch of tall sexy women coming his way, and they surround him and make him dance with them."

Tess cocked her head. The idea had some originality at least. "How did you know who the client was? Did you read my notes, too?"

"Well, sure, I thought that's why you left the envelope. The slogan could go something like 'Faustini makes you feel like dancing.' You know, from the song? But, it's up to you. If you don't want my opinion, I'll keep it to myself."

The slogan wasn't too bad, either, Tess allowed. Of course, she couldn't steal Mitzi's ideas. It wouldn't be ethical, and she really couldn't blame Mitzi for looking at the pictures. If Tess didn't want people messing with her stuff, she shouldn't be giving them the opportunity, which included the information on her PDA.

Meanwhile, Mitzi looked wounded, and Tess felt guilty.

"I really should hire you," Tess said. "Your ideas make more sense than a photo shoot in an S&M club, which seems to be the way my team wants to go."

"S&M? For Faustini?"

The voice came from one of the stalls. It was followed by the music of a flushing toilet, and then the door opened, and Danny Gabriel appeared.

The man had amazing timing. If eavesdropping were an Olympic event, he'd take the gold.

His hands lifted away from his fly, and the graceful movement drew Tess's gaze directly there. Fortunately, he was already busy tucking his tuxedo-front white dress shirt into his pants and didn't notice her gawking. He wore old-fashioned blue jeans, but the fit was killer. The waist was low and the legs were high, stovepipes that shot all the way to his crotch, creating a cupping effect.

She could almost imagine placing her hand there…and squeezing.

Good grief. She would need a lobotomy to remove the image from her brain.

Mitzi slipped off her stool, scurrying to turn on a faucet for him and get a towel ready. Tess moved away from the counter, making way for Mr. Hot Pants. It was clear who got the royal treatment around here.

Tess would have to be very sure not to bow and scrape. "Why didn't you let somebody know you were in there?" she asked him.

He shook water droplets from his hands and took the paper towel Mitzi offered. "Is that a new rule?"

He glanced over his shoulder, as if expecting an answer. She'd forgotten what she said. The jeans worked from this angle too. The back pockets cupped the part of him that seemed to be the birthright of the male gender. A great tight smackable butt.

"I wasn't serious about the S&M," she told him quickly. She didn't want *that* getting back to the client.

"I was. It's a great idea." He caught her reflection in the mirror.

She didn't look away, but she wanted to. He was so *fucking* confrontational. She debated telling him it wasn't his campaign to be serious about, but her covert mission was to teach Mr. Gabriel to play nice, so she held her fire. There would be plenty of opportunities to enlighten him.

In a calm, neutral voice, she said, "In my first meeting with Faustini's head of North American operations, he told me that he didn't want sex, drugs and rock and roll. He was very clear about Faustini's parameters. No nudity, profanity, silver studs or whips."

"Then you have to *give* them nudity, profanity, silver studs and whips because that's exactly what they do want.

They've just given you a glimpse of their libidinal desires. They're telling you what's forbidden to them—and down deep everybody wants what's forbidden, including Faustini's customers."

"You're telling me to try and convince Faustini that an S&M club should be their new image? Who should I suggest as their spokesmodel? Satan?"

His expression brightened. "Can you think of anybody better? However, I'd call him the Prince of Darkness. It's more romantic."

"Now we're romanticizing Satan? Pratt-Summers already has a reputation of not being sensitive to the client's needs," she reminded him pointedly, "and it's losing the agency business. Clients know they can go elsewhere and be heard. And given the cost of advertising these days, they want to be heard. Faustini has hired us to do a job. They're our employer."

"Exactly, they hired us to do *our* job. We don't make leather goods. That's their job, and we don't try to tell them how to do it. They shouldn't tell us how to do advertising."

Tess was momentarily stymied. "Okay...but there's a significant difference. We're not buying their leather goods. They're buying our ads, and they should get what they want."

"What they need, yes. What they want? Never."

Tess sighed. It was axiomatic that you couldn't succeed in advertising by ignoring the client, and yet Danny Gabriel had been doing it very successfully for years. He probably would have gone on doing it had Erica Summers not decided to change the game plan. These days Erica was more interested in expansion than in awards and prestige. She wanted Pratt-Summers to have a global presence, and that meant they needed to attract more traditional clients, like financial institutions and insurance companies, the type who would be terrified of putting their image in the hands of Danny Gabriel.

The hands of Danny Gabriel.

He touched her ankle, innocently positioning it, and streamers of light shot up her thighs, straight to her—

Tess tried to block the image, but she'd had far too much personal experience with his hands. They'd burned sensory impressions into her brain that replayed at the slightest provocation, like now. She felt like a post-traumatic stress victim.

She looked up to see him looking at her too, but not her hands. Her eyes. He was gazing into her washed-out eyes with abject interest.

"Did you know that women can have orgasms that last up to an hour?" he said, his voice dropping to an intimate whisper. "And they stop breathing for minutes at a time, like a deep-sea diver."

Jesus, no wonder he reminded her of Wiley. That could have been straight out of her professor's mouth.

"Well, thank you for sharing," she said, trying to keep her composure. "No, I didn't know that. I doubt if Mitzi did, either."

Mitzi was looking through the pictures and making notes on them with Tess's grease pen. "Of course I knew that," she said, not bothering to look up. "I had one this morning. Forty-five minutes, but who's counting."

What was it with this agency and orgasms? One would think they had the Viagra account. Mitzi spoke from proud personal experience. Tess wondered if Gabriel did, as well. Everyone in the place seemed to have the most incredible sex life. Was it something Mitzi was selling?

"If we're going to talk business," Tess said to Gabriel, hoping to steer the conversation back to exactly that, "maybe we should go somewhere else."

Danny smoothed back tendrils of dark hair, tucking them into his ponytail. "I'm sure Mitzi doesn't mind. She knows everything there is to know about this place, anyway."

"Hopefully, she's not a spy," Tess said under her breath.

"Here's a thought." He glanced at his watch. "You know about our massage room, don't you? I have one scheduled in ten minutes, and the room has two tables. I could ask the masseuse to work on both of us. She won't mind. She can switch back and forth, and we can talk."

He liked the idea. She could tell by his smile.

"A couples massage," he said.

Tess thought about that. She really did. Naked in the same room with him, sharing the same masseuse, a woman who would be moving back and forth between them, her hands all over him and then those same hands rubbing all over Tess. Something about that made her nervous.

"I'll pass," she said. "Massages put me to sleep. I'd never be able to concentrate."

"In that case, sit and talk to me while I have a massage."

Somehow that option didn't make Tess any less nervous. "Not this time," she said.

"Rain check, then?"

"Oh, right, definitely. For sure."

Gabriel took a money clip from his pocket. He pulled out a couple of bills that looked suspiciously like fifties, walked over to Mitzi and tucked them in the pocket of her navy blue duster coat. He thanked her without saying what for, nodded to Tess, and left.

As soon as the door closed, Tess turned to Mitzi. "What the hell was that about?"

"The one-hour orgasm?" Mitzi grinned. "One of his accounts is a pharmaceutical giant that's developed the female equivalent of Viagra. Danny's doing his research."

So, Tess hadn't been too far off about the Viagra. But she hadn't meant the orgasm question. She'd meant the money. Was that an exorbitant tip, or was Gabriel paying Mitzi money owed for something he'd bought? It smacked of something more clandestine, like a drug deal or a bribe, but he'd hardly do those things in front of Tess. Was he buying her cooperation, maybe her silence?

Tess got closer to Mitzi, speaking in whispers. "You said something about Danny Gabriel having a secret."

"I also said I couldn't reveal it."

"Name your price. I'll pay." If Mitzi was an information broker, Tess wasn't above greasing her palm.

Mitzi just smiled. "Here's your dominatrix for the Faustini ad," she said, handing Tess the stack of glossies. "She's right on top."

The model Mitzi had picked was a long-lashed beauty with cat eyes, black-cherry lips and an evil smile. She would be the perfect Mistress of Pain, if Tess were going that route. But she wasn't.

She thanked Mitzi, but did not slip any money into her pocket. The information broker would have to do better than that.

Five

Tess stood on the corner, clutching her tote to her body for warmth as she waved at the cabs sailing by. Someone should have warned her that a standard-issue quilted coat wouldn't cut it this time of year. Was this New York or Antarctica? It was so cold her breath had created an impenetrable fog bank, which might be the reason cabs weren't stopping. They couldn't see her.

It was nearly midnight. She'd just finished working on the Faustini campaign, and her next mission was to get home. Not as easy as it sounded for a native Californian in New York. She'd decided to hail a cab rather than take the subway at this hour. Her furnished two-bedroom condo on the Upper East Side was owned by the agency and used for consultants and commuting executives, but Erica Summers had promised it to Tess, rent free, for as

long as she was with the agency. That had cinched the deal
for Tess. Finding an affordable apartment in Manhattan
was not unlike a quest for the Holy Grail.

"Help the crazy freezing woman!" White steam plumed
from Tess's mouth. She had little personal cab-hailing experience—people drove their own cars in L.A.—but she'd
been coached by Andy to be aggressive. Curse at them,
he'd said. Flip them the bird. Speak their language, and
they'll stop every time, out of respect.

Tess might have to throw her body in front of their
wheels to get respect tonight. Interesting that she was feeling almost ballsy enough to do it. She'd made some incredible progress in the last several hours. She'd actually
come up with a concept and roughed out the print ads
for the Faustini campaign.

Her imagination was still soaring. Brad Hayes had inspired the idea when he'd suggested goth glam, which
didn't quite cover all the bases, in Tess's opinion. She'd
tweaked it a bit and come up with Elegant Goth, reason-
ing that elegance would satisfy the loyal Faustini customers, and the gothic touch would attract the new young,
hip crowd they wanted. It would either be the perfect
crossover, *or* it would miss both markets and totally tank.

But Tess had a good feeling about it. And her team had
liked the concept too, at least the ones she could reach.
She'd arranged an emergency after-hours conference call
to brainstorm the idea, and she, Andy, Brad and Carlotta
had patched together a print layout with the Elegant Goth
theme. Tess had been refining it until moments ago.

"Over here!" she yelled as a cab veered toward her. It

rolled past her at a good clip and stopped up the street, brakes screeching. Tess broke into a run, struggling with her coat and bag, and praying the cab wouldn't take off without her. The back door opened magically as she reached the car, and she piled inside. The only thing on her mind was escaping the cold.

She gave the driver her address as she pulled the door shut. Panting, she turned to throw her tote on the seat beside her and saw that something was already there. Or rather, *someone*. A man.

"Oh! I didn't know the cab was occupied—" Several startling truths hit Tess all at once. She couldn't get out of the cab. The driver had already taken off. They were speeding down the street, and beams from the streetlights illuminated the other passenger's face. His shadow-carved features were disturbingly familiar. She could even see the scar.

"Danny Gabriel? What are you doing?"

The very slowness of Gabriel's smile made it seem sinister. Tess sprang up to get the driver's attention, but Gabriel blocked her. He clamped a hand over her mouth and pulled her back with him, mauling her in a way that would have been quite obscene, if not for the quilted coat.

"The Marquis Club," he told the driver. To Tess he said in a low, mock-menacing voice, "You're coming with me. Don't say a word, and you won't get hurt."

Tess pried his hand off her mouth. "You've been watching too many movies. All I have to do is scream, and the driver will call the police."

Gabriel shook his head in slow motion. "Not after the

wad of cash I gave him. Besides, I told him we were regulars of the club, and we're playing out a little fantasy. It happens all the time."

It was beginning to dawn on Tess that this had to be a joke. Coworkers didn't take each other hostage in taxis in the middle of the night.

"The Marquis Club?" she said. "That's at the Marriott Marquis Hotel, right? On Forty-second Street?"

Danny just laughed. "Sweetheart, it's marquis as in Marquis *de Sade,* and it's the perfect backdrop for the Faustini campaign."

"But that sounds like—"

"An S&M club. You're going to love it. But don't feel like you have to thank me. We all work for the same agency, right?"

"But we're not all on the same *team*. How did you know I was working late? Are you spying on me?"

"*Mmm.*" His voice dropped low. "Your every move."

Okay, maybe this wasn't a joke. Tess weighed her options. She didn't lack nerve. She'd moved to New York on her own, but going to an S&M club with him was about as safe and sane as flipping off a cabdriver. In other words, *not.*

"Pull over," she told the driver. "I'm getting out here."

The driver glanced into the rearview mirror, apparently humoring her with his quick nod and smile. He did not pull over.

"He thinks it's part of the game," Gabriel said.

"Well, game's over!" Tess tapped at her watch. "Do you realize what time it is? I scheduled a run-through with Erica Summers tomorrow at eight-thirty."

"That's why we're hitting the club tonight. You have to see this place to believe it."

"Hey, I already *have* the concept for the ad, and I'm not changing it. I want to go home and sleep." She shot him a hard stare. "Why do you care what I do with the Faustini account? Unless you *want* me to make a wrong move and fall on my face."

"That's cold," he said. "The account was supposed to have been mine, and I put in a lot of time thinking about it."

"Sounds like a reason to want to sabotage me, not help me."

"It would be, if I worked that way. This is a concept you might have learned in kindergarten, Tess. It's called sharing."

Conviction again. And it was very convincing when he decided to turn it on. A shock of dark hair had worked its way free from his ponytail and was flirting with his jawline. He didn't bother with it. She wanted to. It was difficult not to wonder what he'd look like with his hair loose and flowing. Way out of style these days, but probably wildly sensual on him. The man could have invented sex. It was that bad.

"Okay, maybe I shouldn't accuse you," she said, hoping to appeal to his sense of honor. Ha! "But some other night, okay? You can take me to the club and punish me for being bad."

"You said it. I'm not letting you out of this cab, though."

"That's abduction, Danny."

"You called me Danny." He said it as if that had some

kind of special significance to their situation. "And no, it's not abduction in the criminal sense. It's a great sexual fantasy being played out by a man and a woman, whom everyone will believe are two consenting adults. I could throw you over my shoulder and carry you into the club kicking and screaming. No one would say a word."

"That's evil."

"Yeah, it is. You're going to love the place." His smile was panic-inducing. Probably that damn scar.

"I'll love it some other time."

"Come on, check it out. What are you afraid of, Tess? That someone else might have a good idea? Or that you might *like* the club?" He lifted a dark eyebrow. "You're a freak at heart?"

"You wish. How do you know so much about this place?"

"Mitzi, of course."

"Mitzi's freaky?"

"She's adventurous, which is more than I can say for you."

Tess heaved a sigh. Clearly, she wasn't going to talk him out of it.

"I'll take a look," she finally said. "Fifteen minutes, and then I'm out of there, with or without you, agreed? Those are my conditions, but only if you pay the cabbie in advance to wait outside, all night, if necessary."

"Not a problem. I already have the cab for the night, the entire night."

Moments later, the driver pulled into an underground parking garage and stopped in front of an elevator bank.

Graffiti marred the garage walls, making it look more like a tenement than an upscale club. Tess didn't have much hope for the place, and she was more suspicious of his motives than ever.

She'd locked most of the materials for tomorrow's run-through in her desk drawer at the office, but her sketch pad didn't fit in the drawer, and at the last minute, she'd crammed it in her tote bag. She didn't like the idea of leaving the tote in the cab, but it was probably safer than taking it into the club, so she put the bag on the floor, hoping the driver wouldn't realize it was there. As she and Danny got out of the car, she noticed a symbol painted on the wall above the elevator. It looked like a snake, curled in a perfect circle and swallowing its own tail. *How reassuring.*

The elevator rose to an unmarked floor and the doors opened to oceanlike darkness. Things slithered and swam in front of Tess's eyes. Light and shadows? Living beings? She couldn't tell.

She didn't move until Danny took her hand. "Come on," he coaxed, leading her out of the car and onto a path illuminated by red votive candles with white flames. "I'll protect you."

She didn't miss the irony in his tone, but Tess wasn't so sure she wouldn't need protection. Muted screams drifted up from some lower floor. The club probably had a dungeon. Tess imagined floggings and body parts being stretched. But probably it was nothing more than tattoos and piercings being done without benefit of anesthesia.

They'd only taken a few steps when a scarlet spotlight illuminated a scene to their left. Tess's vision hadn't adjusted, but it looked like a woman in stocks. Her head and hands were enclosed in wooden yokes that were secured to low posts, forcing her to bend at the waist. A man stood just behind her, and—

Tess ventured closer. Was she *naked?* At first, Tess thought they were statues. Neither seemed to be moving, but then she caught the rhythmic motion of the man's hips, and the look of utter ecstasy on the woman's face.

Tess jumped back. They were both naked, and he was either having carnal knowledge of her from behind, or doing a very good job of simulating it.

Was that legal in the state of New York? Tess didn't look at Danny. She must be as red as the glow from the spotlight.

Another scene lit up the path to their right. Tess could see a man kneeling in a pool of soft fuchsia light. He was holding on to the thong of a bullwhip, the end of which was wrapped around his neck. He wore a tattered T-shirt and jeans, but the woman who wielded the whip was nude, except for her tightly laced stiletto boots and the snake bracelets coiling up her arms. Clearly, she was the dominant of the two, a fuchsia goddess as she gripped the whip handle in one hand and a branding iron in the other.

"This is all playacting, right?" Tess resisted the tug of Danny's hand. "Tell me it is, or I'm leaving."

"Sure, play-acting."

Tess allowed herself to be nudged along, until a howl of anguish brought her to a dead stop. Not the branded love slave. It hadn't come from his direction, but it was nearby. "What was that?"

"A sound track, obviously. It's all playacting."

"Thanks." It was a sad state of affairs when a smart-ass like Danny Gabriel was your only ally in a hellhole like this. Tess had no desire to see what came next, but the path kept lighting up as they walked, and it was nearly impossible not to look. To their left, a sinuous female creature in black body paint writhed over the supine body of a naked man, who, except for the twitching, looked nearly comatose. And deliriously happy. Maybe he was the one who'd howled.

"She's a succubus," Danny explained.

"And a succubus is…?"

"A nasty little she-devil who preys on sleeping males, drains all their precious vital fluids and leaves them for dead."

"Maybe I could help her pick her next victim." Tess locked her gaze on the path ahead and kept it there. These places were not designed for women who'd sworn off sex, especially if they were in the throes of PMS, which for Tess was the hormonal equivalent of a Siamese cat in heat. Possibly she should have wrestled the whip from the fuchsia goddess and laid claim to the love slave, although the comatose guy was probably more her speed.

More spotlights came on, creating a vibrant rainbow in the red-to-purple spectrum. Since Tess was reluctant to look, Danny was *kind* enough to describe the new scenes, one being a contortionist who could pleasure herself while doing back bends, the other a female magician who was making the clothing disappear, one piece at a time, of a restrained man whom Danny referred to as unnaturally well endowed.

It was too dark to check her watch, but Tess was certain her fifteen minutes must be up. "Well, it's been fun," she said, "but I have to be going."

"Not quite yet." With a flick of his wrist, Danny drew her in front of him, as if he were partnering her in a dance move.

"Is this where I get sold into white slavery?" she joked nervously.

Before he could answer, another spotlight came on. It threw an eerie blue glow directly in front of them. Tess watched it cover her feet like a poisonous mist and creep up her legs. Her denim jeans seemed to absorb the color, but it was turning her oatmeal turtleneck a ghastly shade of red. Bloodred.

Danny had a death grip on her arms. She wasn't going anywhere.

"Heads up," he whispered. "It's our host, the Marquis."

Silhouetted in blue, the Marquis was a towering figure. But as he stepped forward, Tess realized that he wasn't the personification of evil she expected. He was tall and lean enough to be wraithlike, but with his classically sculpted face and slicked-back hair he could have been any haughty maître d' in a tux at a fancy restaurant. Maybe she should have been relieved.

"Welcome," he said in a hypnotic voice that barely rose above a whisper. "I've been expecting you."

Ignoring Danny, the Marquis approached Tess with studied elegance, took her hand and kissed it. His lips were warm, human. That *was* a relief. She wasn't dealing with the living dead, at least not yet. Something rough scratched the inside of her palm, and she felt a mild stinging sensation, but she didn't pull away. That would have been rude, wouldn't it? Who knew about the rules of etiquette in an S&M club?

As he released her hand, the walls opened up behind him, revealing a dark fairy-tale world of red velvet draperies and sparkling crystal chandeliers. He beckoned for Tess and Danny to follow him, and Tess did so automatically, feeling almost as if a spell had been cast over her. She was barely aware of the small voice in her head suggesting that she should have known better than to do it again—pass through doors that magically opened.

They stepped into a hall that could have been a lavish period movie set. It resembled the lobby of a Victorian opera house, but done on a very grand scale. Ebony and gold carpeting covered the floor and staircases. Crushed-velvet drapes the color of garnets set off antique chaises and settees, and richly woven wall hangings added to the opulence.

If it was a movie, it was *The Age of Innocence,* Edith Wharton's turn-of-the-century novel about social mores. But far from innocent, Tess realized as she got a closer look at the wall hangings. Garden of Eden-like scenes were laced with furtive couplings and erotic dalliances of all kinds. Men, women, and fairy-tale beasts copulated with abandon and in all manner of combinations.

Tess glanced overhead and saw that the vaulted ceilings were painted with landscapes, mostly forests and glens teaming with magical animals, horned satyrs and swooning virgins. Women being carried off by Minotaurs was a popular theme, but there were plenty of helpless men getting roughed up by lustful nymphs, and even a princess being ravished by a god in the form of a black swan.

Several dramatic chords of music sounded, and the chandeliers dimmed. Tess turned to find out what was going on—and got the shock of her life. The Marquis had transformed in the seconds she'd turned away. His hair was now long and silvery-white. His eyes were yellow with black slits—serpent's eyes—and the hiss in his throat was a death rattle.

Tess jumped back, bewildered. Was this some kind of joke? The sounds of high-pitched chatter assailed her. Suddenly the empty hall was filled with laughing, costumed people in various states of undress. A lion on a leash was actually a man on all fours, his handler a young woman in snakeskin with a riding crop between her teeth. A magnificently muscled black man in a turban and a diaper-like garment nuzzled with a cobra that was wound around his neck like lethal jewelry.

Where was Danny? Tess spun around, frantically searching the room, only to discover that now the Marquis was gone, too. She found herself in the direct path of a knot of men and women wearing the garish paint and powder of the French court. The men's tight breeches cupped obscene bulges, and the women's empire gowns were cut to expose their jiggling, rosy-tipped breasts.

As they neared Tess, one of the women drew a long, hot-pink feather from her ghostly white hair and stopped to caress Tess's face with it. The woman pursed her violently red lips, inviting a kiss. Tess felt fingers tickling her butt, and she whirled, aware that the group had surrounded her. They were laughing, whispering, touching and petting, crowding closer.

"Excuse me!" Tess pushed through them and nearly collided with Danny. She'd never been so glad to see anyone. "Where did you go?" she demanded.

Danny's hair was long and flowing out of the ponytail. His eyes were dark, fevered.

"I didn't go anywhere," he said. "You turned and looked right through me, like you were in a trance or something. You didn't see me?"

Tess didn't know what he was talking about. Of course she hadn't seen him. He hadn't *been* there, unless she was having hallucinations, which was beginning to seem like a possibility. She did feel a little disoriented, but who wouldn't in a place like this?

Her thoughts raced back to the Marquis' handshake, and the scratch she'd felt on her palm, but she had no time to reason things through. The Marquis' voice boomed in the massive room. Tess was startled to see him just a few feet away from her and looking exactly as he had, black hair slicked back from his severely handsome features. What struck her as different was his voice. It sounded as if it was coming from speakers instead of his body.

"Good evening, my lovelies," the Marquis said, bowing as he addressed the strange crowd. "The last live performance of the evening begins in five minutes. Please take your seats in the Exhibition Hall immediately. The red seats are electrified with a random charge of varying wattage, for your viewing pleasure."

His lovelies began to file through large open arches that led to an auditorium. Tess caught a glimpse of massive chandeliers and gilded box seats and miles of crimson velvet.

"Are you up for a live performance?" Danny asked.

"Of what?"

"Your guess." He shrugged. "We can always leave…I think."

"Sometimes having options is worse than not having them." She sighed, exasperated. "What the hell. I don't want to spend the rest of my life wondering what-if, as I'm sure I would in this case."

They waited until the motley crew had taken their seats before entering the auditorium. A hush had fallen over the room that made Tess feel as if she were at Lincoln Center, anticipating a performance by the Ballets Russes.

Danny found seats in a row near the back, which Tess eyed suspiciously and then refused. It was too dark to see what color they were, and she didn't need another shock right now, thanks. Instead, she planted herself in the aisle and watched the curtain rise, wondering what in God's name she was going to see next.

Six

The curtain opened to an empty stage and a magenta spotlight, circling to find its target. Finally, the light enveloped a young woman, her head bowed, her body turned away from the audience in an attempt to conceal her emotional distress. She wore a slip dress that clung to the taut curves of her dancer's body.

Beautiful, Tess thought. There was inexpressible beauty in every restrained line of her being.

Soft music swelled to fill the auditorium. Tess recognized the passionate strains as a theme from Straus's *Don Juan*, an opera about a man incapable of love yet driven to search for it in the arms of woman after woman.

The music soared, announcing a male dancer in a matador's jacket and tuxedo pants. He was as straight and proud as a military officer, yet limber, willowy. His body language said he'd come to make a plea. He seemed to be asking for forgiveness, but the woman waved him off.

When he persisted, she savagely pushed him away.

The music soared to another crescendo as he disappeared into the darkness. The young woman turned to the audience, her head lifting, fiery and defiant. Tears poured down her cheeks.

Tess hadn't understood much of what she'd seen so far in this club, but she understood this performance. The woman had been betrayed, and she was lashing out, rejecting the man and the pain he'd caused her. She might have wanted to forgive him, but there was a part of her that couldn't forgive anymore. She'd been hurt too much.

Tess had never lashed out. She'd dropped out. The coward's way, she realized now. Her wounds had scarred over and were taking up space that could have gone to something else, like having a life that was more than work, 24/7. Never once had she passionately retaliated or defended herself or her feelings.

But the sadness she felt had no chance against her talent for denial. Grand acts of defiance were for the stage, the movies, she told herself. Life was not an idealistic drama. It was getting through.

At least no one could say she hadn't gone after the brass ring. She'd tried it all, everything from one-night stands to long-term engagements—and come away each time confused and disillusioned. Men had hurt her in little ways. They'd hurt her in big ways. And she had let it happen. She'd even gone back. Eventually, she'd seen the pattern. It was needing things that men couldn't give that had gotten her into trouble. That's when the lightbulb had gone on. *Needing* was her problem.

The hot magenta beam followed the young woman to the other side of the stage where a second man waited, slender and stealthy in his fedora and single-breasted pin-striped suit. With a cold smile, he approached her. And for some reason, she didn't resist him. He tipped her chin high and stared into her eyes until she stopped crying.

She seemed not even to breathe.

With slow precision, he kissed her. His lips brushed, danced. He waited, then drew back to look at her. What did he have here? A wounded bird or an irresistibly clever tease? His tongue flicked the curves of her unyielding mouth. But she didn't respond, even when he lowered the strap of her dress and bared her breast.

His hand cupped her flesh.

Her eyelids quivered and closed. She had slipped back into the pattern. This was her fate, and she was helpless to change it.

Tess understood. She understood too much.

The first male dancer—the matador—sprang from the darkness. He pulled the other man away and yanked off his fedora. Long dark hair tumbled free, waves as beautiful and silky as a girl's. The two men struggled, but the matador was clearly stronger. He ripped open the other man's jacket, revealing breasts as round and firm as ripening fruit.

Tess was startled. A male impostor?

The matador laughed uproariously, kissed the impostor and flung her away. She tumbled to the ground, where she coiled like a snake and spat at him, daring him to come near. The young woman stepped in, as if to protect the impostor. Her fierce expression warned the man off. She would defend even her enemies against him. He had cut her that deeply.

The matador came straight for her, and the dance began. A tango, the eternal struggle for sexual power. She ripped open his jacket, and buttons flew, exposing pectoral muscles that were very much a man's.

She cracked his face with her hand. Cymbals clashed, and the music took on a Latin beat, brooding and sensual. He stepped back, confused, hot with frustration. He circled her, moving in rhythm with the music, seducing her with burning looks. If he'd been an animal, his fangs would have been bared.

He came around her from behind. With a snap of his wrist, he broke the other strap of her dress. The slip floated to her waist, hanging on her hips. Magenta fire lit her shivering breasts. They were the only flesh that moved on her rigid body. Her arms were pressed to her sides, her fingers curled into knots.

Tess watched from the aisle, increasingly aware of Danny who stood next to her. He'd turned his body slightly, perhaps not even consciously, until the curve of his hip pressed against hers. She glanced at him, not surprised that he was fixated, too. He was watching the ménage à trois with a mixture of fascination, undisguised curiosity and something that might have been male lust. His jaw was taut, his mouth parted, poised as if he was imagining himself in the matador's place.

Tess probably shouldn't have expected anything else,

given what was going on. But it hit her wrong. *Men*, she thought. They're all dogs, even when they're women posing as men. She averted her eyes, refusing to watch any more of the performance. She could imagine how the dance was going to end, with the two of them having sex onstage, probably standing up, and she didn't need to watch it.

She heard another whistle and pop and wondered who'd gotten smacked this time. The audience gasped, and finally Tess couldn't stand it. She looked up just in time to see the young woman standing over the matador's fallen body, a smoking gun in her hand.

Apparently she'd taken fate into her own hands. Literally.

Attagirl.

"I need some air." She turned and started for the exit, not caring whether Danny followed her or not. He grasped her arm, catching her midstride. She swung around, thinking she ought to slap him. Everybody else was doing it.

"I'm out of here," she said under her breath.

"I'm right behind you."

The Marquis stepped out of the shadows, blocking them as they reached the doors. "You aren't leaving?" He held the door open for them, gracious to a fault, and undoubtedly evil to a fault as well. "You haven't seen the Boulevard of Broken Dreams, our adult theme park."

"Why broken dreams?" Tess wondered aloud.

She asked the question as she slipped past the Marquis and entered the lobby. Danny was right beside her, but he didn't seem to have anything to say, and Tess couldn't gauge his reaction to what the Marquis had suggested. Danny's expression was as neutral as his sage-green crewneck sweater and blue jeans, but Tess wasn't buying it.

Why wasn't he asking questions? She suspected he had some familiarity with this place beyond hearing about it from Mitzi. She couldn't let go of the feeling that he was not on her side where the Faustini account was concerned, and that she was being set up in some way. And if that was true, she had no idea how far he might take it. She wondered suddenly if the Marquis was involved. But Danny's motives concerned her most. Was this about work, or was it personal, too?

"Broken things demand our attention," the Marquis explained. "They won't let us take them for granted, and we take too much for granted in this life, don't you think?"

"Can't disagree there," she said, "but I think I'll pass on the Boulevard."

"Don't be silly." He gestured toward an elevator, the same one that had brought them up to the opera house. "It's on your way out. You don't want to miss the Vampire Forest. It's our star attraction."

The Marquis' eerie yellow eyes came to mind, even though Tess would have preferred to forget them. Vampire eyes.

One of many lessons Tess had learned in the ad business was to pick your battles. Fight the ones you had a chance of winning. Gracefully concede the others—and save on the wear and tear. In this case, arguing would only prolong the agony, and besides, the Marquis had said the magic words, "It's on the way out."

Moments later, the elevator doors opened to yet another opulent hallway of a castle. Wall sconces designed to look like candelabra splashed firelight across the high vaulted ceiling, and freestanding torchieres threw flames as forked as any demon's tongue. Billowing shadows filled every corner and crevice of the long corridor.

It was a bit medieval for Tess's taste, but then so was the Marquis. They'd only gone down one floor, so this couldn't be the dungeon. Those things cried out for a subground environment.

"Welcome to the Boulevard," the Marquis said. "Where the past they left out of your history books meets the future of your wildest dreams. Look over here."

He gestured to a futuristic archway leading to transparent doors that gave the illusion of being curved like a bubble. They appeared to be glass, and the room beyond looked like the interior of the largest glitter ball Tess had ever seen.

She read the inscription engraved in the doors. "Hypnosis Parlor?"

The Marquis nodded. "It's a circular chamber with mirrored walls, but the eyes that stare back are your own. Just as in real life, we hypnotize ourselves. But if you prefer, you can have one of our Hypnotricks do the honors. Members and guests can take their pick of talented young men and women to entrance them and fill their heads with erotic suggestions."

Danny got close enough to whisper in Tess's ear, "Not a bad place for a photo shoot."

The Marquis produced a remote and tapped a button. Immediately a deep male voice enveloped them, making relaxation suggestions that were as sensual as they were soothing. He could easily have put Tess in a trance with a few well-chosen words.

"I'll bet *he* could defrizz my hair," she murmured.

The Marquis indulged her with a smile. "I'm sure he could, if that's what you want. You also have a choice of two-way mirrors, if you enjoy being watched."

Tess was trying to imagine how that worked, when she was distracted by the sound of splashing water. She noticed an alcove across the hall. The doors were open, and she caught a glimpse of naked bodies drifting back and forth inside.

Curious, she headed over there for a better look, but with no intention of venturing inside. It appeared to be a large spa, tiled entirely in blue and white with at least one pool. But on the far side of the pool was a naked man chained between two pillars. His back was to Tess, and he was being misted by an automatic device that reminded her of a sprinkler system, except that the spray was so fine it looked like steam.

"Why is he writhing?" she asked as Danny and the Marquis joined her. "Is the water hot?"

"Cold," the Marquis said. "It's the duration of restraint that stimulates, not the temperature or the force of the water."

"How long has he been there?" Tess couldn't see anything other than his clenched buttocks, but still, it was pretty unnerving.

"Hours, I'm sure," the Marquis explained. "These are our Roman Baths. They were designed with men in mind, but women are frequent and welcome guests. We have everything from simple soaks to ingenious forms of water games. Some people call it water torture. My favorite is a slow drip on a part of the anatomy that brings even the most resistant woman to a soul-shattering release. Lovely experience, I'm told, if a bit exhausting."

Tess's stomach knotted at the thought. She shot Danny an accusing look, and his response was an innocent shrug. *Hey, what do I know about water torture?*

"Are we almost done?" She skewered both men with the question.

"I've saved the best," the Marquis said, pointing to a large silvery half-moon portal, set apart in its own shadowy alcove at the end of the hallway.

"Our notorious Vampire Forest." He walked to the entrance, which was sealed off by a sheet of gleaming stainless steel. "If you go through this portal and enter the forest, you will be ravished by a vampire, and it will be entirely out of your control. The necessity for surrender is the beauty of vampirism, of course. You don't get to choose the creature or the acts."

He pressed a button in his remote, and the door whooshed open, revealing a courtyard the size of a small stadium, domed in glass. Artificial stars twinkled in the night sky. Otherwise, it seemed to be a fairly normal woods with what looked like a bridge to a path leading into a great thicket of trees. There were hanging vines and abundant undergrowth.

A rustling sound made Tess jump back. Embarrassed, she shot Danny another glare. "Don't you dare suggest a photo shoot in there."

She turned to the Marquis. "Why do people want to be ravished by vampires? Why do they come to a place like this at all?"

"Some of them are sensual adventurers and simply enjoy the variety. Some of them can't experience sexual pleasure any other way. They have what you would call hang-ups and this releases them."

"Such a shame," Tess said.

"Perhaps, but studies have shown that the inclination is nearly universal. Having pleasure forced upon you is the most common sexual fantasy of both men and women."

"Doesn't do a thing for me."

The Marquis arched an eyebrow. He knew it wasn't true. And it was silly of Tess to have made such a claim. Her senses were humming like sonar, taking everything in. Her heart was quietly fibrillating. Why, though? Vampires?

The stainless door swooshed closed without a sign of a vampire.

She was a little disappointed.

Still, she didn't want to give the Marquis any encouragement. The exit door was in plain sight, and she'd been a gracious guest long enough.

"Thank you very much for all the personal attention," she told the Marquis. "Maybe we'll come back and try the amenities another time. It really is late."

She clasped Danny's hand and gave it a tug. He tugged back.

"Wait a minute," he said, glancing around. "What's that noise?"

All three of them hesitated. Tess could hear a faint popping sound, like a balloon being stuck with a pin. She could hear voices, too, but not what they were saying. It sounded like someone was angry. There was another pop, followed by a gasp. Or maybe it was a moan.

What was going on? Were people slapping each other's faces again?

Tess was getting uneasy. The pops were several seconds apart, but the gasps and moans were getting louder and nearly continual. Honestly, it did sound as if someone were being slapped. Or spanked.

Tess's heart began to thunder. "Danny, let's go."

"Ah," the Marquis said, "*that* noise. It's one of our exhibitions. Just this way."

Danny glanced down at Tess's hand, seeming puzzled. "Your pulse is wild. Are you really afraid of a little exhibition?"

Tess pulled her hand away and very reluctantly followed the Marquis to an oddly old-fashioned doorway with a sign hanging on the knob that read: Quiet, Students! Class in Session.

The smallish room inside was dark, except for a brightly lit desk and teacher's chair, where a schoolmaster was sitting, calmly paddling a squirming woman who was draped unceremoniously over his knees with her schoolgirl skirt up and her ruffled panties down.

Tess could hardly believe what she was seeing. It didn't make sense to be shocked at what went on in an S&M

club, but this was too close for comfort. She'd never been spanked herself—nor did she intend to be—but she'd thought about it, thanks to her kinky professor.

It was supposed to be a classroom, Tess realized, but that didn't make her any happier to be there. Shades of Professor Wiley! The seats were filled with adults dressed like students in uniforms.

Tess began to back out the door until Danny blocked her. "Hold on," he whispered. "It's just role-playing."

"That man is *not* playing," Tess whispered back. "Look at how red her butt is."

"Quiet!"

The thunderous command stilled Tess's voice—and her heart.

The schoolmaster searched the classroom, peering into the darkness. "Who spoke?" he demanded to know.

Danny raised his hand and pointed to Tess. "She did, but she apologizes."

Tess slapped at his hand. *"Danny."*

"Not good enough," the schoolmaster boomed. "Bring her up here, young man. Since you reported her, yours is the privilege of administering the lash. Ten swats with your bare hand should teach her a sorely needed lesson."

"Nobody's getting *near* me with a bare hand," Tess exclaimed.

The lights in the room came up, and the schoolmaster rose from his chair, letting his poor charge scramble to her feet. "Who dares to speak such insolence? Come forward. Young man, bring the ill-mannered wench up here immediately."

Tess was prepared to do bodily damage if Danny touched her, but Danny quickly stepped forward to explain the situation to the schoolmaster.

"Sir," he said, "we're visitors here. I'm sorry we interrupted your class. The Marquis is showing us around."

"And where *is* the Marquis?" the schoolmaster asked.

"Right there." Danny gestured toward the door where Tess stood.

But the Marquis was gone. Tess spun around, searching the room, but he wasn't anywhere to be seen. He'd run out on them, probably on purpose, and all eyes were now on her—on Tess Wakefield and the blue jeans they expected to see peeled off her insolent bottom.

"Don't you dare," she said, speaking to Danny, to the schoolmaster, to the entire room. "Don't you dare lay a hand on me, any of you!" A mixture of panic and anticipation rose in her belly.

The room went quiet until a shapely young redhead rose from a seat on the aisle and smiled at Danny, who was not four feet away. "You can spank me," she said in a voice as soft and sugary as meringue pie.

"Thanks," Danny said, "I'd love to, but we really are on a tour."

"Well—" The redhead played with the heavily strained buttons of her blouse. "I wish you would. I've been very naughty."

"Do it!" the schoolmaster bellowed. "Someone must be punished for the wench's transgression."

Tess didn't love being called a wench, but she was even less thrilled when the top-heavy redhead in the thigh-high pleated skirt took Danny's hand and led him to the front of the room. The lights went down, and Tess realized with some considerable surprise that he was going to do it. He was going to spank her.

It wasn't until he was seated on the chair and the redhead had generously arranged herself over his lap that he looked up at Tess with a helpless *I'm doing this for you* expression. He didn't even have to lift her skirt it was so short.

Faintly horrified, Tess watched him draw down the redhead's panties and rub his hands, as if to warm them. "Just how naughty have you been, little girl?" he asked her.

Tess closed her eyes at the first smack. Her stomach rolled, and sweat beaded her forehead. Oh, dear God, she was being punished for her fantasies. Her past had caught up with her, and she was paying for the twisted subliminal wishes that had been festering in her mind all these years.

The redhead began to moan and gasp, but Danny hadn't hurt her. Tess knew pain when she heard it. This woman was loving every minute of it, and her cooing sounds were making Tess ill.

A few more smacks, and Tess was drenched. Anyone would have thought she was getting the paddling. She only wished she couldn't see it so clearly in her mind— Danny and his tequila-gold hands on that little redheaded bitch's pale pink butt. Tess hoped she got blisters.

Her ankles were wobbly as she inched back toward the door. She wasn't sure they'd hold her, but there was only one thing on her mind now. *Not being in this room.*

When no one was looking, she slipped out the school-room door and headed for the exit like a fugitive from justice, praying no one would see her, especially the Marquis. Thank God, there was a taxi waiting.

Seven

The office phone rang, and Tess let out an agonized sigh. The number that came up in the digital display was Erica's assistant.

Tess hit the speakerphone button. "Is she ready, Judy?"

"She is, Tess. You can come up now."

"Thanks, I'm on my way." *Shit.*

Tess turned back to her computer screen, almost forgetting to shut off the speakerphone. Her Faustini files had disappeared. She'd found her locked desk drawer pried open when she arrived this morning. Someone had broken in and taken the material she'd left there last night. And the thief had been smart enough to locate her computer files and erase them, too.

Everything was gone, including the pitch she'd worked on for hours last night. Everyone associated with the account was working around the clock to meet the deadline, even security. Tess had asked Erica to come in on a Sunday morning so she could show her the rough sketches of the print ads and pitch the concept to her.

Thank God, Tess had taken the sketch pad with her last night, but she didn't have the presentation notes she'd prepared on the computer. She'd made a hard copy and left it in the drawer.

Tess watched the computer's search function going at full blast on her screen. Maybe the file she was looking for hadn't been erased. Maybe she'd made a mistake in saving it last night. She could hope.

This morning had started badly anyway. No, that was a lie. Last night had never *ended*. She'd skulked out of the club, leaving Danny to paddle his redheaded trollop, and come home in the cab. But she hadn't slept all night, and it wasn't today's presentation that had kept her awake. It was the visual image of a glowing pink butt, the smack of naked flesh upon flesh, and Danny Gabriel's obscenely wide palm.

Just how naughty have you been, little girl?

Tess might have had an hour's sleep when the alarm rang. Off and on throughout the night, she'd tried various yoga positions to relax, but should have known better. Of course, she'd ended up in her version of the full lotus, the one where the curve of her heel rested against her crotch.

Sparks had flown and bells had peeled. Instantly, Tess was a five-alarm fire. She'd let out a gasp that would have put the club's paddled students to shame. How had that happened? One touch, and she had lit up like New Year's Eve fireworks.

She hadn't wanted to masturbate. She would have felt like a failure if she couldn't control the craziness. But in truth, she couldn't. This was hot stuff, pyrotechnics. And finally, she'd told herself okay, just once. Once, and then you're going to be celibate again. You hear that, missy? *Celibate.*

That's when she'd realized how much trouble she was in.

She was desecrating the solemn tradition of yoga by masturbating to spanking fantasies when her career was at stake? Sad. That was sad.

She had managed to abstain. But she'd also been up all night.

Tess opened the legal tablet in front of her and scribbled down some notes for the meeting. It was the best she could do. She had to go upstairs and sell Erica on the idea this morning, or it was back to square one, which would be a disaster. She and her team had less than a week to put the entire pitch to Faustini together, and starting from scratch would make that virtually impossible. She wasn't certain it was possible with what she had now.

She'd saved the text for the pitch to a file within the Faustini folder, then given the folder a new password, which should have kept it secure. She'd planned to have another look at the file this morning, make any changes that were needed and print out a final copy.

The search function was still going, but it hadn't turned up anything, and probably wouldn't. She hadn't made any mistakes saving the file, and this wasn't a computer glitch. Someone had been broken into her computer files, as well as her desk. Maybe the same person who'd taken her PDA.

Tess rose from the chair, taking the tablet with her. If she survived her meeting with Erica, she would have to bring in the agency's computer security person to help her with this mess. She didn't know where else to search for the folder. There wasn't time, and she didn't have the expertise.

Right now she was late for a command performance and had no idea what she was going to do. Erica might be ready. But Tess wasn't.

"You really expect me to believe that someone stole your presentation? Isn't that a little like the dog ate my homework?"

Erica Summers gazed skeptically across her vast glass-topped desk at Tess. Her reflection rippled across the mirrored surface, emphasizing her Egyptian-green eyes and her reputation for cold-bloodedness. When she blinked, she reminded Tess of an exotic reptile, lazily observing a tasty insect. Not that she wasn't stunning. Erica's beauty was undeniable, but there was no more sympathy running in her veins than there was human warmth.

Maybe it was just as well, Tess decided. Erica Summers's chilly manner brought out the fighter in Tess Wakefield, and the timing couldn't be better.

"Yes, I do expect you to believe it," Tess said. "You have great judgment. I don't think you would have hired me if you thought I'd lie to you about something this important."

A shrug. "Ad people have been known to do anything to sell a product—lie, cheat, steal."

Tess crossed her legs and settled back in the chair, relaxing. There was nothing to be gained by freezing up. Slow insects got eaten.

"Anyone can lie, cheat and steal," Tess said. "How many of them can sell an ad with the truth—and nothing but?"

Another slow blink of Erica's lids. Probably designed to make Tess feel like a beetle grub.

"Faustini needs reinvention," Tess persisted. "Why not take what they have and make it better? If Faustini Leather was a gifted Italian tenor in need of a new image, you wouldn't advise him to change his voice. You'd advise him to sing a new song."

"And you think Elegant Goth is Faustini's new song?"

Tess had already described the ad campaign to Erica, but probably not very effectively. This was her chance to sell it. "Elegance is their voice. Goth is their song. We marry the elegance with some funky hard rock, create a gothic opera, and we have reinvented the Faustini image."

Tess rose and picked up one of the sketches she'd arranged on Erica's desk. "Have another look at this one. I may not have done the concept justice. The idea is to use a futuristic movie set to showcase the luxury leather clothing. Think dark fantasy, think *The Matrix.*"

With some reluctance, Erica perused the sketch, which was a rendering of an agile male model doing a near back bend in a Faustini leather duster coat and their black hessian boots. The setting was the roof of a Manhattan skyscraper, and the model appeared to be dodging what looked like a bolt of red laser fire against the night sky.

Another sketch depicted a Keanu Reeves-like character, looking intent on mayhem as he sprinted through Times Square at night, carrying a Faustini briefcase.

Tess rarely raved about her own work, but she'd fallen in love with the idea of models dressed in Faustini, paying homage to the graceful moves of Neo and Trinity in the original *Matrix* movie. It had always reminded her of a beautifully choreographed ballet. But she was losing hope that Erica might share her vision. Perhaps her boss didn't go to futuristic action movies, but the sketches should have spoken for themselves.

When she'd walked into Erica's office a half hour ago, Tess had decided not to fake it, even though that was typical of ad people, as Erica had pointed out. Tess had told the truth about the missing files, then shown her boss the sketches and described the ad campaign she envisioned, praying her passion would carry the day.

Now, all she could do was wait for Erica to pass judgment.

But Erica seemed to have other things on her mind than sketches. Tess had a sinking feeling she'd struck out. Something hadn't felt right from the beginning. Maybe she'd never had her boss's full attention. She tried to console herself. She'd given it her best shot, but the disappointment that hit her was sharpened by a sense of desperation.

Erica left her desk and walked to the rosewood console

where crystal pitchers of lemon water and iced tea had been arranged on a sterling tray.

"Can I get you something to drink?" she asked Tess.

Tess declined, and Erica poured herself a goblet of water, tilting the pitcher so that not a single ice cube splashed into the glass. It took some dexterity, and she almost finessed it. But as she brought the pitcher back, she lost control for a moment, and a small avalanche of ice cubes created a geyser, splashing water everywhere.

Erica set the pitcher down, seeming composed as she took a napkin and blotted her suit sleeve. But just as she couldn't totally control the ice, she couldn't totally control her hands. They were shaking, Tess realized.

Erica noticed it, too. Abruptly, she abandoned the soggy napkin and the water glass and fixed her brilliant-green gaze on Tess. "Tell me about Danny Gabriel. Are you making any headway with what we discussed?"

"Some, I think." *Too passive, Tess.* The question had surprised her.

"Is he giving you a hard time?"

Only if you call kidnapping me, dragging me to an S&M club, spanking strange women and undermining me in my front of my team a hard time. Oh yeah, and he ambushed me in his office chair.

Tess may have smiled as she realized that she could do Danny Gabriel some harm if he really ticked her off. She could expose him for a kinky bastard. Not without some guilt, given her own inclinations, but she would do it.

"He's a challenge," Tess admitted, "but that's what makes the job interesting."

"I hope you're up to the challenge."

"I am."

Erica didn't seem to hear her conviction. "Don't be so sure," she warned. "He's dangerous. He'll corrupt you, if he can."

"*Corrupt* me? What does that mean?"

Tess's incredulous question was dismissed with a shrug. "It means don't let down your guard."

Tess wasn't sure how to respond, but she had to wonder if there was anything personal in Erica's desire to rein in Danny Gabriel. Tess had heard the rumors of an affair. If they were true, Danny may have given Erica a reason to hold a grudge. Maybe he was the one who'd ended it.

Erica switched gears, but the subject was still Danny. "You know that he would have lost the Faustini account if he'd been allowed to pitch it. That's why I've given it to you, and I'm counting on you to stick the landing."

"*Stick* the landing?"

The other woman's red lips twitched, a near smile. "A million years ago I used to be a gymnast."

"We'll stick the landing," Tess assured her. "My team's fired up and ready. I'll get the art and production people going on these preliminary sketches—that is, if you're giving me the green light."

Erica glanced at the watery mess on the console. If the thought of cleaning it up crossed her mind, she gave no hint. She walked back to her desk, taking her time, and turning to Tess when she got there. "If you really believe someone broke into your computer files, you should have reported it to security."

Tess nodded, confused. "I intend to, as soon as we're done here. Are we...done here?"

Erica pursed her lips. She considered the sketches again and finally, she raised her lids. This time her leisurely blink worked. Tess did feel like a beetle grub. And the giant iguana looked hungry, but perhaps she had a more substantial meal on her mind. Like Danny Gabriel.

"We're done here," Erica said. "Congratulations."

"The good news is we have approval to pitch Elegant Goth to the Faustini brass," Tess told her team. "Erica gave us the green light this morning."

Tess wanted to smile at the group's hoots and high fives, but she didn't let herself. She'd had them meet in a standard conference room in order to convey that this afternoon's meeting was all business, no fun and games, and she herself was standing in the midst of several easels, where she'd clamped her sketches.

She'd known it was going to be a jammed afternoon, no matter how the meeting with Erica turned out, but there was something that had to be done before they got down to work.

"Now, for the bad news." She glanced at each of her team members as she spoke, noting every nuance, from Andy's curious expression to Carlotta's apparent boredom. How they reacted to her news, both good and bad, could tell her a lot. Tess had little stomach for baiting traps, but it had to be done. They were her colleagues, but they were also suspects.

"My PDA has disappeared," she said. "I left it in my office during our Qigong session the other day, and it was gone when I got back. This morning, my desk was broken into, and the entire Faustini folder was missing from my computer."

Andy's eyebrows shot up as if he couldn't believe it. "You lost the whole folder? You're about as swift as I am."

"I didn't *lose* it, Andy—"

Brad cut in, apparently to defend Tess. "Computer files get lost all the time. Folders rarely do—unless someone deletes them, and it's pretty hard to do that by mistake."

"Exactly," Tess said, "and this one didn't get deleted, either intentionally or by mistake."

She let the information sink in, noting that they looked a little perplexed. Only one of the group seemed agitated, Lee Sanchez, but that could have been because of the enormous cup of coffee he was guzzling.

"I don't want to be overly dramatic," Tess went on, "but I think someone's trying to sabotage us. Or maybe it's me they're after. Either way, the account is being hurt. Erica could just as easily have given me a red light this morning. To be honest, my presentation stunk. I wasn't ready. My notes were in the file that was taken from my desk."

Carlotta was beginning to show some interest. Her long pink fingernails rubbed out the matching lipstick on her coffee mug. "How did you get the green light? Was La Summers feeling magnanimous?"

"I told her the truth about the missing files. It was a risk. She could have dismissed it as an excuse—and me as a total incompetent." Tess shot Andy a look to say thanks.

"Mom must like you," Carlotta said, perhaps a little bitterly. "Sympathy isn't her style."

"Maybe she liked the concept. We can only hope." Tess pointed to the easel next to her, wanting to put the question to rest, but she was baffled about Erica's reaction, too. And so far nothing about this meeting had eased her mind about her team members.

"Let's roll up our sleeves and get started," she said. She'd assigned Brad Hayes and Jan Butler to go through the models' portfolios and come up with a shortlist of finalists. "Let's see what you have," she told them now, "and then we can go over my sketches. I'd like to have the material in good enough shape to give to the art department by tomorrow, which means it's going to be a long night."

Tess had announced the thefts to watch her team's reaction. What she hadn't told them was that she'd already met with the agency's security person, and they'd devised a plan to catch the saboteur that involved installing a security camera. Tess truly hoped it was no one in this room, except maybe Carlotta. She was beginning not to like Carlotta.

Tess straggled back down the hall to her office around nine that night. The team had worked straight through dinner before calling it quits, exhausted but triumphant. They now had several preliminary sketches that were strong enough to take to the art studio, where the models would be shot against a blue screen, and computer graphics would be used to complete the ads.

Tess stopped long enough to pull off her heels and groan with relief as she tucked them in her tote. With luck her toes could still be saved from amputation. Her beautiful merino-wool suit was also a little worse for wear. So fresh and crisp this morning, it now looked slept in.

She unbuttoned her jacket, tugged it off and threw it over her shoulder, exposing her black lace camisole bra-top. There was no one around anyway, but if her underwear gave some hallway-lurker a thrill, then it was the least she could do for her fellow man. A small contribution to the constitutional pursuit of happiness, perhaps.

It gave *her* a thrill, shedding the trappings of the high-pressure business world. Maybe now she would be able to take a breather. A cab ride home and just *one* good night's sleep would seem like heaven.

She was tired.

She was happy.

It was good day….

Until she got to her doorway and saw Danny Gabriel sitting at her desk, kicked back in her executive chair like he owned the fucking place.

"Tell me I'm overtired and my unconscious is projecting the demons of my id," she said. "It's Sunday night. What are *you* doing here?"

"Looking for a nail file." He had her middle desk drawer open and had apparently been going through it.

"Did you find one?" *I'll kill you with it.* "Break a nail flogging the naughty redhead?"

"Actually, it's a hangnail, and it hurts."

"Poor baby. Please, don't think I'm unsympathetic, but I am."

She draped her jacket over a guest chair, set down her tote and walked to the desk, slowly, calming herself down.

She looked at him through half-raised lids, registering the boldness with which he looked back. His blousy artisan's shirt seemed designed for topaz skin and long, dark hair, but she had no intention of letting that distract her.

"You might not want to visit my office uninvited again," she said in carefully measured tones. "There's a thief and saboteur in this company, and so far he's stolen my PDA, my presentation notes and a crucial computer folder."

"He? You know who it is?"

Her dead-on stare told him exactly who her prime suspect was.

He shut the drawer. Without a word, he got up and walked around the desk, clearly intent on some kind of confrontation.

He came to a stop in front of her, all hot, dark eyes. "You might not want to accuse me of things I didn't do."

"I haven't—"

He interrupted her with a finger to her lips. "Wait," he said.

It surprised her so much she said nothing, not even when he replaced the finger with his mouth. It surprised her even more when she kissed him back, and her jaw ached with pleasure. Feelings flooded her in a big wet gush. She felt it between her legs and in the breath that steamed through her teeth. Her lungs were flooding, too.

She should have stopped him. Damn, she should have, which made it all the more forbidden and delicious. She just couldn't win with him.

His hands were in her hair, and they were both breathing like sprinters when he pulled back. "*That* you can accuse me of," he said.

In the heat of the moment she jerked her hand back to slap him. Shocked, she stopped herself. "Stop ambushing me like that."

He touched his cheek where her hand would have hit, and heat jetted through his nostrils. "Deal. If you promise to follow through next time."

"You *want* me to slap you?"

A grin pulled at the scar on his lip. "Not as much as you want me to paddle your ass."

"You're sick. You're very very sick. Get out of here."

"Okay." He shrugged, and Tess's throat tightened. He could have made a little more effort to talk her out of it. Her hand wobbled as she adjusted the strap of her camisole. Damn, had he seen that? Her heart was thudding so hard she felt ill.

He was insane. That ridiculous scar drove her nuts. He was also presumptuous, arrogant and appallingly sure of himself. Everything that bugged her in another human being. So why didn't she kick him out of her office? One word. Go. And he would have gone.

Tess felt the tugging inside her. It jerked back and forth like a rope in a tug-of-war. Kids on the playground, fighting. That's what this felt like. Her fiancé had been passive and accommodating. This guy was a challenge every minute of every day, in every way. That was almost an affirmation, but not one she wanted to repeat.

"Sure you want me to go?" he asked. He took her hand and threaded his fingers through hers, enfolding them. It was amazing how that settled her down. And yet.

She nodded her head. *Yes.*

He shook his. "Why can't you admit the truth?"

"That you're a pervert? That's the truth."

He started to laugh. His dark eyes ignited. She was already burning, a fiery little blaze going strong between her legs. How did he make that happen? Desire curled inside her. It snapped like a whip, startling her into a strange, overwrought state of mind. Beautiful, really. Her eyelids felt suddenly heavy as she looked up at him through her lashes.

He looked back, his gaze lit with erotic meaning.

Tess had no idea who made the first move. She may have touched his thigh. Stroked him.

He swore under his breath and lifted her onto her rattan desk, which groaned with the pressure.

God, she was easy. Her legs fell open, inviting him as he moved between them. Her thighs quivered with tension. They ached. She moaned despairingly, astonished at the riot of sensation she felt. Every naked nerve was pleading for his attention. This wasn't natural.

"We're in my office," she pointed out weakly.

"Great place."

"I have a noisy desk."

"Perfect."

He reached down, fingers trailing slowly toward her hot spot. They curled around the crotch of her panties, pulling it away. One of them stroked her gently, then slipped inside her.

His mouth found hers, hot and searching, teeth bared.

"Why did you leave last night?" he whispered.

"I thought you and Lolita might want some privacy."

"This is what I want." He licked her mouth with his tongue and delved inside her with his finger. Words caught helplessly in his throat. "Christ, that's wonderful. You're hot, wet."

The whip cracked again, sweet and sharp. Tess was still reeling over the shock of it when she felt an odd sensation. "Oh!"

He stared at her, puzzled.

Tess's muscles tightened involuntarily, and there it was again. A little catch, deep inside. It wasn't even unpleasant. Kind of nice, really.

"Never mind," she said, her voice a breathy groan. She was getting excited all over again. Her body was taking off without her, like a kite caught in an upgust. She was suddenly, deliriously, out of control. Her walls clenched on his finger, squeezing.

"It must be that damn hangnail. Sorry, I shouldn't have—"

"No, wait!" She gasped as he withdrew. He took care not to cause her any more discomfort, but she gasped anyway, her muscles clutching at the sudden emptiness.

"Wait," she implored. Overwrought nerves sent out jolts of desire. She wanted him back there, his finger, or something bigger and harder, whatever! It must have shown in her face.

"I shouldn't have done that?" His voice softened. "Tess, I shouldn't have pulled out?"

"Well…it wasn't that bad," she admitted.

He studied her, his eyes darkening. "I think we can do a little better than that."

He wasted no time finding a replacement. His jeans sank to the crest of his hips. Tess's face got steamy hot as he inched his zipper down. Within seconds she was sweaty and panting. It wasn't as if she'd never seen a man pull one out of his pants before, but this was different. He was different. And she was avidly curious.

With a few deft movements, he magically produced the gleaming thing between his legs. Stiff was the only way to describe it. Stiff and beautiful. Of course, he would have to have an incredible cock. She didn't even like that word. She *never* used it, but something about this situation elicited it. Something about *him* elicited it. All she could see at the moment was pulsing veins and carnal male muscle.

One of her hoop earrings had come loose and dropped to the desk. She freed the other earring as well. And then she watched in a daze as he not only produced a condom but coaxed it on with one hand.

"What are you doing?" she asked. "We're not going to—"

"You want me to leave now? Leave you like this? Hell, I can't."

"No, you can't," she moaned.

A groan swelled his throat. "How do you want me? Right here? On the desk?"

"I meant no, you can't fuck me."

"Jesus, say that again."

"You can't—"

"No, the other part. *Fuck me.*"

Her face burned, and the fire swept her. She whispered it. "Fuck me."

He kissed her mouth, catching the words on her lips. With both his hands, he gripped her butt and squeezed, lifting, powerful.

The desk beneath Tess creaked and shrieked, protesting.

"Oh, wait," she said as he slipped himself inside her. "Wait, oh—wait, wait, oh…oh, God."

"Oh, God," he echoed. "Oh, God is right."

"No, wait—*really.*"

But he didn't listen, and she didn't stop saying it, a soft cry that became a chant as he plunged deeply.

Eight

Tess steadied the chair by pushing it against the wall next to the bookcase before she climbed onto the seat. With one hand propped against the bookcase, she rose on tiptoe and stretched toward the heating vent near the ceiling.

It was a precarious balancing act but she had no choice. There could be a security camera inside that vent. She worked her fingers into the slats of the grate and tugged until the vent came off, but she wasn't high enough to see inside or even to feel around. Gingerly she stepped up on the chair arms and craned her head to get a look.

"No camera," she whispered, exultant. There was nothing in the vent but dust and lots of it. Her relief was so great she nearly tipped over the chair.

Moments later, the grate was securely in place, and Tess was back down on the floor of her office, wondering where else she could look. The thought of tonight's assignation with Danny on videotape had sent her into a frenzy of searching. But she'd had to get him out of the room first.

She hadn't remembered about the video camera until after their sex on the desk. How awkward had that been? He was still zipping up his pants as she was trying to get him out the door. He probably thought she was angry at him—and she was, plenty angry—but she had only herself to blame.

For the sex *and* the video camera. When Tess had met with Barb MacDonald, the agency's security expert, they had come up with a plan to catch the thief red-handed. Barb had said she would personally install the equipment so that no one in the agency knew. Apparently she hadn't gotten around to it yet. Thank *God*.

There wasn't anywhere else to search, Tess realized. She'd already been through the whole room, including the nose cone of the Messerschmitt. She hadn't found anything, but if she did, she would have to destroy it.

How embarrassing could one woman's life get? And this was her career. It would make more sense if her personal life were dark and complicated and humiliating. Of course, she had no personal life, so there wasn't anywhere else for things to go wrong but her job.

You are going to avoid him like the plague, Tess, she told herself. There will be no more contact with Mr. Gabriel until you've given the Faustini pitch. After that, contact will be kept at a bare minimum. Bare, meaning little, not naked.

She scanned the room one last time, scooped up her bag and coat and walked out the door, believing that she had dodged a bullet. But in the elevator down, her mind went off on another tangent, and she couldn't stop thinking about what would happen if the car suddenly stopped, the doors slid open and in he walked. Stuck between floors with Danny Gabriel. Burning kisses and dirty words. Skirts going up. Zippers coming down. Cables creaking. Minds throbbing. Bodies levitating. Steambath heat.

And from there it only got worse.

She was going to need rehab. How much would it cost to have Meredith flown out from L.A.?

"Tess, what time is it there? Are you all right?"

Meredith sounded groggy, and Tess pictured her friend in cami-style pajamas, hidden beneath the Dacron comforter with the pink roses and the leafy-green arbors. She and Meredith often had sleepovers when they were working late on a project at Renaissance. Of course, they talked about everything, not just work.

Tess missed that. Already, she missed it.

"Sorry, did I wake you?" Tess wedged the phone receiver against her shoulder, freeing her hands for the late-night snack she'd put together from leftover takeout in the fridge. She'd brought everything back to bed with her on a tray, thinking some food might help her get to sleep.

"It's two in the morning," Tess explained, "but it's only eleven in L.A., and you never go to bed before midnight."

"I have an early meeting tomorrow." Meredith yawned

as if she'd just stretched and sat up. "So, what's wrong? Is it the job? Or a man? It has to be one of those things."

"Why?"

"Because it's two in the morning. Women don't call each other in the middle of the night unless it's— This is about a guy, right? You've been there two weeks, and you've already met somebody. And just to keep it complicated, he works at the agency."

"Thanks, Mare, I appreciate the vote of confidence." Tess chose one of the leftover celery stalks over the cold buffalo wings. She dunked the celery in a plastic container of blue-cheese dressing.

"Who is he?" Meredith asked, ignoring Tess's munching.

"There isn't anybody. Why do you doubt me?"

"I can hear something in your voice. You're giving off a vibe."

"What you hear is me, eating celery." Tess set the stalk down and pushed the tray away. Meredith had the intuition of a police psychic. She knew what you were going to do before you did. And infinitely worse, she knew what you'd already done.

"Well, there is my co-creative director," Tess admitted, "but I hate him."

"Oh…my…*God.* Not Danny Gabriel? Based on what you've told me about the job, it has to be him, right? Have you had sex with him yet? Of course, why do I even ask?"

"*Jesus,* Meredith."

"You have!"

Tess winced. With Meredith, you never got a chance to

confess. It was like getting caught in the act. Tess was forced to deny things. It was simple self-defense. But, to be fair, the art of denial had been sewn and cultivated in Tess long before Meredith. In Tess's one conversation with her parents since she arrived, she'd made the mistake of mentioning that she found New York exciting.

Darling, of course you don't. It's noisy and dirty, and nobody there speaks proper English, do they? How could you find that exciting?

It was easier to agree. Tess had learned over thirty-some long years that taking a stand meant that you would be wrestled to the ground and pinned until you admitted the truth. *New York is a hellhole. I hate it here. I want to come home where it's safe, and you can tell me how to think and feel...about everything.*

"Tess? You there?"

"Calm down," Tess growled at Meredith. "It's not that bad. It's not like I'm emotionally involved or anything." *Okay, denial again. There was clearly involvement, just none of it good.*

"It's more weird," Tess explained. "Really, Gabriel is weird. The job is weird. It feels like there's something going on at Pratt-Summers that's not quite right, but maybe it's just me."

Tess didn't mention the missing PDA and file. That would only frighten her friend. It frightened Tess a little, if she stopped to think about it.

"Of course it's you," Meredith said. "You're having sex with your co-director! Don't do that anymore. Just don't do it."

Tess nodded. That was the answer, of course. Life was relatively simple when you lived by Meredith's rules. Tess's rules were pretty simple, too. Work, work, work. She'd just gotten into the wrong taxi was all. She would be fine now.

With the phone still tucked under her ear, Tess picked up the tray of food and put it on the nightstand next to her bed. She snuggled under the goose-down comforter that would have been much too warm for L.A., even in February, and switched off the light.

She also changed the subject. "How's Renaissance doing?"

"Still trying to replace you."

"Can't be done," Tess said, smiling.

"No kidding. You *are* good."

"Did I hear that right?"

"I hope so, 'cause I'm not saying it again."

Tess laughed. "How's *your* love life, Mare?"

"I'm still trying to seduce that cute UPS guy."

"Offer him a coffee, slip some Viagra in it, and then double-lock the coffee-room door. Or follow him out to his truck. I hear cardboard is pretty forgiving."

Tess waited for a response. "Meredith?"

"I'm thinking. You're giving me ideas."

They both chuckled, and Meredith yawned again. "Hey, go to bed," Tess said, getting ready to hang up the phone. "Get your beauty sleep."

"Tess, about the job. Just do the work, and it will all fall into place."

"Of course." Tess was nodding her head again. This was

why she'd called, to put things in perspective. You needed people in your life like that, people who could make everything simple, even when it wasn't. They were priceless, really. Meredith was priceless.

"Want some more advice?" Meredith said.

"Let's quit while we're ahead."

"Call your parents."

Tess groaned. "Are you my friend or not?"

"Call your parents, Tess. It's the kind thing to do. You're over thirty. You can stop punishing them now for not giving you the unconditional love you needed."

"I called them last week when I got here."

"Call again. You're in New York. You know they're worried sick about you."

Tess promised she would, and the minute she and Meredith had said their good-nights, she sank into the bed's king-size pillows. But she didn't drop off immediately.

Meredith meant well. She just didn't know Tess's parents.

Tess's parents meant well, too. They just didn't know Tess.

No, Tess, you're not angry because I went through your things. You're ashamed of yourself for hiding this trashy magazine and forcing me to look for it. Stop moping over that dog, Tess, or we'll give you something to mope about. It's been dead for a month. You couldn't possibly still miss it. Of course you don't like that boy. He's shy and awkward. He won't even look at your father. How could you possibly like him?

Tess rolled to her side and closed her eyes, letting exhaustion overtake her, welcoming it. She'd escaped. She'd escaped them all, and it felt good. Yes, New York was a big, scary place, but it felt good to be here. Risking her life felt good, if that's what she was doing by being here.

Of course her parents meant well. They wanted her to be safe and not make any mistakes. They didn't want her to be hurt. But she still couldn't bring herself to call them. She'd bought them a computer and promised to e-mail. So, e-mail she would, cheery notes, telling them all about her wonderful new job and her friendly and supportive coworkers. As she finally drifted off to sleep, she realized that her parents' unrelenting efforts to protect her had truly backfired if she was actually being forced to lie to protect *them*.

Tess really didn't enjoy hiding in bathroom stalls, although she might have had difficulty making anyone believe that, considering the frequency with which she'd been doing it lately.

As always, she checked her apparel for trailing toilet paper, then waited a beat, listening to make sure the coast was clear before she opened the door. She'd made it through a day and a half without running into him, but nothing had been left to chance. Yesterday, on Monday, she'd worked behind locked doors most of the day yesterday, ordering in food when necessary. When she wasn't in her office, she was in the art studio with the production team or in a conference room with her own team, planning the pitch session to the Faustini brass. And she'd skulked around in the hallways like a spy.

She'd felt pretty foolish, but it had worked. She hadn't

seen a sign of him. Of course, he might be avoiding her too. Wouldn't that be a laugh after all the trouble she'd gone to.

"What's your rush?" Mitzi whipped out a towel and thrust it at Tess as she approached the sinks.

Tess wet her hands, not waiting for the water to get hot, and took the towel. "No rush, just busy."

Tess glanced around at the bathroom door.

"Expecting someone?" Mitzi asked.

"No, not really." Tess checked the door again—and missed the wastebasket with the towel. The mirror bounced back a wary-looking woman with pinched eyes and pale skin.

"He's out of town on business."

Tess jumped. "Who?"

Mitzi gave her a knowing look and busied herself with the stack of inventory sheets she was going through. "The angel, Gabriel. He's in Chicago. One of his accounts is threatening to go into review, and he's at corporate head-quarters, doing damage control."

Hmm. Not a good situation for Danny. Going into review meant the client was about to jump ship and entertain pitches from other agencies. It was generally believed to be tougher to save an unhappy client than to reel in a brand-new one. Danny had taken some blows lately—problems with the boss, having a codirector foisted upon him, and now this. Tess could almost muster some sympathy.

"When did he leave?"

"This morning."

Which meant he'd been around on Monday. Odd that she hadn't gotten a glimpse of him, even with all her stealth machinations. At least she wouldn't have to hide in stalls for a while.

"When's he coming back?" She didn't see any point in pretending indifference. Mitzi already knew anyway. Tess almost wished she could take the other woman into her confidence. Not the sordid sexual details, but Mitzi seemed to know a lot about Danny, and she might be able to give Tess some insight into the man. Strictly for intelligence purposes, of course. A know-your-enemies strategy. Otherwise, she wanted nothing to do with the intimate details of Danny Gabriel's life.

God help her. Nothing.

Her reflection came back into focus, and Tess realized she was nodding her head, a righteous little gleam in her eye. Maybe she wasn't a spineless jellyfish of an excuse for a human being, after all. The tough, decisive Tess was making a comeback. She'd just needed a little breather from *him.*

Tess could feel Mitzi's eyes boring into her. She glanced at the other woman, hoping to ward off any personal questions. "You never did say when he was coming back."

Mitzi shrugged. "I'm supposed to know everything?"

Tess wondered just how much Mitzi did know. Hopefully nothing about the debacle in Tess's office. On the other hand, she probably knew exactly when Danny was coming back but had decided to hold out.

"Are you all right?" Mitzi asked, peering at Tess's reflection. "You look—"

"Pinched and pale?"

"I was going to say a basket case. Is this about Danny? What did he do?"

"Nothing!" Tess caught herself and shrugged, tipped off by the height of Mitzi's eyebrows. "I mean...nothing. He didn't do anything. It's stress. I have a big pitch coming up. Humongous pitch."

"Stress." Mitzi set her inventory list aside and began rummaging through a small box of pills, sealed in tiny Baggies. "I have something here. It's like kava kava, very soothing, but it doesn't destroy the liver."

"That's a comfort." Time to make a run for it, Tess thought. "I'll be fine," she said. "I still have plenty of the tea. Great stuff, that tea."

A buzzing sound caught Tess's ear. She popped her new cell phone out of the case attached to her belt clip and checked the display. It was a text message from Barb MacDonald. The agency's security expert wanted Tess to come to her office as soon as possible.

Tess didn't like the sound of that.

"Here it is, schizandra berries," Mitzi was saying as Tess went out the door.

"I thought you'd want to see what our video surveillance camera picked up last night," Barb MacDonald said.

Tess sat shivering on the guest chair in Barb's frigidly cold office Tuesday morning, watching as she put a cassette in the VCR. Barb's solemn expression had already told Tess she wouldn't like what was coming.

Tess had first met with the surprisingly petite blonde

two days ago, right after the meeting with Erica. They'd agreed on video surveillance of Tess's office in case the thief who'd stolen her PDA and computer files returned to the scene, and Barb had installed the hidden security camera yesterday morning. That was the real reason for Tess's locked door, although she'd told everyone she needed time to work undisturbed.

Tess hadn't expected the camera to pick up anything so quickly, and she was torn between curiosity and aversion. A part of her must have hoped it wouldn't pick up anything at all, and the whole mess would disappear. All that mattered was that she get through the Faustini pitch. She didn't want to deal with professional thievery and sabotage.

Tess crossed her arms and legs for warmth. Her wool-blend pantsuit felt like silk against the chill. She'd mentioned it when she was here the other day, and Barb had said something about the thermostat being broken. Why the hell doesn't she call maintenance? But at the moment, Tess just wanted to get this ordeal over with.

Barb hit the Play button and stepped out of the way of the television screen. She'd actually placed the camera inside the nose cone of the Messerschmitt, which was directly across from Tess's desk. The lights were off in Tess's office as the tape began to play, and suddenly a shadowy figure crossed in front of the camera.

It looked like a man but she couldn't see his face. He moved around the room quickly, checking the desktop and opening drawers. Still, Tess couldn't identify him. The light was too murky.

Finally, he turned, walked over to a locked cabinet against the wall near the model airplane and attempted to open it. As he stepped back, he was staring straight into the camera, straight at Tess, and she had to fight not to close her eyes and shut him out.

"Oh, my God," she whispered. It was Danny. Unmistakably. She'd seen him clearly, and so had Barb.

Within minutes, he was out of eyeshot. The camera's range was limited. It couldn't follow him to certain corners of the room. He only came into view again long enough to retry the cabinet, and then he was gone for good.

"What was he doing?" Tess asked.

Barb used the remote to turn off the TV. "Looking for something, it appears. I watched it several times. He didn't take anything that I could see."

Barb went quiet, and Tess was too shocked to speak. Her mind had already started throwing up all the reasons he couldn't be a common thief, but there was no denying that he had been in her office last night, apparently to finish whatever he'd started the night before when she interrupted him. And *how* she'd interrupted him. He probably hadn't been expecting his target to reward him for his crimes with some white-hot sex.

Tess was gripped with a violent shudder. It was as much a reaction to what she'd seen as the cold, but Barb immediately apologized.

"I decided not to have the thermostat fixed," she explained. "I prefer it cooler in here."

Cooler? The place was a meat locker, and she could tell

Barb was cold too. Her fingers were bluish. But now was not the time to deal with thermostats. "He was in my office, looking for something," she said to Barb. "We have that on tape. Is it enough to connect him to the other crimes?"

Barb shook her head. "He didn't do anything incriminating. Or, if he did, it was out of camera range."

"Then the tape does us no good?"

"On the contrary. He covertly searched your office. It tells us he had some clandestine reason for being there, and it makes him a person of strong interest, as the police say."

"What now?" Tess asked. "Could we bug his office, his phone?"

"Not without a court order, but I can increase the surveillance range in your office by adding another camera."

"And then?"

"And then, we watch and wait."

Tess rose from the chair, aware that she was unsteady as she thanked Barb for her help. She knew there was only so much an agency security officer could do. But Tess had no intention of watching and waiting. Danny was out of town, and she planned to take full advantage of that.

"Ouch." Tess thumped her head on the underside of Danny's desk. She'd heard a creak outside in the hallway. She should have stayed where she was, on all fours, but the noise had alarmed her. It had to be the building creak-

ing. She'd worked late, as usual, and it was after nine
o'clock. There wasn't anyone here at this time of night,
except possibly the janitorial service.

Please God, let it be the building.

She went quiet, listening. Another creak? Was someone in here?

She hazarded a glance over the top of the desk but saw
no one. She'd closed the office door and turned on the
banker's light on the console so she could search the place
undetected. The door was still closed.

Relax, she told herself. There was no one here. Danny
wasn't coming back until tomorrow. She'd checked with
the agency's travel office to verify his flight plans.

A wicked thought entered her head as she sat back on
her haunches. If he did walk in and catch her under his
desk she could always tell him she'd been fantasizing
about giving him a blow job. He would probably believe
it, the bastard. Sadly, it wasn't that far-fetched. The second she got down on all fours, her mind had taken a
plunge into kinky sex-in-the-elevator mode. She'd sunk
like a depth charge, and within seconds, she'd been en-
tertaining some very lewd thoughts about the man who
sat at this desk. It wasn't necessary to unzip his pants. In
her fantasies the material melted away, exposing the most
gorgeous package she'd ever seen—or experianced for
that matter. Even more fun, it was completely unaware
of her. "It" being his masterpiece of a male organ.

He was completely unaware of her hiding under his
desk, and therefore she could take him by surprise—a
butterfly touch here, a curious kitten lick there, some

lovely long strokes of her fingers, and he would be galvanized steel. The very thought thrilled her to pieces—and despite the obvious awkwardness of the situation, she didn't seem to have any inclination to *stop* thinking about it.

Her throat ached as she imagined taking him into her mouth and sucking him gently. She would hold back from more dedicated action until she heard his moan of surprise. Of course, by then he would be a wild man.

Tess's blood began to heat as she imagined him gripping her by the head and driving deeply, nearly choking her with his throbbing cock. He would thrust until he was hard enough to burst. And then suddenly, in a fit of passion, he would rip her off him and pull her out from under his desk.

Tess wasn't entirely sure how it went after that. Her neurons were shorting out, but there wasn't a doubt in her mind that he would fuck her brains out. It would be steamy, screaming, drenched-in-sex sweat, the kind where you didn't even know where you were anymore, and wouldn't have cared if a SWAT team had burst in on you. Car accident sex.

Danny Gabriel was more than capable of car accident sex, and so was she, apparently, when it was him.

God, she had to get out from under this desk, which begged the question why she was so obsessed with having sex with him on, around or under desks?

Obviously, raging female hormones were nondiscriminatory. They didn't care if the fantasy man was your worst nightmare. Maybe they liked it that way.

She needed a good gynecologist. Or more likely, a good psychiatrist. It seemed entirely possible that some of this craziness was being fed by the latent fantasies from her college days, the ones her professor had seeded with his whispers of erotic discipline and pleasure so intense it could make her faint. She'd been little more than a teenager then, but she was a woman now, and she hadn't even had sex that could make her tingle, much less faint—except with Gabriel. She was *still* tingling. And she needed to *stop*.

Back to business, Wakefield.

She pushed up from her hands and knees and smoothed down the creases in her favorite pantsuit she'd put on that morning, strictly for morale purposes. She'd gone over every inch of the office and the adjoining conference room. Unless he had secret compartments or a hidden safe, he wasn't hiding anything other than some pretty raunchy Internet porn.

She was actually relieved. For some reason, she didn't want to think he'd been trying to sabotage her. Not that he fit the nice-guy category, but he didn't come across as a criminal mind, either. She'd like to think she was a better judge of character than that.

She quickly scanned the office area to see that everything was in place. Never one to follow the rules, Danny kept his passwords on a Post-it note stuck to his computer. That gave Tess, and everyone else for that matter, easy access to most of his files except some password-protected ones that she couldn't break into no matter what combination of letters and numbers she tried.

Maybe that was why it nagged at her. His computer was the one area she hadn't been able to search thoroughly.

One more try, she thought, pulling out his chair.

Moments later she was poring over his Explorer index, file by file, to see if there was anything she'd missed. By the time she came across the first secure file, she'd thought of another password variation to try. She typed in the letters of his last name, starting with all the vowels in sequence, then all the consonants, followed by five ones. It was the password combination her former agency had used to allow interagency access to certain files by designated individuals.

She didn't expect the combination to work, but she tried it anyway, rushing to get through the files. She had no luck on the first four. On the fifth, probably from force of habit, she typed in her own last name in the same sequence, plus five ones. Couldn't possibly work, she thought, realizing what she'd done. It had been a reflex on her part.

Tess gasped as the file opened. It was the password she'd used for the Faustini file when it was stolen.

Her heart was pounding so hard she could barely read the screen. It was several seconds before she realized the contents of the file were gibberish. She couldn't make out any of it, and there was no way to know if it was the Faustini material. However, Danny couldn't have known her password unless he was the one who took her PDA, where she'd foolishly stored that information. Maybe when he tried to save the file to his hard drive, he hadn't been able to change the password, so he'd had to use hers. But why save a file full of gibberish? What was the point?

She stared at the screen, wondering if it was some kind of code. During their first meeting, Barb MacDonald had told her about a software program for securing files called PGP, which meant pretty good privacy. It required a two-computer system, with one computer having a lock and the other computer being the key to the lock. If Danny had downloaded the Faustini files into his office computer and encrypted them, turning them into gibberish, then some other computer might be the key to the files, like a laptop he used for traveling or even his PC at home.

Tess glanced at her watch. It was going on ten o'clock, and he wouldn't be back until tomorrow. If she could successfully download the file and get to his house before he got back, she could test her theory. It was crazy, though. He might not have a PC at home. She didn't even know where he lived!

Now she needed Meredith. Her friend would have locked her up until she'd talked her out of this one.

Take a breath, clear your head, get a grip, Tess told herself. Do anything, but do *not* go to his house. That can only be a bad thing.

But mere moments later, she was muttering to herself and pawing through the stuff on his desk. Where would I find his home address? she asked herself. It must be here somewhere. A piece of mail? Personal stationery?

She was going through his in-basket when it hit her. Hit her like a chunk of falling sky. All she had to do was Google him. You could find anything on Google.

Nine

The Fates must have wanted Tess to search Danny Gabriel's condo. Otherwise, they wouldn't have made it so easy. At least that was how she was trying to rationalize the felony crime of breaking and entering—probably punishable by years in lockdown—as she stood in the middle of his entryway.

The multilevel structure had her momentarily confused. It was ultramodern and airy, but there were too many options. Stairways up, stairways down, a sunken living room with a wet bar that was sunken yet again. Thank God, he'd left the recessed lighting on so she could find her way around. An inexperienced felon could get hurt.

At first glance, nothing about this place made her think of Danny Gabriel. He'd seemed rather earthy to her, a man of the elements, but maybe she was being romantic about his Native American roots, if he really had any. She wouldn't have expected his home to be so…minimalistic. It was almost industrial.

The far end of the condo was all glass, and the decor was severe, by Tess's standards. The couches and chairs were either iron-black or bright white with accent pieces in cobalt blue, and the stairs to the various levels had railings of gleaming stainless steel. It was beautiful but sterile.

One thing stood out as earthy, however. Standing in front of the windows and illuminated by accent lights were two very erotic sculptures. Tess's first impression was that the nearly life-size man and woman had been involved in a sexual act. Their bodies looked as if they could actually join like puzzle pieces. But now they were separated by several inches.

Her mind kept trying to put them back together, and perhaps that was the point, she realized. Joined, they wouldn't have drawn the eye and the mind they way they did now. She'd studied art, but she didn't recognize the medium. It wasn't marble or stone. Their bodies looked fluid, seemingly in motion, as if they were made of liquid bronze.

She wasn't getting close enough to verify. Her imagination was overwrought as it was, and she had no desire to wander around in a sexual fog. She had to search this place, starting with his office, wherever that was, and she needed to move fast in case there'd been someone on the other end of the security cameras she'd spotted downstairs in the lobby, who might decide to come up and check her out.

Technically she hadn't actually had to break in. Google had come through with his address, and she'd found some keys on a chain that he'd left in his desk drawer. A couple of them had looked like door keys, and she'd reasoned that she could try them all, if necessary. From there, all she'd had to do was take a taxi down to Tribeca, find his condominium complex and tiptoe past the security guard, who was snoozing at his post.

The first key she'd tried had worked. It was perfect, beautiful. She'd been prepared with a story for the security guard. She was going to flirt with him and say that her boyfriend lived in the building, and they'd had a terrible fight, which was all her fault. Now she wanted to make up and surprise him when he got home from his business trip tomorrow. She would pretend she had a *very* private gift in her tote that needed to be left in their *special* place. Having the door key would prove it was a serious relationship.

But she hadn't needed to say a word.

For once, things were going her way.

She found Danny's office downstairs at the back corner of the condo, and it actually looked like a room he'd spent some time in. There was a storyboard in progress on his worktable and stacks of research material on his desk. She went straight to his desktop computer, plugged in her thumbprint drive and brought up the file that had been gibberish in his office.

"Damn." It was still gibberish.

She sank back, trying to figure out what was wrong. His black mesh ergonomic chair was stiff and uncomfortable—and she was stymied. She didn't understand the PGP concept well enough to know if she'd done it right. If there was some code to be typed in, the program hadn't prompted her.

She pulled up Internet Explorer and went through his files. Maybe the encrypted file was supposed to have been placed in a certain folder before it could be deciphered. But she found nothing that gave her any clue about how to proceed.

Tess bowed her head, rubbing at the furrowed spot between her eyebrows. Damn. Reality was setting in. She really wasn't prepared to break into computer security programs and unencrypt files. She'd gotten lucky with his office computer, but that's all it was. Luck.

She felt something cold seep into her awareness before she could shake it off. Dread? A look at her watch told her she had to get going. The longer she stayed the more chance the guard would wake up, and if he did, she would have to explain her way *out* of the building. Another variation on the fight with the boyfriend story might work. She could say that he'd just dumped her. If the guard asked who the boyfriend was, she would have to break down and sob. Wail and hiccup and run at the nose. Create a mess, and he would be glad to get her out of there.

As she rose from the chair, she tugged at her low-rider slacks, hitching them into place. She'd always thought of the pantsuit as flattering with its cropped jacket and lacy camisole, and she'd also slipped on the Faustini boots. Too bad she didn't have something better to do tonight. All dressed up and a condo to search.

Move, Tess! Where would he hide a stolen PDA?

He hadn't bothered locking things up, she realized as she searched the drawers and cabinets. She went over the area thoroughly, but came up with nothing. The next most logical place was his bedroom, and she was curious anyway, which was just as good a reason not to do it. But she could hardly leave without going through his drawers, as it were.

She found the bedroom as stark as his living room. The king-size bed had a mirrored headboard and a black comforter and pillows. The reading chaise was upholstered in bright white on a black lacquered frame. But what captured her were the sculptures. Another man and woman, but the pose was different. She was facing him, but arched backward, creating a deep curve in her spine. Her arms reached, as if to entwine his neck, and her right leg was raised and curled around what would have been his butt, if he'd been there.

The man was several feet away from her, fully erect, his head thrown back, as if he might be on the brink of an orgasm. Both of them were in a state of terrible tension, every muscle straining. It seemed to go against every law of nature to keep them apart.

Tess wrenched herself away from their predicament and scoped out the rest of the room. A big fluffy robe hung on his bedpost, and she could easily imagine him wearing it. How gorgeous would that snow-white plush be against his tawny skin? That question provoked others, unfortunately. Would his body be hairy or smooth underneath? Relaxed or as hard the sculpture? And why did her mind take her on these X-rated tours?

She began going through the drawers and cabinets in the room with the single-mindedness of a trained spy. She felt no guilt. It didn't have a chance against the fear that drove her, probably because she'd never done anything like this in her life. Maybe the guilt would come later when she was having her mug shot taken. Shame, too.

She found the usual guy stuff in the drawers. Nothing exotic in the underwear department, just standard briefs, all of them white. His T-shirts were mostly white, a few black, and all crew neck. No pajamas. He probably slept in the nude. Jeans of every variety. Condoms, of course. Size: large.

God.

She'd watched him put one on.

Think about something else, Tess.

She rifled through the rest of his dresser and then checked the top, where she discovered a small leather box, probably meant to hold cuff links. But that wasn't what she found inside. Nestled in a bed of navy blue velvet was a large gold hoop earring. Just one hoop, and it was engraved with her initials. It had been a gift from Dillon.

She'd been wearing the earrings the night she and Danny had sex on the desk, but she'd taken them off for safekeeping. Maybe he'd seen her do it. Could he have taken the hoop from her desk the following night when he was caught by the security cameras?

Now, *that* was sick. It made her think of serial killers who took souvenirs from their victims. She wanted to believe there was some other explanation, but it looked like she had Danny Gabriel dead to rights. The cameras had caught him in her office, and he'd obviously taken her earring. But more incriminating in her mind, he'd used her password on his computer, probably to secure the file he stole from her. He was not only a saboteur, he liked playing high-risk games and flirting with getting caught.

Tess closed up the box, leaving the earring. All of this was pretty staggering. She hadn't really expected to find anything, she realized. She was probably still trying to rule him out as the culprit. But this might be so much worse than she could have imagined. The way he was waiting for her in her office that night, the way they had sex made her wonder if he, like serial criminals, really did enjoy taunting his victims.

How ironic that she'd been brought to Pratt-Summers to break the grip of the agency's notoriously autonomous creative director, only to discover things that could bring down his career. This wouldn't break his grip on agency practices. It would break him.

A small prescription bottle peeking out from behind a CD holder caught her eye. She opened it, saw the pharmaceutical logo, but had no idea what the blue and yellow capsules were. Maybe Google would be able to tell her what the letters and numbers meant. If not, a pharmacist.

Tess heard a clicking noise and froze. She dropped the capsule into her jacket pocket, put the prescription bottle back and crept over to the doorway. The noise had come from upstairs. It sounded like a key being inserted in a lock. Someone was trying to get in. The security guard with a master key? Tess must have been seen on the cameras. Maybe they had cameras on this floor, too.

The door creaked open, banged shut.

He wasn't a very quiet security guard.

A moment later she heard what sounded like a brief-case being dropped, shoes being kicked off and steps taken across the tiled entry. She strained to hear as the refrigerator door opened and shut and a pop-top can hissed, followed by a very male groan of exhaustion.

Someone was making himself at home.

"Mailbox number one: You have eight messages."

Tess crouched down, looking for a place to hide. Her heart was racing. The voice she'd just heard had the mechanical sound of a message machine. It wasn't a security guard. It was Danny, picking up his messages. Danny, home early.

It was just a matter of time until he came down to the bedroom.

She hadn't seen any back way out on this level. The only obvious hiding place was his closet. But seconds later, as she closed herself inside the sliding doors, she realized this could be the first place he'd go.

She wasn't going to make it out of here. She was going to get trapped in his condo. An icy shudder caught her as she realized all these things. How would she ever talk her way out of this one?

As she stood in the dark, claustrophobic space, surrounded by his clothing, a completely insane idea hit her, given the circumstances. It was the craziest thing she'd ever done. No, worse than crazy, it was probably suicidal, but what choice did she have?

She began to tear off her clothes.

* * *

"Jesus, Tess! What the hell are you doing in my bedroom? In my condo, for that matter?"

"I needed a little help."

"Help with what?"

Tess stood, facing him, wearing his bathrobe and nothing else, except her Faustini boots, of course. She reached down deep and pulled up the sexiest voice she could find, low, seductive and throaty. "The Faustini account. I have an idea."

"How did you get in here? What's that you're wearing?" He held up his hands. "Are you okay?"

"I'm so much more than okay." She hoped her laughter sounded husky and musical. She smiled invitingly and crooked her finger at him.

His eyebrow shot up. He dumped the shoes and the sports coat he was carrying on a nearby chair, which left him looking as hot as hell in a dress shirt that was open at the neck, and faded jeans. Devastatingly casual. That's what a fashionista would probably have called it.

Thank God, he wasn't close enough to see her hands shaking. She was having a nervous breakdown, but at least she looked like a million bucks. She'd caught a glimpse of herself in his headboard, a huge mirror that arced over his king-size bed like a rising sun. The man's robe and the sexy boots made her look like a stripper taking a break from her routine.

"Here, let me show you what I mean," she said as she pulled the chair from his desk, turned it away from him and sat down, also facing away from him. She glanced back over her shoulder, massively relieved at his per-plexed expression. He didn't seem to have a clue what she was up to, and she needed that edge because she didn't, either. She was bluffing for all she was worth.

Her sole purpose in life at this moment was to distract him. Pretty much everything she held precious hung in the balance—her job, her liberty. House key or not, she had broken into his place, and there was no way to ex-plain it. There would be jail time if he decided to call the cops and press charges. She had to brazen out this crazy scheme and make him think she was here to seduce him. Sure, she wanted a little help on the Faustini account, but what she really wanted was more of what they'd had in her office. Sex. A blatant appeal to his ego on the two levels that men were most susceptible: their careers and their dicks.

It should work.

Theoretically, all she had to do was seduce him to the point of lunacy, create a medical catastrophe—disabling premenstrual cramps should do it. Men were terrified of anything premenstrual—and maybe even have him drive her to the hospital.

Tess, Tess, when did you turn into a sociopath?

She yanked at the bathrobe to keep it from falling off her shoulder.

Sociopath, my ass, she thought. This was exactly what he deserved. He'd done nothing but jerk her around since she'd come to Pratt-Summers. He was setting her up for a fall. He'd stolen from her. He'd seduced her. Twice. The man had shown her no mercy.

Sure as hell.

He deserved this.

Her pulse went nuts as she met his skeptical gaze and whispered the words "Come here." Exactly what he'd said to her when he lured her into his conference room.

He walked over to her, hands on his hips. "What's going on, Tess?"

She drew up one leg, easing the robe apart. "All will be explained, but not yet. That would ruin it."

His exact words. Was he getting the picture? This was a reenactment of that infamous kiss.

"I'd like an explanation *now*."

"I can't." Her voice took on a pleading note. "You don't want to ruin it, do you?"

He was clearly torn. Finally, he sighed. "Okay, what is it you want to show me?"

She stretched out her legs, allowing the robe to do whatever it wanted. And it seemed to want to give him a peep show. The white plush fell open, revealing her knees and just enough thigh to be provocative. Her legs were parted, ever so slightly.

Lashes fluttering, she looked up at him. "Steady the back of the chair, would you? Just to make sure it doesn't tip during my…demonstration."

He gripped the chair, his fingers sliding between her and the wood. She could feel their shape and warmth through the terry cloth. Her shoulders pressed into that warmth as she slid her bottom to the edge of the seat cushion and extended her legs as far as they would go.

It startled her when the robe opened up all the way to

her blond mound. Only a corona of sunny ringlets was visible, but even she was made uncomfortable by the sight. The black stiletto boots were a sensual contrast to the length of her pale legs and the golden curls.

Could he see what she saw?

Her heart began to race. This was so incredibly crazy. What had made her think she could pull this off? Or that he would let her get away with it? Her thoughts were spinning away from her, but she couldn't lose it now. She was naked in his bathrobe, and that hadn't happened by accident. She'd started this seduction thing, and she had to finish it.

She gripped the chair with her hands and bent backward, arching until her spine began to quiver and lock. It was exactly the way he'd asked her to pose before, except that tonight she was going to be a much better Faustini model. He wouldn't believe how good.

She could do this.

She tipped her head back enough to see his expression curl into a frown. Even upside down, it was damn sexy. The scar tugged at his lip, twisting it into a bad-boy sneer, which, for some reason, tightened her throat and sent her stomach into a weightless flip. It was nerves, not pleasure, but even that was unacceptable, she told herself. She would not get all dithery over a ruthless saboteur. She wanted to be in complete and total control when she systematically reduced him to a puddle of melting gelatinous goo.

"Is this what you wanted to show me?" he asked.

"Yes."

"Okay, good, you've shown me. Now—"

"No, we're not done."

He hesitated, his breathing audible. His eyes darkened at a breathtaking rate. With desire, she hoped. "Look down at me, the way you did when I was in your conference room."

It surprised her when he did it, his beautiful, scowling face coming close. His breath lifted tendrils of her hair.

"There you are. Perfect," she purred, echoing more of his words.

His voice was harsh. "What the hell do you want, Tess?"

She arched up toward him. "Kiss my lips."

"No."

"*Please*, this is important. I need you to trust me." In a soft voice, she added, "I trusted you."

He gazed down at her for several seconds, heat steaming from his nostrils. A tough decision, apparently. She moistened her lips, flicking the corners with little pink darts of her tongue. Finally, she released the pent-up breath she was holding, letting warm air rush all over his face.

He swallowed.

She smiled.

"Do it," she whispered, rising higher.

"Fuck," he muttered as he bent and kissed her.

Their lips met in a breathless collision, and Tess trembled with the tension. She tongued him and a strange groan erupted from her throat. Her own boldness thrilled her. Him too, apparently. He swore at her, and then his mouth drowned her in sweetness, plunging and sipping, stinging tender membranes to life.

"Touch yourself," he said against her lips.

She relaxed her arms enough to release the chair, and her hand found its way inside the lapel of her robe. Her breasts were surprisingly hot as she caressed them. Her nipples puckered. She only did it to entice him, but the sensations were exquisite.

She could tell the minute he began kissing her back. His breathing changed. It got fast and hard. She reached up to stroke his face, urging him to continue. Her fingers trailed over the taut lines of his jaw. She found his lips and slipped a finger inside. He drew on it, sucking gently, and her stomach cinched tight, creating the same strange flutters she'd felt before. Sharp and icy bright. If they'd been a color, she would have had to shade her eyes.

She let the robe fall all the way open, revealing the vee of honeyed curls. "These lips, too," she said, spreading her legs wide.

He whispered an obscene word that burned in her ears. "You want me to eat you? Is that what you want?"

His voice was hoarse with disbelief, and Tess couldn't manage much more than a nod. Good God, *was* that what she wanted? Her heart staged a riot, and her nerves jumped as if she'd touched an open socket. Sensations zinged through her, shocking her reluctant flesh to life.

Was *that* what she wanted? How had a woman who'd sworn off penises and everything attached to them gotten into this situation? But this didn't involve his penis, she reminded herself. Not yet, and she was still in control, at least more in than out. Letting him do what she'd suggested might be the only way she would *stay* in control. She could lock herself off, disengage.

The chair groaned as he released it and came around to stand in front of her. She didn't move from the position she was in. It didn't escape her that she was naked, and he was fully dressed. He hadn't missed it, either. His dark gaze was all over her, eating her up, so to speak.

He knelt between her legs and slid his hands beneath her. The way he cupped her buttocks and lifted her to his mouth made her fight back an exclamation. She didn't want to give herself away, but this was nothing like what she'd expected. He breathed more than kissed her. His lips were clouds, his tongue was rain, light and drenching. A lovely warm cloudburst that soaked her and brought gentle, soaring sensations.

A startled moan came from somewhere deep inside as pleasure rippled, radiating from the tip of his tongue. She would have to stop him soon. This was too intense. Her control was slipping. She could feel it, and when it was gone, *she* was gone. She could not let him take her over the edge.

She could not faint dead away from the pleasure. She may have been fantasizing about it all these years, but she couldn't let it happen.

"Oh!" A new sensation startled her. He'd nipped the inside of her thigh, stung her like a bee, and she almost slid off the chair. She gripped his steadying arms, and all the time, he kept murmuring to her, saying things, hypnotizing her with soft, sexy suggestions. She could have been in a trance. She was woozy enough.

Wear Faustini and life will surprise you.

What an ad this would make.

It was her last coherent thought. A lovely aching left her unable to make sense of anything other than her body's astonishing ability to respond. She was as crazy as before, a soaring, runaway kite. Her nerves sparkled and sang. Everything was gushing wet, even her mouth. She actually had to swallow to keep from drooling, and her throat constricted with the effort.

Eventually she realized that he was licking her passionately, with precision and patience, and whispering warnings, telling her every terrible thing he had in mind for her and her vibrating body. But the only thing that registered was the light that burned sharply in the pit of her belly. A signal flare.

"Tess, I want to fuck you on this chair."

"What?"

"You heard me."

Of course, she said no. At least she *thought* the word *no.* His bluntness should have shocked her out of this bizarre state of mind. But he already had her by the hand and was helping her up from the chair. The robe fell to the floor, and she got tangled in it, falling against him. He steadied her naked, shaking body with his. Now she was quivering from head to toe and could hardly move.

He turned the chair toward the mirror and guided her into the position he had in mind, which wasn't sitting, but kneeling. When he was done, she could see herself, curved like a graceful animal, her knees digging into the seat cushion and her fingers curled around the back of the chair.

He'd undone his pants and dropped them. He entered her that way, bending over her body and cupping her swaying breasts. He sheathed himself in her quaking vagina, and she screamed with pleasure. In her mind, she screamed.

Her entire focus flew to the startling pressure of his body as it penetrated. His hands were hot on her breasts, but she couldn't feel them, couldn't feel anything but the radiating heat of his shaft, the length and breadth. She was filled to bursting.

The instant he began to thrust, their rocking bodies became the new focus. His thighs banged hers, hot against her naked skin, and he gripped her shoulders for leverage. Never once did he stop whispering to her and telling her what he was going to do next, shocking her with wildly erotic suggestions. He swore that after a few more strokes, he would replace his cock with his tongue. He would tease and torment the deep, wet, throbbing place until she came, and then he would switch again.

And she would watch it all.

It was no idle threat. She could see everything in the mirror. She watched him slide in and out of her body like a porn star, a look of clenched ecstasy on his face. When the thrusting slowed, and he braced to withdraw, she shuddered and clutched the chair, wondering why she hadn't stopped him at some point before this, wondering if she ever could.

Suzanne Forster

He dropped to one knee, gazing at her terribly vulnerable bottom, and Tess writhed, trying to escape him. She felt his fingertips before she actually saw them caressing her clit, and she closed her eyes. A groan of anguish escaped her. She couldn't stand any more of this.

She wouldn't watch.

She *couldn't* watch, but she could feel.

His tongue slid through her wetness, and her legs quivered like blades of grass. He was as slow and gentle as before. But this time, the cloudburst that soaked her was hot, and the sensations were wild and throbbing. *She* was throbbing, begging, pleading.

Take me, Danny, *take me!*

When had she lost control of this seduction?

When had she lost control of everything?

Ten

Tess could not get out of her apartment door. It was 9:00 a.m., and she was already an hour late for work. Her cell phone hadn't stopped ringing, but she couldn't seem to answer it, either. Her hands weren't working. They had no strength. She stood, clutching the doorknob, but couldn't make herself open it. *What was she going to do about this thing with Danny?*

She'd never been so torn. Even the decision to leave California and come to New York, to uproot her entire life, hadn't been this difficult.

She let go of the doorknob and rocked forward, letting her forehead clunk against the door. What *was* she going to do? The sex was incredible, but the man was not to be trusted. She wasn't at all sure he hadn't played some kind of mind game with her, using hypnosis or subliminal persuasion, and the thought was chilling. She couldn't blame the sex on him. She might well have done it anyway, but the subterfuge was a cheap trick.

What was he going to do next? At this point, he seemed capable of anything. He'd wiped the file of a major account and jeopardized her career, not to mention the agency. He'd stolen things from her office, including her precious PDA. He'd kidnapped her and taken her to a sex club. Why? To help her as he said? Or to confuse and distract her?

They'd gone on a sexual bender last night, and she had *seemed* more than willing to participate, but that didn't negate the rest of it. Mind-altering sex was all the more reason to think she was right about him. Even now her brain was fuzzing things up and disorienting her, which might have been his plan. The subliminal suggestions were still working.

She closed her eyes and swore under her breath. Her forehead would have permanent creases from the door but she didn't care. Nor did she move. Maybe she never would. Just petrify right here in the entryway like a prehistoric rock.

Her seduction had worked beautifully last night. She'd actually distracted *him* for once. Of course, it had spun totally out of control, but in the heat of it all, he seemed to have forgotten all about her breaking and entering. Afterward, he'd been more than willing to believe she'd come there for sex—and with that as her excuse, all was forgiven. He'd seemed bewildered when she'd thrown on her clothes and rushed to leave, using work as her reason, but he hadn't stopped her.

She'd had the security guard in the lobby call her a cab, and because it was nearly dawn, she used the story she'd come up with earlier—that she'd had a terrible fight with her boyfriend. There'd been no need for tears. She was so shell-shocked from the sex that everything was shaking, even her voice. The guard had immediately accommodated her.

Of course, she'd gotten no sleep at all. She'd managed to shower and change this morning, but now she couldn't get out the door.

What was she going to do about this situation with Danny Gabriel?

Despite its bad name, denial was a perfectly good defense mechanism. Plenty of problems did go away if you ignored them long enough, but she couldn't ignore this one any longer. It wasn't just about her, it was about the agency. She had an appointment with Barb MacDonald this morning, and after that, her options only got worse.

Tess had a decision to make, a terrible one.

With great effort, she turned the knob and opened her front door.

"Do you have any idea how important Danny is to this agency, recent problems notwithstanding?"

Erica Summers rose from the redwood bench, exposing every naked inch of her long, supple body to Tess. As she reached for the towel lying next to her, a slight wince marred her perfect features. It had looked like pain, but she snatched the towel up and deftly arranged it around her, knotting the terry sheet over her breasts.

"Yes, I do." Tess was barely able to talk in the suffocating heat.

"Let's get out of this sweatbox." Erica wrapped another towel around her wet hair as Tess rose, fully clothed.

They left the small sauna together and entered the cool, sedate beauty of the sitting area. It was all part of Erica's executive bathroom, a suite of rooms as large as many New Yorkers' apartments. Tess was particularly impressed by the chandelier that sparkled like a canopy of antique diamond necklaces laced together.

"We'll lose clients if I fire him," Erica said, inspecting herself in the softly lit vanity. "It could take down the agency. Are you prepared for that?"

No, Tess was not prepared for that. She'd spent the morning agonizing over her decision to tell Erica about everything from the missing PDA to the videotape to the pills she'd found in Danny's apartment. And she was prepared to take responsibility for blowing the whistle on Danny, so to speak. But now that Tess *had* blown the whistle, it was Erica who would have to make the final decision.

Tess had already met with Barb MacDonald and told her what she'd found in Danny's apartment. Barb had been willing to give Tess twenty-four hours to tell Erica, but stressed that she would have to inform Erica herself at their next administrative staff meeting. Tess had agreed, but realized she'd have to examine her own motives before she said anything to anyone. She'd wanted to make sure it had nothing to do with the sex, that she wasn't punishing him for her seeming lack of control.

And finally, when she was convinced it was about work and work alone, she'd come here.

"I have something to show you," Tess said. She went over to the settee where she'd left her purse, jacket and shoes when Erica had insisted that Tess join her in the sauna. Fortunately, Erica had been nearly through her twenty-minute heat bath, so Tess had used that as an excuse not to undress. One striptease for a stranger in twenty-four hours was plenty, thank you.

She found the Ziploc bag she'd put in her purse and handed it to Erica. Tess had put the prescription medication she'd found in the bag for safekeeping.

"The way he's going," Tess warned, "he'll take down the agency if you *don't* fire him. I found a bottle of these pills in his bedroom with the label torn off. I took it to a pharmacy this morning, and it's a highly addictive pain medication. Danny may have a drug problem."

Erica stared at the capsule. She closed her eyes, emitting a sigh. "All right, I'll talk to Barb MacDonald, as you suggested."

She was clearly angry as she dismissed Tess. "You can go."

Tess gathered up her things and left, having no idea what Erica would do. It was entirely possible that Tess's job was on the line, too. And maybe things she knew nothing about. The hollow sensation in her stomach warned her that she was out of her depth, and the sharks were circling. Even worse, she couldn't be sure who the sharks were.

* * *

"Okay, let's see how it looks." Tess talked to herself as she walked to the back of the conference room to get a better look at the display she'd set up. The client would be arriving soon, and she wanted everything to be perfect. The trials were over. This was the Olympic event, and it was her team's to lose.

It was Thursday morning, and she was pitching her Elegant Goth concept to the Faustini brass today. She'd thought about turning the presentation over to Carlotta, who was quick and good on her feet but didn't have the same passion for the concept as Tess, and in this case, passion was everything.

Six concepts, blown up to the size of movie posters, sat on easels at the front of the room, each one featuring a different product from Faustini's new line of leather clothing and accessories. The conference room lights had been dimmed, and the posters were subtly lit from behind and below to create the drama Tess wanted.

Beautiful, she dared to think. Dark and poetic. Perfect.

Tess was happy. Instead of models, Brad Hayes and Jan Butler had found male and female dancers to emulate the Matrix's Neo and Trinity in the ads, and they'd been perfect, too. Contortionists, but with the grace of ballet dancers.

In her hand, Tess held a stack of brochures with die-cut borders designed to look like Faustini's new line of purses. Even better, you could open the purse to find cutouts of each new product, from the duster coats to the shoes and boots. That was Lee Sanchez's idea, and Tess was thrilled. It had been a grueling week, but her team had really pulled together.

"News flash!" Andy dashed through the open conference room door. "The old man isn't coming. He's in the hospital, and his daughter is taking his place."

Tess nearly dropped the brochures. "Tell me you're joking."

Andy gave a helpless shrug. "Gina Faustini's on her way up. The old man had a minor stroke, and it affected his speech. He's okay, but it'll be a while before he can work. She's taking over for him."

Tess fought to collect herself. She had geared the entire campaign toward Alberto Faustini's more conservative approach. The daughter had wanted a much more extreme look, like the S&M club where Danny had taken Tess.

"Rumor has it that's how Danny got pulled from the account," Andy said. "He went with the daughter's vision."

Tess had heard as much from Erica. Now it seemed like more evidence that Danny was guilty of sabotage. He'd tried to get her to use that approach when he knew the old man wouldn't approve. But Tess couldn't think about that now.

"I'll focus on the Gothic elements," she said, her mind flying in several different directions. "It's good work. I know it is."

"It's *great* work," Andy countered. "It's brilliant, Tess."

"Thanks. We can only hope that Gina feels compelled to carry out her father's wishes, especially now that he's ill. Where's the rest of the team? Why aren't they here?"

"They're on their way. Tess, there's more bad news."

"Okay, but not now." She was already on her way to the front of the room, focusing on the posters and honing new catchphrases to describe them. *Darkly sexy. Erotic menace. Vampire chic.* That was all she could allow herself to think about now. She had to switch gears, and she had only minutes to do it.

She barely noticed her team filing into the room and taking their seats. *Dress for the dark side of your personality. Burn up the night.*

"Tess, she's here." Andy yanked on her sleeve.

Tess turned to see a green-eyed Generation Xer, complete with tattoos and piercings. She was flanked by two blue suits, both of whom Tess had met before. They ran the Faustini marketing department.

"Ms. Faustini, come in, please!" Tess greeted all three enthusiastically and took them to their seats. She presented them with brochures, while Andy loaded up trays with thermal carafes of coffee and tea from the sideboard.

"Open it and look inside," Tess told them, pride in her voice. "This is the mailer we'd be sending across the country and distributing in department stores, along with the Faustini gift, an embossed leather credit card holder for purchasers of a hundred dollars or more."

Tess beamed, but no one beamed back. She waited with bated breath as Gina opened the purse and inspected the cutouts. Gina wrinkled her pierced nose, which rattled Tess, although it shouldn't have. The client rarely showed anything but skepticism at this point. They didn't want to encourage the agency to overcharge, even for a brilliant concept.

Tess forged ahead with her presentation. "The name Faustini means elegance. It means pride of ownership and exquisite handcrafting. It will always mean those things, but today it says something new, something forbidden yet irresistible, something that everyone must have."

She went on, using the catchphrases she'd come up with as she referred to the ads. She'd decided to avoid her audience's facial expressions by looking just over their heads. She was protecting her energy. Passion was a fire too easily extinguished. A raised eyebrow or a yawn were as deadly as a cold draft.

But at some point in the presentation, Tess realized that half her team were wearing black. Head-to-toe black. She had no clue why. Again, the steel trap closed. She could not let her mind go there.

As Tess finished the pitch, she spoke directly to Gina Faustini.

"I would submit to you that this isn't an ad campaign at all. It's a marriage of old and new, a Gothic rock opera. Our graphic designs showcase what Faustini has always been and what it can be. They tell you what it means to carry Faustini, to wear Faustini, to *be* Faustini."

Gina's expression was as stony as the Sphinx. She glanced down at the brochure, clearly not enchanted by it or by Tess's enthusiasm.

"It's a purse," she said. "There's nothing sexy or edgy or new about a purse, even if it's one of ours. It could just as easily be a briefcase, and my family's been making those for a hundred years."

"Of course." Tess quickly conceded. "But what about the movie posters?" She turned to the easels, pointing out the elements she described. "Look at how the female spokesmodel pulls a gun from the bag. There's plenty of edge there. But it's darkly elegant too. Everything your company stands for."

"Lose the elegance." Gina turned up her nose at the posters, too. "It's limp and benign. It's *stale*. I want my Neo to be a villain, and I don't want him on a movie set. I want him somewhere dangerous, the city streets at night, a bad neighborhood or an S&M club, like Danny's concept."

"But your father—"

Gina glared at Tess.

Wrong thing to say.

"My father made his fortune selling to his generation," Gina said. "Now it's my turn." She looked around the room. "Why isn't Danny Gabriel at this meeting? He understands the concept I'm looking for. He took me to a place called the Marquis Club. That's what I want."

Gina *wanted* the Marquis Club as her location? Tess didn't have a chance to respond before Carlotta spoke up.

"Danny's...not available this morning," Carlotta said, clearly flustered about something.

Gina's green eyes flashed with annoyance. "Well, I need him to be available. If he's in another meeting, call him out. Danny can articulate what I want. He understands."

Brad rose from his chair, his features as grim as his

black shirt and slacks. He shot Tess a glare as he spoke. "Danny's no longer with Pratt-Summers."

Tess smothered a gasp. Erica had done it! She'd fired her star player. All of advertising would be talking about this, but why the hell did she do it on the day of the Faustini pitch? Tess fought off a wave of light-headedness. Emotionally, she was in knots. Her arch nemesis had been fired, and she should have been savoring the victory, but all she could feel was confusion and dread. And her meeting was going down in flames.

"Why would Danny leave?" Gina looked as crestfallen as some of Tess's team. "Is it true?" she asked Tess.

"He left this morning," Brad said.

Tess cut Brad off. "I'll handle this." Running on pure adrenaline, she turned to Gina. If Tess didn't cinch this deal now, there was a good chance that Gina would search out Danny and hire him.

"I know exactly what you want," Tess said. "I know, and I can give it to you. Give me a chance—forty-eight hours—and I'll put a new concept together. I'll give you a dangerous locale—the Marquis Club, if we can get it— *and* a spokesmodel to go with it. I'll give you hell and Satan, if you want them."

Gina blinked her surprise. "That might be a little *too* edgy."

"We can always tone it down, make it elegant," Tess said, making no attempt to hide the irony in her tone.

Gina considered her with new respect. "I don't want it fast," she added, "I want it good. Take a week, take two, if necessary."

Tess nodded. "Okay, excellent." She drew in a breath and took another leap into the abyss. "You're going to love what I have in mind. It's everything you're looking for and more. Call it hell on earth, call it the inferno."

Gina stared at her appraisingly. She actually tugged on the ring that impaled her lower lip, distorting her mouth in grotesque ways. Still, she was a beautiful girl. Beautiful and willful and probably totally self-indulgent.

At last, she nodded her assent.

Tess rushed through the maze of hallways to Danny's office. She was perspiring madly but didn't bother to blot the dampness from her face and throat. She'd come out of the pitch session wringing wet. What a nightmare.

Don't let them see you sweat? That was a laugh.

The door to his office was closed but unlocked. Inside, she found the answer to her question. The office and conference room had been cleaned out. Even the framed ads were missing from the walls.

She walked around his desk and sat down in his chair, stunned. He was gone. If Erica had just spoken to him this morning, then he'd moved very quickly. Apparently it had all been done before the Faustini pitch. Maybe Erica wanted to be sure he wasn't around.

Guilt washed over Tess. No, she wouldn't allow herself to feel that. He'd brought it on himself. He'd been ruthless in his behavior toward her. She should be feeling pride, triumph. She'd saved the account for the agency. Gina had been inches from defecting.

Tess did feel a stirring of triumph, but it was edged out

by a growing sense of disbelief. Maybe this was what David had felt after bringing down Goliath. Danny Gabriel had been fired—and because of her? She couldn't quite grasp that reality, and she almost wished it wasn't true. Still, she couldn't let it demoralize her or her team, although she had a bad feeling it had already done some damage.

More than anything, she just wanted to hide out for a while and try to absorb this latest shock to her system. But that might give the gossip a chance to build and do even more damage. If she held a meeting and rallied her team as quickly as possible, she might be able to circumvent some of that. But it would not be pleasant. She could feel that in her bones. And before she did anything, she needed to track down Erica.

Eleven

"Looks like I'm going straight to hell. Also known as the Marquis Club. Who's coming with me?"

Tess scanned the group, waiting expectantly for someone to volunteer. Someone *besides* Carlotta, who was waving her hand like a kid who had to go to the bathroom.

Unfortunately, Tess didn't have any other takers. She'd called an emergency meeting of the team to create at least the illusion of unity after that morning's bombshell about Danny, but no one seemed to be in the mood. Andy was barely in the room. He was leaning against the door frame, his arms crossed defensively. Brad was holding up the other side of the door, and studying the flecked pattern in the carpeting. The remaining three team members sat in guest chairs, and except for Carlotta, were the picture of doom and gloom. Jan Butler was plucking at the sleeve of her mourning garb, a black tunic, and Lee Sanchez was beating a drum solo against his thigh. At least he wasn't wearing black.

It was like JFK had died all over again. Tess hadn't realized the impact of Danny's departure on her team's morale, and she wasn't prepared to say anything to them yet. Apparently, the rumor mill had it that *she* was responsible for his leaving, and even though there was some truth to it, Tess had no idea who'd started the rumor or exactly what had been said. She wanted to discuss it with Erica first, but Erica was out for the rest of the day, according to her assistant.

Talk about a communication gap. Tess could barely fathom it in such a large successful ad agency. Their business was communication! But there were many things about Pratt-Summers that baffled her, and now Erica was at the top of that list.

"What? Am I invisible?" Carlotta rose to get Tess's attention.

"Thanks," Tess said, "but I think it's better that one of the men go with me. You and I alone in the Marquis Club would be like kibble to a pack of wild dogs."

"Whatever." Carlotta sank back down, now as morose as everyone else.

Tess had invited the team to her office to map out the new strategy for the Faustini campaign—and hopefully to whip up some enthusiasm. She'd suggested they stick with the same female dancer as their spokesmodel, relying on makeup to make her look edgier. And then she'd surprised them with the news that she'd already scouted the Marquis Club as a possible location. She'd left out the part about Danny kidnapping her, but she'd assured them the club would be perfect—and it offered a bonus. The club's front man would be the perfect model. The idea for using the Marquis had come to her during the Faustini pitch, and it had been one of those oh-my-god! moments. The Marquis in a Faustini duster coat? Should be memorable.

Tess had been thrilled at the prospect, but she seemed to be the only one. Her team appeared to be going through the motions, more than anything else, and Tess had a bad feeling that she would be carrying this campaign on her back.

"I'm reasonably sure the club can be rented for a price," she said, mostly to fill the silence. She was less sure of the Marquis, but if they could get him, Gina Faustini should be very happy. The Marquis had enough edge to wafer-slice overripe tomatoes.

"Andy, how about it?" she asked. "Be my bodyguard?"

Andy gave her a baleful look. "I can't go in that place," he said. "They'll cook me and eat me."

"Right," Tess said, "a tender morsel like you."

"Take Brad," Andy suggested. "He's bigger than I am."

Brad's arms were folded, too, still apparently protesting his mentor's departure. Tess couldn't say that she blamed him, and he *was* at least a foot taller than Andy, but the last thing Tess needed was a hostile bodyguard.

"I need Brad to stay here and work with the team on the new brochures and posters," she said. "Sorry, it's you and me, Andy. I guess you'd better dig out your black leather thong."

Andy grimaced, and the rest of the group looked a little uneasy about the idea, too. Tess couldn't tell whether they objected to Andy in a thong or the club, but there was little she could do to reassure them. Tess had been brought to the agency to do damage control on their lack of communication with clients, and in this case, the client had made herself crystal clear. She wanted the advertising equivalent of a B horror movie with sex, and she was in charge.

The Marquis' office was dark and funereal, lit only by ornate brass candelabra with flickering tapers. Oppressively heavy with the scent of lilac, the room made Tess think of a mortuary. So did the coffin in the corner, if that's what it was.

She and Andy were alone in the room. The Marquis had already kept them waiting twenty minutes, and Tess was getting annoyed. She'd called right after the emergency meeting with her team and set the appointment up for this afternoon, but who knew if devotees of places like this went by the Gregorian calendar, like the rest of the world. The rather elderly assistant who'd brought them here had looked quite motherly and demure in her skirt and matching twinset, but Tess hadn't missed the exotic dragonfly tattooed on her ankle.

Tess leaned over and whispered to Andy, who was sitting next to her in a chair that had lion's paws for arms and legs. "Overdoing it just a bit, don't you think? I mean, a coffin?"

"I think it's a chest meant to look like a sarcophagus," Andy pointed out. "Could be an antique." He looked around at the exotic decor. There were Egyptian fertility gods sculpted from black stone and emerald-eyed asps carved out of wood.

"Everything in the place looks like an antique," he said. "Check out the papyrus painting on the wall. Is that erotica?"

The room was too dark. Tess couldn't see.

"Guess not," Andy said, walking over to get a closer look at the paper, covered in hieroglyphics and painted figures. "It says here that it's a funeral papyrus. Oh, my God—"

"What's wrong?"

"It's a spell from the Book of the Dead."

Tess's pulse fluttered oddly. "Maybe you shouldn't be reading it. Bad luck or something."

"Yeah, maybe not," Andy said, still glued to the thing.

While he pored over the spell, Tess took a closer look at the office. It was weirdly beautiful, she had to admit, but in a creepy way. On his desk sat a black rhinoceros horn, carved as a goblet. Ibis-headed deities with the bodies of naked men and women decorated the tapestries hanging on the wall behind him. A set of jeweled daggers flanked the tapestries. His bookends were strange-looking sphinxes with female breasts. And then there was the sarcophagus.

Honestly, it made her think of a vampire's lair. At least whoever had decorated the place had skipped the cobwebs. Tess would have to keep her eye out for bats. Was that strange bit of equipment in the corner a torture device of some kind? It didn't look Egyptian, but then vampires were a timeless lot.

"Maybe we should have worn turtlenecks," she said, smiling as Andy glanced over his shoulder. "To protect against fangs?"

She settled back in the chair, aware that her sarcasm was a defense mechanism. She and Andy had joked about the club all the way over in the taxi. She'd been trying to prepare him, but it had also kept the nerves at bay, maybe for both of them.

"Remember what I told you," she whispered as he returned to his chair. "Don't shake hands with him. If he offers his hand, tell him you have a cold."

"Okay, but why?"

"I'll explain later." She didn't want to say that she might have been drugged when she was here before. It would either freak him out or make him think she'd lost it. Neither were good options right now.

Andy shrugged. "I'll just breathe on him. I had garlic for lunch."

No time to reply. The Marquis entered through a back door, much the way a judge would have entered a courtroom from his chambers. Instead of robes, he wore a tuxedo and a black cape with a red satin lining. In the low light, his features were dramatically shadowed, his eyes dark and penetrating.

Could he be any more theatrical? Tess wouldn't have been surprised to see fangs if he'd smiled. Stunt fangs, of course. Those prosthetic things that actors used. Obviously, the Marquis enjoyed playing one of the denizens of the Vampire Forest when he wasn't transforming into demons.

That was why this club existed, she reminded herself. To give bored middle-class Americans another way to spice up their lives of quiet desperation. They were all role-playing—and probably harmless. As long as it looked scary—and so did the Faustini ads—everything would be fine.

"My apologies," he said, walking straight to Andy and extending his hand.

Andy jumped up and grabbed it. "Not a problem," he said. "I'm Andy Phipps from Pratt-Summers."

No! Not the hand. Tess cleared her throat, but not quickly enough. Andy was already in the man's grip. And when the Marquis turned to Tess, she jumped like a teenager. Embarrassed, she surrendered her hand and introduced herself. His skin was strangely cool, but she didn't feel any suspicious pricks this time.

"Pratt-Summers?" the Marquis asked. "Is that the ad agency?"

Tess nodded, trying not to be obvious as she swiped her palm against the leg of her pantsuit. "We'd like to talk to you about renting your club for one of our shoots."

"You want to use the Marquis Club? That must be an interesting client."

"Leather goods," she said, relaxing a notch. Maybe they weren't going to need the turtlenecks. He sounded almost normal. "Is the club available? We'll need it for two or three days, perhaps more."

His eyes were beautifully expressive, Tess realized. One eyebrow had lifted in a subtle arch, and his lashes were pitch-black and preternaturally long. *That* was sexy.

"We're dark on Thursdays," he said. "It's the only day I have available, but you could have the run of the place until, say...midnight."

"Done." Tess wasn't going to hold out for the extra days. She would shoot as much as she could here, and then take the models somewhere else, maybe the streets, as Gina had also suggested.

Andy blurted out, "Can we hire you, too?"

The Marquis' smile revealed perfectly even white teeth and a glimpse of pink gums. No fangs. "I'll be here to oversee," he explained.

"Actually, we'd like you to model." Tess returned his smile. It was time to pour on the charm, but she felt like the apprentice trying to fool the sorcerer. "You have exactly the look our client wants—dark and dangerous, compelling. It's a national ad campaign for a very prestigious account. They're launching a new line of leather clothing and accessories."

He seemed amused. "You think I'm compelling?"

"Yes—and we'll pay you well to be compelling in our ads. You'll get the going rate."

He didn't seem to know whether to take her seriously. After a moment's reflection, he said, "It seems to me that you and I should discuss this in more detail, Ms. Wakefield." He nodded at Andy. "Perhaps your colleague would like a tour of the club so that we can talk alone?"

"No, really, that's not necessary," Tess said. "I've already told Andy all about the club, and I'd prefer that he stay."

The Marquis didn't seem to have heard what she said. He'd already hit a button on his speakerphone. "Find Cassandra and send her in, please."

Mere seconds later, an exotic creature entered the room in a very short black toga and very long black hair. Her feet were sandled in gold, and her eyes were lined with kohl and shadowed in vivid teal blue, reminiscent of Cleopatra. She went beautifully with the room's decor.

Tess couldn't believe Andy's reaction. His Adam's apple actually bounced. He glanced at Tess, begging her with his eyes to let him go.

"I really should take a tour," he said. "I'll look for photo ops."

Tess swallowed a sigh. "All right, but be back here in fifteen minutes. This discussion won't take long."

The Marquis' smile curved into something faintly sinister. "Have fun, Andy—and don't worry about Ms. Wakefield. She'll be perfectly safe with me."

Andy didn't seem to be in need of any reassurance. Cassandra beckoned, and he followed her out the door like a puppy on a short leash. Tess noticed as the light hit Cassandra's toga that she didn't appear to have anything on underneath. Andy seemed to be pretty curious about that, too.

Tess was on her guard as soon as the door shut. "What do you want to talk about that you couldn't say in front of Andy?"

The Marquis opened his desk drawer and took out what looked like a diary, bound in red satin.

"I have a riddle for you," he said. "If you answer it correctly, we have a deal. You can have the club for your photo shoot, and my services as a model, free of charge."

"And if I don't answer it correctly?"

"Same deal, but there's a price."

"How much?"

"Why don't you read the riddle first, then we'll talk cost."

She stared at the red satin book. "This is a business deal, not a game."

"I didn't give you a choice. Here. Take it."

She did, reluctantly. Opening it, she noted the graceful calligraphy, which was almost as ornate as the hieroglyphics on the wall.

"Please," he said, "read."

Something about his voice compelled her. "My life can be measured in hours. I serve by being devoured. Thin, I am quick. Thick, I am slow. Wind is my foe. What am I?"

She had no idea what the answer was. "I hate riddles," she said, looking up to the strange power of his pitch-black eyes. A flame danced in their depths.

A fake. He was nothing but a fake.

"Can you answer it?" he asked.

Tess couldn't, but she wasn't quite ready to admit that. "Why am I sure I'm not going to like these conditions of yours?"

"Because you've already decided you don't like me, so how could you possibly like my conditions?"

It was true. She nodded. "Okay, let's get this over with. What are they?"

"Before you and your people take over my club, I want to give you my own tour of this place, a private tour. I want you to understand this club and what we do here. Intimately."

"Why?"

"Because if you understand what really happens here, you'll treat my creation with respect. I'm sure you'd demand the same for your work. You do value your work, don't you? I don't want my club or its members subjected to ridicule."

"I have no intention of ridiculing them."

"Of course you don't, but I'd like to make sure of that."

"Is that your only condition, the tour?"

"Yes and no. Seeing isn't enough. You have to experience it, too, to understand on a level that touches you, changes you."

"*Changes* me?"

"I'm giving you a temporary membership. You'll be my initiate. I'll take you to places you've never been, train you in the art of surrender and transformation."

"Transformation to what?"

"Not to what, to whom. It's a journey, and I admit it can be a frightening one, but I can't let you use my club if you haven't taken it. I couldn't risk that."

Tess was getting frustrated. Her career was riding on this. "You haven't stopped talking in riddles, Marquis. What do you want?"

"It's not what I want. It's what I insist upon. As my initiate, you will voluntarily submit to me for a period of time and do whatever I ask. I make the rules, and you follow them, utterly and completely."

She handed him the diary. "Over my cold, dead, decomposing body."

His eyebrow dipped. "We don't do necrophilia here."

Tess had heard all she needed to. She reached for the cell phone that hung on her belt clip. Gina Faustini would just have to get over her fixation with the Marquis Club because Tess had meant what she said about decomposing.

"What are you doing?" he asked.

"I'm calling Andy," she said. "We're leaving."

"You're sure you want to do that?"

Tess didn't answer. She was busy with the phone.

"As you wish," he said, "but there's no need to call him. I'll have Cassandra bring him back."

Tess had already tapped out the numbers. Andy came on the line after one ring. "Andy, get back here."

"Tess! This place is awesome. Have you seen the Hypnosis Parlor? We're going to the Vampire Forest next."

"Andy, don't go anywhere else. Come right back here. I'm ready to go."

"That was quick. Did you and the Marquis make a deal?"

Tess glanced up at the Marquis, anger burning in her breathing. And something else, fear. "No, the price was too high."

"What did he want?"

"He wanted me."

"What did you say?"

"You heard me." Tess clicked her phone shut. "I'll wait outside," she told the Marquis. With that, she turned her back on his beautifully expressive eyes and headed for the door, wondering if she'd just been caught up in a waking nightmare. If Danny Gabriel wasn't the incarnation of Professor Wiley, then this guy was. He even had that eerie voice that got under your skin and stayed there. It was hushed and hypnotic and totally subversive.

Tess quelled a shiver as she waited in the hallway for Andy. The anger had burned out, and now she was fighting chills. How bizarre that she kept running into triggers to the very experiences she was trying to push out of her head. She wanted to think it was all a coincidence, but that seemed too easy an explanation. She'd read somewhere that when people had unresolved issues they often sought out situations where they could resolve them, but not necessarily consciously. They were being led by their psyches to deal with the conflicts.

In this case, Tess couldn't seem to escape her past and the predatory Professor Wiley. But if there was something buried inside her that had to be resolved, she wasn't going to do it in the Marquis Club. A woman would have to be crazy to subject herself to a place like this— and a man like that.

"Judy, put me through to Erica." Tess sat on the edge of her chair, the phone pressed to her ear. Judy had been stonewalling her all morning on Erica's whereabouts, and Tess didn't intend to wait any longer to find out what had happened with Danny.

"Tess, I told you. She can't be reached. You've been up here twice already this morning, and I've lost track of how many times you've called. I understand that you consider this important, but—"

Tess hesitated until she could get precise control of her voice. "Do this much for me, okay? Tell Erica it's the Faustini account. If she doesn't want it to go into review, she needs to get back to me. That's it. Just tell her that. Thanks."

"Wait," Judy said. "Hang on."

Tess's finger was on the disconnect button. Several clicks told her that Judy was going to patch her through to Erica. Judy had been using the excuse that Erica wouldn't be in that day, but refusing to give Tess any information. She wouldn't even say when Erica might be available. Once again, Tess was boggled at the agency's lack of leadership.

"Tess? What the h-hell's going on?"

"Erica?" Tess could barely hear her boss's voice. It was weak and halting. She sounded very ill. "Are you all right?"

"What is so important?"

"It's the Faustini campaign," Tess said, instantly changing direction. Maybe Erica was in trouble, possibly in the hospital or even rehab. Otherwise, why all the secrecy?

"How could there be trouble with Faustini?" Erica sounded confused. "I had a good report from Gina herself. She called to tell me she was pleased with your response to her concerns, and that you were going to move mountains to get her what she wanted. She mentioned a place called the Marquis Club."

"Yes, well, that's what I'm calling about." Tess didn't

know what to do except say it. "I can't deliver what Gina Faustini wants. She did request the Marquis Club for a location, but I'm afraid that's impossible. It's not available at any price."

No need to tell her what the price actually was, Tess reasoned.

"Tess, we don't use that word around here."

"What word?"

"Impossible. Gina is dead set on S&M, and she wants the Marquis Club. You have to get it."

Tess was confounded by Erica's insistence. She'd expected her boss to be shocked at the very idea of a kinky underground club. She should have known better. This *was* advertising.

"Hear me out?" Tess said, stoking her courage. "It's a bad idea, Erica. The Marquis Club is a hellhole, to be honest, and Andy and I have already checked out several other S&M clubs. They're called dungeons, and the decor is whips and chains. The members' idea of fun is to be publicly humiliated by doms, who look like refugees from the World Federation of Wrestling. It's bad cable television. Really bad."

"Doms?"

"Dominant males. They're also called masters, and the women are called mistresses. It's underworld sex lingo. Doms and subs, bondage and discipline. Sounds like I've got it down, doesn't it? Scary."

"And just how do you plan to appease our client, Gina Faustini?"

Maybe it was exhaustion or shell shock or both,

but Tess didn't feel like bluffing. "I'm not sure at this point."

Erica's voice went cold. "Listen here, Ms. Whiz Kid. You don't have the luxury of being unsure. If the client wants the Marquis Club, and you agreed to provide it, you'd damn well better do it. That's why I hired you."

"You got it," Tess said faintly. She was already scrambling for other ideas that might appease Gina, like building their own set or renting a horror-movie soundstage and renovating it. All very expensive, though—and this didn't seem like the time to bring it up.

"Tess, this is your account. Why are you calling me? Handle it."

Erica's icy rebuke shocked her, maybe because it was true. This was her account, and her responsibility. That was why she'd been hired. Danny was the one who wouldn't give the clients what they wanted, and Danny was gone.

"I'll handle it," Tess said, her voice as shaky as Erica's.

"Tess, wait." Erica's strength seemed to be ebbing. She could barely get the rest of it out. "Things are much worse than you know. Several of our biggest clients have already defected and gone with Danny. If we lose Faustini, the agency might as well shut its doors. Pratt-Summers won't survive. You have to make this work, Tess."

The phone went dead. Stunned, Tess dropped the receiver in the cradle. She felt the weight of the cosmos descending on her shoulders. Erica had already made it clear that she wanted her to take responsibility not just for the account but for the mess the agency was in. And in a bizarre way, Tess *was* responsible. She had to do something.

But even as she sat there, moments later, sorting through options and coming to grips with the enormity of the trap she'd walked into with the Faustini campaign, she also realized that she'd missed her opportunity. She had not asked Erica about Danny. She still didn't know the real details of his dismissal. Like everyone else, she was relying on rumor and innuendo, and she was as much a target of the gossips as Danny.

Twelve

Maybe Mercury went retrograde, Tess thought. She didn't know exactly what that meant, but it had something to do with life being radically out of sync. And life was. Tess's conversation with Erica this morning was just the most recent in a series of bizarre events, and now even the twenty-eighth-floor bathroom seemed off-kilter.

She'd actually come to pick Mitzi's brain, but the washroom attendant wasn't perched on her stool, adding up receipts, as always. She was standing in front of the mirror, applying makeup and primping.

Tess hesitated, trying to make sense of Mitzi in a black wrap dress that clung to her curves and swirled at the hem. The smock coat was long gone. Tess had noticed a catch in her gait the other day and wondered about an injury, but there was no sign of that now. She was wearing nylons and heels that were low but nonetheless chic.

"Hot lunch date?" Tess asked.

Mitzi looked in the mirror, saw Tess's reflection and went directly back to her efforts with the eyeliner wand. Not even a nod.

For a moment, Tess thought she'd wandered into the wrong bathroom. Maybe it wasn't Mitzi. Or maybe this was an alternate universe. And then it came to her. She must be on Mitzi's enemies list, too.

"Is this about Danny Gabriel?" Tess asked.

"Heartless bitch," Mitzi muttered.

Tess sighed. "I had no choice. I don't know what you heard, but—"

Mitzi slapped down the mascara and picked up a lipstick tube. "I heard you framed him. I got it from the horse's mouth that you told Erica Summers he was trying to sabotage you out of jealousy."

"Erica told you that?"

"*Danny* did. He came in to say goodbye after she fired his ass."

"Did she call him into her office?" Tess asked, anxious to fill in the blanks about the mysterious event.

"No, he went to her home. He said she was sick, and she asked him to meet her there. Afterward, he came back here to get his stuff."

"When? Yesterday morning?"

Mitzi finished with her lipstick and slapped that down. "*Of course,* yesterday morning. It was early. I wasn't even set up for business yet, and I get here at six."

That would explain how he'd been able to vanish without Tess knowing anything about it, although she'd been so wrapped up in preparing for the Faustini pitch she might not have noticed if the building had collapsed. Interesting that he'd taken the time to say goodbye to Mitzi. Tess was very curious about their relationship.

"What else did he say?" Tess asked. "Is he going to another agency? Is he all right?"

Mitzi harrumphed. "Like you care. And like I'm going to tell you anything else. I'm no traitor."

Tess screwed up her courage and walked over to the counter. "At least give me a chance to explain. You gave *him* that much, didn't you? Danny may think I set him up, but I didn't. I wouldn't do that to anyone. I don't *frame* people."

Mitzi began shoveling her makeup back into its case. She was scowling, but she was also blinking furiously, and Tess wondered if she might be fighting tears. "It's not fricking fair," was all she would say.

"You're a pretty good judge of people," Tess said. "Do you think I'd accuse someone of sabotage if I didn't have evidence? He was in my office late at night, going through the drawers and cabinets. It's on videotape. And there's more."

Tess hesitated, aware that she shouldn't say anything else. Who knew what might happen? Danny could file a lawsuit against her and the agency for unfair dismissal. "I didn't want to tell anyone, Mitzi, much less Erica," she said. "I would rather have cut off my hand."

Mitzi's expression suggested that would have been a

better solution. She dropped her makeup bag in a huge tote on the floor. "I haven't got time to be pissed at you," she said. "I have things to do."

Better to gracefully concede, Tess decided. Mitzi was clearly going somewhere. She'd already closed up shop. Her display racks were empty, and she'd probably locked her stock in the cabinets.

"I'll get out of your way," Tess said as Mitzi took another moment to check herself in the mirror. She fussed a bit more with her short dark hair.

"You look great," Tess said. "Love the dress. Special occasion?"

"I have an audition, if you must know," Mitzi shot back.

"Oh! Well, good luck. Or should I say break a leg?"

Mitzi picked up her tote and headed for the door. She'd only taken a couple of steps before she stopped and spun around.

"He didn't do it."

Tess was rocked by the force of Mitzi's passion. She actually did seem to be fighting tears. "How do you know?" Tess said.

"Think about it. He's a brilliant guy. He doesn't need to sabotage anybody. He could have walked away from this business ten years ago, and he would have been the top gun then. He has nothing to prove. Nothing. No offense, but you're just a blip on the radar compared to him. The man is an icon."

Mitzi didn't pull her punches, and Tess could hardly argue. It was all too true. "Did he actually tell you he didn't do it?"

"He said he'd been set up, that someone wanted him out of here."

"And he believes it was me?"

"You're the one who went to Erica. If it wasn't you, who was it? No one else here has any reason to want to hurt Danny. Well, maybe Carlotta Clark, but that was years ago."

"Carlotta Clark? Why would she want to hurt him?"

"That's ancient history." Mitzi brushed past Tess, dismissing the question. The catch in her gait was evident again as she went over to the cabinet by her stool and unlocked it. She pulled out a parka that ballooned like an astronaut's suit.

Tess took advantage of what little time she had. "Mitzi, if Danny's innocent, why didn't he defend himself? Why didn't he stay and try to find out who framed him?"

Mitzi waved her off. "It's more complicated than that."

"I'm sure it is," Tess said. "You told me Danny had a secret. Is it about something that happened with Carlotta?"

"No, of course not."

"Then, could it have anything to do with Erica not wanting him here? You must know about the rumors that they were having an affair."

"It wasn't an affair, not the way people think—and that's all I'm saying."

"Can't you tell me?" Tess said imploringly. "It might help straighten this mess out."

By then Mitzi had herself zipped into the parka, and she was ready to go. Tess held out a hand, staying her. "If you weren't going to tell me what the secret is, why did you mention it at all?"

The other woman looked almost stricken. "I don't know. I shouldn't have. I thought you were different, and that you might be able to see that this is important. He isn't necessarily what he seems." Mitzi hoisted the tote over her shoulder. "No more questions," she said. "I have to go."

She recalled the painkillers. "Just tell me it's not drugs," Tess said. "Tell me he doesn't have a pill habit."

Mitzi's glance was sharp, but she gave nothing away. "We're all addicted to something, aren't we?" Again, she dismissed Tess's concerns. "I have no idea what Danny's monkey might be, but we all have one."

Tess considered that, but didn't agree. She didn't have a monkey. As far as she knew she wasn't addicted to anything. She'd never taken drugs or smoked. She'd given up sex cold turkey. Key lime pie might be a challenge, but she could probably manage that, too.

Mitzi headed out the door without a goodbye, clearly not interested in Tess's opinion. Alone in the room, Tess was left with the uncomfortable possibility that Danny had been framed and wrongfully fired, which made her feel all the more responsible for the agency's plight. What an irony if he were to turn out to be as much as victim as she was.

Slender red tapers gave out the only light in the darkened room. Ablaze in the brass candelabra, they danced macabre shadows across the walls and the ceiling. As Tess sat uneasily in the Marquis' office, waiting for him to show up for their appointment, she prayed the tiny black creatures flitting across the floor were shadows, too.

Even the piped-in music made her uneasy. If the New Age song had a melody, it was obscured by a strange silvery quality that sounded like hisses and whispers. Tess found herself concentrating to hear what was being said, but she couldn't make it out.

The air was still heavy with the scent of lilac, but now she understood why. She'd done some research on the Net and learned that the flower's perfume was considered an aphrodisiac. She'd had quite a dose of that perfume in the last several minutes, especially considering that she was probably hyperventilating.

She wouldn't put it past this kook to keep women waiting on purpose, hoping they'd be under the influence by the time he showed up. Maybe the strange music was part of the seduction, whispering suggestions that could be picked up by the ear but understood only by whatever part of the brain was stimulated by sex.

She glanced at her watch, which, of course, she couldn't see in the dark. Fifteen minutes, at least. That was how long she'd been waiting, by her estimate.

What sort of obscene things was he going to ask her to do? Get wrapped up like a mummy? Wear nipple clamps? Worship his penis?

Not her idea of fun.

Well…maybe the nipple clamps.

"Five more minutes, and I'm out of here," she said under her breath. No PMS sufferer with latent bondage and discipline fantasies should expose herself to more than twenty minutes in an aphrodisiac-soaked environment where naked women in stocks were considered entertainment.

She'd grabbed her coat and bag and was on her way out of the room when she heard a door open behind her.

"I hope you aren't leaving." He spoke to her back in low and sonorous tones. "At least give me a chance to apologize."

His voice sounded as if it was being piped in over surround sound speakers. The first night in the opera house he'd sounded that way, too, as if he was speaking over a PA system. The echoing effect was eerie, but Tess was immune to his attempts to intimidate her. She was here to bargain for her very professional life, and she'd put in hours mentally preparing herself.

She'd realized she had no choice but to come back when it had hit her what was at stake. It wasn't just her job, but Andy's and Carlotta's and Brad's. Everyone's. The entire agency was vulnerable if she couldn't make a deal with the Marquis.

Besides, she reminded herself, his posturing was all for effect. The costumes, the voice enhancement. He was nothing but a fake. And so was that ridiculous music. It was making her hair stand on end.

She turned to a shadowy black form. Almost none of his features could be made out, but she caught the iridescence of his eyes. They were gaseous, like a cat's in the dark.

"What brings you back?" he asked.

"You were apologizing," she reminded him. "Don't let me stop you."

"Ah, yes. I was correcting a wayward odalisque, and those things can take time."

"Oh, I'm sure." Her tone was witheringly dry. "Dirty job. Speaking of which, I've come to accept your offer."

"Really? I'm pleasantly surprised. To be honest, I didn't think you had it in you."

"I don't. It's the lesser of two evils—and there are conditions."

"Indeed?"

He sounded curious. Sensing an advantage, she moved closer to his desk. Something seemed different from the last time she was here, but she couldn't put her finger on what it was, and she wanted to get a better look at him. But the closer she got, the more he seemed to recede into the shadows.

"No drugs," she said, "no bloodletting, no exchange of bodily fluids at any time in any way, and on a scale of one to ten, no pain above a three."

His laughter whispered all around her. She could hardly discern it from the music. "You're no fun at all," he said.

"I don't intend to be. This is business."

Gradually, the room felt silent. Even the music had stopped. Tess could hear his breathing. "Maybe I need to define our roles more clearly," he said. "I make the rules, and you follow them, utterly and completely."

"Not a problem," she said, softening her voice. "I will follow utterly any rules that don't violate my conditions."

"Your conditions *are* a violation. They undermine the

whole point, which is to open yourself to the unconditional, to throw away the training wheels and ride."

"Sorry, no training wheels, no ride."

"In that case, this conversation is over. I'll have you escorted out." He reached for the phone on his desk.

Tess had to wait for her heart to stop pounding. Her bluff hadn't worked, and unfortunately, her plan B was more of the same. Keep bluffing. She would have to play along and made him think she'd accepted his offer. That would get her access to the club and maybe buy her some time. From there she would have to see what she was dealing with, rely on her wits and hope that this initiation of his was nothing more than role-playing, as Danny had said. The important thing was to be able to report back to Erica that she'd made a deal with the Marquis.

She spoke up as he punched out the numbers. "Can I have a safe word at least?"

He looked up, as if she'd somehow surprised him. "You can have as many safe words as you want. You won't need them. Nothing happens here unless you want it to. That's all I can promise."

"Tell me what the rules are."

"The rules are easy. Do as you're instructed."

"But you said I wouldn't have to do anything I didn't want to."

"Exactly, and right now you have two choices. Do you *want* to do this? Or do you *want* to leave? "

Another riddle, she thought, as contradictory and arcane as he was. "Do I have your promise that I won't be forced to do anything I find objectionable?"

"All you're required to do is show up here at the agreed-upon time, and if possible, with an open mind."

"Fine," she said. "We start tomorrow. Eight to five like any other job, and then I'm out of here."

She set down her bag, intending to put on her coat and be gone.

"Tomorrow's fine," he said, "but this isn't a job, and you can't be serious about that eight-to-five stuff. I want three consecutive days with you, twenty-four hours a day. Let's call it a long weekend. Transformation takes time."

"Consecutive? No way! Two days, no sleepovers."

"Three days, around the clock. Take it or leave it."

"This isn't fair. You keep contradicting yourself. You tell me to follow instructions but say I don't have to do anything I don't want to. How does that work?"

"You're free to leave at any time. Actually, I'm surprised you haven't. You must be a very ambitious girl."

She wasn't free to walk out, not in the sense that he meant it. There was too much at stake, but he didn't know that. She drew in a breath and realized she was inhaling essence of lilac again.

"Did you figure out the answer to the riddle?" he asked her.

"No," she admitted, curious enough to ask, "are you going to tell me?"

"Do you remember the lines?"

They had been playing in her head for two days, and she only wished she could blow him away by reciting the riddle word for word, but parts of it had eluded her. "'My life can be measured in hours,'" she said. "'I serve by being devoured.'"

"'Thin, I am quick,'" he prompted. "'Thick, I am slow.'"

She nodded. "And then there's something about the wind?"

"'Wind is my foe.'"

That was the one she'd been struggling with. "Okay, what's the answer?"

"There's one more line."

Apparently he was waiting for her to supply the line, but if she was correct it was nothing more than a simple question. "'Wind is my foe,'" she said. "'What am I?'"

His only response was a smile.

"What am I?" she repeated.

"You're a candle flame."

She'd walked right into that one. *She* was the flame. *Her life could be measured in hours. She served by being devoured.* That was his point, and it was sinister enough to bring a chill to her skin.

She shrugged it off. "I should have gotten that."

"No one gets it. That's why I use it."

She glanced at her watch, but it was still too dark to see. For some reason, her eyes didn't want to adjust in this room. "I really have to be going. What should I expect tomorrow?"

"Surprises, lots of them. If I told you now, it would ruin them."

That sounded suspiciously like what Danny Gabriel had said to her the other day.

"Tomorrow morning you'll be met by the ladies of the Seraglio," he said. "They'll help prepare you."

"In what way?" She wondered who these ladies were.

"In every way. If I can be blunt, you seem to have lost touch with something essential in your nature...if you ever were in touch with it."

She could almost feel his eyes on her, appraising her clothing, which was a basic white silk man-tailored blouse and gray slacks. She'd removed her coat because of the room's warmth.

"And what would that be?"

"Your sexuality."

That was enough for Tess. She was a pro at playing along. She'd been doing it since she was a kid, but even she had her limits. Now this maître d' in a cape was calling her sexless? He'd manipulated her into this insane situation. He'd taken total advantage, but that didn't seem to bother him in the least. This was probably his hobby, preying on vulnerable women.

"When a man questions a woman's sexuality it's often his own sexuality he's unsure of," she said. "Do I threaten your masculinity? Maybe you can't handle a real woman."

"A *real* woman, which implies that you are one?"

Tess came right back at him. He was hitting below the belt. So could she. "At least I'm not some silly fake who wears black capes and uses a PA system to sound scary."

He brought a finger to his lips, as if warning her to be quiet, but she hadn't finished. "You don't really think I'm buying any of this, do you?" she said. "I know it's bogus. You're a fake, probably the biggest fake in this place."

"You think this is all a joke?" he asked softly.

"I think you're amusing yourself, yes. You'll notice *I'm* not laughing."

He muttered something unintelligible, and the candle flames guttered.

"Yeah, right," she said. "Fake."

She was reaching for her bag when all hell broke loose. An explosion nearly rocked her off her feet, and the room went blindingly white. She blinked her eyes, trying to see. The Marquis was a jet-black silhouette, like the negative of a picture. She could see nothing but him and the ice-blue corona that surrounded him. It filled her entire field of vision. If he was from hell, then hell had frozen over.

Tess didn't frighten easily, but this nearly ripped the breath out of her lungs. She knelt to find her bag, trying to shield her eyes from the brightness, but her bag wasn't there. She'd barely gotten to her feet, and he was right in front of her. He thrust out a hand and gripped her shoulder, and his touch was almost painful. It grounded her like an electrical shock.

Her coat slipped from her hands. She could hear herself screaming, but she couldn't move a muscle, not even her head. The room's cloying lilac scent was gone. Fear filled her nostrils, cold and damp.

"Does this feel fake to you?" Very deliberately, he reached out and brushed her breasts with the back of his hand, grazing her nipples and startling them into extreme hardness. Like tiny, faceted gems, they stood out, visible even through her blouse.

The sensation was astonishing, the strangest kind of pleasure she could imagine. It sparkled and stung, creating a path straight to her groin. Tess wanted to throw her head back and gasp. Her thigh muscles tightened, and a sound slipped out as the pressure built. A moan, a cry. It felt like she might have an orgasm.

"Or this?" he asked. She watched him unbutton her blouse with a flooding awareness. There was nothing she could do. She was paralyzed, either by him or by something else. Fear? Excitement?

This was ridiculous. Mind games.

"For the next forty-eight hours, you will be my candle flame," he whispered. "And I will devour you. I will bathe you in oxygen and make you burn high. And if I choose, I will extinguish you."

No fucking way! This was all nightclub magic.

"You are mine. My flame."

His lips curled back, revealing fangs as sharp as talons. They glimmered in the darkness, as blue-white as his aura. She felt his hands slip around her throat, felt his breath on her neck, his fangs sink into her flesh.

She let out a bloodcurdling scream and ripped herself away from him. She clutched herself and screamed and screamed.

She was moving. Not paralyzed. Suddenly she realized no one was touching her. Or undressing her. No one was there.

When she looked up, he was on the other side of the desk, standing there as if he'd never moved. "Are you all right?" he asked.

She rubbed her throat. The skin was smooth and cool where she'd felt him bite her. "What did you do to me?"

"I asked if you were all right."

Her blouse was still buttoned and exactly as it had been. "You didn't touch me?"

"How could I touch you from over here. *Are* you all right?"

She shook her head, trying to clear it. She had watched him, felt his skin on hers, but obviously he hadn't done anything. What the fuck just happened?

"No, I'm not all right," she said.

"Is there anything I can do?"

The room was hot, too hot, and reeking of lilac. She couldn't think. "No, I have to go."

"Are you sure? Can I get you something? Water?"

None of it had happened? She'd imagined all that?

"Tess? Ms. Wakefield?"

His solicitous voice was like fingernails on a blackboard, worse than the sound effects. "No, nothing." She bent and picked up her coat and bag. "I can find my way out."

"Will you be back tomorrow morning?"

Not if she could vanish into a cosmic black hole and cease to exist, but she knew better than to say so. She might even thank him for his hospitality as she walked out the door. But once she hit the streets, all bets were off.

"I'll be the one wearing the cross around my neck," she said.

Thirteen

"Holy shit, Tess. You're going to do it? You're going to play twisted games with that Marquis guy?"

Andy's shocked whisper filled the phone line. Tess had just called him, needing a sounding board. She'd been wrestling with indecision all night long, struggling with where her duty to others ended and her duty to herself began. Whatever had happened in the Marquis' office had scared the hell out of her—and mired her in questions. How much was she supposed to sacrifice to save the jobs of people who were counting on her, and maybe the entire company? Where was that line?

She honestly didn't know. She'd never been good at lines, certainly not when it came to putting her own welfare first. It felt as if she had to take his offer, that she had no choice, but her gut was saying no. Her gut had been churning for hours—and then somehow, despite the turmoil, she'd found the eye of the hurricane.

She'd been struck with an idea that had seemed to outweigh everything else. The moment it had come to her she'd understood what she had to do—for herself, for the company, for everybody. And she'd thought Andy would understand too. He was a creative type. He knew the value of a visionary idea. Like Faust, who sold his soul for knowledge and experience, and had a vision of perfection. No sacrifice was too great.

But clearly, Andy didn't understand.

"This isn't about playing twisted games," she told him. "It isn't even about the Marquis. It's about business. It's about you and me, the team. We're going to make advertising history."

The idea that had blindsided Tess was the realization that the Marquis Club might be the best photo shoot of her career. She had just decided to turn the Marquis' offer down when it struck her right between the eyes why she couldn't. There was power in that place. Her hair stood on end when she was there.

She'd tried to tell herself it was sleight of hand, but even the Queen of Denial couldn't deny that she'd been caught up in something. There was an energy field that took you out of any known sphere, and if she could catch that on camera, the ads would be spectacular, beyond imagining, really.

She'd made it a rule in L.A. to go with her creative instinct on these things, even if the idea frightened her a little, and when she hadn't chickened out, the payoff had been more than worth it. Those ads had won her awards and established her reputation. The question she still couldn't answer was whether the Marquis Club was worth the personal risk, which was hard to calculate when you didn't know what the personal risk was.

"And what exactly do you have to do to make advertising history?" he wanted to know. "Get stretched naked on the rack?"

"Hey, if that's what it takes. However, the Marquis promised that I wouldn't have to do anything I found objectionable." Not the whole story, but why freak him out, she told herself.

"And you believe him? Tess, you do not have to fall on the sword for that fucking advertising agency."

"Andy, you know damn well you'd do the same thing if you were me. This club has tremendous potential, and I want to figure out how to exploit that. And also, to be totally honest, I'm a bit curious."

"About *what?*"

"About the subculture of S&M, the Marquis, the members and why they're there. I want to know what draws them to that place. Can you say that you're not a little curious about Cassandra?"

Tess was way beyond curious. She'd been haunted by some of what she'd seen in the club, including the tango in the Opera House and the woman who'd begged Danny to spank her. She really did wonder what it would be like to be that free to express your sexual desires, that abandoned to your needs. She may have been wild at one time, but she was never abandoned, and she had no idea what it would be like to give up control that way. She'd never allowed herself to feel much of anything when she was having sex. It had all been very mechanical, almost as if she wasn't there. Except with Danny.

Even now she could feel some part of herself stirring, responding in a way she never had before. It was more than fear, it was fascination, too. She'd been just eighteen when her theater arts instructor had ignited her imagination. Now she was a thirty-two-year-old woman—

"Cassandra's different," Andy objected. "I could take her arm wrestling, and if she got funky with me, I would."

"If she got funky with you, you'd love it. And I doubt very much that you could take her anywhere."

"Okay, listen," he said, "if they turn you into the Mistress of the Whips, promise me I get to be your first sex slave."

She laughed, relieved that he was warming to the idea. "I can hardly wait. Now will you relax, please?"

"No," he said emphatically. "But it doesn't look like I can stop you, so do this much for me, will you? Keep your cell phone with you at all times and put my number on speed dial."

"Can do."

"Call me and check in every day," he said. "Let me know you're okay, or I'm coming to get you."

"You're a good friend, Andy. I appreciate it."

"What do you want me to tell the others?" he asked.

"Tell them I'm working on securing the location and setting up the photo shoots. It'll take a few days, and meanwhile, you and the team can scout out alternate locations, just in case. And run interference with Erica. Also, make sure we have everything we need for the ads, including the Faustini clothes and accessories, and all the rest of it. You know the drill."

Tess sounded as if she had everything under control, but Andy's reaction had shaken her a little. She may have convinced him, but she hadn't totally convinced herself that what she was doing wasn't seriously nuts. It was the unknowns that worried her. She had no way of knowing if it was safe to follow up on her hunch about the club. And even more disturbing, she was beginning to wonder if it was the danger that attracted her.

Tess stared out the apartment's bay window like a condemned woman. It was midnight, and tomorrow morning she would take a taxi downtown and turn herself over to the Antichrist. No one was forcing her, although Tess could think of a few people who would make every effort to stop her if they knew. Her parents would have called in an interventionist, and Meredith would have been on the first flight to JFK. Actually, Meredith would have objected strenuously to the mere idea of an S&M club for the ad.

Glad she isn't here, Tess thought. Meredith really was uptight.

Tess took a slug of the generous glass of merlot she'd poured herself, hoping it might help her unwind. So far, she had heartburn, probably because she hadn't eaten, and she was as tense as an unsprung mousetrap.

Andy had finally come around, although she'd sensed

he was only humoring her. Tess doubted even Erica Summers would agree to her going along with the Marquis' demands. But Tess was doing it anyway—and it was for herself more than the agency, she'd realized.

She stared down at the street several stories below, where a couple walked arm in arm, bundled against the cold in coats and mufflers. Somewhere a siren was wailing, but they seemed immune to it as they stopped to kiss, apparently blissful in the knowledge that this was *their* city, and therefore, paradise, sirens and all.

Why did that make her feel so alone?

"Because this isn't *your* city," she observed, watching the couple wander off down the street. "It isn't even your apartment, and you're not immune to anything."

She really didn't think of herself as a risk taker. Advertising was an inherently risky job, but it wasn't physical combat. Her personal life had been pretty mundane, other than the experimental phase, but that was only because she'd felt bad about herself. She felt pretty good about herself now, but she would like to have been able to say that she'd had at least one meaningful relationship.

She was in the third decade of her life and she'd never owned a city the way that couple on the street did. She'd never had that kind of thing with a man. She didn't know why. It was possible she'd never wanted to, but something was missing. She could feel the void. It was there when she breathed, an emptiness.

Turning away from the window, she came face-to-face with an apartment that was beautifully furnished but as impersonal as a hotel room. Her cramped ground-floor studio in Santa Monica had been cluttered with pieces from discount warehouses, but at least she'd picked them out. Funny how she had not expected to miss that place—and here she was.

"I do *not* miss Dillon," she said, just to set the record straight. She hadn't missed Dillon in California.

She took another drink of the wine—and told herself to go to bed. She could probably soul-search all night and not come up with the real reason she'd decided to accept the Marquis' offer. The club had potential, and yes, she was profoundly curious about the place, but in the cold light of day that didn't explain why a reasonably normal woman would subject herself to the whims of a pseudo-vampire. Or why she had an erotic hallucination about him.

Tess hugged herself, aware of the rippling gooseflesh on her arms and the strange pounding of her heart. The answer eluded her, but she had little doubt that it was waiting for her somewhere in the bowels of the S&M underworld that was the Marquis' lair. And she would be captive there for three days with only Andy as her lifeline.

Seventy-two hours in hell, a consort to the devil.

And the mere thought gave her erotic shivers. It thrilled her.

She'd spent her whole life in the cold light of day—and now she wanted a taste of the night.

A supple, toffee-brown male in billowing sultan pants—and nothing else—led Tess into a waiting room worthy of an *Arabian Nights* fantasy. The walls were draped with crimson silk, and the vibrant Turkish carpets were heaped with tasseled pillows. He moved with grace and speed, opening curtains, plumping pillows and adjusting temperature controls the way a bellman would.

"The Marquis asked that you wait here," he said, "and that your every wish be granted. The bar has a variety of drinks and gourmet delicacies. I would be happy to serve you."

"My every wish?"

"Yes, if you wish to be entertained, I could juggle knives or perform contortions. If you prefer relaxation, I could escort you to the baths and help you with your ablutions or give you a massage."

"Sex?"

"With me? Oh, no, I'm a eunuch."

"I see." A eunuch? For real? It was all she could do to keep her eyes off his crotch. Obviously, something was missing down there, but what exactly? *Stop*, she told herself. *This is all playacting. Fun and games for desperately bored adults.*

"Can I get you something?" he asked. "Food? Drink?"

"Thanks, I'll help myself." A bath sounded good, but only if she could skip him and the ablutions. She felt a little grungy in the jeans and black turtleneck sweater she'd worn, thinking foolishly that it was the least sexy thing she owned and would discourage unwanted advances, if she were left to fend for herself.

But she wasn't going to be left to fend—or advanced upon. From what she could see, she was going to be sequestered until the Marquis got around to her, at which point she would probably be expected to fawn and scrape like a harem girl. And God knew what else. She wasn't feeling quite as thrilled and goosebumpy this morning as she had been last night.

"Will he be here soon?" she asked.

"The Marquis? No, not until you're ready. There is preparation first, training in the Sixty-four Arts."

"What are they?" The Marquis had talked about the ladies of the Seraglio preparing her, but sixty-four of anything seemed extreme. Tess couldn't imagine, unless it was like geisha training.

"The ladies will explain. They'll be here presently."

The eunuch bowed and handed Tess a small brass bell. "If you need me," he said.

Tess jingled the bell, disbelieving. "You'll be able to hear this? Wouldn't a pager work better?"

"We don't have phones in the rooms, and cells aren't allowed." He shot a look at the phone hooked to Tess's belt loop, but she wasn't giving it up without a fight. It was her only contact with Andy.

"I'll hear you wherever I am," he promised.

He bowed again and backed out of the room, leaving Tess with yet another puzzle to solve. How *was* he going to hear her? Maybe the room was bugged. Stranger things happened in the Marquis Club, she was sure.

But she shouldn't have let him go without getting some information about the Sixty-four Arts, which were probably not drawing and painting. She considered the bell in her hand and decided against it. Might be better not to know.

The bar he mentioned was an ice-filled silver tub loaded with enough food and chilled drinks for a dozen people. It looked like a crowd was expected. Cornucopias overflowed with fresh seafood, and abalone shells were heaped with rich black caviar, but Tess decided not to have any. She'd already had concerns about being drugged, and she wasn't taking any chances. Right now, she wanted to know what she was dealing with.

Everywhere she looked there were graceful date palms in brass pots and cushioned chaises. The room's centerpiece was a beautifully carved table that sat low to the ground with pillows for chairs. She scanned the ceiling and walls for hidden security cameras and the floor molding for wires, but saw nothing to suggest that she was under surveillance, or that this was anything other than a waiting area.

The brass bell tinkled, and Tess realized she was still holding it.

God forbid she should summon the eunuch. She left the bell on the table and went to investigate some doors nearly hidden by drapes. They led to a small balcony and Tess was surprised to see a pool below.

Actually, it was several pools of varying shapes and sizes, in what looked like a bathhouse made almost entirely of vibrant mosaic tiles. Tess was reminded of the jeweled blue and white solarium at San Simeon, but that was classical Greek. This was another culture, another time period. And it was luxurious enough to be decadent.

The music of tumbling water and female laughter drifted up to her, but Tess couldn't see anyone down there. Rattan chaises decorated the lounging area, and mountains of pillows were piled everywhere, clearly meant for bathers to languish after their soaks.

A perfume drenched the air, so dense and heady it made Tess dizzy when she inhaled. Not lilac. It was white star jasmine. Tess had actually taken the jasmine plants out of the flower beds near her bedroom window in California. In the heat of summer they'd been overpowering and given her dreams at night.

Tess stepped farther out onto the balcony for a better look at the place.

Steam hissed from a cauldron of bubbling water set into the tiled floor. Tess could just make out a human form standing behind the veil of vapor. A woman, she realized as the form materialized and came around to the front. Strawberry-blond hair set off pale features and eyes so blue that Tess could see their color from the balcony.

Draped in an off-the-shoulder gown, the woman raised her arms and stretched like an awakening cat.

From out of nowhere came a turbaned woman, naked from the waist up, her gleaming ebony breasts mostly concealed by the stack of towels she carried. A sarong skirt flowed to her slender ankles, its deep slit revealing long, muscular legs.

She set the towels on the nearest chaise and went over to the blue-eyed woman. They embraced briefly, and Tess watched with fascination as the dark woman began to undress the pale one. Tess felt like a voyeur but couldn't stop herself. She'd never witnessed anything like it.

The dark woman's movements were quick and grace-ful. She unfurled the sheer dress by taking the hem and circling the other woman, who held up her arms and let herself be unwrapped like a confection. When the sheer material was on the ground, she stepped out of it, her ala-baster flesh shimmering with reflections from the sky-lights and pools of water.

She was beautiful. Tess had heard breasts described as globes, but these were perfectly shaped and luminous, lit from within by some mysterious light source. Tess could see blue veins, as delicate as embroidery on lace. She could sense the coolness of naked flesh, dewy with per-fumed condensation from the air.

Suddenly, white fingers caressed a swollen nipple, deeply flushed with color. The woman was touching herself.

Tess felt her stomach lurch. She had always admired feminine beauty, but she'd never felt a compelling desire to touch or caress another woman before. Had it been dor-mant all this time? Perhaps it was more the desire to be touched, in the way the dark woman was now doing. She'd dropped to her knees, and she was tracing her fin-gers over the long pale limbs of the other woman in a highly intimate way.

She almost seemed to be inspecting the woman's body. Her hands glided up the inside of her thighs, then over the milky buttocks, cupping and lifting them. All the while, the blue-eyed woman turned in a slow circle, let-ting the kneeling woman roam every inch of her flesh, in-cluding the golden fleece on her mound.

The contrast of black satin fingers and gold curls left

Tess struggling to breathe. Oddly, though, what they were doing didn't seem to be about sex. It looked like some kind of ritual, perhaps a cleansing or purification.

The first woman walked to a delicate wooden bench and sat, her back to Tess, near a wall fountain that poured into a marble basin. The dark woman wet a sponge then held it above the pale, perfect breasts and squeezed, letting water run all over the glowing flesh.

Tess waited for a reaction but there was none. The pale woman was utterly passive, letting herself be touched and handled, as if that was her lot in life, to be petted and caressed, cared for like a child.

As the ritual continued, other women began to wander into the area from all sides, many of them totally naked, others in various states of undress. They seemed to know each other, but their spontaneous embraces, kisses and displays of affection startled Tess.

These weren't the Roman baths she'd seen on her first visit, she realized. They were probably supposed to be Turkish, and this was meant to be a harem. The dark woman who had done the undressing was a slave, the other possibly an odalisque, the Persian equivalent of a geisha.

Tess noticed that some of the women were now bathing in the pools, but their behavior had subtly changed. They were touching and playing in more sexual ways, and no one showed the slightest embarrassment or self-consciousness. It was carefree, playful and breathtakingly wanton.

One woman sat on the edge of a wading pool, smiling as her feet were seductively washed and fondled by a woman kneeling in the water. Another woman draped herself over a hand railing while admirers caressed her bottom, rubbing lotion into her skin. And, standing naked alongside the pool, two women nibbled on the breasts of a third.

But the odalisque and the slave were still involved in their ritual, and the odalisque remained pliant and yielding as the slave tenderly soaped her thighs. When the slave opened the woman's pale legs to wash the golden curls, the odalisque looked up and met Tess's gaze.

Her lashes dropped seductively low, and Tess saw the invitation hidden in her blue eyes. She didn't know what to do. She'd been discovered, but she didn't want to be seen by the others, so she backed into the room from the balcony.

She didn't realize that she had company in the room until she heard the whispering and turned.

There were four or five women gathered together, speaking in hushed voices, about her, apparently. "Who are you? What are you doing?" she asked as they surrounded her. Tess felt a hand caress her butt, and then her breast. They were feeling her up. One of them lifted her sweater and peered at her midriff.

"We must inspect for blemishes," one of them said. "There can't be any."

The ranks opened up, and a regal, dark-eyed woman of around forty came to stand before Tess. "I am the Sultana," she said, "and you can't be seen by the Marquis in this condition. You must be taken to the baths, stripped naked, washed clean and denuded of body hair."

"Denuded of body hair? Why?"

"Because those are the rules. The women of the Grand Seraglio do not have body hair. In ancient times, it was thought to be unclean."

"These aren't ancient times," Tess pointed out. "And I just saw a woman down there with body hair. It was blond, like mine."

"She is a slave, an odalisque in training," the Sultana explained. "Some day, if she proves herself worthy, she will be an odalisque. The first step is being bathed and scented. The second step is denuding."

The Sultana paused and cocked her head. "Hear those screams? That's her now."

Tess caught the glint in the woman's eye and realized—hoped—she wasn't serious. Still, screams or not, Tess had other plans for her body hair. "No, thanks," she said. "I'll sit this one out."

A beautiful sloe-eyed creature with loosely braided hair came forward, speaking in a soft voice. "Of course you'll be bathed and plucked and made ravishing. It's wonderful. You'll have much more sensation once the hair's gone. Your skin will be tender and pink, like a baby's, and men can have total access to you, every nook and cranny. There is nothing like a stroke of a man's tongue on a freshly shaved—"

"Pussy," someone interjected.

They all laughed, but Tess waved them off. "The Marquis said I wouldn't have to do anything I didn't want to do, and I *don't* want to do this."

"Oh, he always says that." The sloe-eyed creature was

determined to make herself heard on the subject. "He knows how much you'll love this once it's done. That's why you can't be allowed to make the decision. You must trust those who have had the experience."

"Besides, it's beautiful," said a blushing redhead who was undoing the tie of her silk robe. "See?"

She opened the garment to let Tess see the beauty of a plump, pink, totally unfettered mound of Venus. Tess frowned. A Brazilian wax.

Tess thought her heart was going to stop. She'd only recently found the courage to have a *basic* bikini wax. She was not giving up what she had left. She didn't want a freshly shaved pussy, thank you.

"Never," she said, looking at one of them after the other and despairing at their pleased smiles. "No way. Not a chance. Not *happening*."

Fourteen

Tess lay sprawled on the grass matting, woozy and confused. The scent of white star jasmine permeated every breath she took, but it couldn't have made her this light-headed. It was probably the drink she'd had. What had they called it? Lips of the Beauty.

The Sultana had insisted Tess have something in her stomach before they retired to the baths, and Tess had seized at the chance to stall. She'd eaten some cheese and fruit and drank a goblet of wine-laced fruit juice that the Sultana had described as ambrosia. One of the servants had filled Tess's glass from the same decanter she used to serve the other women, and Tess had figured it was safe, as long as everyone else was drinking it, too.

She was only planning to sip, but she'd finished the entire goblet, trying not to guzzle. It was that good. Sup-

posedly it was a recipe several hundred years old that included the essence of violets and roses. Tess hadn't felt
any effects while drinking it, but after setting the goblet
down, she'd realized she was smiling, and quite happy
to be there.

She didn't remember too specifically what had happened after that, but they'd brought her down here to the
baths, where her clothes had definitely come off—and
she'd barely protested. The grooming rituals had lasted
most of the morning, it seemed. First, she'd been inspected, then bathed, pumiced and scraped until she
gleamed. And now she was flat on her back, but with
pubic hair intact, as far as she could tell. The women had
left her here in the bathhouse to rest, with a bamboo
screen for privacy, and off they'd gone. Thank God, because she was utterly exhausted.

She was probably drunk, too. She was definitely naked.

She could feel warm breezes flowing over her, and
when she found the energy to focus her eyes, she saw that
they were man-made. There was a male giant looming
above her with a palm-frond fan. His privates were covered with a loincloth made of some gauzy material. Other
than that, he was naked, sun-bronzed from head to toe,
and gorgeously put together.

Tess continued to gaze up at him, fascinated. But her
focus kept straying to the loincloth, and she couldn't
seem to stop thinking about what he might have stashed
under there. He could probably have smuggled contra-
band, if he'd wanted to, but that wasn't where her mind

was going. It conjured visions of a lovely dark append-age, cradled by two warm, furry sacs, very squeezable. What fun to play with, she thought, feeling a happy lit-tle quiver in her stomach. It didn't bother her a bit that she'd just put his genitals in the category of infant toys. She could hardly wait to get her hands on them.

She smiled up at him, but he didn't seem the slightest bit interested.

Hmm. Another eunuch, no doubt. That *was* the point of eunuchs in harems, she supposed, to guard women rather than molest them. Just her luck. She could have used a little molesting right about then. Interesting the direction her thoughts were taking. They seemed deter-mined to dwell on anything and everything sexual, and there was no reining them in. Some deeply primitive im-pulse had taken over her body as well. She was absolutely alive down there between her legs.

Her *yoni,* she thought, correcting herself.

In the midst of the rituals, the Sultana had given her ladies a little lecture about the care and feeding of the *yoni,* which was what she preferred to call the female genitalia. She'd talked about hygiene and grooming and all the exquisitely sensitive nerve receptors. All Tess knew was that her *yoni* was singing. It felt as if someone had turned up the volume on her internal sound system, and the music was thrumming. Waves gathered inward and rippled outward. Tight. Sweet.

Maybe the jasmine and the drink and all the physical stimulation had impaired her judgment, but Tess was be-

ginning to feel a bit more receptive to some of the entice-
ments the Marquis Club offered. They didn't seem quite
so sinister to her now. From what she'd seen, the members simulated sex rather than actually doing it. And it
wasn't like she'd be breaking a vow if she found herself
having maybe just one little anonymous erotic encounter in this place. It wouldn't be the same as getting involved with another man—another loser—if her track
record was any indication. It would be more like an ad-
venture, and possibly even a chance to experience one of
the fantasies that had been hiding in the dark corners of
her mind all these years.

Whew. Just the thought had her heart going.

The sounds of laughter caught her attention, making
her wonder what was going on beyond the screen. She
burned to know what the women were doing now. Having an orgy, probably. She could hear water splashing and
hushed conversations and excited giggling. If only she
had the energy to go explore.

She looked up at the eunuch, wishing she could get his
attention. He wasn't bound by the no-hair rule, she noted.
His thighs were gloriously dark and downy. On impulse,
she reached over and tickled his ankle, trying not to gig-
gle. She must really be drunk.

"Look at her," someone whispered. "She's flirting with
the guard. I think she's ready."

"Ready for what?" With some effort, Tess raised up to
see who had spoken. The ladies of the Seraglio were
back, and they were surrounding her again. The sloe-
eyed beauty came to stand near one of Tess's shoulders,

the redhead was on Tess's other side, and the Sultana was at her feet. The other two women took positions near her hips.

Tess didn't like the looks of this. There was something calculating in their expressions, but she was seriously outnumbered. Six of them, if you counted the eunuch.

"What are you looking at?" she asked. Not that she needed to. They were staring at her *yoni* with lust and avarice in their eyes.

"We're now at the second step of the cleansing ceremony," the Sultana said. "You were told that your body must be free of all blemishes and hair."

"No," Tess breathed. "He promised. He said I wouldn't have to—"

"This has nothing to do with him. He can't make promises that allow the rules to be broken. Hair is unclean. It must be removed."

This was not the kind of erotic encounter Tess had imagined. She made a halfhearted effort to get up, but knew that even if she'd had the strength to fight, they would not have let her go. This was an initiation, and she was getting the works. The beauty and the redhead held down her arms. The other women took her legs, opening them so that the Sultana could have access.

Tess twisted her hips, the only part of her body she could move.

"Guard, hold her still," the Sultana ordered.

The palm frond dropped to the floor. Giant hands pressed Tess's midsection into the mat, and the four women draped themselves over her, holding her arms and legs with their bodies. Now Tess was truly pinned.

"Relax," the beauty whispered, "it will be over in a few moments." Tenderly she patted Tess's face. "You'll be very happy then. Your virgin flesh will cry out to be stroked, and you will be consumed with desires you never dreamed of."

Tess craned up and saw the Sultana apply a dark gluey substance to her pubic hair with what looked like a paintbrush. The sharp smell of acetone wafted up to her, and she felt a hot sensation.

"What is that? It burns!"

The Sultana kept painting until she'd covered every hair. "This won't take long," she said. "We use arsenic in the depilatory to speed up the process."

Tess dropped back to the mat. She hadn't really said arsenic, had she?

"Not to worry," the beauty assured her. "We only leave it on long enough to dissolve the hair. We won't let it mar your beautiful skin."

Tess wanted desperately to believe her, but the burning was getting worse. She began to writhe, and the women struggled to keep her down.

"Get the water," the Sultana ordered. "Douse her."

Warm water flooded Tess's thighs and abdomen, and the Sultana instructed the women to hold her still. Tess managed to raise her head enough to see the Sultana wipe away most of her blond curls with a damp cloth.

She fell back, exhausted.

All the women hovered over her, oohing and aahing as the Sultana wiped the rest of the hair away from her pubic area. When her genitals cooled down, Tess felt air where she'd never felt air before.

"She's beautiful," one of them said. "Look at how pink and round, like a powder puff."

"Her vulva is so delicate. Look here at the petals, how they quiver."

"Her blood must be rushing into them. They're rosy and fat—and look, she's glistening wet! How beautiful. We must make her come."

"No, we're not allowed. The Marquis has forbidden it."

"But we can touch her, can't we?"

"Of course, but she is not to come."

Tess was amazed at how matter-of-fact they were. They were talking about her vulva as if she wasn't there. She wanted to object, but she felt fingers lightly touching, lifting, exploring—and she was lost in the sensations.

This was true nakedness, true vulnerability. With every caress, the intensity built. She wanted to cry out, she was so sensitive down there. But somehow, she knew it wouldn't do any good to tell them to stop.

"Guard," the Sultana said, "make her presentable. Ladies, give him enough room to do his work."

The guard? "Why him?" Tess asked.

"Because that's his job," the Sultana said, "and he does it well. When he's done, you'll be glowing. Luminous."

The Sultana rose and switched places with the guard. Tess tried desperately to close her legs and couldn't.

Leaning close, the beauty whispered in Tess's ear, "You're missing all the fun. He's a wizard. Let him take you to Oz."

Tess felt a coolness that made her squirm. "What's he doing? Is that soap he's using? It feels odd."

"It's our own special shaving cream made with rose hip, chamomile and passion flower," the Sultana said. "Be very still while he touches you up."

One of the women emitted a throaty laugh. "This will be the closest shave you'll ever have."

Tess went utterly still, horrified at the thought of a blade on her tender flesh. But all she could feel was a feathery-light pressure. Soon the coolness was gone, and in its place was something warm and moist and slightly textured.

"What's that? A washcloth?" Tess closed her eyes, re-laxing a little as the swirling sensations lulled her. It felt almost like water trickling over her like a brook over pebbles, water pooling in sunlit places. She could feel it bubbling around her clitoris and oozing into deep crevices.

"That's really quite lovely," she said. "*Mmmmm.*"

Giggling ensued, and after another moment or two of the bubbling brook, Tess realized what must be going on. It wasn't a washcloth he was using.

"Our eunuchs may have been deprived of their man-hood," the Sultana said "but they have other parts that are very serviceable."

Tess froze. She went rigid, trying to cut herself off from the sensations. "Tell him to stop," she said.

The redhead sniffed. "She really is a pill, isn't she? The Marquis is going to be angry with us because we haven't trained her well."

"The Marquis will deal with her as only *he* can."

The Sultana's warning was the last straw. The Marquis was going to be a dead man when Tess got to him. The deal was over. He'd broken his promise to her repeatedly without even being here. And she could only blame herself for believing him.

I'm not being held prisoner. I can leave whenever I want to. I could walk out that door right now.

Tess paced the floor of her room, mentally repeating the mantra. With any luck, it might even be true. The eunuch had brought her to this dark windowless vault after those lunatic women had burned off all her pubic hair. But he hadn't locked her in or ordered her to stay. The only thing he said before he left was that the Marquis would summon her shortly, and she was to wear a certain red gown hanging in the closet.

Tess had not so much as opened the closet door. She didn't have to stay in this godforsaken place. That was all she cared about at the moment. She no longer had the clothing she'd worn here, her tote bag or her cell phone, so her connections to the outside world had effectively been severed. She didn't even know what time it was. Of course, her personal things could be replaced—and pubic hair would grow back. Her sanity was another thing. But it was already in question, or she wouldn't be here.

At least she wasn't naked now, not technically, anyway. After exfoliating her like a blighted tree, the ladies had draped her in a sarong and top that was as light as air, but not nearly as cool as the breezeway between her legs.

Every movement brought a little chill, a little thrill. The way the silky material caressed her made her constantly aware of her tingling pussy. Even using the toilet was an X-rated experience. It was crazy.

It was exciting, dammit.

It made her breath hitch in. That bright starburst of feeling when she touched herself. *Now she knew what lightning felt like.*

The eunuch had done his job well. She was so sensitive she couldn't sit down. Walking was no picnic, either. In fact, being conscious was almost more than she could manage. It probably wouldn't take much to relieve the pressure. Hell, a deep breath might do it.

Tess came to an abrupt stop. Sex. Why did she keep going there? She needed to come up with a plan to get through this ordeal without losing her mind. Or just get the hell out of here. Meanwhile, she was going nowhere, trapped in the squirrel cage of her own imagination.

This was not good. And yet, the feeling, the humming deep inside of her, that was somehow…very good.

She looked around the room as if she were seeing it for the first time. A roaring fireplace cast golden light on a veiled canopy bed and provided the room's warmth, its heart. Under other circumstances, she might have found it a cozy setting, even a haven. Luxurious animal skins that she hoped were faux hung on the walls and decorated the cool stone floor. The room was actually quite beautiful in a dark fairy-tale-like way. It could have been a bedchamber in a medieval castle. But she didn't want to be part of this fairy-tale, did she?

She could have been gone by now.

The breath she took burned. Her chest was tight. And suddenly it hit her. She knew what the squirrel cage was.

Not sex. It was him. She was angry. That son of a bitch had lied to her—and he was going to hear about it. She had no pubic hair because of him. Let him do his worst. He could turn into a yellow-eyed demon or make her think he was right next to her, breathing down her neck, when he wasn't, but she had some things to say first.

Then she would go.

She went to the closet and opened the door to find the dress she was meant to wear. A sniff of disgust summed things up nicely. It was a red sliplike thing with ruffles around the hem that barely qualified as lingerie it was so skimpy. She gave the door a push, pleased at the bang it made as it shut.

No way would she wear that piece of lint. The women had dressed her up in a lovely floral sarong and camisole top that suited her just fine. But she was going to answer his summons when he got around to making it. And then he would answer to her. She had no reason to sneak out of this place like a thief. She hadn't broken any promises. He'd probably never meant to keep them anyway.

A shuffling sound caught her attention. It had come from the doorway. She looked down and saw a note being slipped under the door.

She knelt and opened the folded piece of paper. A smiled flickered.

This was her summons.

The lobby of the Opera House was dark and deserted. Tess felt like a fly in an amphitheater as she scanned the empty, echoing space. Being utterly alone made everything seem larger and her that much smaller. There were grand staircases on either side of the lobby leading up to the second level, and the dancing shadows looked eerily like people descending the steps, but there was no one there.

Why wasn't *he* here? This was where he'd told her to come.

Tess had brought the note with her. She'd followed its directions to the Opera House explicitly. It hadn't said where to meet him, but she assumed the lobby. Maybe she was supposed to have gone into the theater.

She waited a few moments longer and decided that must have been what he meant. She entered through the double doors, expecting to see him waiting for her, but it was like walking into an enormous cave. The vast auditorium was totally dark. Tess wasn't even sure she could make it down the aisle. She touched the backs of the chairs, using them for guidance, but she'd only taken a few steps before her toe cracked against something hard.

Pain sent streaks of red racing through her vision.

An obscene word caught in her clenched teeth.

Her feet were bare. She'd last seen her clothing when she undressed in the waiting room. And now, she'd probably broken her toe, but she kept going anyway, feeling her way and searching what she could see of the seats. She pictured him sitting somewhere in the audience, taking great pleasure in listening to her knock herself around.

When she got all the way to the orchestra section, she turned and addressed the murky hall. "Is anyone out there?"

She half expected to hear the sound system come on, broadcasting that reverberating voice of his. But nothing happened. No one spoke. Uncertain what to do, she climbed the steps to the stage, knowing it could be dangerous territory. Stages were death traps in the dark. People fell off them with the lights on, and there was all that rigging up above.

Wiley had wanted to tie her up in the rigging and arouse her until she fainted. He'd whispered about pleasures too intense to bear.

Tess had to force herself to keep going. Thank God, her bare feet made no sound as she picked her way across the floor. In the silence, she heard something. A rustling noise seemed to be coming from the wings. Torn between making a run for it and going over to investigate, she hesitated. Maybe he'd show himself. If she couldn't see him, at least she could hear him.

Her heart beat wildly, telling her she shouldn't have come this far. How would she ever find her way down the stairs and out of here? Her eyes hadn't adjusted to the total absence of light, and they probably weren't going to.

Tess turned to go, and ran straight into a web of ropes and netting hanging from the rigging. As she was extricating herself, she heard a loud pop. She whirled, thinking a gun had gone off, and was blinded by a beam of light.

It took her a moment to realize that she was caught in the flood of a spotlight. She could see nothing but the shimmering ball of white fire.

"Glad you made it," a voice said from the audience.

She knew immediately that it was the Marquis. There was no sound system to disguise his voice. Of course, who else would it be?

"I want to talk to you," she said.

"There'll be plenty of time to talk later."

"No, now. And I want the lights on. I want to see your face."

"You don't make the rules," he said.

"And you don't keep your promises."

A faint thump caught her attention. It sounded as if he'd risen, and his cushioned seat had banged up. The hall went quiet. Several seconds passed, and Tess counted every one of them.

"Take off the sarong," he said softly. He was closer, she realized, perhaps just a few feet away.

"Do what?"

"You heard me. I want to see what they've done to you."

Tess stood there, shaking, disbelieving. He couldn't be asking her to strip for him. That wasn't really what he was doing, was it?

Fifteen

Take off her sarong? For one deeply satisfying moment, Tess imagined the pleasure of turning her back on him and dropping the wrapped skirt. Not all the way to the floor, just enough to moon him before she departed the club in a blaze of fuck-you glory.

It was an infantile response, but that wasn't what stopped her.

He might have liked it.

"You lied to me and misrepresented our deal," she said, pleased that she had the control to sound haughty. It was an illusion, of course. She'd been stripped of control—and body hair—in the baths, which made the appearance of it that much more important now. It felt like the only power she had.

She stared past the spotlight in the direction his voice

had come. If she was right, he was somewhere in the orchestra section, near the aisle to her right.

"I didn't misrepresent anything," he said calmly.

"You knew what those women were going to do to me."

"The way I heard it, you were groping the eunuch."

"That was the drugs they put in my drink. I don't know how you do it around here, but I was under the influence of something the entire time."

The hall's acoustics picked up his forbearing sigh. "That's what people like to say when they don't want to take responsibility for enjoying themselves."

"Thanks for the five-cent psychoanalysis, but I didn't."

"Enjoy yourself? That's not what I heard, either."

She shaded her eyes with her hand, trying to see him. "If they told you I enjoyed myself, then *they* lied, too. I was held down by a small army of women, and they got that giant eunuch to sit on me." Okay, slight exaggeration, but no one around here seemed to care about the truth anyway.

"Are you happy with it now?" he asked.

"No, I'm not happy with *it*," she said. "It's cold down there. I'm probably going to catch my death in this damp, drafty place."

He cleared his throat, and she could almost hear him smiling. "This isn't a joke," she said. "I was violated."

"If that's how you feel—"

"That *is* how I feel."

"Then I apologize, Tess. You have my sincere apology, and my word that I'll deal with the people involved."

Tess peered into the darkness. "Deal with them?"

"They'll be fired. The club's policy is mutual consent."

She started to protest that the women hadn't done anything that serious, but thought better of it. This might be another trick.

"Fine," she said.

"You're accepting my apology?"

"I'm thinking about it." He'd caught her off guard. The last thing she'd expected was an apology, and she didn't know what it meant coming from him. Nothing he said could be taken at face value.

She could feel the chill in the room as she pondered. Gooseflesh rippled up and down her arms. It was cold, and the only thing that kept her from shivering was the pain radiating from her foot.

Her toe. Damn, it throbbed.

She told herself to block it out and give him an answer. He claimed to be sincere, but there was no way to know unless she accepted his apology. Still, she held out.

"I don't want anyone fired," she said. "But something was done to me against my will today, and you told me that wouldn't happen."

"It shouldn't have, but keep in mind that a promise, even from me, doesn't trump the club's rules. We have basic laws of existence here, just like any society. If you break a law in the so-called real world, you go to jail. It's not a choice."

"Since when does pubic hair make one a danger to society? They held me down and removed it with *arsenic*."

He hesitated, as if summoning patience. "The mons and the other orifices must be free of hair. Those are the rules of the Seraglio, and they are as ancient as the baths themselves. We honor them—and if you stay, so will you."

"How many other rules do you have? Or do you make them up as you go?"

"There are only two unbreakable rules—self-revelation and surrender. Never be false about your desires, and never fight them. That's how we define surrender. This experience is about desires, Tess. Yours. And they will test you far more than I will."

"I can't do it."

"Can't do what?"

"This!" Tess's heart was going nuts. "I'm not too sure what my desires are, and the ones I know about I'm afraid of."

He went very quiet, as if she might have surprised him.

"Now we're getting somewhere," he said. "The desires that frighten you are the reason you're here. You may think it has something to do with your work, but it really doesn't."

Tess had already figured out this wasn't just about her ad campaign. That was probably what had kept her here, *and* what made her want to run. Exhausting, this shadowboxing. But there was a strange potential in this place, like a powerful magnetic field. It was there to be discovered, waiting to be experienced, and she wanted that for herself as much as for the agency.

Beyond that, she was curious—about him, about the club culture he mentioned, even about what had happened in the baths today. She hadn't understood what the

Sultana meant when she said the Marquis wouldn't permit Tess to have an orgasm. Why in hell not? Wasn't that what this place was all about?

"What do you want me to do?" she asked him.

"You're accepting my apology?"

"I am," she said. *For now*.

The houselights came up slightly, but not enough to see him. The spotlight was too bright. She could see herself, though, all too well. She was looking down at goose bumps and splotchy skin that didn't know whether it was hot or cold. At the purplish toe that seemed to be bent in the wrong direction.

Odd that she couldn't feel anything. No pain, no heat burning her throat, no chill in the air. Must be the adrenaline pumping through her system. She was numb.

A shadow fell across her bare feet. Fascinated, she watched the darkness hover and move up her skirt. Something was blocking the spotlight—and coming closer.

"Dance with me."

She looked up to see him standing at the edge of the light, cutting into its brilliant corona like an eclipse.

"That's what I want you to do," he said.

"Dance with you?"

He held out a hand, and she took it without thinking. "Don't expect graceful," she warned him, stumbling as he pulled her out of the blinding beam. "I stubbed my toe, and it hurts."

"You have a lot to learn," he said. "A little pain can take you to the heights of pleasure."

He was a looming shadow, and Tess felt a crazy need

to yank her hand away as she remembered how he'd scratched her palm in his office and may have drugged her. She couldn't bear the thought of losing control again.

His features were just coming into focus, and she could see the ironic smile that shadowed his expression. He was wearing black again, but it looked like a V-neck sweater and slacks this time. Playing a vampire in the movies would come very naturally to him, she decided. He undoubtedly enjoyed scaring the holy hell out of women, including this one, although she would die before she admitted it.

He brought her hand to his lips, all very gallant. But as he led her into his arms, theoretically to dance, Tess lost her balance again. She stepped awkwardly on her bad toe and a stabbing pain sent her hopping and swearing.

"Shit!" She fell heavily against him, and was startled as he gripped her by the waist and lifted her off her feet. A gasp of laughter slipped out. "What are you doing?"

"Saving your ass? Unless it was your plan to take that header."

"Well, my ass thanks you," she said. "Now, please, put me down."

He did, looking into her eyes the entire time. When her bare feet touched the floor, he sank his fingers into her blond curls and spoke to her in an oddly passionate tone.

"Are you planning on dancing with me anytime tonight?"

"Well…yes." Tess wasn't being demure, exactly. She just couldn't believe she was getting off this easily. All he wanted to do was *dance*? No stripteases or blood sacrifices?

She wasn't being asked to service every man in the place and like it? And then there was that business about the Marquis not permitting certain bodily functions. She'd like to see him stop her from having an orgasm. That would be a good trick.

"We'll take it slow," he promised. "None of the one-armed dips I'm famous for."

He drew her close, but not flush against his body. He was being a gentleman, apparently. If nothing else, they would go through the motions of dancing. Still, she was close enough to feel the heat emanating from him, and she could also feel a rush of cool air between her legs, reminding her that she was naked as a newborn down there.

Holy Mother of God, what a sensation. The silk skirt flitted and floated over her like butterfly wings. Even her clothing was a turn-on. It struck tiny tingling sparks off her skin. She was actually starting to pulse down there. A hot, sweet little throb that made her grateful she wasn't wearing panties. They would have been torture. All that constant friction.

At some point, Tess realized there was music playing, low and sensual. It was coming from every corner of the room, and the volume rose gradually until it seemed to envelop them. She didn't recognize the arrangement, but the beat was syncopated. Latin. A samba?

No, a tango. Tess could see it in her mind. Right here on this stage, the tango master had mercilessly seduced his partner, undressing her down to a black thong. Was that what this guy had in mind? Tess wasn't wearing a black thong—or any kind of thong.

"Where did that music come from?" she asked him.

"Where does all music come from? The celestial spheres."

"Are you ever going to stop playing these games with me?" she implored. "You can do tricks and I can't. It isn't fair."

He cocked his head, his gaze drifting to her mouth. "You know plenty of magic, and you're using *all* of it on me."

"I am not," she said. "I really hurt my toe."

His laughter was sudden, rich and sensual, and the way his black hair fell in a poetic swoon onto his forehead made her think of matinee idols from old movies that played on cable channels. *Suave* and *debonair* came to mind. He really was a throwback to another time.

To be fair, he probably hadn't drugged her that day in his office, and he *was* being surprisingly considerate about her toe. That didn't mean she trusted him, but she was curious. She'd never been with anyone like him, never even known anyone like him, and maybe that was part of the attraction.

Had she mentioned that she was curious?

She might even like the idea that he could hurt her a little or put her in a trance and have his demonic way with her. What would sex be like with such a strange and exotic creature? She'd already started imagining it, which was never a good sign. *What you dream you can do.* It was a catchphrase from an old commercial, and Tess couldn't remember the product, but the message had stuck. She'd made a lot of dreams come true in her younger years, including some bad ones. When her mind had started running, she had, too, even if it was the wrong direction.

She had no desire for history to repeat itself, but this seemed to be different. It wasn't motivated by anger or rebelliousness. She wasn't striking out or trying to prove anything. She *was* curious. Burning.

She could feel the brush of his long legs as he led her through some simple steps that seemed to have nothing to do with the sensual music and everything to do with two bodies being close. His palm molded itself to the low curve of her back. Warmth penetrated her skirt, but it was the sense of movement that got her attention. She could feel something back there, swinging in a gentle arc and realized he was toying with the small of her back. His finger, very probably the small one, glided back and forth, sending shivers up her spine.

"You move well," he commented.

"I don't," she protested.

They turned, and she fell into him again. It wasn't her toe. She couldn't even feel her toe at this point. She just wanted to see what he would do. Immediately, he cinched an arm around her and lifted her off the floor, true to form.

She was facing him now, square on, looking into his eyes. This was a man who seemed capable of shape-shifting, turning into demons. What would that be like?

"Let's be sure and put this in our routine when we enter ourselves in ballroom competition," he said. "We'll call it Tess's Downfall."

She shot him a look. "Fine, but only if we name a move for you, too."

"Maybe this one?" He hooked an arm under her knee and scooped her up as if he was going to carry her over a threshold. She grabbed his neck, hanging on as he spun her around, and thinking he'd gone crazy.

When he set her back down on the floor, the room was moving. She closed her eyes, but it wouldn't stop. With a sigh, she succumbed to the dizziness, feeling a little foolish as she rested her head against his chest. They began to sway, completely ignoring the music. It felt way too much like her first prom, but Tess let herself go with it anyway.

A smile surfaced. Was she actually rubbing her breasts against his chest and getting friendly with his pelvis? Okay, she *was* crazy.

"What do we call this move?" she asked.

He breathed out a raspy sound of appreciation. "He'll never be the same?"

He was a charmer, but then psychopaths were charmers, too.

Gradually, they came to a halt, and he said, "You didn't wear the dress I asked you to. That's a punishable offense."

She drew back and looked up at him. "And the punishment is?"

"You like surprises, don't you?"

"Depends on what they are."

"You'll like this one."

"What's wrong with what I'm wearing? It's a sarong and a camisole top, courtesy of the ladies of the Seraglio. That should make it official."

He stepped back to look at her, clearly disapproving. The skirt was nothing more than a few yards of wispy fabric, and Tess had the feeling he could melt it off her with one scorching look.

"Let's try a few alterations," he said.

He took her hand, raised her arm over her head and turned her, as if wanting to see the outfit from all angles, but then he turned her again and again, and soon Tess realized that he wasn't holding her hand, but she was still turning.

The skirt was unraveling, and she was spinning. It was floating off her body, and before she could get herself stopped, he had all the fabric in his hand, and she was nude from the waist down. Bottomless.

There was nowhere to hide, especially from his gaze.

He held out a hand, which Tess refused to take, but that didn't stop him. He gripped her wrist and pulled her close, covering her nakedness with his body. "Now, don't you wish you'd worn the red dress?"

"I wish I'd mooned you and left when I had the chance," she said.

"Excuse me?"

"Never mind." She was blushing like an idiot. She couldn't believe how utterly exposed she felt. *And aroused, dammit.*

"This is how I want to dance with you," he said, his voice husky and grindingly sensual. "This is what I want. Your naked ass under my hand."

She could feel his hand cupping her, and his amazing erection drilling her thigh.

He nuzzled his face in the soft, honeyed curls near her ear and whispered, "You are my flame. Your life can be measured in hours. You serve by being devoured."

Suddenly Tess was tight and wet. Everwhere.

The music soared, as if on cue.

"I can bathe you in oxygen, make you burn high," he said.

She drew back, but he seized her by the arms and held her.

"Stop fighting this and make a choice." His dark eyes flared. "Stay or go, Tess. If you stay, you will give yourself over to this experience. You will confess your deepest secrets, and until you prove yourself worthy, you will be the lowest of the low. You will take orders from everyone here, even the eunuchs and the slaves. Do you understand?" He hesitated only a moment. "Make your choice. Commit yourself or go. Those are my rules."

Why did that send thrills through her? For God's sake, why?

It suddenly hit her how convenient it had been for him to tell her that she wouldn't have to do anything she didn't want to. If she made the commitment he was asking it would be like saying that she wanted to do anything and everything, for anybody and everybody.

She stepped closer, her breath shaking. "You, but no one else," she said.

"Is that your answer?"

"Yes."

"Go to your room and wait," he told her. "And put on

the red dress, dammit. I'm hungry for the sight of you in that dress."

She half expected him to display his fangs. Instead, he bent and grazed her mouth with his, pouring fire over her lips. It sent pleasure crashing through her. More pleasure than she wanted, really. More than she could know what to do with.

"Give in," he said, as if he'd read her mind. "It's your only hope."

The fire was burning down to embers as Tess fought to keep her eyes open. Her lids were almost too heavy to control. She was curled up inside the red and violet veils of the canopy bed, still fighting the exhaustion that was trying to drag her down into oblivion.

She had no idea what time it was, but it felt as if the night had gone on forever, and if she'd slept, it had been only sporadically. She'd put on the red dress, but not because he'd asked. It was as good a nightgown as any. Okay, maybe it *was* because he'd asked. Maybe some crazy part of her wanted to see what it would be like, giving in. Not feeling as if she had to be in control of everything. That wasn't a crime.

So why did it feel like one? Like she was violating every commandment?

Because he's dangerous, you idiot. Because this place is dangerous for women like you. You're fair game.

Of course, she didn't listen. She was beyond listening to anything that made sense. She'd been in a strange state of arousal all night, not climbing the walls exactly, but restless and excitable. That damn humming between her legs would not go away. It was driving her mad. She'd thought about touching herself. Just a few slick strokes and she could bring that noise to a screeching halt, but she hadn't done it.

She hadn't. And she didn't know why.

Where the hell *was* he? He'd said he was hungry for her in this dress. And she'd actually let herself get caught up in the excitement of seeing him. She'd given in to the feelings, just as he'd told her to. *Give in,* he'd said.

It actually hurt to think he might be playing games with her again, setting her up for a fall, but what kind of idiot was she, getting worked up over the maître d' of an S&M club?

With an anguished sigh, she fell back on a pillow heavily scented with jasmine, and finally, she drifted off to sleep. She didn't dream so much as see visions of fangs and fiends floating through her head.

When she woke up the next time, it was to confusion and total darkness. The fire was out, and she could see nothing. But Tess knew immediately that someone was in the room with her. He was here.

Sixteen

"Where have you *been?*" Tess sat up in bed, straining to see in the darkness. He was definitely in the room somewhere. It was so quiet she could hear him breathing. Apparently, he wasn't going to apologize for keeping her waiting all night.

"Where are you?" she asked.

She rubbed at the sleep in her eyes, waiting for him to say or do something. "Turn on a light," she said. "I can't see anything."

The silence wore on, and finally, she let out a sigh. "Haven't we been through this before? You, hiding in the darkness, and me trying to get you to talk to me? Frankly, it's getting a little boring."

She heard a low "*Hmm,*" edged with disdain. His Highness wasn't pleased? Good. Had it coming.

Her eyelids began to droop, and she fell back, resting
on her elbow. She really was exhausted, thanks to him. A
moment later, her head hit the pillow, and she reached for
a furry throw to pull over herself.

"Go away," she mumbled. "I'm not interested now.
Tired."

She rolled to her side, curling up and fully intending
to go back to sleep. For days, possibly.

"Go away?"

The question reverberated around the room, but Tess
wasn't impressed. "Oh, that silly voice-enhancement
thing again? Get a new trick, why don't you."

She curled up under the throw, clutching it in her
hands. It was a little chilly now that the fire had gone out.

Footsteps thudded across the stone floor. The blanket
flew out of Tess's hands, and a gust of cold air hit her like
a bucket of water. Before she could move, a pair of strong
hands had gripped her ankles.

"What are you doing?" She tried to kick free, but he
moved too fast for her to get any traction. He pulled her
toward him with a death grip on her ankles. He was doing
something, but she couldn't see what. She could feel heat
and pressure, and when he released her, she couldn't get
her feet apart. He'd tied her ankles together!

"Are you bored *now*?" he asked her.

She had no time to respond. He rolled her over on her
stomach and tied her wrists behind her, then rolled her
back. Still bent over her, he breathed a shocking invitation in her ear.

"Now you can fight me," he said. "Should be interesting watching a beautiful naked woman writhe."

She was angry, but she was also unbearably aroused. "I'm not naked."

"You will be."

Tess went very still. *Now* she was frightened. Tied up. Naked. Him. *Not good.*

"You didn't answer my question," he said, his voice thundering softly around the room.

"You're an asshole. What more do you need to know?"

Possibly not a smart thing to say to a man who relished writhing women. She was relieved to hear a snick of laughter come from his direction. At least one of them was amused. Now would have been a good time to invoke her right not to do anything she found objectionable, but she had given it up in a fit of passion. How many unwise things had she done in fits of one kind of passion or another? she wondered.

She struggled to get more comfortable, but it was impossible with her hands wedged in the small of her back. "Could you put a pillow under my head, at least?"

He obliged by lifting her up and settling her back on the pillows, which took the pressure off her arms and spine.

"Better now?" he asked.

"Untying me would make it better. You've made your point."

"And what *is* my point?" He sat on the edge of the bed, right next to her. The fire was gone and the only light in the room came from the fanlight window above the door behind him. She couldn't see his face, much less read his expression, and it was probably better that he couldn't see hers. She was not amused. Matter of fact, she was pissed. He wanted nothing less than total surrender from her, and he couldn't bother to show up all night? And now these caveman tactics?

"Oh, I don't know." Her tone was cold, indifferent. "That you're a big tough guy. But inside, you're really so inadequate you have to tie women up to feel brave and strong? Something like that?"

She could feel his eyes boring into her.

"I only tie up women who pretend to be bored," he said quietly. "And if they want to be untied all they have to do is get real, as Dr. Phil would say."

"You watch Dr. Phil?"

"Around here, I *am* Dr. Phil."

"That must be annoying for the members."

She twisted around, trying to untangle her dress. In all the rolling back and forth, the material had gotten caught underneath her.

"My dress is bunched up," she said. "Could you straighten it? And cover me with the throw, would you? I'm cold."

He rose and stood quietly over her for a moment.

"My dress?" she prompted. "The one you ordered me to wear."

"*I* ordered you to wear it?"

"Of course, when we were dancing." What's with this guy?

He lifted the sheer material as if he were going to straighten it. "Right, I forgot," he said.

"You forgot? How could you—"

"Shh." He took the skirt in his hands, testing a seam that went straight up the middle. With very little effort, he ripped the dress from hem to bodice, cleaving it in two separate pieces.

When he was done, it lay alongside her body like butterfly wings.

"My new trick," he said.

By some miracle, Tess managed to lie still. Inside, she was vibrating like a musical instrument, but he couldn't see it. *Please God, don't let me writhe,* she thought. *Don't let my flesh move or my breasts shake.* Her only cover was the darkness, but it was fading. Her eyes were adjusting, and his must be, too. He'd already seen her naked from the waist down, but this was different. She was bound. She couldn't hide. Or defend herself.

Which raised a disturbing question.

What was he going to do to her?

The answer was painfully obvious. What the hell *did* you do with a bound naked woman besides have sex with her, any kind of kinky sex you wanted?

She tried to quell the panic inside. Maybe he wanted to freak her out, so she wasn't going to give him that satisfaction. "I'm not afraid of you, if that's your goal."

"Tess, Tess," he said, "I could make you afraid of me, if that's what I was trying to do. Men have been doing that to women for centuries. There's a torture chamber in this place. I could start out easy, tormenting the soles of your feet with a feather, maybe drizzling a little hot wax on your belly, or putting clamps on your beautiful nipples."

"*Ugh.*"

"You haven't tried clamps?" He laughed softly. "You should. They tighten with a little twist, compressing until the bud is rosy red and tingling hot. The nipples have more sensory nerves than any other part of the body. Women actually faint from the pleasure."

"Thanks, I'll pass."

"It's not pain, exactly," he explained. "It's more like pressure, and it arouses an entire network of body parts. It's common knowledge that gentle suction on the nipple makes the deep muscles of the womb contract, so you can imagine what a clamp would do. It's intense."

Uncle, Tess thought. Her breasts were already tingling. And something strange was happening in the pit of her belly. It was more a sound than a sensation, like the insistent *zzzzzzz* of honeybees gathered around the queen, their nether ends thrumming, vibrating.

He sat down next to her, the throw draped over his arm. But he didn't put it over her, and she would be damned if she'd ask again. It was getting colder all the time. She could feel gooseflesh prickling her arms and legs, but she wasn't going to give him another opportunity to jerk her around. Let him see her shivering. Let him see her naked, for that matter. Everybody else in the place had.

"This isn't about me," he said. "It's about you. But you don't seem to get that. Maybe you've been missing that your whole life."

"Right," she said sarcastically, "it's about me. It's about *my* nipples, *my* pain. You're not getting anything out of it."

"What I get out of it is sharing it with you. We're only

innocent once, Tess. We only take this journey once, and for me, it was a long time ago. I actually envy you."

It wasn't the answer she expected, and she had no response ready for him. He sounded as if he meant it, and perhaps that should have calmed her, but it didn't. Her body tensed, and she was more aware than ever of the vibrations inside.

"Are you still cold?" he asked.

Through chattering teeth, she said, "Yes."

He bent close to her belly and blew warm air on her. It made her shiver wildly. The hair on her arms pricked as he moved up toward her breasts, blowing great warm jets. She closed her eyes, groaning as another sensation assailed her. She had to fight not to squirm, but this had nothing to do with the cold. He was going the wrong direction. She wanted him between her legs. God, she did. She was throbbing down there. Buzzing, humming, pulsing just a little. She hated that feeling.

It was *so* incredible.

"Couldn't I just have the throw?" she said, her voice going raspy. "It would be a lot easier for both of us."

"You really do lack imagination."

"I *wish.*" She was in imagination-overload hell. She could see what was coming next and everything after that. He would blow warm air over her nipples until they stood up and begged. And when he finally drew them into his hot mouth, taking turns with them just to torture her, he would use his lips like the clamps he described, tightening until she did faint with pleasure.

Why had he told her all that? Now, she would never get

it out of her head. She could almost feel his hands on her naked mons, a finger sliding into her, discovering that she was wet and slippery inside.

Hot, too. Aching. That damn buzzing had been tame compared to this.

What the ladies had promised was true. She was ridiculously sensitive down there. Anything could stimulate her, even the thought of being stimulated. And he must know that. He'd probably invented the damn Seraglio and its rules. He'd planned for those girls to arouse her or why else would he have forbidden them to let her come?

He was saving that for himself. And now that he had her helpless, he would toy with her and tease her until he had her half out of her mind. But eventually, of course, he would bring her around—all the way around. He would make her come undone in one way or another, just to prove that he could.

Somewhere a tiny voice at the base of her brain was saying what's so bad about all that? Who cared what his agenda was? And who would she actually be depriving if she shut down and refused to respond? She wasn't at all certain that she *could* refuse at this point. Or why she should want to when there was every possibility that she would have an orgasm beyond anything she'd ever experienced. Something mind-altering and transcendent.

What was so bad about that?

His dark head was still bent over her, and all she could do was watch him. Warm air bathed her breasts, and she

shivered uncontrollably. She could feel his tongue sliding over her, circling her nipple. She could feel his lips
clamp down.

It was amazing, just the way she'd imagined, but an er-
rant thought flashed into her head and took her right out
of the moment. Suddenly she was back in the baths and
the women were discussing her genitalia and the Marquis'
orders.

"Why did you forbid me to have an orgasm?" she
asked him.

"Forbid you to what?"

"The ladies of the Seraglio said you'd forbidden me to
have an orgasm."

He looked up at her. "Are you trying to distract me?"

She was, but she also wanted an answer. "You did say
that, right? There'd be no reason for them lie."

"You want to talk about this *now?*"

"It's important."

He heaved a sigh and sat up. "Orgasms are too easy.
They're like pressure valves. They open, let off some
steam and close up. Nothing changes afterward."

"Is something *supposed* to change?"

"There should be more. More love, more hate, more joy
or disillusionment. More awareness, at the very least. It
should not be status quo afterward."

"Letting off steam is a bad thing?"

"Not if you're a pressure cooker."

"Sometimes, I feel like one," she said.

"Most people use orgasms like they use drugs and liquor, as tranquilizers. They sleepwalk, and you need to

be awake, present. You need to own your body instead of just using it."

He fascinated her. It wasn't easy to admit, even to herself, but when he talked she wanted to hear more. Clearly, he'd explored these things on levels that she hadn't. And some of what he said made her wonder what he'd gone through in his life. But what really got to her was the realization that this had never happened before, even in her supposedly serious relationships. No man had ever talked to her the way he did.

She tugged at the ropes. She wanted her hands free, maybe to touch him. She wasn't sure why. She just wanted them free.

"Untie me," she said.

"Not yet."

"Turn the lights on. I want to see you."

"Not yet."

"Didn't you tell me to express my desires? Well, I am."

He grasped her churning arm. "Hold still, or you'll get rope burns. Is it possible for you to just let this happen, Tess? I want to see you too, but there's no light in here. There's only the fire, and it's gone, so I'll use my hands to see you."

"How am I supposed to see you? You've tied my hands."

"Then you'll just have to let me do the exploring for now."

He made it sound so easy. Letting someone else take control, even a little bit, was impossible for Tess. She wasn't good at letting people do things for her, and God knew, she didn't give sexual control over to anyone. She wouldn't have known how. Besides, a woman was supposed to be responsible for her own orgasms these days. It was politically correct.

He touched her face, and she closed her eyes, uncomfortable as he traced her eyes and her nose, her cheekbones and jaw. He spent considerable time on the contours of her mouth. Either he wanted to know if she was smiling—or he just liked her mouth.

Her lids flicked open when she realized it wasn't his fingers anymore. It was his lips. His breath was pungently scented with liquor and mint. "Give me your mouth," he said, "or I'll punish you."

Astounding the effect of those words.

Tess's jaw fell slack and her lips parted. She lifted toward him, ready to give him anything. He gripped her face, his thumb curving into her cheek as he ravished her mouth. Abruptly, he released her and she fell back against the pillow.

His head dropped to her breast, and Tess arched with pleasure. She felt steam heat and a flash of teeth. The buzzing inside her was deafening. His bite made her gasp. He stung her sweetly, stung her to life.

He began to massage her breast with his palm, and Tess felt a thrill of desire. She lifted up, every muscle straining. She wanted it harder.

But his other hand was in her hair, tugging. He forced her to look up at him, and suddenly she realized why he'd been blowing warm air on her. She was the candle flame. He was the oxygen.

"And will you devour me now?" she asked him.

"Devour you?"

"The riddle. 'Your life is measured in hours. You live by being devoured.' You know, the riddle you asked me to solve."

She sensed his hesitation and was confounded. How could he have forgotten about the riddle?

"Devour you, yes," he said, "like a decadent dessert."

He dropped her into the pillows and moved to her legs. She would have opened them if she could, but he had tied them, the fool. Now he couldn't get at what he wanted. Still, he managed just fine.

His breath bathed her bare mons with exquisite sensations. Who knew that virgin skin could be so much fun? Her back arched as she felt something slide through her wetness. She looked down and made out his dark head between her legs. It was his tongue. He fluttered it back and forth, circling her clitoris with tantalizing strokes. He lifted her hips right off the pillow. She could actually see what was happening, see the petals rising, quivering, as he teased them into a state of frenzy.

He moved up to look at her. "So…you *can* writhe."

"Just torture me," she pleaded, "and get it over with."

"No one has to torture you, Tess. You do it too well."

"Don't tell me you didn't like tying me up, that you're not enjoying this."

"Of course, I'm enjoying it. And so are you."

"I am not—" But she was. and it was absurd to deny it. She'd never been kissed with her hands tied. There was something wildly exciting about it. Anything could happen, and just the thought made her weak.

"Kiss me again," she whispered. "Kiss me hard."

She wanted to be pressed into the pillows, held down and taken. He obliged with breathtaking force. It was a wild and reckless kiss. She heard him growl as their mouths clashed and their teeth clicked together. His fingers burned her skin. They sank into the flesh of her arms as he lifted her off the pillow. This could go anywhere, Tess realized. They could turn savage and kill each other. That's how reckless it felt.

As his mouth ravished hers, she felt something ridgelike and rough. *What was that?* A scar? She'd only known one person in her life with a scar like that on his lip.

No. It couldn't be. She stopped kissing him and stared at him, breathing hard.

"Who are you?" she demanded.

"What do you mean?"

"You're not the Marquis."

"You *are* trying to distract me."

"No, really." It all came together in her mind. He hadn't known about the dress or the line from the riddle. "What's the answer to the riddle?" she asked him. "If you're the Marquis, you'll know."

He pressed his fingers to her mouth, not letting her say anything else. Her heart was pounding wildly as he tried to talk to her.

"You ask too many questions," he said. "And you do it to stay in control. Every time your feelings start to overwhelm you, you bombard me with questions. You start thinking so you don't have to feel."

"Prove to me that you're him, and I'll be quiet. Not another word."

"I'm not proving anything to you. I'm leaving now."

Tess tried to sit up and couldn't. Who was she kidding. She wanted this, Marquis or not. "No! I don't want you to leave. I won't talk anymore." Her voice grew seductive. "Kiss me."

"You want sex?"

"Yes."

"Like this? Tied up?"

She nodded, but he left her anyway. "What are you doing?" she asked as he sat up and moved away from her.

"Sex isn't what you need, Tess. And even if it was, you're not ready for it."

"I'm ready. For God's sake, I am."

He shook his head. "You haven't earned that yet."

"Earned what? I don't need to *earn* anything. I don't need you, either. I can do it myself."

"How? You don't have the use of your hands."

"After you untie me."

"Who says I'm going to untie you?"

"You *have* to," she breathed.

"Let's just say I should—and I would if I wanted to protect you from yourself—but I don't. I want just the opposite, Tess."

He touched her face, then got up and walked to the door. "Don't fight it. Fighting is not the solution."

"You are not leaving me like this!"

"Get some rest," he said. "Someone will be in later to check on you."

"No!" she cried. "No! The deal's off. I'm calling it off. I want out of here. I—"

She doubled over, a moan dying in her throat. He'd already gone. The door to this place was as thick as a bank vault, and he'd shut it and gone. No one could hear her now.

When Tess woke up the next morning, she felt something tickling her cheek. A strand of hair, she realized as she touched it. By the time she'd brushed it away, the obvious had dawned on her. Her hands weren't tied.

She sat up, blood pounding into her brain, waking her up.

She was free.

She rubbed her wrists, aware of the tenderness. Apparently she couldn't write off last night as a bad dream. It had happened. Those were rope burns on her skin.

The Marquis had teased her half out of her mind and calmly skipped out on her, but there were several moments when she'd actually found herself wondering if it was Danny.

She really did need to get Danny Gabriel out of her mind. Maybe it was guilt that made her conjure up his image. Maybe she felt like he should torture her for what she'd done. Everyone else at Pratt-Summers probably thought so.

As Tess was mulling over the questions, she noticed an old leather trunk in the corner by the door. On it someone had placed her bag, her watch and her cell phone. Next to the trunk, hanging on a wall hook was an outfit that definitely wasn't hers. The sheer black lace gown had a graceful ballerina skirt and a fitted corset bodice.

She wrapped the throw around her, left the bed and walked over to the trunk, reaching for the cell phone first. It was her lifeline. She opened the flip top and stared at the screen. She'd momentarily forgotten how to bring up her messages.

She glanced over at the outfit, drawn to the delicate material and the daring bodice. It was wickedly sexy, but the note pinned to the bra strap ticked her off.

"Wear this for me today. I want to see your legs. No panties."

It was signed M. He really was pushing it.

What astonished her more was her reaction. She really wanted to try on the outfit. She wanted to see if it was as sexy as it looked, and if it would make her look sexy. More important, would it give him whiplash? Because that's what she wanted—to drive him half out of his mind.

Seventeen

"You're sure you're okay, Tess? Just say the word, and I'll break you out of that freak show."

"I'm fine, Andy, really." Tess talked softly into her cell phone, trying to calm Andy down without being over-heard. She was alone in the bedchamber, but there was al-ways the possibility that she was under surveillance of some kind. There was no end to the surprises this place dished up. She'd been shocked at how late it was when she turned on the cell moments ago. One-thirty in the after-noon. After her "visitor" had walked out on her, she'd slept through what was left of the night and all of the morning.

"Is that what I'm supposed to tell Erica?" he said. "It's Monday. She's back at work. She's asking questions. *Ev-erybody's* asking questions."

"I've only been gone since yesterday, Andy. Tell Erica

the story we came up with—that I'm doing fieldwork, scouting locations, setting up the photo shoots. It'll take another day, at least."

"And why aren't *we* there with you? Your team? How do I explain that?"

Tess clutched at the throw she'd wrapped around herself, trying to stop it from falling. With the phone tucked under her chin, she knotted the blanket like a bath towel, securing it over her breasts. She felt a tug of alarm as her fingers brushed her skin. The warmth of her own flesh startled her. Why did that feel so unbearably erotic? All she had to do was breathe, and desire sparkled between her legs like water reflecting light. Bright and glittery. It almost hurt.

She glanced up, fighting light-headedness, and saw the black lace outfit. She'd hardly taken her eyes off it since she noticed it hanging on a hook by the door. The attraction was pretty obvious. It had been created for the sole purpose of seduction. Merciless seduction. What man wouldn't want to fuck a woman wearing that thing? And Tess wanted him to *want* to fuck her.

Listen to you. Fuck is now your new favorite word?

Her heart began to pound again. It never seemed to *stop*.

"Tess? You there?"

Tess's face turned fiery hot. She felt like a teenager who'd been caught doing something dirty, which was pretty close to true.

"I'm here," she said, clearing her throat. "You can tell whoever asks that the Marquis has concerns about how his club will be used, and he insists on approving the shots in advance. He nixed the team idea because he doesn't want his members gawked at or ridiculed. Hey, we should be glad he's willing to deal with me."

"Is he ever going to let us in that place?"

"Once he's satisfied we're sincere and not out to exploit him, he'll turn the club over to us, after hours, of course."

"Is any of that true, Tess? What's really going on?"

"Of course it's true." Tess quelled a bubble of near hysteria. It should have been true, and maybe it was, but she had no idea anymore. She couldn't seem to tear herself away from all these bizarre new feelings and sensations. Right now there was an icy flutter in her gut as she studied the gown's sinfully sexy corseted bra. The skirt flared from the hips, saved from being transparent only by the black lace pattern. Could the fabric be as tissue soft as it looked?

Andy's questions echoed in her mind, but they couldn't compete with the dark turns her thoughts were taking, or with her abject fascination for what might be around the next corner. It was nearly irresistible. Her own mind was a siren, calling to her. Even now, another impulse had taken over her awareness, and it was frighteningly strong, especially since she seemed to be losing the desire to fight it.

"What kind of shots are you thinking of?" Andy asked. "Cassandra took me to a couple of rooms called the Walk of Shame and Redemption. Now, those were pretty hot."

Tess touched the gathers and folds of the gown, smiling with secret pleasure. Exactly. The fabric was as soft as tissue paper. Softer.

"There are so many possibilities," she said absently. "Really, this is the perfect location. Did you see the Turkish baths?"

"Leather goods in a Turkish bath? Get serious. Listen, we don't have to use the Marquis Club. Jan and I scouted some other great locations. There's a body-art bar near Forty-second Street. Incredibly weird ambience."

"Body art?" Tess ran her fingers along the bra's deeply cut décolletage, and then traced her breasts in the same way. She had to fight not to moan. The aching that flared was intense, and it shot straight to her female parts, feeding the nerves with pleasure.

"Yeah, it's all about self-decoration," Andy explained. "Some of the regulars don't wear anything *but* their tattoos and piercings…"

He continued to talk about the bar, but Tess was no longer listening. Shivering in the cool morning air, she undid the throw and let it drop to the floor. Her pulse went crazy, her breathing turned shallow. She drew the gown from the hanger. "Andy, I have to go."

"Tess? What is it? You don't sound right."

The urgency in his voice made her pause. She glanced down at the throw on the floor, at her own nudity. She really had lost touch for a moment.

"Don't hang up!" he said. "You haven't heard the rest of it. Brad's on a rampage. He doesn't believe Danny stole your stuff. He says he knows who did it."

"Brad Hayes?" Andy had her full attention now. "Who does he think it was?"

"You, Tess. He thinks you framed Danny to get control of the creative division."

"Andy, that's ridiculous." Brad been one of *her* chief suspects, although there hadn't been any need to pursue it with all the evidence against Danny.

"I know," Andy said, "but he found a video camera in that model plane in your office. He thinks you put it there to trap Danny."

"Barb MacDonald installed the camera. She suggested surveillance, and I agreed. Someone was *stealing* things from my office. And if Brad's after me, he's on a wild-goose chase. He has no proof of anything."

"Yeah, but the talk isn't good, Tess."

And she wasn't there to defend herself. "You have to talk to Brad," she told him. "Will you do that? Remind him that we're a team, and we're up against the wall with this Faustini thing. You can even tell him I'm a virtual prisoner here until I get the green light from the Marquis."

"I already did that, Tess. I made sure he knew you were putting your career on the line to get the club, and I told him to back off his witch hunt until we have Faustini in the can. I bought you some time, but I don't know how much."

If only Andy knew what she was putting on the line. Her career might be the least of it. But he couldn't. No one could. "Thanks, Andy. *Thank you.*"

"Just get the hell back here."

Tess shivered and knelt to pick up the throw. "Has anyone seen Danny? Do you know what's happened to him?"

Her thoughts spun back to the night before and her feeling that the man with her had been Danny. It was only intuition, but powerful. She'd felt what might have been a scar on his mouth when he'd kissed her, but she hadn't been able to reach up and touch it to find out for sure. *Maybe that was why he bound my hands, so I couldn't touch him.*

But why would Danny show up *here*—and go to such trouble to deceive her? Revenge, possibly, if he really believed she'd gotten him fired. Could he have put Brad up to implicating her in the sabotage of her own work? Or maybe this was about humiliating her sexually?

"There's talk he might be opening his own agency," Andy was saying, "but I also heard he was offered a job in Japan. No one seems to know for sure."

She nodded, wrapping herself tightly in the blanket for warmth. Her skin was nothing but gooseflesh. The room was ice cold, but she hadn't noticed it until now.

"Danny always was mysterious," she said, trying not to think about the last time she'd seen him—wearing his bathrobe in his condo. Revenge didn't seem quite as far-fetched when she thought about breaking into his place and seducing him. Still, her hunch about last night had begun to seem crazy to her now. Surely he had better things to do with his new life than to disguise his voice and torment her. He might even be thousands of miles away.

"Tess, let me come and get you."

Andy's voice sounded very far away. She knew he was worried, but she didn't know how to reassure him. She could have walked out of this place several times. She was obviously free to go now, but she'd just been trying to convince Andy that she should stay. She hadn't secured the club yet, and that *was* her reason for being here. Everything was riding on her ability to do that, except that she'd barely given a thought to the job the entire time she'd been here.

That was frighteningly out of character for Tess Wakefield—and may have scared her more than anything else. Having someone take control from you was one thing. Giving it away was another.

"Andy, stop worrying about me," she said. "I'm probably in less danger here than I would be there."

"Tess—"

"Promise me you'll deal with Brad. I'm counting on you to keep everything on track for me there at Pratt. Andy, *promise*—and let me get back to work."

"All right," he said grudgingly. "But hurry up, dammit."

She shut off the phone before he could say anything else, and as she flipped the top shut, guilt and confusion swamped her. What in God's name was she doing? It felt as if she was losing touch with everything she knew. She only wished she understood her reasons for staying, all of them. Or maybe she *did* understand, but couldn't face them. She was being driven by impulse, and it was terrifying.

She'd always been motivated by reason and rationality. Now she was being taken in another direction entirely, and she couldn't explain why, even to herself. That made her feel helpless...which seemed to be the point.

Helplessness.

Why?

Of course, the answer evaded her. So much of this was outside her grasp, but something compelled her to stay and see it through. It was more than a professional obligation. It was gut instinct. What if Danny was actually here in this club?

The black lace gown was on the floor. She knelt to pick it up and her hands began to tremble. A strange sound caught in her throat. She had never heard it before, not from her own lips, but she knew instantly what it was.

A whimper of surrender.

She was going to do this.

Tess walked openly among the members of the club, most of whom were wearing costumes of one kind or another and paid no attention to the blond, blue-eyed seductress in black lace, whose bosom was perilously exposed.

Tess hadn't realized just *how* exposed until she had the outfit on, but it wasn't as though she had anything else to wear. When she'd left her room earlier, intending to have a look around the club, she'd found an elevator with a control panel that told her there were two subterranean levels in the building, and she was on one of them. At least it wasn't the lowest one, which featured the Walk of Shame and Redemption rooms that Andy had mentioned, and possibly the dungeon she'd heard so much about.

According to the eunuch who'd taken her to the balcony room above the Turkish baths, the club had two floors belowground and three above. The rest of the building apparently housed commercial businesses of one kind or another. Tess wondered if they knew about the orgy going on in their midst.

She'd pressed the button for the third floor. The ground floor was the Boulevard of Broken Dreams with the baths, the Hypnosis Parlor, and the other bizarre venues she'd visited the night she came with Danny. The Opera House was on the floor above, as was the balcony room she'd waited in. The rest of the area had reminded her of a luxury hotel with numbered guest rooms. There'd also been a rather normal-looking lounge and restaurant.

The only level she hadn't seen aboveground was the third. So, up she'd gone, only to discover that it was mostly unused offices. The small clerical staff, hard at work in their cubicles, could have been employed by an accounting firm. Even a fantasy sex club had to make a buck, she supposed.

She'd come back down to the ground floor, reassured that this place was made of brick and mortar like the rest of the world, and now she was looking for one more dose of reality. Danny Gabriel. If it *had* actually been him last night, maybe she wouldn't feel quite so disoriented. It would just be strange, not crazy. She didn't expect to find him in the flesh, but it was possible someone had seen him or knew of him.

How odd if this club were to give her the chance to talk to him about what had happened at the agency, the sabotage, and all the rest of it. He had much to explain—and she had a few things as well.

The Marquis should be able to tell her if Danny was a member, but Tess had it in mind to avoid the Marquis for the time being. She wanted to explore on her own, and he had a way of short-circuiting her brain with his black magic. She wasn't sure how she felt about him beyond that, except that there seemed to be an odd bond forming between them, as if they were conspirators in her growing desire to learn what was around the next dark corner.

Tess hadn't expected to see the club so crowded in the afternoon. All the hustle and bustle made her think of an adult Disneyland with the Boulevard of Broken Dreams as its Main Street. Men and women in white togas thronged the entry to the Roman Baths, no doubt to enjoy some water sports. Tess wondered if there might be a special exhibition. A mind-boggling thought, given what she knew about the baths.

A juggler on a unicycle wheeled his way through the congestion, getting close enough for Tess to see that he was lobbing dildos. A woman at least six feet tall strode by, leading another woman on a silvery mesh chain attached to a dog collar that looked like jewelry. The second woman wasn't naked, but she might as well have been. She wore nothing under her sheer chemise except gold nipple rings and a matching belly chain. No underwear of any kind, of course.

Tess must be getting used to going commando. She'd barely noticed the breezes cooling her privates. That was too bad, really. The sharp awareness had been pretty exhilarating, even if it had made her tense. Now, it was her bobbing breasts making her tense. The corset bones had propped her up and displayed her like fruit in a bowl.

Tess noticed a small cluster of people gathered at the entrance to the Hypnosis Parlor. Curious, she stopped to see what was going on. They seemed to be waiting to go inside. She peeked through the crowd and saw someone moving around in the mirrored room, dressed in a black hooded robe. The Marquis had mentioned assistants called Hypnotricks, who could put guests in a trance and give them hypnotic suggestions. This must be one of them.

Tess assumed she was watching a man, but when the hypnotrick turned, she got a rude shock. It was a woman, and she was a dead ringer for—Tess gaped at her, unable to believe it. She looked like Mitzi from the rest room at the agency!

"Excuse me," Tess said, trying to edge her way through the crowd. "Sorry, I need to get to the door. Please, let me through."

She made several attempts, but no one would move for her. One after another, they stepped in front of her, almost as if intending to block her. Tess had to forcibly push through them, and by the time she got to the door, Mitzi's double had vanished.

The door handle gave when she turned it. Over the protests of the crowd, she entered the glittering glass ball, and was instantly disoriented. Her reflection was everywhere, bouncing at her from the walls, the ceiling, even the floor. Dizzily, she took a seat in one of the sleek white leather reclining chairs, as if to signal that she was there for a hypnosis session, like everybody else.

She could have been inside a jeweled space capsule. Even more bewildering, she was every facet of the gem. What bounced back at her now was a million reflections of her eyes, as blue as stars. Too bright to bear. What was she doing in this disco dome? All she wanted to do was find the assistant who looked like Mitzi, but the voices had already begun whispering to her. They were soft and unintelligible, like rustling leaves.

She glanced around to see if the others could hear them, too, and realized she was totally alone in the room. Mitzi wasn't there. No one was.

From outside, angry faces peered through the glass. Tess wondered why they didn't come in. What was going on?

It was difficult to avoid the mirrors, but she tried. She didn't want to see the eyes. They were too invasive. She tried to block out the whispers, too, but they grew more insistent.

Don't fight, Tess. Fighting's not the solution. You are.

Gradually the voices began to sound familiar, like someone she knew. It almost sounded like her own voice. Her mind was talking to her. And just beneath the words was a deep, steady heartbeat. She closed her eyes and was nearly lulled into a trance by the sound, but she couldn't make sense of what the whispers were saying. Maybe she didn't want to.

Tess, plumb the depths. Go deeper. The darkness has your secrets. The darkness has what you want—

She strained to hear the rest of it, but a woman's voice intruded, angry and accusative.

"You think you're better than the rest of us?" she snapped. "You can cut in front of people?"

Tess opened her eyes to see a gray-haired woman hovering over her, furious. She reminded Tess a little of Jan Butler from the agency.

"Wait your turn, bitch," the woman said as she took the chair next to Tess.

"Sorry," Tess said weakly. "I didn't know there was a line."

Tess didn't realize she was shaking until her feet hit the floor. She went straight to the door and let herself out, rushing past the angry glares of the people in line. This place *was* like Disneyland.

She'd seen a women's lounge on the ground floor, and she went looking for it. She needed a place to clear her head, anywhere that she could feel safe. She had no idea what the whispers meant. Another damn riddle. The darkness had her secrets? This whole place was dark.

One of her destinations today had been the Vampire Forest. She couldn't leave without taking a closer look. Maybe it was the darkness she was supposed to seek. But there was another place she hadn't been, too, the lowest level, the belly of the beast.

Plumb the depths.

She hesitated and looked around. Where was that elevator? It was time to visit the dungeon.

* * *

Tess could still hear the heartbeat. It seemed to be pulsing all around her as she made her way through the maze of dimly lit corridors in the lowest level. It was plenty dark down here, and if there was anyone around, they were well hidden. She hadn't seen a soul.

She could hear them, though. Occasionally, a gasp or a moan would tell her if she was going in the right direction. It sounded like people in pain, and she was nervous about what she might see, but curiosity had taken over—and something else that was much more personal. Maybe the voices were right, and she had impulse lurking inside her that only this place could touch. It was a frightening thought.

She rounded another corner, wondering how she would ever find her way out of the maze. She should have marked her path, but it was too late now. There was another turn ahead, and the noises were getting louder. She picked up her pace—and saw the portal as soon as she'd taken the corner. A large open arch bore the words *The Walk of Shame and Redemption* painted on the transom in ornate black letters.

Tess entered the portal to a disturbingly familiar landscape. The long hallway-like room was dark, except for areas lit by the hot red glow of a spotlight, where various punishments were being meted out. She and Danny had seen similar tableaux on the walkway into the club that first night.

Tess felt like an intruder, but no one seemed to notice her. Everywhere she looked something strange and fascinating was taking place. A burly, bearded man on his knees lovingly washed the feet of his mistress and begged her to forgive him. A handsome older woman had filled an entire blackboard with the words *I touched myself in an impure way* and now she was cradled in the lap of a young man who gently caressed her hair, a graceful gray chignon, as she sobbed.

The place was aptly named, Tess decided. The Walk of Shame and Redemption, where transgressors were punished for their sins.

In a pool of violet light, a curvaceous young woman, dressed like an eighteenth-century milkmaid, leaned over a low table, straight-armed and supporting herself with her hands. Her panties were down around her ankles, her skirt hiked up to expose her lush bare buttocks. A man, costumed as a preacher, wielded a paddle that gave out a soft *whap* when it connected with her blushing flesh.

Tess winced as the paddle found its mark again. It startled her to see the woman's eyes nearly roll back in her head. She was the one gasping and moaning, Tess realized, but she wasn't being hurt. By the look on her face, she was in ecstasy. It was about pleasure, not pain.

Suddenly the paddling stopped. The man seemed to be done, but the woman wasn't. She began to writhe and moan, calling him a bastard and berating him for stopping. She wanted more, but what riveted Tess was the sound she made as the man told her to spread her legs. Tess had heard it before. That same sound had caught in her own throat when she'd knelt to pick up the gown in her room. A whimper of surrender.

Tess felt her chest tighten and her throat burn. She had to get out of here. But as she glanced up, she saw the man asking the woman if she was ready. The woman nodded her head eagerly, swearing that she was. He grew very stern, warning her that she would be punished if she wasn't telling the truth. She begged him to believe her, begged him to touch her and prove it to himself.

Tess was astounded. She wanted to run, but her legs wouldn't move. They barely held her up. She stood there, practically paralyzed as the woman continued to plead. Finally, the man smoothed his hand back and forth across her bottom, giving it a little swat before he dipped his finger between her legs.

The woman moaned and arched her back. Her whole body shuddered.

That was it for Tess. She clamped a hand over her mouth, afraid she was going to be ill. This was too much. She didn't understand it, nor did she want to. She was ready, too. *Ready to get the hell out of here.*

But when she turned, she saw a man standing in the arch of the doorway, watching her intently. She had no idea how long the Marquis had been there, but her pulse kicked up immediately. She had not wanted to be caught here, especially by him.

"What brings you to the Walk of Shame and Redemption?" he asked as he joined her.

She shrugged and tried to sound calm. "I came to see what all the screaming was about."

"See anything that interests you? The paddle, perhaps? That's my personal favorite."

Her voice went chilly. "Don't be ridiculous. Sorry to chat and run, but if you'll get out of the way, I'll be leaving."

"You're walking out on the deal?"

"No, I'm leaving this room. I've heard enough whimpering, thank you."

She tried to go around him, but he caught her by the hand. "What are you doing?" She watched him press his fingers to the pulse in her wrist, as if he was counting the beats.

He nodded. "This is your area of greatest excitement," he said, searching her expression. "You were meant to be here."

"No—"

"Never be false about your desires and always surrender to them. You've broken the first rule many times. The only way you can redeem yourself it to keep the second."

He waved his arm, encompassing the entire room. "Pick your poison, Tess Wakefield. You've been a bad girl, and you have to be punished."

Eighteen

"Andy, don't ask any q-questions." Tess spoke into her cell phone, her teeth chattering from the cold. "I'm almost out of b-battery time. Just send a cab over to the Marquis Club for me. I'm at the underground parking entrance. Tell them to hurry."

"One sec, Tess. I'm on a call. Let me get rid of her."

He was gone before Tess could speak. Rid of *her?* Tess's eyes rolled up. Wretched little Casanova, that one.

Tess prayed the battery held out.

Her breath created contrails of white vapor as she waited for Andy to come back to the phone. She rubbed her bare arm vigorously, trying to keep warm and not drop the phone or her bag. Shoes hadn't come with her costume, and her bare feet were aching blocks of ice.

She was lucky it wasn't snowing yet. It felt like snow

to her, except that being from southern California, she had only a vague idea of what that meant. She'd always liked the phrase, but that was before she'd had to deal with weather that could produce the real thing. *Brrrr.*

She was wearing nothing but the black lace gown, and her skin was chalk white in contrast. It had drained of all color. There hadn't been time to swipe a coat. She'd flown out of the club before she or anyone else could talk her out of it.

There was only so much humiliation one could—

"I'm back," Andy said, breaking into Tess's thoughts. "What's going on? You okay?"

"Just send the cab, Andy, *please.* Do it now." The beeping in her ear meant the battery was dying, and any second they'd be cut off.

"Okay, but borrow another cell and call me back. Let me know what's going on."

"As soon as I can," Tess promised and hung up the phone, aware that she hadn't asked about Pratt-Summers or Brad. That would have to wait until she'd gotten the hell out of here. She was just glad to have an excuse not to talk. She couldn't possibly have explained her situation to Andy. It was beyond embarrassing.

She had chosen the paddle as her punishment, and she'd responded like a repressed Victorian housewife. God help her, she had. Moaning and whimpering and loving every second of it. She couldn't remember being more turned on in her life! What was wrong with her? Did she secretly yearn to be dominated? Or worse, was she was a closet masochist, who got off on public humiliation? Was she an exhibitionist to boot?

She wasn't sure about the first two, but at least the last one didn't play. She'd absolutely refused to be publicly flogged, so the Marquis had taken her to a private room, which, in retrospect, may have been a mistake. When they were all alone, he'd worked his black magic like he was the devil's answer to David Copperfield, whispering in her ear and caressing her until she was so woozy she would have let him do anything. *Anything.*

And worse, afterward, she had not been able to deny any of it. Lying wasn't an option. That was the unbreakable rule that had gotten her into this mess. She'd had to admit to enjoying it, as if her body's response wasn't proof enough. She was wet and throbbing from head to toe, with rosy-red blotches that weren't limited to her backside. They mottled her pale skin wherever it was exposed, which was *too* many places. And the sounds that came out of her, the pathetic little whimpers, the clutching and writhing!

He must have loved that.

He had her caress her own butt to feel how hot it was. And then he'd had her stroke herself and one touch was all it had taken. She was steamy wet and all hot, sparking nerves. And when *he'd* touched her there—well, more than touched, he'd shamelessly played with her pussy— she'd had an epiphany. She'd lost it utterly.

She'd been totally humiliated at her own lack of control. He'd tried to tell her that it wasn't about control, it was about freedom, and she'd told him to shove his stupid freedom and run. She couldn't bear to be in his presence.

At least he'd had the good grace not to try and stop her.

Now, if only that taxi would show up.

Tess was nearly blue before it did. The cab pulled into the driveway and the driver got out and opened the door for her.

"Ms. Wakefield?" he said. "Please, get in. I have the heat going, and there's a goose-down comforter in the back to keep you warm."

Some service. Andy should get a raise for this.

Tess tossed her bag inside, then scrambled into the car and nearly mummified herself in the comforter. Perfect for hiding from the world, as well as from hypothermia. She gave the driver her home address, and then pulled her knees up to her chest and buried her face, burrowing in the goose down. Her nose was an icicle.

She was free, safe, and probably not permanently scarred. Except her ego. That damage might never be repaired. She wasn't terribly concerned about the domination stuff or the masochism. Those things hadn't come up before and probably wouldn't again, as along as she stayed away from places like the Marquis Club. The career situation was anybody's guess. She had no idea how she was going to deal with that. There was no way they'd be able to use the club now.

As warmth seeped into her, she closed her eyes, and possibly she even drifted off for a bit. It was all a little vague, but at least she was feeling slightly more human when she roused herself and looked up. She peered out the window, trying to figure out where they were. It definitely wasn't the city, and Tess lived in the city. It was more like the countryside, possibly even the hills. They were heading up a tree-lined street where large estates were walled off and hidden from view.

"Where are we?" she asked the driver. "I live on the Upper East Side."

"Right, ma'am," he said, glancing in the rearview mirror. "This is where I was told to take you."

"*Told* to take me?" Tess frantically checked out the taxi and realized something was wrong. There was no fare meter on the car's dashboard. Every taxi she'd ever been in had a meter and a special license clipped to the visor. This one didn't.

It *wasn't* a taxi. *What the fuck?*

Tess fought her way out of the comforter, but kept it around her just in case. "Where are we? Where are you taking me?"

"Right here." He drove a few more feet and pulled through a gated entrance. The road that stretched ahead of them was lined with towering white birches, with frozen ponds on either side of the road and statuary as stark and terrifying as it was beautiful.

"Whose house is this? Does it belong to the Marquis?" Tess was certain it did. Somehow he must have intercepted her phone call to Andy. Cell phones were never secure.

"Sorry, ma'am, I'm not at liberty to say."

Tess reached for the door handle. "If you don't tell me, I'm getting out. Whether you stop the car or not, I'm getting out."

She heard a loud click and realized he'd locked the

doors from the inside. Ahead of them the road forked in two directions, one running under a graceful portico with classical Greek pillars that led to a manse of marble and glass, the other to a multicar garage. Seven or eight doors? There wasn't time to count before one of them opened, and the car rolled in.

The driver cut the engine and let himself out. He opened Tess's door and extended his hand, but she didn't take it. "This is kidnapping," she said, trying not to sound frightened. "I asked you to let me out of the car."

Tess didn't like anything about the man's buggy eyes and bald head, which she suspected he'd shaved to look more formidable. It hadn't worked. He was probably in his late twenties and bore a passing resemblance to a young Bruce Willis.

"Your choice," he said. "You don't have to come in, but it's going to get cold tonight. They're calling for single digits, and this garage isn't heated. It could be dangerous."

"Not nearly as dangerous as coming inside. Now answer my question, or I'll stay out here and freeze, which might be a little awkward for the Marquis. A dead body in his garage, I mean. This *is* his house, right?"

The driver glared at Tess. Finally, he nodded. "I didn't say a word."

Deciding she would have to be satisfied with that, Tess got herself out of the car, awkwardly carrying the comforter and her bag. She followed him into a spacious kitchen that dazzled the eye with its bright white cabinets and brushed stainless-steel appliances. There was a bottle of champagne chilling in a silver bucket on the white marble countertop. Right next to it sat at least two dozen ruby-red roses in a sparkling crystal vase.

Tess noticed her name on the card but didn't comment on it. She still felt as if she was a prisoner here, not a guest. She wasn't about to acknowledge a welcoming bouquet of flowers.

"Why am I here?" she asked.

"Your host will be with you shortly," the driver said, evading her question. "Meanwhile, please make yourself at home. Can I take your bag and the comforter?"

Tess handed him the comforter but kept her bag.

"Would you like something to eat or drink?" he asked. "There's champagne on ice or hot sake, if you're still feeling chilled. If you're hungry, a buffet awaits in the dining room. It's been set out on the credenza, and everything was freshly made for you."

"Am I locked in?" Tess asked, ignoring his efforts to put her at ease.

"No, you can leave anytime you want. But if you decide to stay, you might need this." He handed her what looked like a pager. "I'm in a room off the garage. Just press the button if you need anything."

Tess went to the door and checked it after he left. She wasn't locked in, which had the paradoxical effect of making her want to stay, at least long enough to look around.

She left her purse and the pager on the island countertop, and then she turned her attention to the rest of the house, which was breathtaking. The entire ground floor was open concept. From the kitchen she could see through to the living room, where a fire roared behind an etched-glass screen and furry white area rugs graced the marble floor. Beyond the living-room windows, she could see the white birch forest outside. The entire structure seemed to have been built of glass.

Was that snow outside? She thought it must be an illusion, dust motes caught in the pale, slanting rays of the rising sun, but the longer she watched the more she realized it was snowflakes. There was already a light dusting of white on the ground, and when she got to the window and looked up, she saw it drifting down from the thick gray sky like confetti.

Snow. Tess had only seen it on trips to the local mountains in California. This was her first snowstorm, and she had a ringside seat. She stood there for a few minutes, turning slowly and gazing at the world outside. It was snowing in every direction she looked. And she was beginning to understand why people might make decisions in moments of weakness that they would never have made otherwise. She *wanted* to be snowed in here. Trapped by the elements. Not with the Marquis. Not with anyone. All by herself, warm and sleepy in front of the fireplace. A little drunk on sake. For some reason, that seemed magical to her right now.

Of course, it was crazy. She couldn't do it. But what *was* she going to do? She still had a job, obligations, and people counting on her. Somewhere along the way she'd lost track of all that. She'd wandered into a bewildering erotic maze and couldn't seem to find her way out.

"Call a taxi," she told herself, "a real one this time. Get out of here before you get snowed in."

She'd slipped her cell phone inside the strings of her corset for safekeeping. She fished it out, flipped it open and saw immediately that the battery was totally gone. It was probably dead before she turned it off. Or maybe she'd forgotten to turn it off. Nearly freezing to death must have dulled her senses.

There had to be a phone around here somewhere. The kitchen was made up of built-ins disguised as cabinets. Even the refrigerator was cleverly hidden from view by two brushed-steel panels. Push buttons on either side seemed intended to open the doors. Nevertheless, Tess spotted a phone attached to the flat-screen television that folded up under the upper cabinets. Everything was hidden in this place, Tess realized, and yet nothing was.

Her relief evaporated as soon as she picked the phone up. There was no dial tone. She hit buttons at random, and suddenly an automated woman's voice spoke to her from the earpiece.

"I'm sorry, but you are not authorized to use this phone. Please enter your password to activate."

"What?" Tess tried every combination of numbers she could think of and got the same message. She hung up the phone with a bang. She couldn't call out? She didn't dare try to walk out of here, even over to one of the neighbors'. She had no shoes, and they probably wouldn't let her through their gates anyway. Hopefully the gate to this place didn't lock from the inside. She would never make it over the wall, and then there was security to think about. She hadn't noticed guards, but a place like this was likely to have them, although it might be an outside company rather than guards on the premises. Still, if she tried to open the gate without a remote, it would probably set off alarms.

Her stomach rumbled, and she sniffed the air. The smells wafting from the dining room were tantalizing, and she was hungry. No, ravenous to the point of being ill. Maybe just a peek at the buffet…

As she lifted one lid after another from silver chafing dishes, her mouth began to water. To hell with worrying about being poisoned. She needed food. She tried some of the domburi, a luscious Japanese rice dish with tempura chicken, using the serving spoon to eat straight out of the dish. The fusilli with green pesto sauce and pine nuts looked delicious, and was. There were spring rolls filled with crunchy Asian vegetables, and her favorite— coconut shrimp with apricot wasabi sauce.

She washed it all down with a shot glass of warm sake, which was surprisingly fruity and lively. The slight burn warmed her up.

She went into the living room with a piece of shrimp and a glass of sake in her hands. The glass walls must be state of the art, she decided. She couldn't see any seams, even where the walls met at the corners. It was almost dizzying to have the feeling of no barriers, as if you could be inside and outside, everywhere at once.

Tess spotted a city skyline beyond the white birch forest. It was nestled in a valley that seemed to span the entire horizon, and Tess had to assume it wasn't Manhattan. Possibly they'd crossed the bridge into New Jersey.

She ate the last bite of shrimp, swallowed the sake and

set the glass down, aware of the wasabi's bite and heat. It surprised her that she was eating and drinking as if it were perfectly normal to be here, enjoying the hospitality of her absent host. Of course, he would make his presence known at some point. He loved keeping her waiting—and off balance.

Meanwhile though, she had a deadline and pressing problems to deal with. She ought to have been searching the house for the clothing she needed to get back to her life, boots and a warm coat. Before she stepped foot in the Marquis Club, she would not have thought it possible to be thrown off course this way. She would have been clawing her way out of here, rushing to get back to her obligations. Now she wasn't even sure she wanted to go. Bizarre.

A sigh welled unexpectedly, bringing back that sense of something missing in her life. She had a great job. Well, maybe not after all this, but she could always go back to L.A., and advertising was her career of choice, so what was the problem? She couldn't have too much sympathy for herself. She was sure no one else would. Most people would have killed for the opportunity she'd been given. It was the chance of a lifetime. Hers to blow, as a matter of fact.

So, why *wasn't* she frantic? Why was she standing here staring out a window?

Outside, the snow feathered the birch boughs like lace, and Tess could only imagine the utter quiet. She looked up to see a bright red cardinal land on a nearby tree, high in the topmost branches. It was beautiful beyond description. Perfect.

She moved to the nearest chair and sat down. It was a chaise lounge very near the glass, and resting in it made her feel as if she were on a magic carpet, floating through the forest. She didn't intend to sit for more than a minute. She'd never seen a sight like this before. Mother Nature was putting on her own theater, and Tess wondered if this could be what was missing. Stillness. Serenity. Feeling as if she was inside and outside, everywhere at once.

When Tess woke up she was covered with a velvety blanket, and the house was dark, except for the glow of indirect lighting around the perimeter of the room. She was still lying in the same cushy chair. She could have slept there for days. Her body felt limp and heavy. Even her thoughts were sluggish. Something had knocked her out. Maybe all that food and sake. But who had covered her up? The driver?

She got to her feet in stages, making sure that she was steady enough. A cursory look around told her she was alone in the room, and probably in the house as well. The quiet was a presence all its own. Still needing to clear her thoughts, she stepped off the cloud-soft rug and walked to the window. Icy marble tiles chilled the soles of her feet, waking her up.

The birch forest was beautifully illuminated by accent lights, and Tess could see that it had stopped snowing. But there was a heavy covering of white on the ground, and the trees were loaded down. A glimpse of something red caught her eye, but it wasn't the bird at the top of the tallest tree. This was on the ground, some twenty feet away from the house.

Tess peered harder, bewildered by the sight.

A crimson rose rested atop a snowdrift, as if someone had very deliberately placed it there. As Tess stared at the flower, she realized that she was also looking at a head-stone, partially covered by the snow. There was a grave out there.

Her breathing turned shallow. The rose hadn't been there before. She would have seen it. It had been placed there after she fell asleep, and she doubted the driver had put it there. She turned back to the house, searching the shadows. Maybe she wasn't alone after all.

A dramatic spiral stairway was tucked into a large cres-cent-shaped alcove between the dining room and the liv-ing room. Tess headed for it, assuming it led to the second floor. She avoided touching the wrought-iron railing, fear-ing it might creak. Luckily, her bare feet made no sound on the marble steps, and even though she was wobbly, she made it to the top without a problem.

The second floor was also lit by indirect lighting. She could see her way from room to room, but it was nearly impossible to see what was inside them. This part of the house had walls and windows, but the light was muted. Tess wondered if the heavy snow clouds were blocking the moonlight.

She counted what she thought were three bedrooms and a media room, and they all appeared to be empty, but she was now faced with the double doors at the end of the hall. It was probably the master bedroom, where he was most likely to be. What would she do if he was in there? Awake?

Ask him what the hell you're doing here, for starters.

The door opened soundlessly. It was a large room and as dark as the others, but this one was occupied. Tess could hear his breathing.

She approached the bed cautiously, trying not to make any noise. Scenes from horror movies played in her mind, where the sleeping spring to life in terrifying ways. She couldn't make out any more than the outline of his body, even when she was right next to the bed.

He was lying on his stomach, his legs tangled up in the sheets. His head was turned her way, which meant she should have been looking at his profile, but he'd bunched the pillow up with his arms around his head, and she couldn't tell where it ended and his features began.

Praying she wouldn't wake him, she touched his head and felt his hair. Silky strands slipped through her fingers.

This wasn't the Marquis, she realized. This man had long hair.

It was Danny.

Nineteen

Tess had no reason to believe the sleeping man was Danny, except for the long hair—and the megaphone in her gut that was shouting at her like a hostage negotiator. No, it made no sense. But for a second, she'd been completely convinced. She was still convinced. She was shaking.

Danny? Why did her mind keep going there?

She'd had the same gut-wrenching premonition last night in the club, and she hadn't been able to explain that, either, which was exactly why she couldn't trust these crazy hunches. This could as easily be about what she *needed* to be true as what *was* true. People altered reality to fit their needs all the time. It was human nature.

For all she knew, the Marquis had long hair. She'd never really noticed. It had been dark and surreal every time they were together. She couldn't be sure of anything.

But, if it *was* Danny, then she had a news flash for him. She didn't appreciate him screwing with her life this way.

The floor creaked, and Tess froze. She hadn't moved, but she may have shifted her weight without realizing it. *Don't wake him up.*

Her thready pulse reminded her that a confrontation could be dangerous. She should leave now while he was asleep. She would still have to search the house for cold-weather clothes or tromp through the snow barefoot, but that was only part of what stopped her. She knew she would always wonder. If she left without knowing who he was, and why he'd brought her here, she was certain to regret it later.

All she had to do was get a look at his face.

She quieted her mind and listened to his breathing. It sounded like the rhythms of deep sleep, so she crept closer and bent over him, getting as near as she dared. It hadn't occurred to her before now that Danny and the Marquis might be the same man. They seemed very different, one dark and otherworldly, the other earthy and very much of this world. But they both had a powerful presence, and she could feel that here. This man gave off heat. He had an energy field, even asleep.

She needed to see him.

She traced her fingertips lightly over his jawline. He stirred, and she hesitated. Her pulse slammed into high gear, but she couldn't bolt now. That would almost certainly wake him.

She dug her toes into the carpet to anchor herself. She was bent at an odd angle, and her thigh muscles ached.

It took all of her balance to hold the position. *Please God, don't let me fall on him.*

Finally his breathing deepened, and she tried again, but it was hard to tell if she was making contact. Her inability to see seemed to be affecting her other senses. She managed to pull away a corner of the pillow and revealed part of his face.

From there, it wasn't difficult to find his mouth. She traced her finger over the rough patch above his lips. Was that a scar? It might be razor stubble. Her shaking legs forced her to make a decision. She had to have some light. There was a lamp on the nightstand. If she could turn it on and off quickly enough, she might be able to see him without waking him. Even a quick flash of light should do.

She reached for the lamp, and nearly jumped out of her skin as a hand shot out and clamped her wrist.

"Don't do it," he said.

"Danny?" The name exploded from her lungs.

"You don't know who I am?"

At the moment she didn't know anything. Her brain waves had turned to static. If his voice had sounded familiar for a second it didn't now. She couldn't blame it on magic tricks or voice enhancement. There were no reverberations, except in her head. Her senses weren't functioning. She couldn't see, couldn't hear things right. Maybe her sense of touch was off, too. Maybe she hadn't felt anything by his mouth.

"God," she whispered. "I'm going crazy."

"There are worse things, Tess." He tugged on her wrist,

pulling her down to sit next to him on the bed. "Take off that thing you're wearing."

His voice shocked her. It was full of carnal passion, of kindling heat, but it didn't bring about any recognition at all. Still, he knew her name. If it wasn't Danny, it had to be the Marquis.

"Take it off," he said. "I want you naked in bed with me."

She ripped her hand away. "I'm not taking off anything else for anyone. Who the hell are you?"

His silence fed the fire.

"Turn on the light," she snapped. "Show yourself, you coward."

"The light stays off."

"Then my clothes stay on." She rose from the bed. "I'm leaving."

"You won't get very far in this weather."

"Anywhere that's not *here* is far enough."

The bed springs creaked as he threw the blanket off. "I'll call my driver. You'll freeze out there."

Tess was shaking again. First, it had been fear. Now it was anger. "Don't do me any fucking favors."

She turned and walked to the door, stopping only as another wave of indignation hit her. "There's something I forgot."

He was rising from the bed as she turned around. "What is it?" he asked.

"This." She curled her hand into a fist, walked over and landed a surprisingly solid right to his jaw. The blow stung her knuckles, but it was worth any amount of pain to see his hand fly to his face.

"That's for humiliating me this morning," she said. It should have been a one-two punch for the sabotage mess, but she couldn't be sure who she was dealing with.

He rubbed his jaw. "I thought you didn't know who I was."

"You insist on playing stupid games, you hide in the dark, and you won't tell me who you are. What more do I need to know?"

"I *can't* tell you who I am."

"Why not?"

"Because it would make this about me, and it's not about me."

"That's not good enough." He'd said almost the same thing the night before—that it wasn't about him. It was about her. Nice words, but they were beginning to sound like a Hallmark card.

He let out a weary sigh. "It would be all over if I told you. You'd walk out."

"I was on my way out anyway."

Light flickered over his face, and Tess's heart went nuts. Her eyes adjusted to the darkness, and she'd just gotten a glimpse of his features, or thought she had, but she couldn't seem to hang on to them. It was like a jigsaw puzzle that came together and fell apart. She'd had it and lost it, like his voice. He could only be one of two men. How difficult could it be to identify him? But something in her psyche was blocking it.

She was fighting herself, and conspiring with him, she realized. Maybe, on some level, she believed what he'd just told her. If she knew his identity, it would all be over.

This was not an experience she could allow herself to have with Danny Gabriel, given the turbulence of their brief relationship. It had to be clean. It had to be someone anonymous and powerful, a man who could take her to a place she'd never been. And what if that place wasn't a wild sexual experience? What if sex was only a means to an end?

God, she was confused! She understood everything and nothing. She had to go on faith, and that in itself was unthinkable. She'd never done it before. She had to trust, but not him, herself.

An exquisite thought. Just leap. Fly.

An insane thought. Who did that? Who leaped? Suicides, that's who. Either she wasn't brave enough or crazy enough. She didn't understand why she was even considering it. She didn't understand anything. Her mind kept giving her glimpses of things. Him. Herself. Something more. Something exquisite.

And then ripped it away.

Finally, she blurted, "What's the big deal anyway? It's just a stupid sexual escapade, right? I don't even know why I'm here."

"Do you want me to answer that for you?"

Obviously, he couldn't see her withering expression. "Maybe you should tell me why *you're* here? Haven't you got anything better to do than to watch women come unglued?"

"No, I don't. There's nothing better than that."

"That's sick. You're sick."

He sighed. "Maybe I know something you don't—that

life has no meaning except what we put into it. Otherwise, it's empty and only fleetingly pleasurable. Nothing lasts."

She could hear that world-weary resonance in his voice again, and yet he didn't strike her as the melancholy sort.

"And *this* is meaningful to you?" she said. "Having sex with me, dominating me, or whatever other freaky thing you have in mind?"

He was quiet for what seemed like a long time. Perhaps she'd made him angry. That would be an interesting change. But when he spoke, his voice was oddly soft.

"If you wanted those things, they might be meaningful to me, but not otherwise."

"Then why am I here? And no more riddles, please."

Pale light crept into the room, and Tess wondered if it was moonlight or the breaking dawn. He was wearing pajama bottoms and nothing else. She could see that as the light illuminated the lower half of his body, revealing the black drawstring pants that hung on his hips. She could even see his belly button and his *ripped* stomach muscles.

It was totally unexpected—and pure male animal. She fought for control as her heart started to pound. She was not going to lose it now, not before she had some answers.

"No riddles," he promised. "This may be your only shot at accepting yourself, Tess Wakefield."

More Hallmark cards? "And if I take this shot?"

Tess didn't move, and neither did he, except to relax his stance a little, and continue in a low, deliberate tone.

"Then, for the next several hours, Tess Wakefield is mine. She will give over all control, all cares, all burdens to me and it will set her free."

He raised a hand, as if he didn't want her to speak yet. "Have you ever surrendered completely to anything, or do you fight to control every experience? Most people do. They have a deep terror of letting go, but there's no other way to find yourself, no other way to end the lies."

"I don't lie."

"*Everyone* lies, but you won't have to anymore. No more lies, Tess. When it's over, you will have surrendered every secret, every defense against intimacy, every shred of false pride."

"And I will be magically healed and glued together again? Perfect as the day I was born?"

If he heard her sarcasm, he ignored it. "No, you'll be *im*perfect in every sense of the word. You'll be a mess, but it will be okay."

Tess realized she was fingering the laces of her corset. In her nervousness, she'd already loosened them. But it was dark. He couldn't see her, thank God. What he didn't know wouldn't hurt him.

It would hurt her.

Her fingers went still. The lying *had* hurt her, she realized. He was right about that. Somewhere, a long time ago, she'd read that every lie took a little piece of the soul, and it had scared her because she lied all the time. She was pathological when it came to her inner life. She couldn't tell the truth. Her parents had never really allowed it. She'd been told who she was, how to feel.

Tess, stop moping over that dog… You couldn't possibly still miss it…

Everything Tess felt was wrong, so eventually she'd

stopped feeling. It was the only safe way to exist. She'd shut her emotions off and learned to fake it instead. She could put on a great show of not being angry or hurt. She'd never given anyone an inkling of how badly she quaked during thunderstorms, least of all her parents. She'd even hidden the blood where her fingernails had cut into her palms.

No one knew what was going on inside of her. They never even suspected. Maybe she wasn't perfectly glued together, but she was liquid-cemented to the max. Tough. Unbreakable.

But that was the outside. The inside was…

A mess, to use his word. Over the years, she'd started eliminating things from her life that she couldn't control. It was the only safe way. But now she was losing control of what little was left, her work. Her precious work.

"Can't I keep *anything*?" she asked him.

"You can't cling to something and let go at the same time."

"Shit." She went quiet, her fingers tangled in the corset ties. They had come partially undone, and she began to work at them, slowly, painstakingly, but with an entirely different sense of purpose.

Finally, he spoke. "What are you doing?"

"Taking this thing off…like you asked me to."

"I didn't ask you, Tess. I told you. You're mine now."

"I know." She bowed her head, an emotion sweeping through her that she didn't understand. After a moment, she began to weep, overwhelmed by relief, and by a wild, coursing desire to be touched and held.

"Come here, beautiful girl," he said.

She walked to him on unsteady legs and let him untangle the mess she'd made. Entranced, she watched his hands work.

"No more lies," she said, looking up at him, his face still too dark to make out.

He gripped her face, stroking her lips with his thumb and boring through her last defense with his gaze.

"I'll do everything I promised," he said. "I'm going to shake you to your core."

Her heart was beating too furiously to speak. She touched the hanging ties, the unlaced corset. She touched her own burning skin. This was what it felt like to be under someone else's control. Utterly subjugated to their whims. Naked for their pleasure.

"Yes."

His mouth was soft, hard, heaven. She actually moaned when he kissed her. So much pent-up feeling. So much pressure without release. *Too much time without a man who made her moan.* She was ready for this. Her nerves were tying themselves into knots as sweet as they were tight. She wanted to fly, even if it meant falling from the skies.

He put his hands around her waist and lifted her onto the bed with him.

Tess fell against him and their mouths came together, softly crushed by the pressure. The kiss went deep and dizzy, and she sank like a rock, spiraling, moaning, getting deliciously lost. She was absently aware of his hands buried in her hair and drawing her back. But she didn't want to be drawn back. She was too much in need.

Their lips clung as he broke the kiss, and she felt something rough. It could have been a scar, but her obsession with knowing who he was was gone. Maybe the real confusion had come from within her—from not knowing who *she* was.

He pulled her on top of him, and they rolled together. Breathless, she landed on her back with him above her. Her corset was mostly unlaced, and he had only to lay it open to feast his eyes.

He watched her breasts tremble as she laughed and tried to catch her breath.

"This is enough to make my blood rise," he said.

He was blocking the light, and she couldn't see. But she could feel him, and his rising blood was turning him into brute matter. He was hardening, and it thrilled her.

He toyed with her breasts, purling his fingertips lightly over the pale mounds and tickling her nipples, as if it amused him to watch them tighten and tingle. He circled and swirled, never giving her satisfaction.

Pleasure pricked her. She moaned as her swelling flesh ached to be handled firmly.

"More, dammit," she whispered.

"More?" He rolled a nipple between his fingers, twisting it hard.

She let out a cry, but nothing stopped him. Tears stung her eyes as he cupped her breast and brought it to his mouth. He pampered the flaming bud for a moment, soothing it with the softness of his lips, cooling it with his tongue. He gentled her until she sighed with bliss, and then he began to pull deeply again on her nipple, pulling and releasing until he'd built a rhythm as raw and sensual as the feelings.

It was good. She wanted more. She wanted to burst.

He brushed the tears from her lashes. "See the power you've given me," he said, his voice roughening with passion. "I can make you weep with joy, or I can make you scream with pleasure. Which do you want more?"

"Either." She said it almost angrily. "Anything. *Everything*."

Pain or pleasure? She didn't know which it was that made her dig her fingernails into the flesh of his shoulder. His hand floated down the center of her belly to caress her naked mons, and she arched up, desperate for his touch. Her whole body lit up, and every nerve quivered. Every fiber ached.

She was barely able to hold herself still as his fingers played in her wetness. Her body went red with anticipation, blushing madly. His fingers glided up and down and around, joining her throbbing clitoris and her opening in a vibrant figure eight, until finally she begged him to enter her.

"Finger-fuck me," she whispered, barely able to make herself heard. He made her want to talk dirty and use words she'd never used with a man. He made her ask for what she wanted. God, that frightened her.

She burned with pleasure as he slid a finger inside. She writhed with sexual need, but it was the deep vulnerability she felt, the utter abandon, that brought tears to her eyes again.

"This is terrifying," she whispered.

He kissed her mouth and nipped her lower lip. "I'll spank you until you're hot enough to catch fire, and then I'll soothe you with kisses and whispers."

A thrill shot through her. She clutched inside, and her toes curled, echoing the sensations. She could feel herself getting wetter.

Her ass tingled as if he'd already laid a hand to her, and her stomach muscles jerked like high-tension wires. She couldn't take it. The throbbing was instant and intense. She'd had the same reaction at the club when the Marquis had taken her into the private room. Her body had gone nuts, and as hard as she'd fought for control, she'd lost it entirely. She'd never felt anything like that. It was too much.

Was this her professor's fault? Had he turned her into a discipline junkie with just a few horny suggestions breathed in her ear?

"What else do you fear?" he asked.

The lump in her throat made it difficult to talk, but she had vowed not to lie. And there was something else. "I'm afraid that I could need this too much."

"We fear most what we need most. It's a rule of life."

"No *way* do I need to be enslaved." Tess shook her head. Was he smiling? "Are you smiling? Why are you looking at me like that?"

"That's exactly what you do need," he said. "It may be the *only* thing you need."

A deep inner shiver touched her. It was almost painful. She wanted to deny what he'd said. She might have tried, vow or no vow, if she'd thought she could make him believe her.

"Undress," he ordered. "I want you totally naked."

Something in his voice put the fear of God in her. He was no longer the sensitive mentor, her patient and giving teacher. He was deadly serious. He fully intended to shake her to her core, reduce her to nothing.

"I need a minute," she said. Her chest felt odd, and it burned when she tried to breathe.

"I said *now*."

"No, really, I can't breathe." Suddenly in a panic, she scrambled around him and out of the bed, clutching the corset to her breasts. "There's something wrong."

He fell back, not looking at her. "You're not ready to be here. That's what's wrong."

"No, I am. I just need a min—"

"Obviously, you're not. If you're going to run away like a frightened child, then keep running."

Tess's voice was almost shrill. "Please understand what you're asking. I am frightened. Maybe you could—I need you to—"

"You need me to what?"

"Force me?" she said, her voice losing strength. She felt as if she'd somehow failed. "Don't give me a choice. If you want me to do this, you're going to have to force me. Make me do it, please."

"It doesn't work that way. This isn't about physical force."

She shook her head. "I'm sorry."

"Don't waste my time being sorry. Or yours. Just go. You're not ready."

Instantly, she was angry. "Waste your time?"

"You heard me."

"Waste your *time?* Fuck you! I'm not going anywhere."

He rolled up to look at her. "Good," he said softly.

She was breathing like a runner, staring at him in the darkness.

"It's not me you're angry at," he said. "You hate that you could respond the way you do. It's a part of you that you can't accept. There's so much you can't accept, Tess. You want to cut yourself off, and you think I won't let you. That's what you're afraid of."

She closed her eyes, but there was nowhere to hide.

"Now do what I said," he told her. "Strip. You're going to be punished for that act of rebellion."

A sigh came shaking out of her.

When her heart had quieted, she walked to the window and stood in the pool of muted light so that he could watch her take off her clothes. It was her first tribute.

The corset was already undone. All she had to do was peel it away and let it fall. She did so, shivering as cool air rushed over her flushed skin. As she stepped out of the black lace gown and kicked it away, he got out of the bed and came to her. He took her hand and drew her back into the darkness. He was naked, too. The low light revealed his muscular torso and runner's legs. His erection was a wonder to watch. She'd never seen such physical precision, such beauty.

It made her stomach knot, her legs ache.

She reached up to touch his mouth, but he caught her hand. Was she trying to feel the scar? Her curiosity wasn't totally assuaged?

"Off-limits," he said.

"That's not fair," she protested. "I really should know who I'm entrusting myself to."

"You do know."

She did. She'd always known. And it was what she wanted. "Take me to bed," she told him. "I want to be in bed with you as lovers."

"Tess, Tess, I give the orders. What do I have to do to get that through to you?"

He whipped her into his arms, hissing soft threats in her ear and messing her blond curls with his hungry hands. He aroused her in shocking ways with his voice alone. You are *a wanton little seductress at heart and you have made the dire mistake of seducing me. Now you will pay.* And he very nearly made her faint when he told her what was coming next.

Twenty

The feeling never went away. Weakness everywhere. It was beautiful. She loved being limp with passion, having no control whatsoever. Her body was limp, too. He had to pick her up and carry her. She could do nothing, not even hang on to him properly, and it was the purest sensation she'd ever experienced. The vibrations running through her felt like a never-ending chain of tiny orgasms, barely felt, and yet profound in their effect. Small, silent killers, she thought, robbing you of motor skills and speech, leaving you helpless, like ischemic strokes in the brain.

He was sitting next to her on the bed. She'd heard the springs sigh under his weight, and she'd swayed toward him when the mattress sank.

"Look at you," he said, "floating on the surface of the pond like a water lily. You can't be real."

He touched her breast, and she shuddered.

Her hands were flung over her head. She couldn't quite imagine herself having done that, having displayed herself like a voluptuary, but she liked the feeling. She was feeding on her own vulnerability, glorying in it. Nothing more thrilling and risky in life than this, which made it so deadly sweet. He could have done anything to her, anything, and she would have quaked like a new leaf, transparent and tender.

What did they call this? Swooning? She tried to imagine the expression on her face. It must have been Mona Lisa-esque. Now, perhaps she knew what that legendary secret smile meant. This delicious weakness. This utter abandon.

She'd never given over control to anyone, even during her wild days. That had been about power, never about pleasure. The only emotion she'd experienced was the delicious terror of breaking the rules, and a certain satisfaction that she had the boy's undivided attention, usually for as long as she wanted it. But it had seemed imperative to keep a tight leash on her responses, just as she'd always done. Defying her parents was reckless enough.

Now she couldn't control anything. She was bursting like a grape bursts in the mouth, between the teeth. She couldn't stop fizzing. Despite her weakness, the deeper vibrations never let up. The drones crowded around their fertile queen, thrumming like musical instruments. And that sharp light in her belly grew brighter with every breath.

"You haven't stopped trembling," he said. "I don't even have to touch you."

"I can't stop." She dropped her hand to where the light was brightest. "I'm lit up…in here."

He flattened her belly with his palm. "Here?" When he pressed down, the light scattered. Brightness everywhere. More bursting stars.

"Make me come," she whispered. The ache in her voice was palpable. She was a puppet and someone had taken hold of the strings. Her buttocks tightened and her spine arched. Her limbs danced helplessly.

"Not yet," he whispered back. "There's plenty of time for that."

He tried to calm her with his hands, but it was no good. Or maybe it was too good. He was everywhere, soothing her skin like a hot wind, tickling her thighs with his tongue, suckling her breast, kissing her mouth when she moaned. But at the very center of it all, she throbbed.

It wasn't what he did as much as the way she responded to it. She didn't understand the power. It took everything she had. Where did it go? Was her energy transferring to him? Was he becoming more powerful as she became weaker?

Perfect. He could be strong. He could have it all. Someone had to have strength because she had nothing. Nothing and everything.

He stretched out beside her, and she rolled into his arms, loving the heat of his body and the pounding erection that was caught between them. Soon she would have his hardened flesh inside her. They would be lovers in the bed. That was all she wanted. All.

"Take me inside," he said. "Show me what it feels like to be held from the inside out."

She opened herself to him as he moved over her, ready. Achingly ready. Enticingly fragrant with female juices. But once he was between her legs, with his hands on either side of her, he held himself at arm's length, gazing down at her for what seemed like forever. It was almost as if he was trying to imagine the experience of making love with starlight.

She rocked her hips, sliding her naked pussy along his shaft. The friction sent a fork of lightning through her. Blue-white and hot.

"Don't make me wait," she implored.

They never broke eye contact. Still braced high above her, he found her opening and eased himself inside her. An arc of energy connected their gaze, streaming through her mind and body, connecting their loins in a vibrant loop.

For several moments, he didn't touch her, other than to hold her with his eyes and his thrusting penis. As the pleasure mounted, she reached for him. The energy came from somewhere, but he'd drawn back, she realized. He was watching her, sheathed tightly in her body, and just watching her.

"Come with me," she said, meaning only that she wanted him to feel what she was feeling, to quake the way she did.

"Not yet. There'll be plenty of time for that."

He might be able to hold back, but she couldn't. "I think it's now or never." Her muscles tightened around her, forcing a hard sigh of pleasure through her clenched teeth. The release that shook her body was sharp, but incomplete, like a sluice gate opening, but only releasing enough of the pressure to sustain equilibrium.

"It can be much more than this," he said.

Still, it was beautiful, and she told him so.

"Only the beginning," he promised. "I'm going to make you my hostage, Tess."

"Never let me go."

"Never," he said. She touched his face, and he kissed her fingertips. "No matter where you are or who you're with, you will always be a hostage. *Mine.*"

When Tess opened her eyes, she was resting in the curve of his arm, and he was sitting above her, lying against the headboard, and caressing her hair. "Put yourself in my hands," he said. "If you can do that, if you can allow yourself to trust that deeply, it will change you."

"You're going to change me?"

"No, the experience will change you, but it takes more courage than most people have."

She sat up and faced him. Without a qualm, she held out her hands, crossed at the wrists.

"What are you doing?" he asked.

"I'm offering myself as your hostage."

Tess opened her eyes to suffocating darkness. Her eyelashes caught on fabric, reminding her that she was blindfolded. And bound. She was lying on her stomach, her hands behind her, tied securely and resting in the small of her back.

He was good with ropes. She had to think he'd had some practice, and on women. His Boy Scout leader probably hadn't taught him to tie feet such that when you release a certain knot, the still-bound ankles open, effectively creating shackles. She also doubted that he'd been taught to put a pillow under the tummy to ease the strain on the lower back.

Her back was fine. She would rather have risked the strain than have her naked booty waving in the air, but he'd insisted. And she wasn't about to buck the Fanny Master. Her term, not his.

She had no idea how long she'd been asleep. It was probably morning by now, and the thought of light flooding into the room made the prospect of her nakedness even less appealing, at least to her. She wasn't glorying in her vulnerability now.

She tested them, rotating her wrists and then her ankles.

"Good luck," he said. "Those knots could hold Houdini."

His calm voice frightened her badly. "Why didn't you tell me you were in the room?" she snapped.

"Watch your tone, young lady. You're primed for some corporal punishment, and I'm just the man to do it."

Tess felt a hand on her ass, and she jumped like a startled cat. She'd known he was close, but not that close.

"Do you want to be paddled or petted?" he said.

"Petted."

"In that case—"

"Ouch!" The smack he gave her stung like nettles. She bit back the fiery epithet on her tongue. It didn't do him justice, anyway.

"Pink is your color," he said, laughing softly.

"Black could be yours. If my hands were free, I'd aim straight for your eye."

She winced, preparing herself for another whack, but instead she felt something light and feathery tickle her smarting skin.

He leaned close enough to whisper in her ear. "If I haven't told you before that you have one beautiful ass, let me apologize now."

"Well, you can just kiss my beautiful ass," she whispered back.

"With pleasure."

Tess bit down on her lower lip as he caressed her extremely bare and vulnerable bottom. It had to be his lips gliding over her. All she could do was feel—and it was intense. He didn't miss an inch of her tingling skin.

He'd tied her so that he could open her legs, and she made no attempt to resist him. She wasn't that foolish. This was too incredible anyway. She fought to breathe as his hand slid between her legs. The first contact with his fingers told her that she was burning hot. Ringing wet.

How was it possible to be this aroused?

She didn't understand that. Or how he could slide in a finger and caress her with his thumb at the same time, but it was happening, all of it. The twofold stimulation sent her into throes of ecstasy. She arched her back, offering herself, wanting more, but suddenly he was gone.

"Why did you stop?" she gasped.

"You're getting too close."

"I want to get close. I want to get all the way *there*."

"No."

"No? Are you going to tell me I'm not ready? Are you going to do that again?"

"Readiness is a state of mind, not body."

"Would you stop with the freaking platitudes?"

"Sure, I'll stop. Happy to."

Chilly air touched the spot where his hand had been. She heard him turn and walk to the door. "Are you leaving? Don't leave!"

Quietly, he said, "Are you going to ask nicely?"

She forced herself to breathe deeply, to calm down. "Please...please stay."

She was still shaking by the time he got back to the bed, part of it anger, part of it raging sexual arousal.

"You're fighting me every inch of the way, Tess. And you're fighting yourself." His voice was heavy, harsh. "Are you listening?"

She didn't respond, but the quiet was soon broken by the creak of springs and the slanting mattress. He was on the bed with her, though she wasn't sure of his position. He wasn't lying down, and he didn't seem to be sitting.

She felt his hand in her hair, drawing her head back. His breath hissed lightly against her mouth as he whispered, "Are you listening now, Tess? Remember that baby swat I gave you? There's more where that came from.

Want to be a smart-ass? Then your ass is going to smart—
and that's not all."

She was dealing with the devil again. What had happened to the wise, understanding mentor? She wanted
him back.

He released her hair, making Tess think he was going
to walk out on her again. That would have been worse
than the punishment, she realized, although she didn't
know why.

"I'm listening!" she said.

After a moment, he spoke in a firm and unwavering
tone. "I'll tell you when you're ready. Then, and only
then, are you allowed to have an orgasm. You will come
when I tell you."

"But— What if it just happens?"

"Don't let it."

"You can't be serious! Why are you doing this to me?"

"Stroke me," he said, "and see what *you've* done to me."

She didn't know what he meant, so he showed her.

Tess's last impression was the burning silk of his shaft
as he knelt next to her on the bed and guided one of her
bound hands over him. He was roped with swollen veins
and vibrating with tension.

For some time after he left, she breathed in shaking
gulps of air, painfully aware of how easily he could have
released her with that stunningly hard organ of his.

"Whatever you do, Tess Wakefield, do not have an
orgasm."

Had she actually said that out loud? Tess tried to open

her eyes but her lids were uncontrollable. They quivered and drooped, too heavy to lift. God, she must be glowing like a beacon. They were lighting her up from the inside, crackling like the filaments of a neon tube.

Had he heard her? What would he do? Take it as a challenge and increase the pressure? Or lighten it and drive her utterly mad? It wouldn't take much. He could so easily sweep her up and fling her over the edge.

With one finger.

With his breath on her aching nipple.

A feather stroke.

Why didn't he get it over with? Why did he leave her alone for so long? He came when she least expected him and touched her in intimate places. One finger gliding through her wetness, and then he was gone. The way a child steals icing from a cake.

Two fingers rolling her nipple.

Tight and tender.

Teeth on her ass.

How long had he been doing that? Hours? Days? She didn't know anymore.

But he didn't know how strong she was, how ardently she had fought to take back control of her life. She could not be broken, even if it was joy that poured from the cracks.

Someone was laughing, shaking with laughter. Him? No, it was her. Tears soaked her face and salted her tongue.

Was he even there? Or was she imagining a lover worthy of the Marquis de Sade? A demon with the patience for whatever time it took.

Was any of this really happening? The water dripping on her body, splashing between her legs and becoming more intense with each drop. It was a torrent now. She was becoming the water, flowing, dripping, melting like a glacier in spring.

She forced her eyes open and saw them staring back at her. Eyes. Everywhere. Hypnotic and black as cherries. Her own eyes, heavy with sexual desire. Begging. Release me. Don't let me writhe and thrash like this, helpless. Electrical current grounds me. Lust cracks me like a whip. You made me this, a whore for pleasure, but I will fight you to prove that I'm not. And I will win.

"Put your hands against the wall. Spread your legs."

Was that his voice? Was he speaking to her? Was that his hand on her naked flank?

Oh, God, no. Another touch. Another feather stroke, and she would be gone. Shattered.

She was ready to climb out of her own body, shed it like a snake, anything to escape him. She grabbed hold of the metal bars, quivering, waiting for pleasure that was unbearable. It took her all the way to heaven and back. All the way to hell. She could not let go. She would shatter into pieces.

One touch and he would break her in half.

Whatever you do, Tess Wakefield, do not—

"I'm not ready!"

He laughed. "Yes, you are."

"No, it's too late. I can't."

"You can do anything, Tess. You're more ready than anyone I've ever known. I would give my soul to have what you have."

"What is that?"

"A flame that nothing can extinguish. You surrender everything, and yet you conquer. It's humbling to watch."

He wasn't even inside her as he spoke. He wasn't physically a part of her, but he was everywhere. He was everywhere.

A feather stroke, and Tess was gone. Every sense was blinded. Every thought was erased. A feather stroke, and she ceased to exist. She was a mote in the eye of God, a ship on the horizon, a child being born.

The catharsis stripped her to her core, just as he'd said it would. She had no idea how long it lasted, but she could easily have flown to the stars and back. She'd never felt anything like this. It was liberating, cleansing. She must be changing in every cell of her body. Altered forever. How could she not be?

"It's cold." His voice was low and somehow sad. "Let's get some clothes on you."

She *was* cold. She could feel the gooseflesh crawling up her back, but she didn't understand why he didn't come to the bed with her this time. He'd walked in moments ago and put the black lace nightgown in her hands. It would hardly keep her warm.

She stared in the direction of his voice. He'd released the ropes when he'd had her brace herself against the wall, but he'd never removed the blindfold, and he'd told her not to, either.

"What's the point of getting dressed?" she asked. "I'm not going anywhere."

"It's time, Tess."

"Time for what? I told you I'm not going anywhere." She thrust out her hands. "Here! Tie me up."

"Tess, put on the nightgown and rest a while. I'll come back."

"No, dammit. Do it!"

Her arms were rigidly extended, and finally she heard a resigned sigh. She felt the nightgown being drawn over her head, and she cooperated with him in getting it on, but when he was done, she thrust her hands out again.

"You don't need ropes anymore," he said.

"I *want* them."

"All right." He tied them loosely, and then looped another rope around her ankles. She could have kicked it off.

"Now, compose yourself," he said. "I'll be back."

"No, wait, stay with me a little longer, tell me about yourself. Is this your house?" She searched frantically for some way to engage him in conversation. "I saw a grave outside, a headstone. Is that someone you—"

He made a strange sound, as if he was choking, and she caught herself, aware that it might be something he couldn't deal with. "I'm sorry. Don't go yet, please."

But he did go. She heard the door close, and she collapsed on the bed, despairing. What was happening? What would become of her? Eventually, she fell into a restless, aching sleep and woke up, still blindfolded. Still vibrating. She didn't care. All she could think about was when he would come to her next.

Tess started at the sound of the door opening. A painful shock ran through her. Deep vaginal muscles rippled and cramped, aching sweetly in anticipation. He was here.

When he left the last time, she'd curled up on the bed, facing the door. Now she tried to calm herself as she waited for him. But she wasn't calm. She was desperate. "I thought you were never coming back," she said.

He didn't answer.

She tried to track his footsteps, but they seemed to be going off in another direction. Suddenly she felt his weight on the bed behind her, and she panicked. He'd gone around to the other side of the bed. What was he doing back there?

She felt something tug at her wrists. He was untying her, swiftly, and with great ease. He was good at ropes. When her hands and feet were undone, he loosened the blindfold, but it didn't fall away from her eyes.

Tess lay on the bed, unmoving. She felt the mattress recoil and knew he'd risen. "Why are you doing this?" she asked. "Is the time up?"

She heard him come around the bed and stop in front of her. He removed the blindfold from her eyes, but Tess couldn't see anything for several seconds. Her brain seemed to be struggling to process images. She'd been blindfolded for several hours, but it was probably something else. Exhaustion. Shock.

She saw nothing but scattered dots. But gradually they began to coalesce into a face, a body, and Tess was staring at the unsmiling countenance of her captor. Her mouth went dry. Her chest began to hurt, as if she'd swallowed something too large, and it had caught beneath her breastbone, a burning lump.

"It was you?" she finally said.

The Marquis' expression was neutral. Kind, but neutral. "You thought it was someone else?"

Her disappointment was so sharp she couldn't answer. Obviously, she had thought that. She'd bonded with a man she believed was Danny, and that bond had gone much deeper than she'd realized until this very moment. She was a little old to be struggling with loss of innocence, but that's what it felt like. It hurt like that. It wasn't possible to give yourself to someone, even to an experience, the way she had, and not become attached in some essential way.

It was like Siamese twins, joined by a vital organ. Danny *was* the experience. She couldn't separate him from what had happened to her any more than she could separate him from every strange and exquisite sensation.

But now she wanted to.

He'd been right, she realized. There was nothing left. She'd given it all, but to the wrong man, a Las Vegas magician, a circus act. She felt horribly betrayed, but she didn't know who had done it. Was it him or her own senses? He'd said she was a flame that couldn't be extinguished. He'd said things that touched her and opened her up. They *mattered*.

She couldn't imagine the Marquis saying those things. It hadn't sounded like his voice in that bedroom, but maybe her senses had been playing tricks the whole time. From beginning to end, the club experience had been hallucinatory. She'd seen bizarre visions and heard strange whispers in the music. How could she be sure whose voice she'd heard in this bedroom? She might not have recognized her own voice.

She bowed her head, unable to fathom her reaction. She couldn't even seem to comprehend that her hands and feet were free. What had he done to her? She couldn't move. She was destroyed. It was the Stockholm syndrome, where captives confuse gratitude with love, but she had thought he was Danny. There was no getting around that now.

Her whole body ached as she sat up. She was just beginning to comprehend what she'd done, how she'd flung herself into something without knowing the risks, without even knowing her partner—and it frightened her. Really, it was terrifying how narrow her escape had been. She'd begged him to tie her up, to let her stay. What if he'd taken her up on it? Anything could have happened. She could be dead.

"I think I need to get out of here," she said. "I *do* need to."

He shrugged, but there was a hint of surprise in his voice. "Of course, that's what you do. You run away. Apparently you've learned nothing about yourself. Sad, really."

"I need to stop doing things that make me want to run away. That's what I've learned."

It was daylight now, and the room was clearly lit. Tess moved to the edge of the bed, dropped her legs over and looked around. The bedroom had more color than the rest of the house, but it was mostly as white as the ground outside. There was a colorful modern painting on the wall with lots of red accents, but that was about all Tess could take in. No torture devices. Interesting.

The Marquis was quite a contrast to the decor in his typical head-to-toe black. This time he was wearing boots, jeans and a loose silk shirt. Her heart began to ping as she scrutinized him more closely. He did not have long hair.

"When you're ready," he said. "I'll be downstairs."

"I told you, I'm going home."

"Of course, I'll have the driver take you. There's a bathroom through that doorway." He pointed toward a room of black marble, trimmed in white "You'll love the tub," he said. "Take your time."

He left her alone, and Tess went to the bathroom where she found a large shopping bag with her clothes, her purse and her other belongings. She began scrambling to get the jeans and sweater on. She wasn't taking a shower. All she wanted to do was leave and never see this place or him again.

Minutes later she headed down the stairs and into the kitchen, where she saw him adding fresh water to the roses.

"I suppose I should thank you for the flowers," she said.

"You could, but they aren't from me."

"Really? Who are they from?"

He touched the card. "It's made out to you. It's not signed, but there's a message. Shall I read it to you?"

She shook her head. No more confusion. She wanted to stop the hallucinations, not make them worse. It wasn't Danny. She'd been stupid and foolish, but this wasn't the first time. That was all she needed to know.

"When can I go?" she asked.

"Whenever you like. The car's warming up in the garage."

She turned to leave, never expecting to see him again.

"What about our business deal?" he said. "Off or on?"

"Our business deal." She almost laughed the thought was so ludicrous. "Someone will be in touch."

Twenty-One

Tess's cell phone began ringing almost as soon as she plugged it into the charger. She'd walked into her apartment only ten minutes ago, after being left off downstairs by the Marquis' driver. The first thing she'd done was plug in her cell. The *last* thing she wanted to do now was answer it.

It was probably Andy calling, frantic that she'd disappeared. It pained her that she couldn't pick up the phone and let him know she was all right, but she needed a little more time. She was still too scattered.

She'd had the limo ride to try and make sense of the last few days, but much of it eluded her. Even so, the ride had been oddly cathartic because she'd come to a surprising conclusion. She didn't have any regrets. She'd felt profoundly shocked and betrayed, and a little foolish for having been so fixated on the man being Danny. But right now she wasn't certain it mattered who he was. It was the utter bliss of letting go that resonated in her mind.

Even the risk she'd taken didn't seem so frightening. It actually made sense if you applied the stock market's risk-reward ratio, which was what Tess had found herself doing. Less emotionally guarded people probably got all the reward they needed from taking small, sane risks, like expressing anger to a loved one or revealing hidden emotional needs. But Tess had had to rip open the seams she'd sewn and resewn all her life. Her risk had to be as great as her need to protect herself, which was huge.

Now she had to deal with the fallout.

Her cell phone sat silently on the writing desk, no longer vibrating like a battery-operated toy. It had stopped ringing, and she hadn't even noticed. Her relief was so sharp it hurt.

Now, what was her next move? Coffee? A shower? Something simple to ground her and bring her back to reality before the world crashed in on her?

She went to the apartment's small golden-maple kitchen and took a bag of dark French roast from the re-frigerator. Decaf. She didn't need jangling nerves right now. As she spooned the fine-drip grind into a ten-cup pot that had come with the furnished apartment, she thought about the firing squad she would have to face to-morrow.

Somehow she had to explain her absence to Erica's sat-isfaction, and Tess didn't have the heart for more lies and excuses. It had even occurred to her that she should offer to resign. She wasn't giving everything she had to the job, and she couldn't take the title, the salary and the perks, and not give it her all. That wasn't the way she did things.

Also, she may have jeopardized the ad campaign for a major account, and she'd just gotten the company's star player fired. She wasn't doing Pratt-Summers any favors, even she could see that. Maybe she wouldn't be given the opportunity to resign.

Abruptly, Tess set the coffee measure down. The cell phone. How long had it been since she'd listened to her messages? Just a few days ago, that would have been the first thing she'd done. She would have played them back in the limo.

Moments later, standing by the apartment's bay window, she hurried to get through a voice-mail box full of messages, most of them from Andy, exhorting her to call him back. In one of the messages, he admitted to panicking when he didn't hear from her, and calling the club directly. He said he'd spoken with the Marquis, who told him that Tess couldn't be disturbed but refused to explain why.

That was last night, Tess realized as she replayed the message and listened to the time it had come in. It sounded as if Andy had been speaking to the Marquis at the club at the same time the Marquis was supposed to have been with Tess at the house in the birch forest.

Tess's thoughts began to back up and collide with each other. There was too much conflicting information, and she didn't have the energy to sort it out. But one disturbing thought stayed with her as she saved the message, promising herself that she would play it again later. She couldn't dismiss the possibility that someone was playing a very elaborate game with her.

Andy also left her several updates on the Faustini account, one explaining that he and Carlotta had mapped out some great new locations, and gotten Gina Faustini's okay to use them. That was a huge relief to Tess. It sounded as if the campaign might be salvaged after all. But the news about Brad Hayes wasn't good. Not good at all. Andy's last message said that Brad had already gone to Erica with his suspicions about Tess. No one had been able to talk him out of it.

Tess was numb as she hit the Off button. He'd already gone to Erica? It had never occurred to her he would take it that far. She stared out the window for several moments, wondering how she was going to defend herself. Surely Erica wouldn't believe Brad's crazy accusations, but even if she didn't, they were more proof that Tess had failed as a team leader. She hadn't secured the club as a location, and one of the team's key members had accused her of immoral behavior, of criminal acts.

This was more surreal than where she'd just been.

Tess dropped the phone on the window ledge, barely aware as it tumbled off and landed on the carpet. She went over the details of the sabotage in her mind, step by step, including her attempts to investigate the thefts, but nothing stood out. No one's behavior struck her as unusually suspicious in retrospect, even Brad's. More than likely, he was simply defending a mentor he idolized.

Eventually Tess began to realize that the only way to

prove her innocence was to find the guilty party. All the evidence had pointed to Danny, but something Mitzi said when Tess last spoke with her had just come back. Mitzi had inadvertently revealed a secret about one of Danny's coworkers, and Tess was very curious about what she'd meant.

But there was something else Tess had to do first. She dreaded the thought, but given Andy's messages, she had no choice.

"Were Danny and Carlotta ever lovers?" Tess sat on the window ledge in her office, her back to a skyline that glistened like quicksilver under the icy morning sunshine. More snow was predicted, but Tess's mind wasn't on the weather.

"You didn't know?" Andy stepped back to appraise the cat whiskers he'd just drawn on the nose of the Messerschmitt with a black felt tip pen. He and Tess had already checked the nose cone and the heating vent for the security cameras Barb MacDonald installed. Apparently they'd been removed while Tess was away.

"It's part of the Pratt-Summer's legend," Andy said. "Carlotta was madly in love with Danny, and he threw her over for Erica. Yup, there was one big nasty love triangle here at the agency. Happened a couple years ago. Everybody knows about it."

"Where have *I* been?" Tess had only heard the rumors about Erica.

"Talking to the wrong people, I guess."

Tess had been talking to Mitzi, who knew everything and said nothing.

"So, Carlotta was a woman scorned? Did she retaliate?" Tess looked at her watch for the zillionth time. She had a meeting with Erica in a few minutes, and she was sick to her stomach. Obviously, a bad case of nerves, but she had cramps too—and a serious need for some Midol. Her period had started this morning, to her great surprise and relief. Maybe her body had decided to function normally again.

"Well, that's the sad part," Andy said. "Apparently, Carlotta turned all that scorn inward and became self-destructive. The way I hear it, she'd probably be dead if not for Barb MacDonald."

Tess's head snapped back up. "Barb MacDonald? How does she figure into this?"

"Where *have* you been? Barb and Carlotta are friends. Carlotta got Barb her job here. I guess they've known each other all their lives—grew up together, went to school, the usual female-bonding stuff."

"Friends?" Tess said. "Just friends? Or something more?"

Andy looked pained. "Don't be silly. Carlotta's hot for me." He slipped the pen in the pocket of his denim shirt, apparently satisfied with his desecration of her decor.

"Maybe, but it sounds like Barb was hot for *her.*"

"Hey, Carlotta's not gay. Trust me, I'd know."

He winked, but Tess stopped him with a head shake. "Not a word about your sex life, Andy. My stomach isn't up to it this morning."

His shrug said it was her loss. "I know nothing about

Barb's sexual preferences, but she's a lioness to Carlotta's cub. Fiercely protective. Rumor has it she thought Carlotta was being taken for granted by Erica—and she was furious when Carlotta didn't get your job."

"Carlotta didn't seem too happy about that, either." Tess was still trying to put this together with what Mitzi had said, and possibly the sabotage. "How does Carlotta feel about Danny now?"

"She's so over him." He grinned and raked a hand through his dark curls. "She's got me."

"How about Barb? Danny must have been on her shit list."

"It would figure, especially since Carlotta had been carrying a torch for Danny for years, and she went a little nuts when he blew her off. She became obsessed with her looks and had one plastic surgery after another, trying to lure him away from Erica."

What a waste, Tess thought, that a beautiful, talented woman would mutilate herself, thinking that could make a man care about her.

"One of the operations, a tummy tuck, nearly killed her," Andy added. "Barb nursed her back to health."

Mitzi's reference made sense now. *You're the only person who'd want to hurt him, except maybe Carlotta, but that was a long time ago.*

Not that long ago, Tess thought.

"What's so fascinating about your watch?" Andy wanted to know. "You haven't taken your eyes off it since I got here."

Tess rose from the window ledge. "I have a meeting

with Erica. Do I look all right?" She was wearing a black wool pantsuit with a wide pinstripe and a silk man-tailored blouse. Elegant yet somber, an advertising professional in mourning for her job.

"I like the lines," he said. "Sexy. Are you going to tell Erica the real story about your escapade at the Marquis Club?"

Tess hadn't told anyone the real story, including Andy. She wasn't sure she knew the real story herself, but she was tempted to ask Andy about his phone conversation with the Marquis the night she was supposed to have been with the Marquis at his estate. It had been on her mind ever since she heard Andy's message. As much as she wanted to verify the time and what was said, she wasn't ready to open herself for questions.

"Actually, I'm going to offer Erica my resignation," Tess said.

"What do you mean *resignation?*" Erica Summers stood in the doorway of Tess's office, her eyebrows arched in disbelief. "What kind of chickenshit idea is that?"

Tess was truly taken aback. "I just thought—"

"You thought *what?*"

Erica marched on in, and Andy wedged past her to the door. "Just leaving," he said, flashing her a giddy smile. "Nice to see you again. You too, Tess. Glad you're back."

And out the door he went.

Chickenshit, thy name is Andy Phipps.

Tess took a breath—and then she took charge. It must have been survival instincts at work. Erica might be on the rampage but Tess had little to lose at this point.

"Please, have a seat," she said, indicating one of the guest chairs in front of her desk.

Erica cocked a hip and planted a hand on it. She was as stunning as always in a lime green skirt and sweater, but Tess noticed the smudges of purple beneath her eyes and the deepening lines of fatigue. She did not look well.

"Could we get to the point?" Erica asked.

"Of course. I thought you might want to bring Danny back, and it would be easier if I weren't here."

"And that's a reason to resign?"

"One of the reasons," Tess said, hesitating. The rest was very hard to admit, but there was no point in sugar-coating it now. "It's pretty obvious I'm not doing the job I was hired to do. My leadership skills stink, and I'm not focused on the campaign. I'm not giving it my best, and I'm not used to giving anything less."

"I see."

Fear gripped Tess in that second. She had no idea what Erica was going to say next, and the thought of being fired was paralyzing. Apparently she did have something to lose. A sense of pride in her achievements, undoubtedly— and in her rapid ascent to the top. This would be her first professional setback, and it was a big one.

"Trust me, Danny won't come back, and even if I wanted him to, that doesn't let you off the hook. You have a commitment to this agency, Tess, and a mess to clean up as well. If you take the easy way out, you won't be working at Pratt-Summers, or anywhere in this city. I'll see to that."

"I'm sure you will," Tess said softly. She didn't like

being threatened. It made her wonder whether Erica wanted a commitment or the opportunity to exact punishment, but Tess had already made up her mind. She needed some time. She did have a mess to clean up—and her own name to clear. If Erica wouldn't give her the space to do that then Tess's answer would be no.

She had the letter of resignation ready in her drawer, and she would hand it to Erica, pack up her things and leave.

"Andy, hurry up! It's freezing in here."

Tess struggled to steady the chair as Andy climbed up onto its back. His tennis shoes clung to the chair's narrow metal framework, putting him just high enough to pull off the heating vent grate and look inside. He wasn't much taller than Tess, but he'd been elected to do the dirty work because he wasn't wearing good clothes, and she was.

The grate came off in his hands with a terrible screech, spewing dust and corrosion everywhere. Andy began to cough and the chair wobbled. Tess climbed up on the seat and pushed on his butt to anchor him.

"Can you see anything?" she asked.

"You mean through a foot-thick cloud of toxic waste? Why is it so damn cold in this place?"

"Barb claims the thermostat is broken, but I have my doubts. That's why we're here, Andy. You have to get a good look inside that vent."

"Easy for you to say!"

Tess and Andy were in Barb MacDonald's office, following up on Tess's latest hunch. The puzzle pieces had started coming together during her talk with Andy this morning, and by the time she'd finished with Erica, Tess had been almost certain what her next step should be. Of course, she couldn't do anything until Barb had left for the day.

Andy rose on tiptoe and peered into the opening.

"Bingo," he said softly. "Somebody's been using this place for storage."

He reached inside and pulled out a very dusty PDA. Her PDA.

Tess allowed herself a smile. She wanted to scream, but she couldn't let herself get that excited yet. "I thought so," she said.

The next thing he handed her was a grungy file folder. Tess opened it, saw her missing pitch notes and swore with glee.

"That's it," he said. "We found the smoking gun. Now get me off these stilts."

Tess helped him down—and smothered him with a huge hug. When she released him, they were both coated with pale powder. "How can I ever thank you for helping me solve this?" she asked him.

"Feel free to grab my ass anytime. That's thanks enough."

Their conversation this morning had made her realize that Barb may have had a stronger motive than Carlotta. Obsession. She'd not only been Carlotta's protector, but her avenging angel. And Barb's icy office had been another tip-off. The offices all had similar heating vents, and Tess knew Barb had hidden a security camera in the vent in her office. It seemed likely she might hide something in her own.

Tess set the crumpled folder on Barb's desk, aware that it was now evidence. "This is why her office feels like a meat locker. The file wouldn't let any heat through."

"It was Barb all along," Andy said, awe creeping into his voice. "And her goal was to frame Danny?"

"Obviously, but she probably wanted to get rid of me, too, and conveniently open the way for Carlotta to take my place. With Danny and me both gone, who else could Erica give the job to?"

"I wonder if Carlotta was in on it, too." Andy sounded dejected.

"And which one of them planted the drugs."

"What drugs?" Andy asked.

Tess had been thinking aloud, and she quickly dismissed the question as confusion on her part. Andy didn't know what she was talking about because Tess and Erica had agreed to keep silent about Tess's clandestine trip to Danny's condo. They hadn't told anyone else, including the police, and Tess didn't see any reason to tell Andy now. But she hadn't forgotten about the prescription bottle with the label torn off.

Even if Carlotta was involved, Tess had to assume that Barb did most of the dirty work. Carlotta wouldn't have had the skills for computer sabotage, whereas Barb was an expert. And whether she'd operated alone or not, Barb had gone to great lengths to accomplish her plan.

In addition to stealing Tess's PDA and computer file,

she'd broken into Danny's computer, created a password that only Tess could figure out, then told Tess about the interlocking PGP security program, apparently hoping that Tess would go to Danny's place to search for the file that was the key.

It really didn't hit Tess until that very moment what she and Andy had just done. They'd cleared her name, but that wasn't what rocked her. She grabbed the chair Andy had been standing on and sat down, raising a cloud of dust.

"Danny didn't do it," she said under her breath.

The following morning, Pratt-Summers was host to two of New York City's finest. The police detectives awaited Barb MacDonald in her office, armed with Tess and Andy's evidence, and within a half hour of Barb's arrival, she'd confessed to everything—and exonerated Carlotta, whom she swore knew nothing about her scheme.

Andy was hyper and wanted to get the team together for a celebratory lunch, but after watching the detectives take Barb away for questioning, Tess wasn't in the mood to celebrate. She also had more questions that needed answering, so she sent Andy off to find Carlotta and give her the news. And Tess went in search of the one person she hoped could put her remaining questions to rest.

Tess found Mitzi pondering the deep-sea mural in the hallway on the twenty-eighth floor. Tess had stopped by the washroom first and been startled to see Mitzi's display of products dismantled. Her stool was gone, too. A moment of raw panic had gripped Tess. No one had said anything about Mitzi leaving. Surely Andy would have mentioned it. Mitzi had been here longer than anyone else, probably even Erica.

Tess hesitated, not wanting to interrupt the other woman's meditation but tremendously relieved to see her. And concerned at the same time. Something wasn't right here.

While Tess waited, she noticed the sleek killer whale and the frolicking brown-eyed seal. The former bore a striking resemblance to Erica, and the latter looked like Jan Butler. Tess spotted Barb McDonald, too. She was the octopus.

Finally, Mitzi looked over her shoulder and nodded a greeting.

"Do you know who painted the mural?" Tess asked.

"The mermaid over here." Mitzi stepped over to a shimmering green creature with feathery tail fins and a seductive smile.

Tess recognized the facial features as Carlotta's. If she was the artist, that probably explained the octopus and the killer whale.

Tess tapped the dolphin, whose human face had Danny's features.

Both women were silent until finally Mitzi said, "It's not the same without him."

"Do you have any idea where he is?" Tess asked.

"Exactly where he chooses to be, I hope."

"Mitzi, I have to find him. It's important." Tess grasped the other woman's hand and turned her around. "Is he at the Marquis Club? I know he's involved there somehow."

Tess squeezed her hand. "Is that his secret?"

Mitzi looked surprised. She quickly averted her eyes, and Tess knew she'd struck a chord.

"I saw you there too," Tess said, "in the Hypnosis Parlor. I know it was you."

Mitzi jerked her hand away. "So, I was there," she said. "I work there some nights, and I tell people it's the theater. That's not a crime."

She started down the hallway, as if to get away from Tess but unable to make much progress. Her gait was too uncertain.

Tess followed her helplessly. "Of course it's not a crime, I—"

Mitzi whirled, her voice an emphatic whisper. "It isn't the club," she said, pulling Tess into a doorway alcove. "Danny's an investor there or something, but that's not what I meant when I told you he had a secret."

Danny was an investor there? Tess's heart lurched painfully. It seemed more and more likely that he could have been involved in her initiation, as the Marquis had called it, but the only man she'd actually seen at any point was the Marquis. Could she have been with both men? Her head began to spin, drowning her in terrible confusion. She couldn't let herself get mired in that now.

"So, I could find him at the club?" she asked Mitzi.

"No, don't go back there. He's not there."

"His condo then? Please, tell me. Is it drugs? Is that his secret? Because I found these in his place." Tess drew the capsule from the pocket of her jacket.

Mitzi grabbed it as if to shield it from prying eyes. Heat reddened her face. Tess couldn't tell if she was angry or embarrassed.

"These aren't Danny's," she said. "They're Erica's."

"Erica's?"

Mitzi slipped the pill into her purse. "It isn't Danny who has the problem with pills. It's Erica. She's been on painkillers for years—an injury when she was in college, competing as a gymnast."

"But Danny was involved with her, right? Romantically?"

"Yes, before he knew about her problem. When he found out she was using, he gave her an ultimatum. She could use or she could lose."

"Lose what?"

"Him, as her creative director. He told her if she didn't quit the pills, he'd quit the agency. She went to rehab and stopped using altogether until a few months ago. That's when he found her with a bottle of pills in her hand and took them away from her."

"How do you know all this about him?"

"Maybe he'll tell you that. I can't."

"But you will tell me where he is."

Mitzi took a card and a pen from her purse. She scribbled an address and a phone number on the card and gave it to Tess. "This is the most likely place. If he's not there, I don't know where he is."

"Thank you," Tess said. "Really, Mitzi, thank you."

Mitzi shook her head. "I'm not sure I'm doing either one of you any favors, especially Danny. He's already lost too much already."

Tess had a feeling Mitzi didn't mean his job, but she didn't press. "Are you leaving Pratt-Summers?" she asked.

"For a while. I need a vacation."

"But you'll be back, right?"

"We'll see. It feels different around here."

Tess felt a welling sadness as she realized this place was changing and would never be the same. One of its institutions was gone and another soon would be. She had the feeling Mitzi's vacation would be a long one.

It was no accident that Tess was a half hour early for her one o'clock appointment with Danny Gabriel. She'd called him right after her meeting with Mitzi, and even though he'd sounded surprised, he'd agreed to see her today. And now, here she was, standing at his front door, under the cover of the porte cochere, and hoping he wasn't quite ready. That way she might be left on her own long enough to have a look around.

It wasn't just déjà vu at work as she rang the doorbell of the spectacular glass structure that apparently belonged to Danny rather than the Marquis. She had been here before. This was the house where she'd been taken hostage and turned into a veritable sex slave, albeit voluntarily.

Tess's head was swimming with questions, and she'd come to get answers, one way or another. But she also had another purpose for the visit, which felt more important to her right now.

Frosty air jetted from her lungs in shallow breaths, giving away her nerves as she pressed his doorbell again. But it surprised her how little it mattered to her that he might see her this way, anxious. No more lies, she thought. It made life so easy. It might even be the antidote to tranquilizers, antidepressants and booze.

Huddling in her pinstripe pantsuit and too-thin quilted coat, she wondered what she would do if no one answered. She'd let the taxi go, and it was too cold to wait outside for long. Most of yesterday's snow was already gone, but more had been predicted, and Tess was beginning to imagine herself as an ice sculpture in his entranceway.

She pressed the doorbell once more, and then she tried the door handle, surprised when it gave. "Hello?" she called out as she let herself into the foyer. Certainly, he'd understand that she had to get out of the cold.

She got no response, and as she entered the wide-open ground-floor area with its marble tiles and pristine white furniture, she sensed that she was alone in the house. It had that same still feeling as when she'd been here before.

She shivered, resisting memories that were too fresh and raw.

"Hello?" she called again, wondering if he'd decided not to meet with her after all. She couldn't imagine why his door would be unlocked, especially if he'd left the house, unless he'd been in such a hurry he'd forgotten. But that made no sense, either. There was no need to disappear. He could have refused to meet with her.

The bouquet of red roses was no longer on the counter. It was the first thing Tess noticed as she crossed the expansive living area on a diagonal path to the kitchen. She glanced at her watch, checking the time, and then she turned back toward the spiral stairs, wondering if she dare go up there.

Moments later, she was on the second floor, checking the media room and the bedrooms. She opened the doors very carefully but found no one inside and nothing unusual until she reached the room nearest the master. It was a child's room, she realized, a young girl's, judging by the decor.

Tess hadn't been able to see in the rooms the night she was here. It had been too dark, but now light flooded through the sheer lace curtains, illuminating the canopy bed and the doll collection arranged on the white wicker dresser.

But what caught Tess's eye was the poster hanging on the wall opposite the bed. It was a girl on a swing, and Tess had seen it before, singled out from all the other ads on a separate wall of Danny's office. Because it wasn't an ad, she realized.

Her heart began to pound. She turned and hurried out of the room. Once she was downstairs, she looked for a back door to let her out, but there was nothing but glass. Damn impenetrable glass. A prison of it. There had to be a way to get to the birch forest behind the house.

She found the door in the first garage.

It was an icy and treacherous walk to the birch trees, and Tess was wearing sky-high Faustini boots. They would almost certainly be ruined by the time she was done, but that was the last thing on her mind. Nor did she give a thought to her favorite suit as she finally found the grave she'd seen out here.

She knelt next to the headstone, scraping enough snow to read the inscription. It was a child's grave just as she suspected. *Dorie Gabriel*. She'd died four years ago, and she'd been just three years old.

"What the hell are you doing out here?"

The bellowing voice nearly knocked Tess off balance. She looked up to see the driver who'd kidnapped her standing in the open garage doorway. She didn't have a chance to answer him. He sprinted over and grabbed her by the arm, pulling her away from the grave.

Tess fought to keep her balance, but the boots wouldn't hold her, and she sprawled to the ground. As the driver pulled her to her feet, Danny appeared in the doorway, his long dark hair flying around his clenched face. He had a red rose in one hand, but he didn't look like a man bearing gifts. He looked angry. Very angry.

Twenty-Two

Tess's arms burned from the driver's grip. He pulled her to her feet and held her as Danny strode toward them. Tess wondered if Danny was going to get physical. She was actually frightened for a moment.

"Let go of her," Danny told the driver. His voice was measured, but his eyes were shards of ice.

The other man released Tess, and she nearly went down again. A blast of adrenaline turned her legs to rubber and the ground to a skating rink. She made it to a patch of grass, and when she looked up, Danny had transferred his angry glare to the driver. He was haranguing him about manhandling women and bullying guests.

Gradually, Tess realized it was the driver Danny had been angry with all along.

"I thought she'd broken in," the driver tried to explain. "The front door was open, and I found her out here."

"It was freezing outside," Tess explained, brushing at the melting snow on her coat. "I called before I let myself in but no one answered."

The driver looked sheepish. "I may have dozed off."

The long-stemmed rose ticked in Danny's hand. "I leave for twenty minutes to get a flower, and you fall asleep? You're supposed to be providing security for this place." He waved the guy off. "Pack up your things. You no longer work here."

Shock registered on the driver's face, and then anger, but he nodded and left. It wasn't Tess's intention to get him fired, but she had little sympathy for him, given how aggressive he'd been. It made her wonder if he'd taken it upon himself to intimidate her the night he brought her here—and if Danny knew.

Danny looked Tess up and down. "Are you okay?"

She clutched her arms, her breath flooding, partly in relief. "I'll be fine if I don't freeze."

"Let's go inside," he suggested. "There's a fire going, and I'll get you something hot to drink."

Tess hesitated, glancing down at the headstone she'd uncovered. "Dorie Gabriel? Was she a relative?"

He cut her a look that shimmered with pain. His eyes were narrowed, his brow clenched. But when he spoke, his voice was strangely toneless. "She was my daughter, Dorie."

A daughter? The thought sucked the breath out of her. Maybe she should have guessed, but she wasn't aware that he'd been married, or seriously involved with anyone.

"I'm sorry," she said. "I didn't know. I didn't mean to intrude."

He held out his hand, apparently intending to help her through the snow. "You haven't," he said, "yet."

Was Dorie Gabriel his secret? Tess tried to observe him without being too obvious. She wanted to ask about the child, but it would take more courage than she had to breach the barrier he'd just raised. Mitzi would know, but Mitzi was gone.

"Tess," he said, "it's cold."

It felt awkward taking his hand. She'd exposed herself to him in ways she didn't want to think about, but the warmth of his palm against hers felt almost too intimate.

She didn't notice the weather's biting chill until they reached the living room, and the heat from the fireplace hit her. She shivered as he took her coat. He went to the kitchen to get them something to drink, and she settled on the couch in front of the fire, covering herself with the soft woolen throw he'd given her.

He'd left the red rose on a glass tray on the coffee table, and Tess couldn't take her eyes off it. When he returned moments later it was with two cups of steaming hot chocolate, fragrantly laced with some pungent liquor.

Tess took the mug he offered, noticing that he'd removed his coat and pushed up the sleeves of his sweater. The rustic white cable-knit set off his tawny skin and dark eyes. But his striking looks were almost an afterthought, Tess realized. They didn't play into why she was here in any way. She wanted to expose him the way he'd exposed her. It was only fair.

"Did you mean to leave the rose on the grave?" she asked.

"No, it's for you." He stood by the fireplace, gingerly holding the hot cup in his hands. "A peace offering."

Tess was caught completely off guard. She'd prepared herself to pursue the truth like a forensics expert, but she wasn't prepared to have it volunteered. There wasn't going to be a confrontation?

She brought the mug to her lips and drank, grateful for the drink's heat, its flame. Cognac. It seared her nostrils as she breathed out.

"It was you, wasn't it?" she said. "You were the man asleep in the bed. And the night in the bedchamber, that was you, too."

He cast his eyes down, but only for a second. "Yes."

She hardly knew where to start with the questions. "Why didn't you tell me? I asked, but you talked in riddles."

"It would have changed everything if I'd told you. You wouldn't be here, and neither would I." There was no hesitation in him now. He searched out her gaze and held it. "I was in the auditorium when you danced with the Marquis, and after watching you, I became convinced that you wanted to go through with the initiation he described to you. I'm still convinced. I think you wanted to do what we did."

The games were over. She could feel it. They were going to be brutally honest with each other.

"I did want it," she said.

"But I didn't want you with the Marquis," he admitted. "That's another reason I didn't tell you who I was. I thought you might turn to him."

She was forced to ask, "Was this about jealousy? Male rivalry?"

"I was afraid he would miss what was obvious to me— that you weren't at the club just for an exotic sexual experience. It was about control and trust."

A silence settled in around them, accented by the low roar of the fire. Tess stared at the flames, taking a moment to consider what he'd said.

She set down her cup. "I couldn't even trust my own feelings."

"And now?" he asked.

"What do you mean?"

"Can you trust your feelings now?"

She shrugged.

"Think about it, Tess. You stripped away everything that wasn't you, everything you *couldn't* trust. What you got down to was real."

"I didn't strip it away. You did."

"That's not true. I had no control over you except what you gave me. But at the end it was total—and you surrendered it all in an act of blind faith. That took some courage."

She stared at him a long time, trying to understand how she could have done something like that. Right now, the answer eluded her, although at other times it had lit her mind like a beacon.

"Whose idea was it?" she asked him. "Yours or the Marquis'?"

"Mine, all of it. I had the Marquis set it up, and then finally, I found the courage to be part of it. That was the night I came to the bedchamber."

Odd how he kept using that word. *Courage.* She had it. He didn't. She wanted to know more, but asking questions felt like taking a suspension bridge that she wasn't sure would hold her.

"Do you and the Marquis often conspire to seduce women?" she asked.

His brows knit in a frown. "First time for me. I can't speak for him. Listen, if you're going to blame someone for what happened, blame me. I was the mastermind."

"I have no one to blame. I made my own choices, and I wasn't forced or drugged." She pushed the blanket aside, suddenly warm. "I wasn't drugged, was I?"

"Never."

"Not even the drink, Lips of the Beauty?"

"Lips of the—? How did I miss that?" A quizzical smile appeared. "Hard drugs and hard liquor aren't allowed in the club. The Marquis has a zero-tolerance rule, so whatever was in Lips of the Beauty, it couldn't have been too potent."

"Try some, if you don't think it's potent." Absently, she smoothed the leg of her pantsuit with the tip of her boot. "What is your connection with the Marquis?" she asked. "Business? Personal?"

"Both. I spent a couple years losing myself at the club— the exact opposite of what you did, I suppose. It's a good place to run away from your feelings, if that's where your head is."

The suspension bridge again. She could feel it swaying beneath her feet. "What feelings were you running from?"

He took a long swallow of the spiked chocolate. "Maybe I'll get all that figured out one day."

Tess didn't sense that he was evading her as much as he was deeply unresolved about something, probably that grave outside. And she was continually weighing whether or not to question him about it. "Mitzi said you were an investor in the club."

"Alex wanted to expand." At Tess's puzzled expression, he added, "Alex Burton. The Marquis has a real name, although don't say I told you. Anyway, I was intrigued by his vision of what the club could be, so I loaned him some money."

Tess rested her head on the sofa pillows and gazed at Danny. "Is that guy for real?"

"Alex? Your guess is as good as mine. He's an interesting man with a penchant for sexual intrigue, which makes him a natural for the club."

"But the two of you are friends?"

"We're close enough that I trusted him with you, to a point. I also knew he was the only one powerful enough to gain your respect, and that you wouldn't accept his offer otherwise."

"But you were sure I would accept?"

"I would have bet my last dollar on it."

"I was that obvious?"

His smile turned knowing—and sexual. Tess was instantly uncomfortable.

"We were together twice," he said, "once in your office, and—"

"I *know* we were together."

"It gave me a pretty good sense of what you were about."

"Right, a freaky basket case who gets her thrills from the occasional spanking."

His mouth set in disapproval. "You talk that way, and I'm going to think you didn't learn a thing about yourself."

She ignored him. "Were the other members in on it, too? The women?"

"No, they were just doing what they always do. They thought it was the fantasy you'd chosen. That's how this place works. You get to live out your secret dreams, and no one questions or judges you."

"That *wasn't* my secret dream."

His dark eyes narrowed. "In that case, I got it wrong."

"Okay, it was close," she admitted. Obviously, closer than he knew, but the truth didn't need to get *that* brutal. And she still wasn't satisfied that she understood the sequence of things.

"So, the Marquis was paving the way for you to come to the bedchamber that night?"

"It wasn't quite that cold-blooded. And I was involved well before the bedchamber. When you came to the Marquis' office to accept his offer, that was actually me—and I did my best to scare you away. I think I hoped you wouldn't go through with it because then *I* wouldn't have to."

"You were afraid, too?"

"It was pretty arrogant of me to think that I was the right one to take you through the experience. Yes, I was afraid."

Behind him, through the window, Mother Nature was putting on another show. It had begun to snow again, and mercurial gusts captured the sparkling flakes, whipping them into lacy flurries. It made her think of women dancing in gossamer dresses, sprinkled with sequins.

It was quite magical, and apparently, so was he. "You frightened me half to death that day. How were you able to make me think you were right next to me?"

"How do you know I wasn't?" He smiled. "The Marquis has his office rigged with some interesting special effects. Other than that, it was a little hocus-pocus, a little hypnotic suggestion, and possibly a little desire on your part to be frightened half to death."

One day she might debate that last thing with him, but there was too much ground to cover now.

"From the beginning I thought you might be involved," she said, "but I assumed it was about revenge. Payback for getting you fired."

"You didn't get me fired. I quit."

"Well, okay, but the point is you wouldn't have had to if I hadn't accused you of something you didn't do. Was this ever about revenge on your part?"

"Maybe, at first." He set the cup on the fireplace mantel. "And don't say you didn't deserve some payback. You were playing serious games—searching my office and breaking into my home, and then seducing me to try and cover your tracks."

She didn't attempt to defend herself. He knew her reasons. "There were moments during the initiation when I was certain I was being taught a painful lesson."

"There were moments when you taught *me* a painful lesson. But for the record, I wasn't playing teacher."

"Then what *were* you doing?"

He took a moment. "Admiring you."

"Right, my naked ass?"

"Your naked soul would be closer to the truth. I was amazed at the way you put it all on the line. I told you if you could trust deeply enough, it would change you— and you didn't hesitate. I envied that."

"So…you admired me, and you envied my ability to trust? That's it?"

"You want me to say it was the sex? It *was*. You're beautiful and desirable, and I wanted to be with you. And yes, I was feeling protective and probably even territorial. I didn't want you with Alex or anyone else."

She could feel warmth creeping up the back of her neck. "Well, thanks, but I wasn't fishing for compliments. I confess I'm still confused, Danny. You say you envy me, but you gave yourself to the experience almost as totally as I did, and I can't help but wonder if there's some deeper reason, something you're holding back."

He walked over to the window that faced the grave and stared out. "And if there is?" he asked.

"Then you're doing what you accused me of doing—cutting yourself off from something."

"Everyone finds ways to cut themselves off from pain," he said, "but some of us are better at it than others. Sometimes I feel like a surgeon who's cut away so much, it's a miracle there's anything left."

The bridge began to feel steadier, as if it might hold her. "I felt like parts of me had gone dead and no longer existed," she said. "Any thought or feeling that wasn't acceptable to my parents had to be killed off."

"Which is probably why I had to take you through the experience. I couldn't explain it, but I felt compelled to be your partner."

"What do you mean?"

"Maybe I needed *you* to do what I couldn't."

Did he mean give up control? Surrender?

She got up and joined him at the window. He'd taken the time to try and understand her in a way that no one else had. He may not have been entirely right about who she was, and what she needed, but at least he'd made the attempt.

"Can you talk about your daughter?" she asked.

A muscle tightened in his cheek. "There's not much to talk about."

"Tell me what there is."

"She died before her fourth birthday. She spent half of her short time on this earth in hospitals and suffered like hell through one treatment after another, just about everything known to medical science. You have no idea what kids with leukemia go through."

"I'm sorry." Words were completely inadequate, but silence would have been worse. "That must have been horrible for you."

"Nothing compared to what it was like for her."

She studied his impassive profile, aware that he was probably dealing with survivor guilt, in addition to the grief he'd never allowed himself to express. He looked as if he were made of stone, as impenetrable as the marker on the child's grave. He probably wished he was.

"I didn't know you were married," she said. "Where is her mother?"

"I'm not married, never was. Dorie's mother left her with me when Dorie was diagnosed. She had her own problems and couldn't deal with a healthy kid, much less a sick one. And I didn't know I had a child until she showed up on my doorstep with a toddler. Dorie was the product of a one-night stand."

Tess stayed silent—and prayed that he wouldn't.

"She left before I woke up the next morning," he said, "and she hadn't given me her real name, so I couldn't contact her. A couple years later, she got the devastating news about Dorie's leukemia. That's when she got in touch with me."

"And you kept Dorie? You raised her?"

"She was mine. DNA testing proved it. And her mother *couldn't* keep her. I only had her for a year."

But it was long enough to fall in love with her, Tess realized, watching him recede even farther. She thought back, remembering the beautiful but sterile apartment in Tribeca—and wondering if he'd moved there after Dorie died, at a time when he may not have wanted to live in anything resembling a home. He'd also talked about getting lost at the club.

Something made Tess ask, "What would you have done if she hadn't been yours?"

"Would I have taken her anyway?" He shook his head. "I'm not that noble. Watching her suffer took me to a place I don't want to go again. I don't tolerate pain well, especially other's."

Tess found herself saying, "You tolerated my pain pretty well."

"I knew you were going to live."

There were hints of censure and cynicism in his voice, but the only person he wanted to hurt was himself. As punishment, Tess imagined.

"You must have needed help with Dorie's care," she said. "Why didn't you tell anyone about her?"

"The leukemia was advanced. I didn't know how long she had, and I didn't want her exposed to questions and curiosity, possibly even media speculation about Danny Gabriel's love child. She deserved some happiness, some peace, whatever I could give her."

Finally he looked at Tess, and the stress that creased his eyes gave her a glimpse of what he'd been dealing with.

"It seemed like the best way to handle things," he said. "And I did have help. I hired a full-time nurse."

"But you also told Mitzi?"

If he was curious how she'd known that, he didn't say. "I went to Mitzi when it was clear that traditional medicine wasn't going to work. I didn't really believe anything could save Dorie at that point, but Mitzi had herbal remedies that were gentle and noninvasive. They seemed to help with the pain."

His shoulders lifted and fell. "I sometimes wonder what would have happened if we'd started Mitzi's treatments sooner."

"Playing what-if won't change anything, Danny. You did everything you could to save her. If you'd taken her off conventional therapy, you would have wondered if that was a mistake. I've always believed if you look for something bad, you'll find it—and it seems to me that you're looking for ways to blame yourself."

He didn't respond, but she pressed on anyway. "Wasn't it you who said that life has no meaning except what we put into it? Maybe it's time for you to forgive yourself for what happened to Dorie. You're not God. You did for that little girl what her own mother couldn't."

He nodded, but she didn't seem to be getting through. Until he'd forgiven himself, he would never get in touch with his feelings of loss, she realized, which might be why he couldn't. It was another way to avoid the pain. Guilt was more tolerable than grief.

"I am intruding," she said. "I should go."

She stepped back, wondering where he'd put her coat, but he stopped her with a hand on her arm.

"I have something of yours." He drew a piece of delicate gold jewelry from the pocket of his jeans. Tess recognized it as her hoop earring. She'd found it in his apartment the night she was there, searching for evidence.

"Where did you get that?" she asked.

"Somehow it got impaled in the sleeve of my linen shirt. It must have gotten hooked there the night we were in your office, but I didn't find it until I got home."

The night they'd had sex on her desk was what he hadn't said.

As she took the earring, she remembered her suspicions when she'd found it in his bedroom. She looked up and met his gaze, curious. "Did anyone ever tell you that a security camera caught you searching my office? I never had a chance to ask what you were doing."

"I was running a little investigation of my own. I thought it was Carlotta who'd tried to sabotage you—and to incriminate me—and I figured she'd try again. I was looking for any evidence I could find of that."

"You weren't too far off. It was Carlotta's lifelong friend."

He nodded, but their eye contact was soon broken, and his thoughts seemed to have drifted elsewhere. Clearly, he didn't want to talk about his daughter anymore, and that disappointed Tess in ways she couldn't express—and probably didn't quite understand. But he wasn't ready to let go. He might never be, and she had to respect that.

She slipped the earring into the pocket of her jacket, aware that she was reluctant to leave. It didn't feel as if they were done, and yet she couldn't imagine what else she might have to say to him. If he'd wanted to throw up barriers, he'd done a good job. But there *was* something, she realized.

"I haven't done what I came here to do," she said. "I want you to come back to Pratt-Summers. They need you. Erica needs you."

"They'll do fine. They have you."

"I'll quit if that's what it takes to get you back."

"Tess, my decision to leave was a selfish one. I need to move on, branch out. I've known that for some time, but it was comfortable there. Too comfortable. I'm not going back."

He was solid in that decision. She could hear it in his voice and that pleased her. And somehow, it was also the impetus for a question that she'd been reluctant to ask, and might have left without asking.

"It was the Marquis who untied me. Why?"

He stared out the window at the swirling snow. "When you asked about Dorie's grave, I realized I wasn't ready to deal with it. And I think I knew you wouldn't let me get away with that for long. Like I said, you scared the hell out of me. On some level, I believed you would require more of me than I could give."

That thought had already occurred to her, although she hadn't wanted to analyze it too closely. In the club, he was her guide. Now it felt as if she might have to be his, but it wasn't clear that he was willing to take the journey.

The fire crackled behind them, a comforting sound. His gaze had a certain measure of warmth as he turned his attention to her. His shoulders were hunched, his head tilted.

"What about you?" he asked. "What are you going to do?"

"Me? Oh, I'll stay with Pratt-Summers to finish the Faustini account, and then I'll reassess things. I'm not sure the New York ad scene is for me."

"Somehow, I knew that." He regarded her with a certain amount of pride, the mentor about to send his protégée packing. "I guess you're ready to find your way now, your true path."

"That sounds a little scary."

"You'll be fine." He went to get the rose on the table. "Don't forget this," he said as he handed it to her.

She immediately brought the flower to her nose and breathed in. The fragrance flooded her, eliciting a poignant mix of emotions. It was snowing, and she was in a beautiful place with, from what she knew of him, a beautiful man. This was a fantasy, much more so than her experience with surrender had been. She could stay.

"Were the roses from you?" she asked.

"Yes."

"What did the card say?"

"'Your life starts now. Don't live it too wisely. You've already done that.'"

She smiled. "Then you know what I'm going to do."

He nodded and held out his arms. She walked into his embrace, grateful and sad at the same time. They were saying goodbye, and it felt as if she was leaving someone important. At least she had the solace of knowing that she was leaving as a different person. Her life had been changed, simply as a result of knowing him, and she wasn't sure what impact she'd had on his. But he was the one who'd told her that trust changed people, and if that was true, then he knew all he needed to.

"I won't live it too wisely. Promise you won't, either."

"I promise," he said.

Epilogue

One year later…

"Tess, you *promised*."

"Meredith, stop waving that thing in my face. I'm trying to drive."

"It's not a *thing*. It's an invitation to a bitchin' party, and you promised we'd go."

"Bitchin' party?" Tess wasn't sure she'd ever heard Meredith use surfer lingo before. "If you keep that up, we won't be going anywhere. We'll be in a multicar pileup."

Tess batted Meredith's hand away so she could see the street, not that she relished the view. It was rush hour on a Friday afternoon in downtown Manhattan, and the taxis were deadly weapons. The only thing crazier than trying to hail one at rush hour was driving the streets with swarms of them.

But Meredith, a Californian to the marrow, had insisted they rent a car rather than use the subways and cabs to get around the city. And since Meredith wasn't familiar with Manhattan, Tess had to drive.

Tess took the next one-way street and squeaked out a left turn, braving squalling horns and bawled insults.

"Where are we going?" Meredith asked. "The invitation says Greenwich. That's the other way, isn't it?"

"We're going back to the hotel," Tess explained. She and Meredith were in the city on a working vacation, looking into the possibility of opening a small agency of their own in the Tribeca area. Tess had stayed on at Pratt-Summers to complete the Faustini campaign, which had made quite a splash with the Marquis Club as its backdrop. Shortly after that, when it was clear that Erica was ready to take over the reins at the agency, Tess had wished everyone well, especially her buddy, Andy, and headed back to Los Angeles.

It had always felt as if she'd left L.A. in great haste, and maybe even been running away from something. But the trip back proved there'd been nothing to run from. Her parents hadn't changed and never would, and if her relationship with them was different, it was only because *she* was different. She'd revisited all her old haunts, and eventually, she'd even gone back to work at Renaissance, but that hadn't felt right, either.

It was all she'd needed to know. She was a New York girl after all. And since there were no Merediths in Manhattan, she'd talked her friend into coming back with her to test the waters for an exciting new venture.

"Why are we going back to the hotel?" Meredith asked.

"We need to change." Tess tilted her a sly smile. "We're not dressed appropriately for a party at the Marquis Club."

The elevator in the club's parking garage whisked Tess and Meredith straight up to the Opera House. Tess was grateful they'd avoided the entrance with the erotic tableaux, lit in shades of red and purple. One look at the naked woman in stocks, and Meredith might have run screaming, although Tess wasn't so certain of that now. Possibly, New York had a liberating effect on the libido, because her friend seemed much more open and adventurous.

"Shazam," Meredith whispered as the elevator doors parted, revealing the opulent lobby of the Opera House. The invitation that had been forwarded to Tess in L.A. said the party was in celebration of the club's tenth anniversary, and a Lolita-like strawberry blonde waited at the door to greet them. Her dress was a rustling evening gown that appeared to be made mostly of tinfoil, and she held a huge bouquet of roses with petals that were crimson on one side and silvery foil on the other.

"I'm the club's tenth-anniversary present," she announced, breathy-voiced and pouty-lipped as she drew a rose from her bouquet for Meredith.

Tess recognized her from the classroom where Danny had so heroically stepped in to administer some discipline. It looked to Tess as if he hadn't administered enough. This unrelenting nymphet needed to be locked in the stocks with her clothes *on*. That should ruin her day.

Meredith actually brought the flower to her nose and sniffed. "Is tinfoil the official tenth-anniversary gift?" she asked.

"*Aluminum.*" The nymphet adopted a slightly superior tone as she presented Tess with a rose.

"Ah, yes, *aluminum.*" Tess accepted the rose with a gracious nod. "So difficult to wear. Too bad it's not your color."

The nymphet's nose wrinkled. Tess hooked Meredith's arm and tugged her into the lobby, which had been lavishly decorated for the celebration. The heavy curtains were roped with garlands of foil roses and twinkling lights, and on the stairway landings, velvety bunches of authentic red roses were arranged in enormous cut-glass vases.

It was all very strange and beautiful. The piped-in music was the same whispery New Age fare Tess remembered, and the air smelled of something exotic, perhaps lilac?

"Look up there." Meredith pointed to the ceiling, where swings hung from a wheel that spun around a crystal chandelier like a carnival ride. Seated on the swings were androgynous creatures costumed as brightly colored lovebirds. The club's own Cirque du Soleil, Tess thought. The rest of the party guests seemed to be dressed for a turn-of-the century masquerade ball.

At least they had clothes on. Tess had been worried about that.

"This is where you shot your ads?" Meredith asked.

Tess nodded. "Pretty amazing, huh?" She'd told Meredith very little about her personal adventures, but it was widely known in the advertising world that Tess had done an ad campaign in an S&M club, and Tess had shared some of the details with her friend. After this, she would have to confess everything. Meredith wouldn't let her live, otherwise.

Tess saw the Marquis coming toward them, and her stomach actually fluttered. He was over the top, as always, in a white tie and tails, but there was something undeniably dashing about the man. She'd already decided that he was a throwback to an age more sophisticated than this one.

Perfect for Meredith, she thought.

He held out his hands. "How have you been, Tess?"

She allowed herself to be pulled into his arms—and was assailed by a memory of dancing bottomless on a stage. "Better dressed than the last time we were this close," she said, drawing back. "How are you?"

He pretended to be bereft. "Wishing you *weren't* better dressed."

"Let me introduce my friend?" Tess smiled as his dark eyes slid over to Meredith, who had the sense to look uneasy.

The Marquis gave Meredith a subtle once-over while Tess did the introductions. He was clearly intrigued. But Meredith didn't seem to know what to make of him, which didn't surprise Tess at all.

"Would you two like the grand tour?" the Marquis asked when Tess was done. He beckoned for a server, who was dressed like a French maid and carrying a tray of sparkling wine that looked suspiciously like Lips of the Beauty. Tess was fairly certain the maid was a very attractive man.

Fortunately, Meredith didn't want anything to drink. Tess declined, too.

"I've *had* the grand tour," Tess said, catching the Marquis' eye. He acknowledged her with a smile but said nothing.

Meredith's voice took on a pleading note. "You're not taking the tour, Tess? Well, I'd like to, but I don't want to abandon you."

Tess couldn't tell whether Meredith was more interested in the tour or the Marquis, but she did seem to want to go.

"I'll be fine," Tess assured her. "I know my way around."

"It's settled, then." The Marquis was all innocent smiles, probably for Tess's benefit. "I'll take the lovely Meredith, and Tess can wander around and visit old friends to her heart's content."

Meredith looked at Tess askance. "She has old friends here?"

"I wouldn't call them *old* friends," Tess said. "I met some people."

"Check out the Hypnosis Parlor." The Marquis gave Tess a tip of his head, and then he offered his arm to Meredith and began to list the events they could visit, including the Walk of Shame and Redemption.

Tess prayed Meredith wouldn't choose that one.

Of course, she did.

"What did you call that walk?" she asked him.

The Marquis beamed. "My kind of girl."

Tess's voice was firm. "I think the tango exhibition might be a good place to start. Meredith loves ballroom dancing, *don't* you, Meredith."

Her brow pleated. "I do?"

The Marquis patted her hand. "You'll love the tango," he said. He mouthed the word *chill* to Tess.

Tess had a few qualms as the two of them walked off, her childhood friend arm in arm with de Sade himself. Meredith was five foot nine and strikingly lovely in the skinny black sheath she'd chosen to wear. Tess would never have described her as angelic, but she did look almost innocent next to her tour guide.

Elvira would have looked innocent next to him.

As they disappeared through the auditorium doors, Tess told herself to take the Marquis' advice and chill. He wouldn't bite her, at least not on the first date.

Smiling at the thought, Tess made her way through a dazzling array of masqueraders. She spotted the French court contingent with their bright red lipstick and feathers—and felt quite underdressed in her silver-flecked off-the-shoulder sweater and gored skirt.

The crowds hadn't lightened by the time she reached the Grand Hallway, and as always, there was a line for the Hypnosis Parlor. But Tess was able to get close enough to see what was going on inside. She'd figured the old friend had to be Mitzi, but both of the robed and hooded attendants looked too tall. Strange things happened around this place, but Mitzi couldn't have grown a foot since Tess had last seen her.

Before Tess had left Pratt-Summers, Mitzi was back at her post in the agency's rest room, seeming refreshed and happy. She'd taken a month's hiatus, and though she hadn't gone into detail about her adventures, she'd implied there was now a man in her life. Tess had been pleased for her, but at the same time, she'd remembered the man and woman she'd seen on the sidewalk below her apartment window, the couple who owned the streets—and the pang she'd felt at seeing them.

That sense of something missing had been replaced, she realized, by a feeling of anticipation. Her life had opened up, and she was slowly but surely discovering the vital parts of herself that had been negated. There were things locked inside her she hadn't known existed. Who could have guessed she would want to live in New York, that she could be happier here? And she *still* missed her beloved dog, dammit. She always would.

Maybe she also missed having a partner to wake up with in the mornings and to share things with in the evenings. It surprised her how much she missed sex, given that she'd sworn off gladly about this time last year. But she was still busy getting to know who she was…and there was plenty of time. Everything had its season, even love.

At last, one of the attendants turned Tess's way—and Tess saw that it *was* an old friend. Andy! He must be moonlighting at the club. She'd kept in touch with him by e-mail, and he was still at Pratt-Summers, working with Carlotta, who'd been made creative director at long last.

Instinctively, Tess ducked. She adored Andy, and she

hadn't intended to leave New York without seeing him, but this wasn't the right time. He would be all over her with questions about her plans, and she didn't know what they were just yet. Not knowing was half the fun, she'd discovered.

Quickly, Tess moved on down the hallway with a specific destination in mind. She'd only had a glimpse of the Vampire Forest when she'd been here before, and she'd been intrigued by the idea of it ever since. Perhaps she secretly wanted to relive that delicious thrill of letting go, spiraling like a leaf in a strong breeze—and putting yourself totally in someone else's hands.

But Tess realized there was a problem when she got to the silver door and didn't know how to open it. She ran her hands over the portal and the walls that framed it, thinking there might be a hidden pressure-sensitive spot. The Marquis had had a remote, but there must be a way to open the doors manually. Unfortunately, nothing budged.

She scoped out the area, hoping to find someone to help. The entrance was in its own shadowy alcove, and there was no one else around. Odd, was her first thought. She would have expected this to be one of the most popular events. Her second thought was to go and find the Marquis.

She hadn't taken two steps when a whooshing sound stopped her. Cool air flooded her back, and she turned to find the door had opened, revealing a virtual forest of darkness. What was that noise? She could hear something coming from inside. It sounded like the rustle of a small, scurrying animal. A sudden hiss made her think of snakes, slithering through the grass. And then there was the distant hooting of an owl.

"Well, you wanted to do this, didn't you?" she said under her breath. The shivers she'd felt were now goose-flesh, and the delayed beat of her heart was painful. The slower it got, the harder it seemed to thud.

The silver panel whooshed down just seconds after she stepped inside. If she'd been any closer it would have closed *on* her. She could see nothing. The darkness was total, and terrifying. She wanted to run, but there was no-where to go, except deeper into the void.

As her vision cleared, she was able to make out what looked like a bridge in front of her, and the rustling sound she'd heard was water. There must be a creek running through the forest, and the bridge seemed to be floating on it.

Tess stepped onto the rickety structure and stayed close to the railing as she made her way across. Above her and beyond the treetops, stars seemed to be twinkling. That had to be rigged, a clever electrician's work. Everything about this place was rigged, obviously. She doubted even the trees were real. Her senses were being tricked by the sounds and smells.

She breathed in the wet, loamy scent of dirt and decomposing leaves. The woodsy smell of pine and laurel surrounded her, and the wooden bridge creaked under her weight. When she stepped off, onto the ground, she heard twigs snap beneath her feet.

Sounds effects, of course. The Marquis even used them

in his office. This place was the equivalent of a haunted house at a theme park, only not as good, she told herself. It was a little disappointing, really. She'd expected more.

An eerie howl stopped her short. Sounds effects or not, the fine hairs on her arms prickled like tiny wires. She really did want out of this place. There had to be an emergency exit somewhere. The city's safety codes must have required one.

She could just make out a path leading away from the bridge. It looked as if it would take her into the bowels of this horror-movie set, but that might be the quickest way to the exit, and she couldn't see well enough to forge her own path. Branches snagged at her sweater as she started along the trail. It was cold, too. She could see her own breath.

She grabbed her arms, hugging herself. Climate control, she told herself. It had to be. This was actually the middle of April.

"Is anyone else here?" she called out. The question echoed, growing fainter each time it repeated. Something slithered over her feet. A snake?

She leaped back. "I'm looking for the exit. I want out of here!"

"Don't we all?"

The question had come from behind her, a man's voice. It was low, evil. He was laughing.

She whirled around, her breath flooding out. "Stay the fuck away from me, or I'll kill you!"

The laughter grew louder. Gradually, it turned into the

howl of a baying animal. And as the howl became a shriek, Tess began to shake.

"Where are you, dammit? I'm not playing these games. I want out of here." She couldn't see. It was too dark. And the sudden silence was as unnerving as the chaos.

Tess couldn't figure out where the howling had come from. She didn't know which way to go. She backed up, and hit something.

No, someone. *Him.* Behind her.

The snake hissed, an evil sound. She felt a warm caress, and then something sharp pricked her neck. *Sweet Jesus.*

Tess screamed. She struck out blindly, but his arms whipped around her. A cape flew, enveloping her.

"Don't scream again," he whispered, "unless you *want* to arouse me."

His hold was powerful. There was no pain, just power, and something seemed to have stunned her into submission. Had she been bitten? She didn't have the strength to scream again. Her heart was pounding too hard, and her body was fiery hot with the blood rushing through it. That would probably arouse him, too.

This was crazy, insane. It was a carnival ride, nothing more. She was in the haunted house, and apparently she'd met her first bogeyman.

Was it Danny?

Where the hell had that question come from? She seemed doomed to think that every man in the dark was him. *Stop it, Tess. You're being ridiculous.*

Her legs were shaking so hard she could barely stand.

He drew her close and whispered in her ear, his breath warm and steamy, "You're only fighting yourself, Tess. Give in to what you want most—the freefall through space, the release from this mortal coil."

"Fuck you," she said, startled at the pleading note in her voice.

His hands tightened on her arms. He gave her a firm shake and pulled her closer. "There's nothing to fear. I'm not going to hurt you. I'm going to make the pain go away."

He knew her name, of course. He probably knew her social security number, driver's license and bra size, too. It wouldn't have surprised her if the club did deep background checks on its members. Not that she was one, but that wouldn't stop the Marquis.

"You're shaking," he said, "but it's only fear. Let go of everything that frightens you and lean on me. Give it to me."

His arms gathered her close, urging her to relax.

Give it to me. Lean on me.

For some unknown reason, she did, and her legs nearly gave out. As she slumped against him, she felt the tension draining from her body. His cape surrounded her like a heavy curtain. It captured the heat emanating from his body.

"If you think you've known pleasure, you're wrong. This is pleasure so intense it could kill you, but such a sweet death."

The animal howled again, keening in some kind of urgent need.

The sound was beautiful. It ripped through Tess's defenses. An answering sound caught in her throat, and she was suddenly swimming in weakness. Her body went limp. If he weren't holding her she would have been on the ground.

"Who are you?" she asked him.

"You know who I am."

"I don't know anything. This isn't real. You're not real. It's a ridiculous fantasy."

"Yes, it's a ridiculous fantasy. A beautiful, perfectly ridiculous fantasy. And it was tailor-made for you, Tess. Give yourself to it. Hold back nothing, and you'll get everything you need."

What made it thrilling was her willingness to surrender, she realized, even to a stranger in the dark. The not knowing was thrilling, too. But a question echoed in her mind as he picked her up in his arms and walked deeper into the darkness, carrying her off to his lair like the great lonely beast in a horror movie.

Was it Danny?

Suzanne Forster

New York Times bestselling author Suzanne Forster has written over thirty novels and been the recipient of countless awards, including the National Readers Choice Award for *Shameless*, her mainstream debut. Suzanne has a master's degree in writing popular fiction and teaches and lectures frequently. She divides her time between homes in Newport Beach, California, and Olympia, Washington. You can contact Suzanne through her Web site at www.suzanneforster.com.

Spice

SPICE & BootyParlor.com

live your fantasy CONTEST

For the launch of our Spice line of books, we've teamed up with our friends at BootyParlor.com™ to offer you a chance to win an irresistibly sexy contest. Why not enter today?

Live Your Fantasy Romantic Island Getaway Contest

You could win a trip for two to the beautiful Jalousie Plantation Hotel™ on the gorgeous island of St. Lucia! Nothing is sexier than spending a full week at this tropical all-inclusive resort. All accommodations, airfares and meals are included! Even spa treatments— nothing's more sensuous.

Simply tell us about your most romantic fantasy—in 100 words or less— and you could win!